TO

Relative
Fiction

ALAINA ROSE

Thank you so much for always supporting me!

Alayna

Copyright © 2023 by Alaina Rose

All rights reserved.

Cover art: Ashley Ranae Quick

Cover design: Murphy Rae

Editing: Samantha Maffeo

ISBN: 9798987598009

No part of this book may be reproduced in any form or by any electronic or mechanical means, including information storage and retrieval systems, without written permission from the author, except for the use of brief quotations in a book review.

This book is a work of fiction. Any names, characters, companies, organizations, places, events, locales, and incidents are either used in a fictitious manner or are fictional. Any resemblance to actual persons, living or dead, actual companies or organizations, or actual events is purely coincidental.

AUTHOR'S NOTE

Thank you so much for picking up Relative Fiction. I want every reader to have a safe and enjoyable experience, so I have included this list of content warnings.

I endeavored to make this list as inclusive as possible. If you feel anything else should be included, or if you have any questions or concerns, please contact me.

Relative Fiction includes: discussions of mature, consensual, graphic on page sex, terminal illness (lung cancer) and death of a parent (not on page), on page wake/funeral scene (not at funeral home), in-depth discussions of death, discussions of grief, mild medical discussion (nasal cannula and oxygen use), cheating ex (no on page cheating), swearing, alcohol use, marijuana use, brief scene observing body suspension, two scenes with anxiety-induced vomiting, a fist fight, mild emotional abuse from a parent.

*This is all thanks to, because of, and for Andrew,
my great love story*

ONE
JULIA

JULIA CLUTCHED the box of the ivory toned Le Creuset butter dish as her heart shattered.

Again.

She balanced it on top of a growing mountain of returned kitchenware in a fantastically humiliating display of her failed relationship, right in the middle of the Downtown Home & Garden for all of Starling Hills to see.

Again.

She'd pinned this exact, damned dish to her Pinterest board years ago, crafting an entire fantasy around this one, ridiculous piece of expensive stoneware. To Past Julia, the butter dish was the emblem of her domestic future. Which had been about to become real at thirty-one, because Josh was finally ready to Settle Down.

Until a few months ago, Julia was going to marry her high school sweetheart.

Instead, the Saturday in September passed without fanfare, marked only by Julia eating an impressive number of fancy cupcakes during a Star Wars marathon with her sister.

"That fucking butter dish," Heather said, wagging her head back and forth as she gazed wistfully at the thing, thumbnail between her teeth in contemplation.

As Julia's younger sister, she knew how much Julia had pined over that dish. Almost as much as she used to pine over fandom pairings, typing out one-shots on the internet.

Julia loosened her chipped-manicure grasp on the package, surrendering it for good. The bored sixteen-year-old cashier opened her hand for the gift receipts without the slightest hint of concern for Julia's plight. Yet Julia was sure the teen, like everyone else in town, knew the whole damn story.

She passed over the stack of receipts, then stuffed her fists in her jean pockets. How ridiculous that her stunningly bright 'Agent Orange' bridal shower gel manicure still survived in slivered chips, yet her soon-to-be-nuptials were no more. The last vestiges of any sort of hope she had over salvaging her future flickered and faded away with each beep of the cashier's scanner.

Yep, she could curl up right here and nap for a couple years. That'd be fine.

"That fucking butter dish," Julia echoed Heather.

This was miserable. Each day in the aftermath of her breakup—which seemed like a pathetically simple phrase for over a decade of her life down the drain—brought some new fresh hell of embarrassment. Julia thought she'd gotten past the worst of it, but returning the bridal shower gifts sent shock waves pulsing through her body. Lightning bolts of shame, regret, and doubt. She shuddered, the hair on her arms standing up.

The day Julia and Josh spent at Downtown Home & Garden scanning gifts for their registry, she felt so powerful. Like she'd won the game of Life. Josh kept his hand linked in hers, as she held the scanner, squealing with delight at each overpriced piece of flatware, stoneware, and glassware she added.

"Anything you want, babe," he purred in her ear, his arms snaking around her and grasping her hips. "You're the queen here."

"I love imagining our kitchen." Julia turned and met his lips just over her shoulder, visions of quartz countertops and farmhouse sinks dancing in her head.

As she broke their kiss, she snorted, remembering their small, outdated apartment kitchen that barely had a functioning dishwasher. "Well, not our current kitchen, obviously. The lighting is awful, it's basically fluorescent. But, I mean, in the home we're going to buy...soon?"

"Soon." Josh smirked. "I knew what you meant." He pinched her hip and she jumped under his touch.

"Stop it, babe!" She laughed and scanned the Le Creuset butter dish.

A lifetime ago. She wasn't that naive woman anymore.

How ridiculous. Julia's heart thudded against her chest. That was barely six months ago, when she was still smack dab in the middle of fantasyland. She had no idea, zero clue, that her life was about to implode. Not only did it take less than two weeks from the bridal shower for their engagement to dissolve, but Julia had also gotten stuck with the lion's share of the items from the shower to return.

Sure, she needed the cash after moving back in with her parents, but returning all this stuff was an errand of epic proportions. And Julia hated errands. Months later and it still wasn't done.

"You couldn't have just kept all this beautiful stuff?" Heather could barely keep her hands off it all, running her fingers over each matte box of the *meringue* colored Le Creuset pieces. She was almost worse than Julia herself at letting it go. Almost like Heather had really lost something with the dissolution of Julia's relationship.

Heather flashed her a puppy dog look. It was a look that Julia knew well. It was the same over-exaggerated look she saw from her mom and dad. It was a look of pity, but also with a little question behind it. Like everyone wondered if Julia was doing the right thing.

Late at night, Julia wondered, too, if she was doing the right thing. The thought of starting over curdled her stomach. She was thirty-one after all, with over ten years spent with Josh. She had trusted him, implicitly, since she was seventeen years old.

What a mistake that had been. And now she could barely tell which way was up because her instincts were shattered.

Julia sighed, tamping down the anxiety that stung her insides. "Well, Mom threatened to throw all this stuff out with the trash if I didn't take care of it this week."

It had all been situated in a neat maze of boxes in her childhood bedroom, but even Julia could see she was on track to become a modern day Miss Havisham.

"She's so dramatic." Heather rolled her eyes.

Their mom really was. Yet Julia bristled, still jumping to defend her after all these years. "Yeah, well, I am living in her house again."

"But like, have a little compassion?"

Julia made a little snorting noise through her nose. Her mom wasn't exactly the queen of compassion. She welcomed Julia back into her house, but that wasn't without its own little strings. And it's not like Julia had anywhere else to go. She'd lived with Josh since they graduated from University of Michigan nine years ago, in a two-bedroom apartment in downtown Starling Hills that she couldn't afford on her own while they were saving up for a down payment on a home. Which wasn't the easiest thing to do while also paying down student loans.

Josh always had this strange rule that they couldn't get

married before they bought a house, and the stars were about to align for Julia. So they were waiting, this whole time.

Now it all made sense.

Turns out, Julia's share of the savings had been just enough to hire a moving company to get her back into her parents' house—because her parents had refused to help. That was really the cherry on top of this shit sundae.

But the wad of cash that the cashier whipped from the till and began counting would definitely make this all less shitty. If there was a silver lining to any of this, it was the cash.

In her pocket, Julia's phone vibrated, but she ignored it. She was with Heather, so it was probably her mom, and her mom could wait. Because the cashier had finished counting out Julia's money and was about to hand it over.

"One thousand, one hundred and twelve dollars and ninety-seven cents." Her eyes widened just slightly at the number but then she quickly went back to completely disinterested.

Julia's palms started to sweat at the amount of money she tucked into her wallet. And that wasn't even all of the stuff she had to return. Maybe returning all of the bridal shower gifts wasn't the short end of the stick after all.

Her phone vibrated again—the second alert to an unwelcome text message—as Julia tucked her wallet away in her purse. She groaned, not eager to check in with her mom.

"You know what, screw this. I need a margarita." Julia needed at least three drinks and she needed them quick. At least they were already in downtown Starling Hills, right around the corner from all their favorite bars.

Heather was all smiles now. "That's what I'm talking about."

"My treat." Julia patted her purse, ignoring how hard it was to leave behind the stupid mini-mountain of her imagined future. How each pump of her heart sent heat searing through her veins, flushing her peachy white skin. "I got cash."

The sisters laughed and linked arms, the bell tinkling above the door as they left the Downtown Home & Garden a couple boxes of fucking fancy stoneware lighter.

* * *

JULIA GROANED into her pulled pork nachos at the Prickly Pear Cantina bar, picking a fresh jalapeño off the top and popping it into her mouth.

There was a lot of groaning. And moaning. And a decent amount of sighing. A deep, gaping cavern yawned in her chest that only happy hour blood orange margaritas could fill. With the cash in her pocket, she could buy a lot of discounted margaritas. Heather sat by and occasionally patted her sister's knee or squeezed her shoulder. At a certain point, there wasn't much more to say.

Julia leaned her head on her sister's shoulder, letting

out another massive sigh. As far as sisters went, the two looked an awful lot alike. Long brown hair, blueish eyes that changed tone with the weather and their moods, and a splash of freckles. They were often confused for twins, especially when they were younger.

But as the older sister, Julia blossomed into a more reserved person—whether by nature or function of Josh, she'd never know—whereas Heather was easier to smile and dance. For better or worse, Heather often leapt before looking, and Julia found herself envying that casual attitude. She wanted more of it in her life.

"You know," Julia's words were starting to slip from one into the next, "I never really liked Josh's mom."

Heather giggled and booped her sister's nose. "You're drunk."

"I am drunk, and you know what?" She took a loaded nacho and shoved it in her mouth. The sour cream melted on her tongue. "I like it."

"Let's be real, I like it too. You're feisty when you're drunk."

"And," Julia poked a finger in her sister's forearm, "I'm honest. Which I guess is really saying something these days."

Heather's smile faltered, her perfect eyelashes fluttering.

Julia could feel herself flying headlong into an utterly embarrassing rant about her ex-fiancé that Heather had heard too many times. One that she didn't want to have again, this time in public. But the margaritas, the anguish that made her head swim, and the cash in her wallet combined to form a reckless stew.

Maybe she was too drunk, but she didn't care.

"Some people just can't keep it in their pants!" She picked up her margarita, sloshing the sticky, melting beverage over the rim and onto her fingers. "I'm telling you, it's a real problem." Julia shook her head and pursed her lips matter-of-factly.

"We started dated when I was seventeen, Heather. Fourteen years," she cried, waving her glass through the air. She felt herself unhinging. It was like watching a TV show trainwreck, cars accordioning and flying off the track in slow motion. "Fourteen years I gave that dishonest fucker and he lied through every single one of them."

"Okaaaay." Heather drew out the word, looking around with a wide-eyed, apologetic smile. She leaned toward the bartender, who was now watching the disaster in front of him instead of the one on the news.

"Bad breakup," she whispered, conspiratorially.

"Oh I know. Heard all about it," Angus, the bartender, said. "You think I work behind this bar and don't get all the gossip?"

Heather stared daggers at him on behalf of her sister.

"Of course Angus knows. Just like everyone else in town. Probably," Julia said, licking some sugar off the rim of her drink.

Heather plucked the drink from her sister's hand and pushed the plate of nachos toward her. "Girl, listen. Josh fucking sucks. I know it, you know it, but it's six PM on a Tuesday and these people just want their tacos."

Julia scooped another chip and rolled her eyes but she couldn't stop herself. Didn't want to stop herself.

"Nope, I deserve a little something after all these years." Julia closed her eyes indignantly, nacho paused halfway to her mouth. "I deserve to be angry! I found out by an encrypted email, Heather. An *electronic letter*," she stage-whispered dramatically.

An email followed by a massive interrogation in which Josh confessed to years of cheating on her.

That she had absolutely no idea was the worst part. Josh had always loved how delightedly delusional she was. He found her naïveté endearing. Now she understood why. Poor, sweet, blind Julia. Completely bamboozled by her ex-fiancé's adultering ways.

"I know that, but the entire bar doesn't have to hear this," Heather said.

"*I couldn't, in good conscience, not tell you this before the wedding, in case you didn't already know.*" Eyes still closed, Julia rattled off the email for her reluctant audience. Heather patted the back of her hand. "*I didn't know he was engaged...*"

Julia's skin flushed as the words crept through her body. Not only engaged but who was supposed to have been monogamous the whole time. It's not those women's fault. Not really. And there were so many women.

"It's my fault. And it's everyone fucking else's fault who knew and didn't tell me."

Who knew that Josh was never loyal to Julia since the day she got on her knees for him behind the mess hall at church camp their senior year of high school. He moaned as he ran his fingers through her long brown hair, after they'd just finished singing worship songs as a group.

Josh was the kind of boy who sat with Julia's family in church on Sundays. They innocently laced fingers in the auditorium, the picture of chaste compared to what they did most Friday nights after football games.

At the time, he was exactly the all-American, church going, football playing, pick-up driving, hometown boy that her mom wanted her to marry one day. And if Josh could keep Julia from following her fanciful writer dreams to New York City, all the better.

Even then, he was with other girls.

In college, more than one of Julia's supposed friends slept with him too.

She let herself get wrapped up in the fantasy. The Le Creuset filled domestic dreams.

Julia dropped her head onto the bar, her hair fanning around her.

"I didn't know about any of it. So sweet and so stupid." Julia's voice dripped with bitterness, talking, literally, to the bar. "It was a fucking email."

An encrypted email sent to her personal inbox that Julia thankfully hadn't immediately purged as junk. Otherwise she still never would have known.

Julia sat up, bits of queso and beans strung in her hair. She lost her edge then, the fight draining from her, and her face crumpled into tears.

"Okay, time to go then!" Heather wriggled Julia's wallet from her purse and laid down too much money for their bill as an apology to the bartender for Julia's performance. She plucked the keys out, too. "I'll be driving us."

Though smaller in stature and build than Julia, Heather wrangled her sister from the barstool, out the door, and into her car. Which was no easy feat considering that she was sobbing and stumbling the entire way.

It wasn't until much later when Julia woke up, still fully dressed in her bed and her mouth dry like it'd been stuffed with rancid cotton balls, that she looked at her phone again. Just to see the time. After eleven, but the text message from earlier still sat unread. She'd completely forgotten about it in her margarita-fueled haze.

An unsaved number flashed at the top of the screen, but the bare digits thrummed memory awakening deep in Julia's gut. Sweat instantly prickled her palms. Her mouth dropped open as the phone fell from her hand, the dull thud on the carpet echoing in her chest.

Jules, I'm home.

TWO
THOMAS

PRESSURE PULSED behind Thomas's eyes as he stared at the backgammon board. The early autumn sunlight dappled through his parents' sun room warming his bare, olive-toned arms. He rested his chin on his hands, his elbows carving divots into his thighs. Instead of masterminding his next move against Dad, the text message consumed his thoughts.

The text message that he sent as a distraction. A distraction from the mess that had cycloned around Thomas ever since he touched down in Michigan last week. A break from the tension that radiated from the marrow of his bones after being home for the first time in three years.

Yes, three years. He actually couldn't believe it. But there had always been some plausible excuse.

I need to write. I'm broke. Just started a new internship.

Now there was no excuse. He couldn't continue to pass off the brunt of the family responsibilities—the emotional and actual ones—on his siblings.

Danny and Ari had done so much over the years that Thomas had straight up ignored. He couldn't help feeling a little bit like a dick about that. But he had his life in New York City. That wasn't so easy to give up but, this time, he had to be there. At least for now.

And so of course now he stressed about his family *and* the text message. A perfect storm of guilt, grief, and embarrassment constantly waged for control in his gut as he tried not to check his phone every two minutes for a response to his, admittedly, kinda shady text he shot off after a Scotch or two the other night.

Julia Ward's number, tucked away in his phone after all this time, had finally been put to use. He didn't consider until after he texted that she likely didn't have his number anymore and probably had no idea who was texting her.

He should have signed his name. But Thomas didn't think about that until hours later when a follow up text would have been even more mortifying.

"Son, your turn," Dad wheezed, watching Thomas over the game board as he positioned his cannula with a little more purchase in his nose. The oxygen whistled slowly, steadily, as they leaned toward each other over the game.

"Sorry." Thomas shook his head, chasing away the

thoughts of the now two-day-old text. Maybe she would never respond. No use obsessing over it.

Easier said than done.

"What are you thinking about?" Dad took a deep inhale through his nose, tapping a finger on the board. "I know it's not this game."

Thomas's stomach flipped. A famous Dad question. Or maybe it was just his question for Thomas. So often he wasn't paying attention to what was in front of him, instead daydreaming about something else.

But this wasn't a daydream. This was anxious scenario running. Another delightful quirk of his.

Did he want to tell Dad? If he didn't, and made up some other story, he would know straight away that Thomas lied. He'd never been good at hiding stuff from his folks.

Maybe that was part of why he left. Why he wanted so desperately to go to school at New York University. Thanks to stellar grades and test scores, and enough scholarship money, he was able to. Much to everyone's chagrin, he stayed there after graduating. Which, he was self-aware enough to admit, was a convenient way to avoid the not-so-subtle hints from his mom about coming home, settling down, and taking over the family restaurant, Callaghan's Coney Island. Not that he didn't want those things, just that he wasn't ready for them, then or now.

Possibly never.

He assumed he would be ready for it someday. But

that *someday* was now hurtling toward him way too fast and that thought curdled his stomach more than he dreaded the responsibility.

Instead, he made his own life until that fabled *someday*, pulling pints at Bushwick's hip XYZ Brewing, taking any internship in the entertainment industry he could, and writing romance novels in all the odd hours that he wasn't working those two other jobs. Even with two published books, he barely made rent and had a pathetic social life, but it was a life all his own.

A life that, once upon a time, he'd dreamed of sharing with Julia.

Tell Dad all of that? No thanks.

Did he already guess eighty percent of it without needing to be told? Of course.

Dad knew his first-born too well and his eyes softened. "I know this is hard for you."

Guilt flooded Thomas's veins. Hard? For him? He sat up straight. He wasn't the one dying. "Please, Dad. Don't be silly. I'm glad I'm home. Of course I'm here. It's nothing."

Home. For how long? It was impossible to tell. Mom hadn't even told Dad that Thomas was coming home after she'd called him sobbing three weeks ago.

Three weeks ago, when Dad made the decision to stop the chemotherapy treatments that weren't likely to help his stage four lung cancer anyway.

So Thomas cut his losses. He shipped home some

belongings, mostly books, and packed the rest up in tidy boxes that he tucked in his shared apartment's living room. Thanks to word of mouth, mostly from his three roommates, Thomas found a subletter in record time, too. One who agreed to a month-to-month arrangement. Then he flew home, fully intending to go back to New York when…when he wasn't needed in Starling Hills. Thomas swallowed, not ready to think about that.

"Ahh." Dad brushed a hand at the air and his eyes locked on his son. "I know you'd rather be back in New York than in Michigan helping at the diner every day."

Dad could always read Thomas like a book, mysterious though he wanted to be. Thomas wouldn't admit that Dad was right about this, not ever, but he wouldn't lie to him either.

Instead, Thomas clenched his jaw and gave a small nod before rolling the dice again.

Backgammon was their game. The two of them had spent countless hours playing in the sun room. In the summer, while drinking Cokes, windows thrown wide open to the sound of bugs chirping all evening. And in the winter, with hot chocolate or Scotch, a powerful space heater, and huddled under wool blankets.

Today was in between it all. Early October but still warm enough to wear a t-shirt and drink Coke. The breeze had a crispy fall edge, tangling through the trees under a bluebell sky crisscrossed with wisps of fluffy clouds.

Thomas counted his pieces across the board, happy to concentrate on his turn and not what Dad had said. The longer this conversation went on, the more likely Thomas would admit to something that he didn't want to. That he wasn't ready to.

"I just want you to be happy, Thomas." Dad stared at the dice, not picking them up for his turn.

Thomas clicked his tongue and leaned back in his chair, crossing his arms over his chest. "I am. Living the dream."

But after he said it, his jaw tightened.

His dream had been the same since sixteen. Since he first met Julia and they had the same dream: to write. Novels, TV shows, screenplays—anything and everything, and they were going to chase that dream. Study at New York University, do the whole starry-eyed New York, struggling artist thing, and do it together.

In the end, only Thomas went.

If he wasn't happy, he'd been living this way for a long time. Too long now to give up the ghost.

"How are the roommates? Rick and Janet and Trixie?" Dad always liked to say their names, proving he remembered them all.

"Fine," Thomas sighed, then amended his statement as Dad's eyes pinched just slightly in concern. "I mean, good. Ya know? We've all got our hustles we're working on so we're all busy but overall fine. Good."

Thomas swallowed and hoped that his bumbling

words convinced his dad enough that things were *good*. Though Thomas spent most of his life with Rick, Janet, and Trixie—an actor, comedienne, and installation artist respectively—he didn't miss them. It disgusted him a little, but it was true.

"Are you dating anyone?" Dad leaned back in his chair, his voice getting more wheezy.

"No." Thomas hoped this trip would have been less about his dating life and more about family. But his family wanted to know all about his dating life.

"It's been a while since you talked about anyone *special*." Dad wiggled his eyebrows unevenly and Thomas had to laugh at that.

But the laughter didn't last long.

No doubt Dad was referencing Micha, his writing partner and the closest thing to a *special person* in Thomas's life. The man his parents met the last time they visited him in New York. He...well...he wasn't exactly special but he was fine. Fun. Great looking and an amazing writer. More of a special writing partner than a special partner-partner.

Micha was a distraction who Thomas latched onto to convince himself that things were fine.

Someone *special* would have been given an explanation for why he was leaving the city for an unknown amount of time. XYZ Brewing got more information than Micha had.

Thomas sat back in his chair, the breeze rustling

through the trees and yellowing leaves. The two were quiet, not playing and not really talking either. The silence was comfortable. But Thomas could feel the emotional energy building, like when he stood in the Florida ocean as a kid and the tide pulled at his ankles.

Dad sighed. "I haven't seen you happy in a long time. That's all I want."

Thomas sighed harder, his exasperation winning out. "I *am* happy. I don't know how I'm supposed to prove it to you."

Dad shook his head and opened his hands as if he didn't know either. "It's just…it's good to have you home."

Thomas flicked his eyes up from the board to meet Dad's gaze. His chest burned as he saw the shining tears there, built up but not falling. He followed the nasal cannula looping across his father's face, around his ears, and down under the table to the oxygen tank. His whiskers needed trimming and his clothes hung off his shrinking frame.

This man, who moved his family through hard times, working extra shifts on the auto assembly line to squirrel away some money and chase his own dream of opening a restaurant one day. Who helped all of his kids through school, eager to give them a better springboard than he had.

Thomas paled in comparison. More selfish and stubborn than his dad, Thomas left Michigan to *study English* of all things and create his own life away from the self-inflicted shadow of him.

Still such a proud man, his dad was different now. Sick. Not able to care for himself.

Thomas's throat tightened, again at a loss for words. Not willing to tell Dad the whole truth, but not trusting his ability to say anything right now without falling apart. He nodded again and fidgeted with the dice in his hand as a single tear streamed down Dad's cheek.

"Okay, boys. Been out here for a while now and it's time for your afternoon meds, sir," Sienna said as she opened the sliding door to the sunroom, breaking the tension.

Sienna, the hospice nurse, came in the afternoons when Dad finished up at the restaurant. Thomas knew her from high school so it was still a little weird to see her in scrubs, in his parents' house. But she looked after Dad before Mom could be home to help. Though he wasn't receiving chemo, he still had a litany of medications to take and it was all a lot for Mom to manage alone.

Dad sniffed, pulling a handkerchief out of his pocket and wiping his nose.

Thomas helped Dad out of the chair.

"Good to see you, Thomas." Sienna smiled and nodded before following Dad into the house.

Out on the porch, Thomas drained his bottle of Coke and checked his phone for messages: nothing. Nothing from New York and nothing from Julia. Not even a read receipt. Just said "delivered." Maybe she had the read receipts off, but he couldn't even get the humiliating satisfaction of being left on read, the confirmation that she'd at least *seen* it. Anyway, Julia probably deleted the message, thinking it was some prank.

Should he try again? Maybe in a couple days. If Thomas could manage to ignore the shame that rolled over him in waves every couple minutes, causing him to second guess even reaching out at all.

Admittedly, it had been a risk. It had been twelve years since they talked, but he was home and heard about the breakup with Josh. Mom heard it from someone else, who got the story secondhand, and on and on. That's how news traveled in Starling Hills. Bad news moved faster. Unfortunately, his mom shared a startling amount of detail about how Josh had apparently been cheating on Julia for years and she found out via an email. An *anonymous* email.

And the dirtbag was going to marry her.

Thomas flexed his fingers. The whole thing made his blood boil. Not only because Josh was an asshole of epic proportions, but because of his history with Julia. Their intense friendship, and friendship-ending fight, and his botched apology—history that he'd tried for years to forget.

Being in Starling Hills made it all flood back to him, bittersweet and thick like honey in his veins. Though he was thirty, sleeping in his childhood bed with his feet hanging off the end, he felt sixteen again. Driving down Main Street in the same Toyota Corolla that he drove in high school, past the park and the playground, the hospital and shops: it felt like his first fall in this town.

It all felt like Julia.

His scalp tingled with anticipation. If he could see her, just once, maybe he could remember how to be happy again.

How to not have to worry about Dad. Or what Mom's going to do without him. Or what's going to happen to the Coney Island when Dad dies. Or question all of his choices up until now and doubt his career.

Thomas ran a hand through his almost-black tousled hair and down his beard, stretching the skin around his eyes. Some homecoming.

"Stop being ridiculous," he chided himself, picking up his Moleskine journal and flipping absentmindedly through the pages. As he did, his phone lit up but didn't make a sound, permanently on silent.

He saw the name.

Jules.

Julia.

His heart immediately kick-started, a galloping rhythm keeping time in his chest, as he swiped to the message.

And just like that, he was sixteen, it was three in the morning, and he had just gotten a text from Julia about the placement of the constellation Orion in the sky that night. Or some song lyrics that she really liked and reminded her of him. Or just the simple fact that she couldn't sleep.

Those texts used to be his favorite. The hopeless, restless ones that made him picture her face just barely glowing from the phone screen, hair a mess, lip between her teeth, waiting on his response.

His mouth went dry. His stomach dropped completely past his toes, through the floor, and into the soft, dark earth.

There was no preamble. She didn't even ask. She knew who sent the text.

Can I see you?

THREE

THOMAS

FOURTEEN YEARS AGO

BEING the new kid at sixteen, just before junior year of high school, was tough. It required all sorts of social gymnastics skills that Thomas didn't possess at all. More comfortable with a Moleskine notebook and ink smeared over the side of his left hand, the idea of forced small talk at the Summer Music Theater wrap party with the intention of "making friends" was a special kind of torture.

So, he decided, he wouldn't do it at all. He only came to the party anyway because his mom had somehow gotten wind of it and she'd guilt-tripped him into going.

"It'll be so fun! Who knows, maybe you'll meet a cute girl...or boy...or person! Do it for your mom who can no longer enjoy her youth." Then she flashed her most pleading stare. Thomas had definitely inherited her puppy dog eyes, droopy at the corners and always earnest.

As her oldest child, he was powerless against her begging eyes, serious request or not.

Fresh off their run of *Les Misérables*, this party marked the final hurrah before back-to-school time. Half the kids floated in the pool—a big *nope* from Thomas—and a few definitely smuggled warm vodka in water bottles that they chased with sips of Diet Vanilla Coke. He shuddered at the thought.

In classic wallflower mode, Thomas tucked himself into the quietest spot he could find to people watch as the summer golden hour faded into lavender dusk. He sat on the edge of a picnic table, tapping his checkered Vans on the bench as the playlist switched between pop punk bands and a medley of show tunes. Strings of patio lights crisscrossed overhead and citronella candles burned at even intervals around the periphery. The night smelled of chlorine, bug spray, and freshly mown grass and Thomas realized that he actually enjoyed the whole thing, even if it wasn't in the way that his mom had intended.

Out of nowhere, a girl with long, dark hair, wearing a maroon bandeau bikini top with a rainbow striped beach towel wrapped around her middle, plopped down on the table next to him. She crossed her arms over her stomach, her white skin cast in golden shadows from the twinkling overhead lights.

"I don't know you," she said. "I feel kinda bad that we worked backstage on the musical this whole summer and

I have no idea who you are so I thought I'd introduce myself. I'm Julia."

The neurologic pathways from Thomas's brain to his mouth completely shut down and sweat prickled his palms, momentarily speechless.

"Um," he stuttered, lifting his eyebrows, his forehead crinkling. This was why he didn't do small talk. He couldn't even spit out his name on command.

"Ha, sorry, kinda awkward to just sit down next to you uninvited, but you found the best perch in this place. Had to test it out." She lifted her eyes toward the string lights, the blue of her irises igniting deep and pure like Lake Michigan waves on an endless summer's day.

He cleared his throat. "Thomas Callaghan."

"Hello, Thomas Callaghan. My full name's Julia Ward. But, like I said, you can just call me Julia."

Was she making fun of him? No, probably not. She smiled at him, wide and easy, and he wondered how someone could be so effortless.

"Nice to meet you." He rubbed his palms on his thighs to dry them. Then stopped when the movement seemed too conspicuous.

"Are you new here?" Her smile still glowed, her hair flashing almost magenta in the dying evening light.

"Uh yup, my family moved to Starling Hills earlier this summer. My dad's opening a Coney Island—Callaghan's Coney Island—in a couple weeks and he wanted to be closer to the location." Not that she asked for all that information, but Thomas felt compelled to justify the situation.

"Ohmygod, I love a coney." Julia placed her hand on his forearm, closing her eyes in adulation. "Extra onions."

Heat laced up his arm from her touch and he immediately wanted to pull away but forced himself to stay put. She was just a girl excited about a hot dog, that's all this was. He didn't need to freak out about her friendly touch.

"My dad's wanted to open one for a long time. Grew up on them in Detroit. Second generation Irish immigrant and all that." *Okay Thomas, TMI. She doesn't need your family's life story.*

But she seemed to enjoy the TMI. Julia leaned in toward Thomas, finally moving her hand off his forearm as she talked animatedly with her hands.

"I was wondering about the cultural mixed metaphor. Don't often see an Irish Coney. Oh—that would be a great menu item. Coneys loaded with corned beef. Corned beef hash!" She narrowed her eyes and nodded. "Lots of potential there."

"Hot dogs aren't my favorite." More useless info.

"Well I, for one, would not want to live without hot dogs. It's like the perfect vehicle for a myriad of condiments." Her towel loosened around her and drooped at her waist, a wide swath of skin peeking out.

Thomas quickly looked away, as if they weren't already at a pool party and in *bathing suits*. "Except for ranch."

"You're so right." Julia nodded solemnly. "Ranch doesn't work on a hot dog. And I would know, I've tried."

Thomas laughed, a full guffaw that sent his upper body reeling backward. He caught himself on his hands behind him. "You're joking."

"I don't joke about ranch, Thomas. It's a condiment that's very near and dear to my heart."

"That's very Midwestern of you."

"Well, we are in the Midwest, aren't we?"

They smiled at each other, the banter between them immediate and easy. It wasn't always like this with new people. It was barely like this with anyone.

Thomas's words came out more easily on the page.

That's why he liked the backstage of the theater. He could never get up in front of an auditorium of people and act. Sing. Dance. Hell no. But he loved being a part of the magic of it all. Wearing all black and scampering around behind the scenes. If he couldn't write for the high school stage, at least he could be one of the magicians helping it all happen.

Julia kicked her legs. "Well, this worked out better than I anticipated."

"What do you mean?"

"I lied a little when I came over." Julia wrinkled her nose. "My sister dared me to come talk to you."

She pointed to someone in the water who looked like she could be Julia's twin. Who wiggled a wave when she noticed Julia's attention. Thomas recognized her: she played Cosette in the musical.

"That's your sister?" Then Julia's words actually landed in Thomas's brain. "She dared you to talk to me?"

Julia's cheeks flushed a peachy pink. "Yeah. Sorry for the lie."

"Why the dare?"

She shrugged, casual. "It's summertime. Why not?"

They chatted for the rest of the night. Until ten-thirty when Julia had to corral her sister from the pool to get them home for their eleven o'clock curfew. But not before Julia asked for Thomas's number. Casual.

Thomas left the party shortly after, too. By the time he got home, there was a text waiting for him. Already, something tingled hot through his veins at the thought of Julia.

Nice to meet you tonight, Thomas :-)

FOUR
JULIA

A COUPLE DAYS passed before Julia returned to the text. It was easy enough to pretend it never came. But every time she looked at her messages, there it was sitting open in her inbox. She had her read receipts off so there was no harm in opening and just staring at the message. Though letting it linger in *delivered* limbo wasn't very nice either. She just wasn't sure what to do with it yet.

She couldn't deny the fact that each time she read his message, a little trail of warmth danced over her skin.

And now she paced in her cubicle at work, phone clutched in hand and staring at the words. Tiny circles back and forth in her block-heeled mules, blazing a metaphorical trail in her miniscule workbox.

She'd read the text so many times that the excitement had numbed her. Over-sensitized her. The words were like a little dagger right to the heart, over and over. They repeated on a loop in her brain.

Jules, I'm home.

She knew exactly who sent the text. Thomas Callaghan.

Her best friend before she was progressively sucked into Josh's orbit. Her friend who showed up out of nowhere. One day he didn't exist, and the next, there he was, like a constellation rising in the sky. They met under the stars at the Summer Musical Theater wrap party, talking until it was too late and the mosquitoes ate them alive.

Somehow, Julia and Thomas instantly bonded.

She stretched her fingers, shifting her phone to the other hand as she paced another mini-turn, tendrils of apprehension and shame sneaking through her shell. Her limbs grew heavy with it.

Did he know what happened between her and Josh? Did someone tell him? Not like it was splashed on her socials or anything, but maybe one of his high school friends might have told him, if he still talked to anyone. Then again, news—especially bad news—traveled fast around Starling Hills.

She stopped pacing, started to type a response for the millionth time, the cursor blinking at her, but she didn't know what to say. Backspacing, she locked her phone and continued her mini-march.

God, why had this text sent her into such a tailspin?

She hadn't thought about Thomas in years, but now all she could think about was that summer they met fourteen years ago.

Thomas had puppy dog eyes. Earnest, deep brown eyes that pulled slightly downward at the corners. Crowned with black caterpillar eyebrows that would take him years to grow into, his eyes always asked a question. Even at sixteen, he had a sprinkling of a mustache so that you knew one day he would grow a beautiful beard. Back then, he kept his hair buzzed short.

He sat perched over the party, watching everyone with the most intense stare. More intense of a gaze than she'd seen on any other sixteen-year-old boy. From her vantage point in the pool, warm and wet and full of glee at what this group of kids had accomplished in a month's time, she knew she wanted to talk to this stranger. And when Heather dared her to do just that, she wrapped her blossoming curves and round hips in a towel and sauntered over to him.

They hardly left each other's side after that moment. When they weren't driving aimlessly around Starling Hills, switching out burned CDs in his Corolla's player, or eating fries at Callaghan's Coney Island, they texted late into the night.

One night, Thomas wanted to stargaze.

He came over to her house and they laid in her backyard. The grass tickled the backs of her knees, itchy like a million bugs crawling over her bare skin. She tried not to look at his calves rising out of his checkered sneakers. Her heart fluttered at the sight; she never knew calves could be so attractive.

They just laid out in the yard, talking, as the power lines stood tall and crackling nearby. No wind. Just the crickets chirping their slow song and Thomas's steady breath beside her. Their arms tucked down by their sides. Thomas on Julia's right. Their hands didn't touch but were so close to each other that she felt the grass twitch with his movements.

"What do you want to be when you grow up?" She stared at the sky as they tried to pick out constellations.

He thought for a moment. "I want to be a writer."

"Me too," Julia said, flicking her pinky in the air, brushing past his.

She had never told anyone that before. Between the friction in her smallest finger and the butterflies dancing in her stomach, she felt breathless.

"Really?" He turned his head to the side and looked at her, but she stayed staring at the sky.

She forced herself to breathe. To tell him her secrets.

"Mm-hmm. I write fan fiction online already. But I don't know what I want to write when I'm older. Fantasy novels, probably? What about you?"

Her cheeks flushed with the thrill and utter embarrassment of admitting her life's dream to another living, breathing soul. She had never told anyone about her online writing, either. Especially not her parents.

"Novels. But screenplays, too, I think." He paused. "Wait, you write fics? Can I read them?"

"I mean, yeah. They're on my LiveJournal." Her heart pulsed in every inch of her body. "What do you want to write?"

"Romantic comedies." Now it was his turn to blush. He distinctly fixed his eyes on the stars as he said it.

"You're joking." She propped herself up on one elbow, a grin plastered on her face. Leaning over him, her long, brown hair dragged on his arm.

"I wouldn't dare. I take my romcoms very seriously."

Their eyes met then. She, surrounded by a cascading waterfall of hair looking down at him. And him staring up at her with the stars reflected in his eyes. Serious as a heart attack. Until Thomas broke out into peals of laughter. Julia laughed so hard that her arms got weak and she rolled onto her back in the grass.

They made a plan to meet outside of school on the first day, and after that it just became a thing. He carried all of his binders in his backpack and never had to go to his locker. They darted back and forth to Julia's locker, through the teeming halls of high school that smelled like Axe body spray and Love Spell perfume, day in and out, always a duo.

Until one day, they weren't anymore.

Julia paused her pacing, considering, for the millionth time. Did she even care that Thomas was home? Did she want to see him? Their last conversation at the end of senior year wasn't exactly pleasant. She was so awful back then. The whole thing was all her fault.

God, had it really been twelve years?

Julia crossed her arms over her stomach, shielding herself from the memory of that fight.

Now those in-between years all seemed so hazy, spent glued to Josh's side. And for what? She barely recognized herself anymore. She never wrote anymore. All of the dreams she had as a teen were tucked away in a dark corner of her heart. But her fingers still ached to hold a pen and scribble story notes. To fly over the keyboard in the middle of a brilliant scene.

Eventually, she lost Thomas's number when she got a new phone and purged him off all socials with the rest of the high school people that she no longer talked to.

But his phone number was still burned in her brain from the marathon text sessions they had late into the night in high school. She leaned onto her desk chair, closed her eyes, and saw his number seared into the back of her eyelids.

Why was he home? He always said New York was a ten-year town and it had been eight or so since he finished his degree.

I'm home. Simple but at the same time, not. No explanation.

A knock outside Julia's cubicle snapped her out of her daydream, her eyes flying open.

"Earth to Julia," Susan, another purchaser on her

team, sing-songed. Her strawberry-blonde-peppered-grey hair was twisted back with a tortoise shell barrette and the lines of her forehead jumped higher than normal in an expectant look.

Susan was Julia's ride-or-die, the only person who truly and one hundred percent backed her when she left Josh. In large part because she'd also been cheated on in her marriage and was left a single, working mother of two middle grade girls.

Julia quickly locked her phone and turned it face down. "What's up, Susan?"

"I could ask you the same thing. You've been pacing for like an hour." She leaned into Julia's cubicle and scanned the place. "Quality meeting. You coming?"

"Morning ladies!" Michelle trilled as she paused next to Susan. Her pastel pink nails clutched a Starbucks cup, her laptop in the other. "Meeting time!"

Julia's skin tightened. She fought the recoil reflex that she got whenever Michelle, the third purchaser on their team, was around. Admittedly, Julia had no real reason to dislike her; she just didn't think Michelle was a good person. Bad vibes. Julia secretly considered Michelle her office rival. Friendly competition that Michelle had no idea existed, of course. Susan knew though. They complained about Michelle a lot.

"Good morning!" Julia forced a smile and enthusiasm. "Didn't realize it was ten o'clock already!"

She had literally done nothing this morning except

obsess over the text, typing and un-typing things she didn't know how to say.

Susan smirked and turned away, shoving her hands in the pockets of her pantsuit. "Distracted this morning?"

"It's nothing," Julia mumbled, grabbing her sticker-covered Nalgene water bottle and undocking her laptop. She slid her phone into her pencil skirt pocket.

Michelle fluffed her voluminous blonde hair over her shoulder. Her strong perfume wafted as she did.

"Well!" she sang, "I'll see you both in there!"

Michelle strutted away and Susan huffed before turning to Julia, who rolled her eyes. They communicated their silent complaints about Michelle with just those two looks.

"Yeah, well looks like you've been doing nothing all morning," Susan laughed, getting back on topic.

Julia blustered in protest, afraid someone might overhear their conversation as they walked down the hall.

"Girl, your cubicle is right across from mine and you haven't complained or freaked out about the promotion once all morning. Just doing little power walking loops around your cozy cubbyhole there. I know when you're distracted."

Julia's stomach plunged. The promotion that would solidify her trajectory with Contrakale Logistics, with her life. It was something that Josh had encouraged her toward back when they were together. Now that seemed like such a farce. He probably only wanted her to be working more so he could have more time to philander.

Contrakale, the main industrial employer in Starling Hills, specialized in logistics automation software solutions. What a mouthful. Did she really want this to be her *life*? She didn't want to think about it right now.

"Fine, it's just a text," she huffed, clutching her laptop tighter. "They're supposed to email about the next round of interviews today."

"Hmm." Susan quirked an eyebrow, sizing up Julia's anxiety with one sweep of her gaze. "Let's stay on the important topic here. Some text. Or sext, maybe?"

"Ohmygodstopit." Color rose into Julia's cheeks and she changed the subject. "They're gonna ride us about that piece that's on backorder. I just know it."

"Interesting choice of words there." Susan tried to remain serious but she shook with suppressed laughter. "Freudian slip regarding your mysterious text, or?"

"Shut up!" Julia groaned, knocking into Susan's shoulder as they walked down the hall.

"Ah you're just too easy, Juju. You're right, the engineers are always riding us about something or other." Susan could barely keep a straight face.

Julia clamped her lips shut, not willing to give into Susan's teasing—she was the only person allowed to call her Juju—as her cheeks flared with heat. It was just a text. She was being ridiculous about it anyway. It didn't mean anything. It couldn't. It had been years since they talked. It was all just weird. But in a good way.

"So..." Susan still wanted information, her impatience clear in the way she drew out the syllable.

Julia stayed silent for a couple more seconds, just to rile her friend even more.

"Julia, are you seeing someone or what?" She fell onto Julia's arm, clinging in faux desperation. "Give a single mom with no time for dating all the details."

Julia sighed. "There's nothing to tell. Someone I know from high school is moving back. I think."

"Someone? Male or female, friend or foe?"

Julia side-eyed her.

"What? I said all the details." Susan shrugged. "You know I live vicariously through your youth."

"Stop, thirty-eight is hardly old." Julia rolled her eyes. "And I'll remind you that being publicly humiliated by my ex-fiancé is really fucking great."

"Hey." She grabbed Julia's elbow, stopping them outside of the board room. "Don't let that fucker steal everything from you, alright? You can still be excited about stuff. Life. Mysterious text messages."

She gave Susan a half smile. "You're right. Thanks."

"I know I am. Now let's sit quietly as far tucked back in the corner as we can, staring daggers at anyone who questions the lead times, eh?"

Julia smiled, the lightness of relief fluttering in her stomach. Susan could be counted on for a pep talk. Or a stiff drink. Whichever the situation called for. When Julia found out about Josh, Susan was the one who got her drunk. For weeks they went out to happy hour at Gratzi!, Starling Hills's best (and only) place for Italian, and drank too many dirty martinis and ate too much fettuccine Alfredo.

"Fuck men and fuck their peckers," Susan growled as the first toast at exactly five thirty every evening. "Just be glad you found out now, Juju. And praise be, you're still young and hot."

Her support lessened the burn but didn't make it easier. Too many happy hours, Julia cried into her fourth martini as Susan patted her back and plied her with pasta until she sobered up enough to drive home.

It took many, many happy hours until Julia didn't need four rounds and everyday happy hours anymore.

And now it was a cavernous, ever-present ache. A hole Julia thought she'd carry for the rest of her life. A reminder that she couldn't trust her inner compass. Though Susan continually assured her that one day it would be better, Julia didn't believe her. This void wouldn't end with nothing but stupid work meetings and deadlines to fill it.

It's hard to care about anything when there was just corporate numbness inside.

Back at her desk, just before she signed off for the day, an email whooshed into her inbox with a little chime.

Dear Ms. Ward,

We're pleased to inform you that you've moved on to the next round of interviews.

Please visit the attached link to schedule your interview.
Sincerely,

Christopher Wu

Her stomach plunged. This was happening. She was one step closer to a fully corporate life.

After work, Julia lounged in bed, cradling her phone and staring at the text message.

Jules, I'm home.

It was almost like the years hadn't passed and she was seventeen again, in the same bed, texting the same boy.

Something lingered just at the edges that pulled at her. A context for the message that Julia didn't know, but wanted to. Why was Thomas home now? And why was he texting her?

She pulled her bottom lip between her teeth, deciding to respond. So many questions ricocheted through her mind, but there was only one that she needed to ask right now. Only one question that could lead to so many more. More questions than even Julia was ready to ask of herself.

Her thumbs shook from the adrenaline and she bit her lip to ground her, but it didn't help.

Can I see you?

As she hit send, she breathed out, and before her next inhale, Julia already had her response: *Yes.*

FIVE
THOMAS

THOMAS TAPPED HIS PEN, the empty page of his journal taunting him. He could think of nothing to write, fearing that any words he put down would be too whiny, too self-incriminating, too much like the self-obsessed entries he wrote back in high school. He feared that he would only write about Julia. Which was not much different than what sixteen-year-old Thomas wrote.

So instead, he anxiously beat out an abstract rhythm with his pen and watched the bartenders work.

Salt Cellar Distillery wasn't busy. He hunched toward the bar, leaning on his elbows, and kept an eye out for Camden—Danny's best friend and the manager of this place. But she didn't appear to be here today.

Thomas sighed. This laidback bar tucked into a side street in downtown Starling Hills with its industrial farmhouse vibe was nothing like the nights that he worked at

XYZ Brewing in Bushwick. He mostly tackled that chaos with his roommate, Janet. The place would be full every night, no empty seats, and most nights it was four plus deep at the bar, people hollering for drinks.

He missed New York. Or parts of it, at least. How it was so busy that he could never really think properly. The frenetic way that it all fit together. He was never really alone in New York. Now the Michigan silence unnerved him.

The littlest creaks of his parents' house would wake him up. Someone flushing the toilet, or the house settling. In his apartment, the cacophony of traffic and people yelling eventually became a lullaby. It droned on, constant and consuming, so much so that Thomas didn't need to fill his head with always thinking of *something else,* because something was already there. He didn't have time to stop and think about whether or not he was happy. New York was a container in which all of his emotions settled and diffused until he was a new kind of numb.

In Starling Hills, he didn't have that container. And he had so much more to think about here. He couldn't ignore his family, his past, because he relived it constantly. He couldn't use the allure of two published novels to make fake friends or get someone in his bed. Here, he was forced to reckon with who he was. The trouble was…he didn't really know who he was anymore.

On top of that, trying to write his next novel with his knees shoved under his childhood desk, surrounded by bookcases stuffed with his old journals and walls plastered with classic musical posters, had contributed to his writer's block in a big, tragic way. Hurray.

He sipped his Manhattan. It was good, balanced, and he was surprised by how impressed he was by it.

Downtown Starling Hills's glow-up had really started when Camden's parents started this place in the mid aughts. Over time, Salt Cellar became an institution.

The drink was good, but he had to admit that he still preferred an ice-cold Coors Light.

All because of one memory: a trip with a bunch of theater kids to canoe on a river up north.

He and Julia snuck a lunchbox stuffed with Coors Light into their boat and passed cans back and forth as they paddled down the river. Alcohol would never again taste as good as when they drank from the same can, getting burnt and exhausted from the sun. When Julia tossed her head back, neck extending long, her maroon bikini top a wide swatch of fabric stretching to contain her breasts.

His heart literally quivered at the memory. *Oh my god.* He cleared his throat, leg bouncing incessantly. Thomas needed to stop thinking about all that immediately.

That was over ten years ago and they were different people now. Grown up and grown out of their friendship. Though Thomas distinctly *didn't keep tabs* on Julia, he did look up her Instagram (private), TikTok (no posts), Twitter (locked down), and Facebook (non-existent) to see what she looked like now or suss out what she was up to. He couldn't find her online and therefore couldn't get the image of Julia at seventeen out of his head—not for lack of trying.

He needed to get control of himself. Coming out of the gate all flustered wouldn't be a good way to rekindle their friendship. Just as Thomas took another sip, someone appeared at his elbow.

"There you are," she said with a smile on her voice. "Hi."

There she was. Julia.

She looked, somehow, exactly the same, just more mature. A more round face, more curves. Same long brown hair tied back in a braid and thoughtful, storm cloud blue eyes that sucked him in immediately.

Caught by surprise, heat flared through Thomas's entire body and he quickly swallowed the liquor before he coughed it all over her. It burned going down and he did cough, mouth closed. Real cool. He swallowed again, his throat thick and Adam's apple bobbing. She leaned toward him, elbow on the bar, and the shorter pieces of hair falling loose from her braid tickled his arm. His heart nearly stopped.

Oh no.

No this wasn't good at all. Those damned butterflies still fluttered alive and well all these years later.

She smiled widely, her blue-grey eyes sparkling as she blushed pleasantly.

Thomas adjusted in his seat and then shook his head.

"What am I doing?" he said, before dropping down from the slight height of the barstool. His mind whirred a million miles a minute. It had been years since they'd seen each other. Did they hug? Should they hug?

Then his arms, as if working under their own control, opened widely to Julia. He guessed they were hugging now. Taking quick stock, he noted that his choice of faded black t-shirt wasn't showing his sweat even though he could feel it beading on his forehead.

Fuck.

Julia hesitated, apparently the same doubts going through her mind. But she laughed politely, awkwardly. His six-foot-four height tucked her just-over-five-feet neatly under his arms. She still smelled like the same warm vanilla sugar body spray she wore in high school.

Thomas thanked whatever god might be listening that Julia still smelled of vanilla sugar.

In a dizzying rush, memories flooded Thomas. The night they met at the *Les Mis* wrap party, sitting on that picnic table until curfew. Laying on the grass when they first confessed their dreams to each other. Her in that long, purple-blue dress at Homecoming that year. That last, horrific day that they ever talked in person, when Julia revealed the secret she hid from him for months.

Thomas didn't like thinking about the last one. A memory that haunted him. They all melded together, tight in his chest. Bittersweet hunger.

She stepped back, breaking their hug.

"You look great, Julia." He exhaled, rubbing his sweating palms down his jeans.

Her blush traveled higher up her cheeks and into her forehead.

"Yeah, thanks." She said it like a sigh, running her hand over her braid. "You too," she tacked on.

Thomas cleared his throat, pulling back a stool. "Please."

"Oh." Julia laughed again. "That's nice. Thanks."

Heat prickled the back of Thomas's neck as he attempted to smoothly scoot the stool back to the bar. Julia adjusted her hips in response and the tingling continued up and over Thomas's scalp.

All he needed to do was play it cool. Casual. Just two friends catching up after years of not speaking. Totally fine.

"I know they don't have Coors Light here." Julia scrunched her lips to the side as she scanned the menu then flicked her eyes up to Thomas at the last second, giggling conspiratorially. "You know, that's the only time I've been canoeing on that river."

"Not since?" Thomas relaxed back into his chair, the awkwardness easing up between them. He flagged down the bartender and took a sip of his drink. "I haven't either actually, so I don't know why that's surprising to me." He smirked.

When the bartender arrived, Thomas nodded toward

Julia. She took a breath and smiled, biting down on her lip just before she ordered. "The Botanical G&T, please."

"You got it, Julia." The bartender nodded. Of course the bartender knew her.

Julia folded her hands in her lap. She turned to Thomas, opening her eyes wide, expectantly. Neither of them spoke for a beat, trying to find their rhythm with each other.

"Still journaling, eh?" She flicked the pages of his journal, still open to a blank page.

"Ah yeah." Thomas flipped the cover shut, suddenly very self-aware. "Nasty little habit I can't seem to give up. I realized a couple years ago I should probably burn the old ones. Incriminating stuff." His lips pulled into a wry grin.

Julia nodded, sighing a laugh through her nose.

"It's good to see you," she said as the bartender put her drink down. Little edible flowers floated on the surface, and she smiled at it. She licked her lips and turned back to Thomas. "It was a wild summer."

"Was it?" He tried to sound casual, but he did not. Not the least bit. It didn't help that his voice cracked just a little. Thomas winced as Julia's lips smashed into a thin line.

"You've heard then, I guess." It wasn't a question but a forlorn statement of fact.

Oh no. Of course this would come up immediately, the elephant in the room. Josh, the shithead wedge that drove them apart, spinning further away from each other, until years stood between them.

And then, they weren't so far apart at all. They were here, in this moment, having this cringe conversation.

Thomas swallowed. Might as well get this part over with.

"I did, yeah. My mom heard it from someone who..." He trailed off as Julia's face fell.

"Cool. Really love that everyone's talking about the catastrophic end to my happiness." She stared into her cocktail, lips turned down. "You know what, I don't have anything against polyamory, but I do have a thing against liars. And cheaters. And I really can't deal with the fucking ugly dishonesty."

Her voice grew higher and tighter as she went on, staring at some point in the middle distance. Thomas hated to see her like this. No one deserved what was happening to her. Thomas stared into his whiskey with his lips pulled back, baring his teeth in a grimace. If he ever ran into this Josh guy, he wasn't sure what he would do to him.

"How are the drinks?" the bartender asked, breaking Thomas out of his trance.

"Great, thanks," Thomas said after a beat when it was clear that Julia wasn't going to respond.

"This drink almost makes me feel better," she said when he walked away, but she still frowned.

"Listen, all that Josh stuff was really fucked up and I'm

sorry that it happened." Thomas hadn't been sure how he wanted to address the whole situation, but it rolled off his tongue. The sincerity behind the words burned in his chest. "You deserve better than him."

He finished his drink to make himself shut up, the large ice ball knocking into his front teeth. It would be too easy now to say something really ridiculous when all he really wanted was to be friends again. The person who she texted about good movies and excellent books.

"Anyway," he cleared his throat, "do you still write?"

"Oh god no." She laughed it off like it was a silly suggestion and grabbed her drink, nonchalantly taking another sip.

Thomas furrowed his brows, honing in on her. "Your fan fiction was some of the best I've read, to be honest. Especially when you started to get steamy. And I've read a lot of fics."

She ignored the compliment. "Ha, well, I mean, I just haven't had the time, with work at Contra and all that. I'm just exhausted, ya know?"

"I know exhausted, yep." Thomas pulled his lips between his teeth and widened his eyes. "I've got two published books, but I'm still working basically three jobs just to make rent."

"Three? Thomas, really?"

His name spiked in his ears, so casual on her tongue but it was the first time he heard her say it in years. His stomach vaporized into a fine mist. Like liquid nitrogen. Nothing there to stabilize him.

"Yep." He hoped that he nodded in a casual way. A way that didn't suggest his world just slid completely off-kilter.

"I've read your books." She smirked. "You said *my* steamy fics were good, but your sex scenes are *hot*. Very tender stories, too."

He melted, now simply a puddle of goo attempting to sit in a chair.

She read his books. He supposed it made sense. They weren't a secret or anything and they were published by one of the big houses under the name "T. Callaghan." Not exactly a pseudonym. With his picture on the back, too. Not a mystery. But she indirectly inspired so much of those stories. The tropes: the girl that got away in one, the guy next door in the other. Did she see through it?

"Well, thanks," he said. He didn't dare say more.

"Of course." She caught his gaze. "I'm so proud of you. And a little jealous." Julia narrowed her eyes, considering. "A lot jealous I guess."

"Yeah. It hasn't been easy exactly. I constantly have to fight to make time for what I love. And I love writing." He felt a bit like a douche explaining this to someone outside his writer world. He cleared his throat in an attempt to recover. "You used to too, remember?"

Julia frowned and raised her eyebrows, over-exaggeratedly haughty. "Yeah, well we don't all have that kind of luxury."

He snorted. With his two books floundering on the mid-list, his third had sold, but just barely. It wouldn't release for another three years, and the advance was laughably small.

"Did you forget about the working two other jobs part? Not to mention the crippling writer's block I'm struggling with. Luxury? Hardly."

Julia huffed, a derisive *huh*, and crossed her arms. She stared at the live edge bar with a frown on her face.

The minutes passed in silence, the curtain of awkwardness firmly pulled between them once more. Thomas's mind raced to catalogue the moment that their conversation had gotten so off track.

This was different to his social circle in New York. Everyone he knew there had a side hustle or a third hustle or some kind of gig that was actually the reason they were there. Writing, acting, comedy, singing, some medium of art. They were all hiding their misery behind a marquee of lights, updating their social channels with the highlight reel of their successes. All while eating sad cup-o-noodles for every meal that cost less than a dollar but would probably give them all scurvy in the end.

He opened his mouth to apologize, but Julia spoke first.

"Are you happy? In New York?" she asked, holding her chin in her hand with her elbow propped on the bar. Her gaze locked on him, the grey in her eyes highlighting the depth of her thoughts.

Thomas couldn't look at her and instead watched their drinks. That question again. He couldn't lie to his dad, so he didn't say anything. But he wasn't sure what he wanted Julia to know or not know or how long he wanted to keep up this charade.

In truth, he wasn't even sure what he felt. New York was New York. Exactly what he thought it would be, and yet totally different at the same time. But his life was there, in Brooklyn. Everything he worked toward since he left high school. It just was what it was.

But he loaded up some bullshit answer about all the great opportunities he'd come across in New York. A list of things that had changed since the pandemic, like how he lived in a better place now for marginally cheaper rent. But just as he opened his mouth, Julia kept going.

"I mean, I just ask because I was supposed to be there too, you know?" She stared down the bar, gaze unfocused. "And now I'm up for this huge promotion that I've been interviewing for for months and it'll be a major step in my career. It's supposed to be a good thing. Josh pushed me to go for it even though it would mean way less time at home because it would be like true *corporate* life. I have the final interview in a couple weeks. Seeing you reminds me that New York City was always our plan and it didn't happen."

Thomas's stomach hardened. Memories flooded back to him, the shape and feel of the shame and regret as he lost his best friend to an absolute prick of a guy.

"It happened for me, Julia. Whose fault is it that it

didn't happen for you?" The bitter words escaped before he could stop them. He didn't reel them back in—they were true after all—so he let them lie.

"Wow." Julia shook her head at him, her mouth falling open. "If I had known you'd be like this, I never would have agreed to see you again."

"Like what?" He wanted to hear what she thought of him. He wanted to feel the pain of her words deep in his marrow. It was better than the silence that had lasted over a decade.

"Like a pompous asshat who's too good for the life you left behind!" Her cheeks mottled a deep red.

Asshat? He wasn't *that* bad, was he?

"I didn't leave anyone behind, Julia. You were already gone." The words grated like sandpaper.

"Not that you deserve an explanation but, yeah, in hindsight, I might have made some questionable choices in my life, but I wouldn't wish this shit on anyone. Zero out of ten, do not recommend." She sliced her hand through the air and her lips turned into an exaggerated frown. "And I don't need more snark piled on top of it from you."

Julia chugged half her cocktail in one go as Thomas stared, his nostrils flaring.

Thomas and Julia sat in silence again as the bar got more crowded with the pre-dinner rush. He kicked himself. He didn't mean to be such a dick; it just came out that way.

Thomas took a breath. "I'm sorry. That wasn't what I meant."

"Yeah, well, whatever," she mumbled, running her thumb over her glass, sparkling with condensation. "It's always so easy in your books."

"What is?"

Julia's thumb traced a smiley face on her sweating glass. "Being happy."

Thomas's gut twisted at how hopeless she sounded. "Romance novels are tidier than real life."

"Is that why you love them so much?"

"It's part of it. And also because they're a reminder that no matter how bad things get, there's always a happy ending."

"You don't really believe that?" She looked at him from the top of her gaze.

He shrugged. "You don't?"

"I used to." Julia curled in on herself, leaning toward the bar. The shorter pieces of her hair dragging along the top.

Thomas's heart shattered watching her, her posture totally devoid of hope. This wasn't how this meetup was supposed to be. This wasn't how they imagined their lives when they were sixteen and full of promise for the future. When they still had their dreams to lift them up.

Thomas's jaw tightened. He had to do something. Anything. He had to make it better.

"What if I could prove it to you?"

"Prove it to me? You can't prove that happy endings are a guarantee." She rolled her eyes.

"Sure I can. We'll study the best romance films and we'll build a body of evidence so compelling that you'll have to agree with me. There's always a happy ending." He swiveled his chair toward her. His long legs swung freely, his checkered Vans kicking through the air.

"You're enjoying this." She smirked and swung her stool around too. Her lavender Chuck Taylors nestled between his feet.

Their knees didn't touch, but the space in between them tingled. Electricity jumped back and forth. Thomas's breath hitched as sparks raced over his body. If Julia felt it, too, she didn't show it. He rubbed a hand down his thigh.

Stay calm.

"I'm enjoying this very much." Thomas smiled, his beard moving with his lips as the corners of his eyes pulled downward.

"I don't believe in your hypothesis, but I'm curious to see what you come up with." Julia narrowed her eyes. "In the name of science, I propose we make it more interesting. You've got your writer's block and I'm out of practice. Let's take the theory out of the classroom. First person to write 50,000 words wins," she paused, casting around for a decent prize, "a burrito."

Thomas quirked an eyebrow. This *could* be interesting. "A burrito bet? For 50,000 words? Low stakes."

"Friendly competition, let's say. And I'm rusty."

They lifted their cocktails in the air and drank to it.

That night, Thomas doomscrolled in bed. The same nightly routine of Instagram, Twitter, and TikTok of all of his peers (friends?) back in Brooklyn. Then the major news outlets for any new fresh hell. And then once more all over again for good measure.

His eyes burned, straining in the dark, one hand clutching the phone and the other hand running absent-mindedly over his beard. A text notification popped up at the top of his screen and he immediately clicked on it, read receipts be damned.

So which movie are we watching first?

SIX

JULIA

HEATHER BURST into Julia's bedroom, startling Julia from the mild Sunday afternoon coma she'd fallen into on her bed.

"Mom said you saw Thomas Callaghan yesterday."

"Leave me alone. I'm stressed." Julia huddled down further in her blankets as her sister pranced across the room between the remaining bridal shower gifts that needed to be returned.

"Thinking about the interview?" Heather loomed over her sister, hands on her hips, wearing leggings and a well-worn Michigan State University hoodie. Her Sunday uniform, since the two refused to go to church with their parents anymore, despite how often their mother requested it.

Julia nodded, trying not to think about it. "Final one is next week. And Mom shouldn't be telling you things about who I see and how I do. Also, how dare you wear Sparty around me."

"Go green!" Heather said, referencing her alma mater and sticking out her tongue.

Julia wrinkled her nose in response. They were a house divided, through and through. Fifty percent University of Michigan Wolverines, and fifty percent Michigan State University Spartans. Even their parents rooted for different football teams.

Heather shrugged. "But you know how Mom is. Can't keep her mouth shut."

Julia frowned, thinking about how Thomas's mom heard from someone, who heard from someone else, about her imploded engagement. That all had to start somewhere, hadn't it? Julia sure wasn't broadcasting the news. She would die if she knew that her mom was gossiping about her. With her Bible study group? Her book club? The thought made her feel ill.

Letting out an uncontrolled moan, Julia flipped over in bed and pulled the duvet over her head.

Heather flopped onto Julia's bed, cuddling under the covers next to her older sister. Julia scooted closer to the wall, huffing.

"Do you really need to get in my bed with your day clothes still on?" The blankets muffled her voice.

Heather tore the blanket off her sister so that Julia's head peeked out again. "Whatever, I'm not dirty. They're clean."

Julia rolled her eyes.

Heather nuzzled into Julia's arm. "So what's up with Thomas?"

Warmth flared in Julia's belly. *That* wasn't particularly convenient. Fresh off a trashed relationship, attraction to someone new wasn't exactly what she wanted. But Thomas wasn't new, was he?

Yesterday had been a mild disaster anyway. Their conversation oscillated between the ease of comfortable old besties to bitter rivals and back again. And she certainly felt the electricity crackling between them. The one that she was never really sure was mutual. The one she'd given up on back in high school.

But now, the warmth traveled into her chest, inflating like a crinkling mylar balloon. No, Thomas was one of her oldest friends. All the others lost to marriage, or babies, or careers. Some lost to Josh. And they were going to spend a lot of time together this fall, with their "happy ending" research sessions and little friendly burrito bet on the line.

Her stomach curdled. None of this was convenient at all. She couldn't even trust these feelings. The same feelings that had urged her to fall head over heels for Josh and rearrange her plans for him. She changed for him, and now it was safe to say that it wasn't for the better.

Julia sighed. Best to stay ambiguous, especially with Heather. "He's fine."

But that traitorous heat flew from her chest into her cheeks.

Heather turned her chin up toward Julia. Like a bloodhound on a mission for the truth, Heather could always smell a lie. This finely tuned skill of hers led to the summertime dare to talk to Thomas in the first place. Julia had spent the entire summer watching Thomas backstage, too nervous to talk to the cute new kid. Until her sister sussed out the truth and forced her hand at the wrap party. Julia never could turn down a dare. Not that Heather would have let her. If Julia had ignored the situation, it would have gotten worse, until Heather did some humiliating thing like talk to Thomas for her.

Heather narrowed her eyes. "Just *fine*?" She drew out the middle syllable.

"That's what I said." Julia cleared her throat and shifted against her pillows.

"Well," Heather said, dropping that line of questioning and switching tactics. "Is he dating anyone?"

"I don't know. We didn't talk about that."

"Ah, a convenient oversight."

"Not like it matters."

Heather was not dissuaded. "It *matters* because he was always in love with you."

Julia's entire body surged, her stomach dropping like she'd been pushed into a pool unexpectedly.

"Excuse me?" She didn't dare look at her sister, risking giving something—too much—away.

"I mean, it was obvious, wasn't it?"

Julia opened her mouth and closed it again, but not before a tiny, confused whine escaped her lips.

"Oh sweet Julia." Heather's eyes were wide with faux pity. She patted Julia's leg.

Her younger sister was always savvier in the dating department, hitting all of the milestones before Julia. At sixteen, when she heard a story about fourteen-year-old Heather making out with her boyfriend backstage, Julia's stomach twisted into knots, never having even kissed anyone yet. Not that she hadn't *wanted* to, it just hadn't happened yet.

"Thomas was obsessed with you." Heather shrugged. "I always thought he was The One for you."

Julia sputtered, speechless. Even her toes tingled. The One? What kind of nonsense was that? "Whatever. There's no such thing as The One," she grumbled as she crossed her arms over her stomach.

Heather jumped onto her knees, bouncing the entire bed in the process. "Wow, I like seeing my perfect older sister all unsettled like this." Heather smiled, the slant of her lips pulling to a smug angle.

"I don't like it." Julia frowned. "And anyway, you're wrong."

"Please, what teenager wouldn't have been obsessed with you?" Heather fluffed a lock of her sister's hair. "Great hair, huge boobs, sweet little backstage theater nerd. May I re-emphasize the huge boobs? That's all kids really care about."

"Stop it." Julia pulled her hair over her opposite shoulder. "And thank you, but I can assure you no one was obsessed with me in high school. No one even showed interest until Josh," she mumbled.

A long list of failed crushes and extremely embarrassing moments of attempted flirtation burned in the back of her brain. Until the now infamous church weekend with Josh in her senior year of high school, there hadn't been anyone remotely interested in Julia. Which was part of why their romance was a whirlwind. Absolute and all consuming.

"Well, fuck Josh. I think we can both agree on that. And I'm telling you: I'm right about Thomas."

"Can you please just not? You're not helping."

"Fine." Heather nestled up against the headboard. "What's the story here? What's Thomas doing in town anyway? Did he text you? Did he slide into your DMs? Give me all the juicy deets." Her eyes widened, desperate for the story.

Julia really didn't want to give Heather the *deets*. She wanted to live in this secret bubble as long as possible. The bubble that burned in her chest and made her giddy with possibility. Even though it was very obvious that Thomas didn't have a crush on her in high school, the distant possibility that he *could* have made her feel buoyant. He came back to her, and that had to mean something. Right?

But Heather's reaction made it shockingly clear that Julia's little private bubble had already popped.

Why did she tell her mom again? That was her first mistake.

Julia put on her best casual voice. "He texted me, and we met for a drink at Salt Cellar. That's it," she said, not adding that she didn't know why he was in town again. It didn't come up in their conversation, and Julia didn't want to ask. After all this time, she had a sneaking suspicion that whatever he was in town for wasn't something good. She kept that little nugget of a feeling to herself.

And, of course, he'd go back to New York City eventually anyway. Where his life was.

Heather clicked her tongue against her cheek. "See? Why would he text you, now, after all this time, if he wasn't still obsessed with you?" She pursed her lips.

Julia groaned, but she couldn't stop the burn from traveling up her neck and into her cheeks. "Oh my god Heather, shut up, he's not. We're just friends."

"Classic excuse. I've seen the movies, Julia Gulia, I know how this goes. This is your butterfly moment." Heather's eyes widened as she nodded for emphasis.

Those damn movies again. Leave it to her little sister to come in like a wrecking ball and demolish this tidy *thing* that Julia and Thomas were starting up. The tidiness of the situation was imperative. Julia was not in the mood for complicated. Despite what her instincts may have told her during their get-together yesterday, Julia would not listen to them. They had been wrong before.

Julia shook her head, clearing all thoughts of romance from it. "There's a lot of history between us. Like, complicated stuff. It doesn't matter anyway because I'm definitely not in the position to date anyone."

Complicated like that the last time they talked all those years ago, it devolved into a yelling match. In front of school. When she finally told him the secret she harbored from him for months.

Heather raised her eyebrows. "No one's saying you need to fall in love, but some casual and extremely hot sex never hurt anyone. It doesn't have to be *complicated*."

Julia threw a pillow at her sister, heat prickling all through her body at the mere suggestion of *sex with Thomas*. Heather shrieked, losing her balance and laughing as she tumbled from the bed.

"Ew, you're so annoying. Get out of here!" Julia yelled. "And shut the door!" she called after Heather, who most definitely did not shut the door.

Julia grabbed the pillow from the floor and snuggled back down into her bed. Back into her cocoon of fantasy, where she could pretend things weren't complicated.

It wasn't that she didn't want to consider that Thomas had a major crush on her in high school. It was more that *she* was actually completely obsessed with Thomas back then. She lived for their late-night texting marathons. The ongoing conversations they had. The dreams of their future in New York City powered her through the annoying shifts at her high school job throwing pizzas.

When her crush never materialized into a kiss or a date, she figured that there was nothing really between them. Just friends.

The memory of that junior year homecoming dance came back to her, the one she used to think about all the time. The closest they'd ever been to *something*. At the time, she thought that was it: the moment when things would change.

But nothing came of it. Julia, too scared to say anything herself, just went along with it. Crushed, she tried not to let it hurt their friendship, which was better than nothing.

It wasn't long after that that Josh came along.

Popular and with beautiful hair, his interest surprised her. But also encouraged her to fall fast and hard. To ignore whatever red flags might be there. On paper, Josh checked all the boxes. Especially her mom's boxes.

Heather's words snaked back to her. *I always thought he was The One for you.*

The corner of Julia's lip pulled up. The One. Not that she ever really believed in the concept, but hearing Heather say that did something to Julia. Something extremely inconvenient and not at all conducive to spending the next couple weeks seeing Thomas. As friends.

And besides, she couldn't trust herself anymore. Her poor tender heart wasn't ready for another round, hot sex or not.

As it was Sunday and a cool breeze came through her window, Julia rolled over and willed herself to forget it all and fall back into her indulgent mid-afternoon nap.

SEVEN
THOMAS

THOMAS PULLED his forearm across his forehead, wiping away the sheen of sweat and balancing the plastic tub full of dirty dishes on the edge of the industrial sink. Bussing tables was no joke, especially when helping out his mom during the Sunday "after church" rush. Right at the end of downtown, Callaghan's Coney Island sat at the driving epicenter of Starling Hills, making it classically full of too many old folks and screaming children after any kind of religious service or school function. Hiding in the back of the house was the only way to get some semblance of peace and quiet.

With a sigh, he straightened his shoulders. Seeing Julia yesterday immediately teleported him back to high school. Taking up the same after-school duties at the family diner had cemented him there.

He even blasted an old mix CD—from Julia of course

—on his way to work today. Amazed that the CDs had survived over the years, he found them tucked under the passenger seat in a black zip-up binder. A dusty, crusty relic from his years driving the Corolla that his siblings had either never found or hadn't bothered to remove. He flipped through the pages, browsing the different burned CDs, no longer recalling the track list for any of them. Back then, he could find a specific song on any given CD, depending on what he needed to hear.

In the end, he settled on one that Julia had titled "Summer Songs for the Road," signed simply "from Julia." From the opening chords of *Semi-Charmed Life* by Third Eye Blind, he was back in the car scream-singing the words with Julia. Windows down, her hair and vanilla sugar scent cycloning around the car. With 7-Eleven Slurpees in the cup holders—he always preferred classic Coke, while she mixed whatever random flavors that melted into a disgusting green-brown flavor confusion—they never drove anywhere in particular. Driving just to drive.

"Did you have a nice time with Julia yesterday?" Mom interrupted his thoughts. She leaned against the sink, a white apron tied around her waist and sleeves rolled up past her elbows.

So much for peace and quiet.

Thomas ducked his chin. Like Dad, Mom had an unfortunate knack for reading her son. He wasn't sure what she would interpret in the dark circles around his eyes and the second day stubble that trailed down his neck. He didn't want to know what she surmised. And he definitely didn't want her to know that his little get-together with Julia had thrown his entire world for a loop.

But that seemed to be a theme these days.

"It was fine." He braced the plastic tub against his hip. It pinched his skin as he offloaded the dishes. Despite the racket from the dishwasher, the three teenagers that worked in the back froze to half-listen to their conversation.

"Hmm." His mom's telltale sound that meant she didn't believe him.

What was it really? It was fine. Yeah, totally. Was it bad though? Or terrible even? She had texted basically right after so it couldn't have been all bad.

Though he certainly misstepped a couple times, like when his douchey coastal tendencies came out, but it ended okay. He hated some of the things he had said to her. The snarky comments that he couldn't hold back. But it ended with their friendly bet and a promise that they'd see a lot more of each other this fall.

Fall, the season of Julia.

Their history was just that, though. History. Long in the past. History that didn't matter. She never felt the same way about him, so what was the point of bringing it up again? But just the thought of Julia sent electricity over his skin, even now, fourteen years after his first whiff of a crush on that night they met.

Yet he could have sworn that something sparked between them yesterday. The lightning storm of emotions overloaded his senses.

Because, yeah, they were best friends for a time. But really, he'd fallen in love with her all those years ago. For him, their friendship was a thin veil over the emotional dominoes that fell down his spine whenever she texted him. Or when a song reminded him of her. Or when he thought of their future in New York.

He never had the nerve to tell her, to ask her to be more. He'd hoped that years and other people would have dulled the chemistry between them. But when they met yesterday, it was impossible for him to deny the lingering attraction that still flooded his veins.

For better or worse, Julia Ward was The One That Got Away.

He edged away from Mom, desperate to dodge anymore conversation about Julia lest he say something that he really shouldn't. "I need to get back to work."

But she wasn't buying it.

"I need more information than that, Thomas." She crossed her arms over her chest and the eavesdropping teenagers leaned closer.

Thomas wrinkled his nose. Despite his age, being home meant his mom was in all of his business. "Come on, Mom, I don't need you spreading rumors about Julia and me around town."

Mom sucked in a breath and pressed her hand to her

chest, the image of shocked offense. "I would never do such a thing."

The teens snickered and she glared at them. "Hey, back to work." She waved a towel at them. "This is a private conversation."

They all immediately jumped, returning to their duties. Thomas snorted softly through his nose when Mom winked at him.

"Honey, you know I only gather information. I wouldn't dream of telling anyone more than the strict need-to-knows about you."

Thomas balanced the dish tub against his waist, preparing to launch back into the dining room. He rubbed the back of his neck, putting a moment of pressure on either side before letting go. "Thanks, Mom. This is all just a lot, with Dad and being home and Julia. All that. I don't really know. There's nothing to say. We're going to hang out some more but that's it, ya know?"

Mom tutted, a little frown creasing between her eyebrows. "You're so handsome. My first born. She doesn't know what she's missing."

Thomas barely dodged Mom's hand coming to ruffle his hair. "Come on, Mom." As if he needed to feel more like a bashful teenager.

The dishwashing observers all snickered.

"Hey, what did I say?" Mom called over the clanging of dishes.

They just laughed more. This time, Thomas did too. It

was just like high school, cornered by Mom in the back of the diner. Thirty years old and still at the mercy of the dish room, the humidity cementing his jeans to the back of his knees.

"Thanks, but that's really not what this is. Julia just got out of a really long relationship and I doubt she's looking to date right now. We're just hanging out. Just as friends." He knew nothing he said would convince Mom that this was the truth. Some tiny piece of him wished that they could be more than friends, but he wouldn't push Julia. He never had, and he never would.

"I always liked her, you know," she said.

She and Dad always welcomed her when she came around. And she came around a lot in those couple years. Even after she started dating Josh, she still came over. They still dreamed of New York City. It was still possible then, still their plan. Rock solid.

At least, Thomas never questioned it. That all changed in the spring of senior year, but he still went through with it.

Thomas suspected the same memories flit through Mom's mind, because her eyes actually twinkled. Her cheeks pulled high and tight as if holding back tears.

"Mom, are you...crying?" He barely concealed a wry grin.

"Don't be silly." Mom sniffed and then wetly laughed it off. "But I have missed Julia all these years. You two were inseparable! Part of me thought she'd always be around."

What Mom actually said prickled through his gut. Always be around. Part of him hoped she would have always been around, too. But Julia made her choices. Thomas couldn't do anything about that.

"Mom," he sighed, resignation heavy on his shoulders.

"I know, I know, I shouldn't say things like that. Your sister doesn't like it either."

Twenty-five-year-old Ari was full sass, and Thomas smirked, picturing his youngest sibling telling Mom off for making earnest comments about her fickle love life. "She's a full on zillennial, Mom, you can't tell her anything."

Mom fixed him with a dead-pan look, zero recognition on her face. "I have no idea what you just said, but I believe you."

That earned another chuckle from the peanut gallery and she flashed the teens a look of venom.

Her features softened once she returned to her son. "And, you know, if this is about Micha, he's great too. Dad and I like him a lot."

"No, it's not about him." Thomas sighed, getting more aggravated by this conversation. He bit his tongue to stop him from saying anything else about Micha. He didn't want to broadcast that the man he'd introduced his parents to the last time they were in the city was only to make it appear like he has a semblance of a social life. Micha was little more than a fuck buddy in that regard. A mutually beneficial casual arrangement that suited both of them just fine.

Nope, she didn't need that information.

"Don't worry. Soon things will be back to normal and you'll be back in New York before you know it." But even as she tried to plaster a smile on her face, her features crumbled.

Because there was no returning to normal.

Thomas's stomach swooped. He held on to the edge of the sink to combat the fierce and sudden vertigo that washed over him. Thomas being back in New York meant that he was no longer needed in Starling Hills. And when he was no longer needed back home, that would mean Dad was dead.

Thomas took a shuddering breath as he put down the plastic tub and wrapped Mom in his arms. She was tall, but, at six foot four, he still had a couple inches on her. He squeezed her soft upper arms and smelled parsley on her hair.

"It's going to be alright, Mom," he whispered, fiercely willing it to be true. "We're going to be alright. Between me and Danny and Ari, we'll make sure everything will be alright. For however long it takes, I'll be here."

Mom nodded but had no words.

Thomas's stomach twisted, knowing that "however long it takes" could be a very long time. When would he be able to get back to Brooklyn? The whole life that he made for himself was there. *He* was there, the person he blossomed into after leaving the suburban bubble of his youth. In Starling Hills, on this unfamiliar ground, he wasn't quite sure who he was anymore.

On his break, he sat in the parking lot, the October sun streaming hot through the windows, and ran a hand through his thick, sweaty hair. Thomas slid his phone from his pocket, only wanting to do one thing right now. He re-read the last text from Julia, *So which movie are we watching first?* He punched the response and hit send without letting himself think twice.

It's a surprise. Friday at 7pm? Do you remember where I live?

Her response set his insides fluttering away, completely outside of his control.

As if I could forget. See you then.

EIGHT
JULIA

JULIA SWUNG her Jeep around the corner, hand over hand turning the wheel as she pulled onto Thomas's family's street.

Like her own family, the Callaghan's lived outside of downtown Starling Hills that quickly turned into shrouded country, dirt roads with little neighborhood-like streets that branched off deeper into the woods. Her stomach pretzeled as she caught sight of Thomas's house. Already from the end of the block, she recognized it. The roses that Mrs. Callaghan kept out front. Pots of autumn mums on the porch. As she parked on the street, she noticed the Michigan State University gnome—the alma mater of Thomas's younger sister, Ari—hiding in the bushes. It all looked the same.

Inside, she wasn't the same, no longer the starry-eyed dreamer she'd been in high school. But Julia allowed herself to remember that girl. With Thomas back in her life—and Josh gone—it wasn't difficult. The little dork pounding out stories late at night, keyboard clicking as she switched between windows. Instant messaging Thomas in one, and her fevered stories in the other.

That girl was gone.

Josh never encouraged that side of her. He didn't want to hear about her niche interests or the fandoms she adored. Under his influence, she became more concerned with bending herself to fit into her fiancé's life, soaking up his interests like a sponge, morphing into someone she no longer recognized. Sports and boating and craft beer. If she was honest with herself, she hated all those things.

But now that woman was gone too. Or at least, Julia wanted her to be. With the last of the bridal gifts finally returned, she hoped she finally exorcized that woman.

Scrubbed clean. Fresh. New.

Afraid.

She sighed against the steering wheel, biting the inside of her cheek. Was this a good idea? Things didn't go totally smoothly with Thomas last time. He wasn't the same shy, story-obsessed boy who somehow always had ink on hands. He was T. Callaghan, published author, who judged her life choices. At least a little bit. He made that clear with his testy comments.

But she needed something good. Maybe if she saw some kernel of sixteen-year-old Thomas inside him, she could access the adult woman that little Julia always dreamed of. Perform her own complete metamorphosis. Sixteen-year-old Julia didn't dream of Le Creuset butter dishes or the perfect tailgate party. She yearned over her OTPs and obsessed about series and books like it was her job.

Who was thirty-one-year-old Julia now? She didn't know.

Julia wiped her sweating palms on her jeans and turned off the car, suddenly unsure if she wanted to walk up to the front door. In high school, she'd mostly walked through the yard, wet grass tickling her ankles, down their slanted backyard, to reach the walkout basement door and slip in that way. The basement where the big TV and the good sound system was.

This was different, though. They were different. No longer comfortably casual with one another.

Taking a deep breath, she grabbed her bag, holding onto it like a life vest.

Could they just move forward, now, as friends? Whatever Heather said about *casual* was wrong. Sitting in Thomas's parents' driveway, with war waging in her stomach, alternatively hardening and fluttering, this definitely felt *complicated*.

But she couldn't trust the damn butterflies. Or the icy dread. She couldn't trust her own body. Her gut had led her astray before.

She walked up the driveway toward the door. Someone, somewhere was mowing their lawn, the distant humming reminding her of easier times. The freshly mown grass scent tickled her nose, fresh, and at the same time, nostalgic. The memory of the night she met Thomas, sitting on the picnic table, sent a shower of goosebumps down her arms.

The door opened before she even hit the porch. Thomas, in a red flannel button down and faded jeans, stood barefoot, beaming in the doorway.

"Hey," he said, his voice gravelly. He cleared his throat and his smile slipped away.

The way that simple greeting made Julia's stomach swoop was definitely not convenient.

"Hey yourself." Pausing on the porch, she tried not to groan, unsure if she sounded chill or ridiculous.

They stood staring at each other for a moment, an invisible energy building between them until Thomas laughed and Julia pulled her lower lip between her teeth.

"It's weird seeing you standing there." Thomas's knuckles whitened on the door handle.

"It feels weird. I'm more used to sneaking around the back." Julia tucked a piece of hair behind her ears.

"That's not a bad idea. Parents, ya know?" He stepped out of the entry, pulling the door shut behind him. He moved so unexpectedly that Julia didn't step back. Now they stood too close on the porch, face to face, mere inches between them.

The hair stood up on Julia's arms as Thomas smiled down at her.

"Hi," he said, so warmly that it made her toes curl in her shoes.

She laughed through her nose, trying to keep a grasp on "casual," but her chest tightened. This close she saw the fresh, close shave around the edge of his beard and smelled the difference between his cologne and piquant aftershave. He must have just showered because his hair was still a little damp as it curled away from his face. The honey brown warmth of his eyes danced in the dappled October light.

Julia wet her lips. She stood stock still, standing in his way for a beat too long.

"Sorry." She stepped to the side.

"Come on, I've got a surprise." Thomas weaved around her and jumped off the front porch steps, the cardamom-cedar of his cologne trailing faintly behind him.

As soon as he moved out of her space, Julia missed his heat, his presence. She shook her head, almost violently, trying to stop feeling like a kid again. This wasn't the time for a crush. She couldn't crush on Thomas Callaghan. Especially since he lived in New York City, not Starling Hills.

Stop thinking about it. All of it. Just casual, normal friendship.

She turned on the spot. "Oh? Another surprise? Not just the movie?"

"You'll see."

Julia kicked her floral-lavender Chuck Taylors through

the grass as they walked around the house. The weight of not running into his parents lifted slightly off her shoulders. Still possible, though less likely since they took the back way in.

Thomas pulled open the sliding door and gestured for her to go in first.

"Thanks." She smiled.

Julia thought she mentally prepared enough for this whole thing, but she didn't come prepared for what the smell of Thomas's basement would do to her. It hit her like the force of a seat belt tightening when slamming on the brakes. Downy fabric softener, pine needles and cinnamon, whatever garlic-based food was cooking upstairs, and a hint of wet cement.

She cleared her suddenly thick throat and continued to step through. "It hasn't changed."

"Dad updated the TV a couple years ago, but beyond that, no not really."

It was half finished, with a Persian rug, a slightly sagging L-shaped couch, and a TV tucked in one half of the open basement. Clear plastic storage bins sat neatly on shelves along the unfinished side.

Julia hadn't even realized she'd missed this place. She hadn't thought of it in years, which now seemed wild. But she kicked off her shoes and made a beeline for the couch. When she plopped on it, she immediately sank deep into the cushions.

"It's nice." She pulled her bag into her lap, still

huddling around it. "Not sure I'll ever be able to get out of this couch though."

"Trusty old couch. Oh, let me get my stuff. The other surprise. Be right back." Thomas sprinted up the stairs two at a time.

Julia opened the lid of the rattan storage trunk next to the couch, looking for a blanket. She grabbed a fuzzy one for her now bare feet that she pulled up next to her on the couch. Behind the couch hung the same patterned tapestry. Upstairs, Thomas stomped around, and Julia caught muffled bits of conversation.

He reappeared a couple minutes later, armed with frosted animal crackers, two movie theater boxes of Hot Tamales, and two glass-bottled Cokes in hand. "Our favorites."

"You remembered." Julia smiled, warmth spreading through her body at his use of "our." She reached for a box of Hot Tamales, which drew a wide, crooked grin onto Thomas's face.

"Surprise." He ran a hand over his beard, his forearm twisting and flexing as he did. He stared at the table. "Listen, I'm sorry for how things happened the other day. I said some brutal and unfair things. I wanted to make it up to you," he gestured to the snacks, "with snacks. Our favorites. Your favorites. I took a guess that they still are."

He turned to her then, the corners of his eyes pulled down and squinting at her as if to gauge her reaction.

Then his thick eyebrows jumped high, waiting for her response.

"Oh." She hadn't expected his apology. "It's cool. Well, I mean it's not cool, but I appreciate it." She took a steadying breath. "What I'm trying to say is thank you."

Thomas nodded and scooted back into the couch, pulling some of the blanket over his legs too. "Mind if we share?"

Her bare feet flexed under the blanket, so close to Thomas's legs that it sent a thrill out from her center. But she nodded.

This is casual. This is fine.

Thomas clicked on the TV and grabbed a box of Hot Tamales. "I couldn't find this one streaming so I loaded up the DVD. Oh, my mom says hi." He tossed a handful of candy into his mouth.

"Tell her I said hi." Julia leaned and snatched the bag of animal crackers off the table, adding to their snack stash between them on the blanket.

"I told her it might be a lot for you to see them today."

Julia smiled softly into the bag of animal crackers, touched that Thomas would take that into consideration. They hadn't talked about how awkward this all was. How awkward it could be. How it felt like a huge step forward and backward at the same time. Did she want to go back to the person she was before Josh? Was that even possible?

But she just shrugged. "I've been through worse."

Thomas paused, considering for a second, and then nodded to the TV, the DVD menu now loaded.

"Are you ready for your first Happily Ever After lesson?" He smiled, a little goofy.

"*When Harry Met Sally.* Nice." Julia smiled back. "50,000 words, here I come. That burrito is mine."

"Unlikely," Thomas said, a laugh on his voice, as he leaned forward to put the remote on the table, sending the scent of cinnamon candy in her direction.

His shirt rode up just a couple of inches, revealing an expanse of olive skin and one perfectly round mole. Julia wiggled her hips back into the corner of the couch, tucking her feet more directly under her as warmth flushed up her neck.

Thomas popped the Cokes and leaned back, offering one to Julia, her tongue suddenly heavy and dry.

"Thanks." Even her voice sounded parched. She took a drink, the bubbles tingling her tongue, and put the bottle on the couch side table. Thomas stretched—those few blessed inches of skin peeking out again—and put his bottle on the table at the opposite end of the couch.

As the old couple on the loveseat at the beginning of the movie appeared on the screen, something inside Julia wound tight with lightning speed.

"I was sitting with my friend..." the man started.

Julia took a sharp inhale, her chest concave. Maybe she wasn't ready for something like this, her nerves still frazzled from the fallout of her engagement.

Great. Josh wasn't even around anymore and he was still ruining things for her.

"You see that girl? I'm going to marry her," the man on screen continued.

Marry her. Her eyes burned, her sinuses cottony, and she shoved two more cookies in her mouth, willing the tears not to fall. Barely twenty seconds into the film and she couldn't handle it.

Keep it together. She didn't want Thomas to see her tears, but it quickly became an exercise in futility. Her vision blurred, the couple on the screen becoming a watery human portmanteau. Two becoming one.

A tear slid down each cheek. Tears she could hide, for the most part, but she knew what came next.

Uncontrollable sniffles. She tried just one as inconspicuous as possible. Immediately, she knew one subtle sniffle wouldn't be enough. Her chest tightened, from the threat of tears and the effort of keeping them in.

"It's over fifty years later, and we're still married."

Thomas shifted beside her. "They're so sweet—wait, whoa, Julia are you okay?" He turned to her, pulling a leg up onto the couch. "I didn't...I mean." Thomas stopped talking and exhaled a sigh. The dark brown pools of his eyes pinned on her as he shook his head.

Julia smiled, shaky and tenuous. Over Thomas's shoulder, a virtually prepubescent Billy Crystal loomed on the screen.

"Sorry." She rubbed her cheek with the back of her

hand and openly sniffled, a virtual snot machine. "I didn't think this would happen."

Thomas cocked his head. "Do we need to stop watching?"

"No, no, I want to watch. Thanks." Julia leaned toward Thomas and meant to rest her hand on his forearm—give it a friendly pat—but she overshot.

She watched it happen in slow motion, the moment slowing down like maple syrup from the fridge. As she got closer, he flipped his palm up. It rested on his thigh, fingers twitching, almost calling her hand into his. Her hand landed right in his.

She sucked in a surprised breath as his fingers closed around hers, lightning scattering over her entire body. Thomas's gaze fell to their entwined hands on his leg. After a moment, he ran his rough thumb over the back of Julia's hand, sending sparks up her arm.

What was going on?

No, this was very bad. Warning bells clanged in Julia's head, a voice insisting that she pull her hand away right now. But a much smaller voice repeated Heather's words back to her. *But some casual and extremely hot sex never hurt anyone.* The little devil. Julia was going to strangle her.

No. That was not happening right now.

And yet, as Meg Ryan and Billy Crystal drove away from the University of Chicago, less than five minutes into the movie, Julia twisted her hips toward Thomas, facing him straight on, their hands still clasped in his lap.

From this angle, she could sense the ghost of the sixteen-year-old boy, the Thomas from when they first met. With a buzzcut, shy eyes, and a whisper of a mustache. That boy still folded and tucked into this man. He had curls now and an impressively full, black beard, but his eyes still had the same sincere, melancholic turn to them. Always asking a question, always wondering.

Was he thinking the same thing about her? Could he see the girl that worked the theater lights and walked the high school halls with him every day? His eyes bounced around her face, and she thought that maybe, yes, he saw that girl she used to be.

The moment froze between them. And then Thomas moved toward her just slightly, a suggestion of closing the gap between them. It was a question. The air fizzed around them, their bodies mere inches apart.

Julia saw what would happen next. She saw the next few minutes...days...weeks...months. It all ended with her alone, again. Because Thomas would leave again, and she would still be in Starling Hills, Michigan.

She opened her mouth and the tiniest crack of a sound came out. With it, the spell between them broke.

Thomas let go of her hand like it had burned him. She snatched her hand off his leg and he rocketed back into the couch, putting space, feet, between them.

"I should go." Julia stumbled over her words. "I don't know, I'm already crying and I'm kind of a mess and I have that interview coming up and I just have a lot going on right now."

Thomas looked at the floor as he rubbed his beard up and down, creating a disheveled mess of it. He didn't say anything.

"I'm sorry," she whispered. Her toes curled into the corner of the fuzzy blanket that had fallen onto the floor. She didn't want to ruin this, she wanted tonight to be good, fun, easy between friends. But fucking Josh—the memory of Josh and their failed relationship—still messed things up for her.

"It's fine," he said, hand still worrying his beard. "It's... totally fine, Jules. I get it."

Her heart clenched. *Jules*. His nickname for her. She hadn't heard it in years.

Though he said the words, he didn't look fine. Not at all. His eyes hung full and sad. But he wouldn't say any of that, if there was anything else to even say. Julia knew he would spare her what he could. He always had.

"I'll text you," she said as she rose from the couch, grabbing her purse.

He just nodded, didn't even look at her. She stuffed her feet into her shoes and ran out the door without looking back.

Julia sat in her Jeep, hands braced on the steering wheel. Her heart rate only barely returned to normal.

When she turned the keys in the ignition, the music came to life. The first four chords to *Semi-Charmed Life* by

Third Eye Blind floated around her, and she finally let the tears fall. All of them, a disgusting, snotty, hyperventilating mess. But not for Josh. No, not for fucking Josh. Instead, the tears were a tribute to the women she had been and in anticipation for the one she would grow into. Whoever she would be, Julia couldn't wait to meet her.

Before the song ended, her tears dried. Still idling in park, she grabbed her phone from her bag. She sent off a text to Thomas before tossing the phone into the passenger seat.

Raincheck?

NINE
THOMAS

THOMAS KEPT one hand on the grocery cart as he and Dad strolled up and down the aisles of Meijer, the large chain grocery store on the outskirts of Starling Hills. Dad wanted lamb for dinner, and he wanted to do it all himself. It was more and more rare that he had energy for anything beyond his morning shifts at the Coney Island. So when he declared his intentions, Mom shooed Thomas out of work too, insisting that he accompany Dad, just in case.

Now they browsed in silence, eyes scanning up and down the shelves.

"I really just wanted a break from your mother," Dad said, both hands gripping the cart as he shuffled along.

"What?" Thomas laughed, something fragile splintering in his chest.

Dad winked, his playful demeanor still alive and well.

Mom and Dad were Thomas's original blueprint for joy. How he would laugh in the kitchen as Dad cooked, then handed him the spatula to take over flipping the pancakes. Playing twenty questions about his life while folding the laundry with Mom. His parents doing intricate 1,000-piece puzzles together on the formal dining table and drinking Scotch late into the night.

"She's been so worried about me, she barely lets me out of her sight. I knew she'd make you take me to the store. She never leaves work this early."

"She didn't *make* me take you."

Dad chuckled and it turned into a cough, his eyes watering. "It's what I wanted to happen anyway."

"So it all worked out?" Thomas cocked an eyebrow at his dad.

"It usually does." Dad hummed a contented little tune as they continued walking.

A warmth flared through Thomas's body, and he looked sideways at Dad who had a smug little grin pulling at the corners of his lips. "Are we still talking about Mom?"

"I don't think so..." he mused, narrowing his eyes down the aisle, focusing on the fridge full of rows of milk at the end. "Are you going back to New York, Thomas?"

Thomas's stomach clenched. He hadn't thought about the city that much in the last couple days. In part because Michigan just felt sort of normal again, but also because his thoughts were consumed with Julia Ward. Someone he used to think about all the time but had in recent years managed to somehow mostly forget.

He still planned to return to the city. Always had. Get back to the hustle, the haywire rhythm he'd settled into. But not yet.

"Not anytime soon." He cleared his throat to stop himself from adding more words like, *I hope*. He didn't want to talk to Dad about death. His death.

He nodded, processing Thomas's answer.

Thomas scuffed his checkered Vans on the shining linoleum floor. "I'm not done there yet."

Even as he said it, he wasn't sure if it was true.

Maybe he was done there. At one point, New York City had been a promise that things could be better. That there was something to work toward. But was slinging pints every damn night of the week just to make rent really worth the tradeoff of access to some unpaid industry internship? Was that supposed industry experience actually getting him anywhere of consequence with this writing career? He used to believe it was. He convinced himself that it was. But distance slowly distilled into perspective.

"Would it be so bad for you to come home?"

His dad whispered the question, and each word dropped like polished Petoskey stones into Thomas's stomach, weighing him down. Thomas stuffed his fists into his pockets, scrunching his shoulders up to his ears, not wanting to have this conversation. Not right now in the middle of a grocery store.

"I am home."

Physically, he was. Mentally, his thoughts wandered hundreds of miles and an entire world away. It seemed impossible that Starling Hills and New York City—Brooklyn—existed on the same planet, let alone in the same country.

"Yes, you are. But what about coming home for good?"

Dad's question threw Thomas for a loop so hard, he felt like he rode a Tilt-A-Whirl. Thrills a minute. The unspoken implication of *when* hung in the air. *When* Dad dies.

Dad stopped walking but Thomas kept going for another few steps before he realized he'd left the cart behind. When he turned, it struck him again how frail his dad had become. Standing behind the cart, shoulders hunched forward, he was a physical shadow of the man Thomas idolized growing up.

The chef, the manager, the partner. The father. Somehow all things at the same time.

He was still that man. Still his dad.

Still the backgammon master who went to the diner every day, forever asking Thomas the hard questions.

"Your mother is going to need someone to help her with the restaurant." Dad's jaw tensed.

The Tilt-A-Whirl flung Thomas around for another pass. "Don't talk like that."

A rare frown graced his dad's face, deep and cutting, and he banged one hand on the grocery cart's handle, not meeting his son's eyes.

"Thomas, goddamnit, this is happening. I'm dying. I won't always be here," he said, voice firm.

Usually such an even keel, Dad rarely raised his voice. His outburst shocked Thomas to attention. They stood in the cereal aisle, surrounded by sugar and marshmallows, six feet apart, tinny muzak playing over the speakers. Neither of them spoke.

Thomas didn't want this to happen. Not this conversation and not Dad's death. A twisted part of him wished he'd stayed in New York and skipped this part. As much as he willed all the hard stuff away, he would never be free of it. This was life.

"It's something we need to think about." Dad started walking again, leaving his surge of emotion and Thomas behind, in the middle of the aisle, still looping on the carnival ride.

It was just like Dad to ambush him in the middle of some mundane task with these kinds of questions. But Thomas did the same. They were pulling weeds in the garden together when Thomas first told him of his plan to study at New York University. Painting Thomas's bedroom, freshly moved to their new home, when Thomas came out as bisexual.

In the cereal aisle when Dad asked Thomas what he's going to do with his life when he dies.

Fair is fair.

"I know one thing Michigan has that New York doesn't," he called over his shoulder as he shuffled away. "Julia Ward."

Damn him.

Thomas jogged to catch up with Dad. "That has nothing to do with anything."

"No?" Dad pushed his chin up in a faux-quizzical look, eyes narrowed and weighing. "Huh."

Warmth spiked Thomas's cheeks. "You're as bad as Mom."

Dad shrugged, back to cool as a cucumber. "So maybe your parents want you back home, and maybe we made a coordinated plan of attack. Maybe."

Thomas groaned. He would be more offended if they weren't half right.

Starling Hills seemed like a dream, New York a fantasy, and Thomas floated in the nebulous space in between those two far off worlds that supposedly existed in the same universe. He found it damn near impossible to reconcile those two cities existing on the same plane.

"Coordinated? Really?" Thomas cringed. His parents had always meddled in his love life, under the guise of *wanting him to be happy*. In high school, they had tried to matchmake him with every high schooler that worked at the Coney to less than stellar results. He wasn't interested. Even then, it had already been about Julia.

"Can you blame us?" Dad's eyes twinkled, not with tears but with delight. "Old habits die hard."

Thomas snorted a laugh at his dad's macabre sense of humor. "I guess so. But Julia and I are just friends."

That's all we have to be. All we can be.

"But why?"

"There is no why, Dad. It is what it is."

It wasn't what Thomas wanted it to be though.

All those years ago, at sixteen driving around with the windows open in the winter and the heat blasting, listening to Blink-182, he'd wanted Julia.

Last night in the basement, on the same couch they'd watched *The Princess Bride* fourteen years ago, he had to admit that he still wanted her.

Her tears and the way that she bolted out of there made it clear she was barely ready to be friends with him, let alone anything else.

But he was going back to New York. Back to this life there. The one he dreamed of since high school. He wasn't going to give it up, despite the unrelenting pressure from all angles.

And Julia would still be in Michigan. There was no future between them.

As much as Thomas wanted there to be, there was nothing between them. And there never would be.

"Oh, I've been craving Apple Jacks," Dad said, reaching for a box, and effectively changing the subject.

Thomas hummed, grateful for that conversation to be over. For now.

* * *

THOMAS RETURNED to the Coney Island after bringing Dad back to the house. And it was a good thing he did.

"Two servers called off, we were already short, and it's dinner rush. I need you to step in as waitstaff," Mom said, her eyes wide and white from the stress of managing the evening.

"Uh." Thomas looked around.

Orders lined up under the warming lights, more seated tables were bare than had food or drinks, and no one looked happy. Especially not his mom. He rarely served at Callaghan's, usually bussing or working in the dish room—backstage, just like in the theater.

But bartending had to have some transferrable skills, right? Thomas chewed the inside of his cheek. He had to give it a shot.

"Yeah, yeah, you got it."

Mom's face crumbled with relief. She leaned over to kiss her son on the cheek. "Thank you, you're a lifesaver."

New to the manager role herself, she still struggled working out the kinks of running the dining room as smoothly as Dad always had. After retiring from the line at General Motors—a job he worked since sixteen—he knew how to run a tight ship. A skill Mom didn't quite have yet.

So of course Thomas agreed to help. He pulled a black apron around his waist and picked up a stack of guest checks. He walked over to the closest table, squaring his shoulders, trying to look like he knew how this all worked.

"Hi folks," he said. "What can I get y'all?"

The whole table of four looked up at him, their annoyance laid plain on their faces.

"We've been waiting for ten minutes and no one's come by yet," one with a short, asymmetrical blonde haircut said, her lips pursed.

"Sorry about that, ma'am. Short staffed today. But I'm here now." Thomas gave a curt nod. Thrown right to the sharks. Lovely.

The customer clicked her tongue and rolled her eyes. "I just hope we don't have to wait so long for our food."

"Why don't we just order, honey?" The man with her widened his eyes, and the kids bounced in their seats. One of them screamed.

Dear lord. Thomas looked down the line of booths. The orders from all these tables would slam the kitchen, but by the looks of it, they'd all been seated for too long without anyone coming by. He needed to get all their orders now otherwise things would only get worse. As he scribbled down this table's order, he looked over his shoulder, spying his brother Danny working the fryer, a frown on his face and his shoulders hunched. An all-hands-on deck kind of day. But he didn't see Ari. His little sister really could wiggle out of anything.

Every table greeted him with the same irritation, the same frowns. By the end of the line, his helpful mood morphed into a peeved headache, tension radiating down his neck. He made a beeline for the kitchen to drop off all the orders, making a mental note to circle back around to the table that somehow still needed time to decide.

"What the hell, dude?" Danny asked, looking at the row of tickets that Thomas hung. "You trying to kill us back here?" He crossed his beefy arms over his chest. The two didn't look much alike. Danny stood a head shorter than his brother, and he kept his dark brown hair cropped short. Though they had the same thick eyebrows, Danny's facial hair covered more cheek and neck than his brother's but he didn't keep a beard. His impressive five o'clock shadow grew in by noon though.

Thomas's cheeks warmed, knowing a pissed off kitchen wasn't the best first step to helping anyone out. "I know, man, sorry. The people were all just sitting there. No one took their order for like ten minutes."

Danny groaned. "You think this will help that?" He marched off to drop a fresh batch of fries into the sizzling grease.

Thomas whirled around to the drink machine. How the hell was he going to get all these drinks out in a timely fashion? With only two hands, he wasn't. And he'd need to make multiple trips. Usually his dad would stick mostly to the drink machine and fill cups for the servers, an effective time management trick that the servers all appreciated. But Mom circled around the tables, too, nowhere near the fountain dispenser. She took orders along with the rest of them, apologizing for the chaos. Thomas hadn't seen the restaurant this bad in a while.

And still no Ari in sight.

Thomas frowned into the Cokes and Sprites and Vernors as he filled them. He balanced twelve full plastic cups on a tray and then eyed them. This could very easily end in disaster. At the bar, he usually just pulled the pints and slung them this way and that for the patrons, or left them at the end for the actual servers to bring out. He decided on a two-handed grip on the tray.

Walking back to the first table, he put the tray down and started passing out the drinks.

"We want waters, too. Four of them," the blonde said, the same pursed lip expression on her face. She seemed like an unhappy person.

Thomas's stomach dropped. "Uh, right. Let me drop these other drinks off and I'll be right back."

The woman huffed and rolled her eyes.

He moved down the line of tables, dropping off drinks. The table he promised to circle back to waved him down while his tray was still half full. Great.

"Hello!" they called. "We're ready to order."

"Be right with you folks," he said, breezing by to deliver the rest of the drinks.

"Order's up!" Danny called from behind the window, raising a withering brow at Thomas as he stood in the middle of the restaurant, pulled in too many directions at once.

Fuck. Thomas definitely had more talent behind the bar than on this side of the counter.

When Thomas finally made it back to the warmer, Danny pointed at the plates.

"Table 2, 4, and 6 up. We're still working on the rest," he grumbled.

Thomas filled up a food sized tray, balancing it on one shoulder and grabbed a tray stand as he passed. His muscles seized and shook under the weight. But he wouldn't topple the tray. He couldn't. It would only add to the train-wreck.

"Alrighty," he said as he flipped open the tray stand.

"Finally," the sour, blonde woman said, rolling her eyes. "And waters. Which I've asked for three times now."

Thomas really didn't like her. "I'll be right back with those." He served the food, and the woman looked down at her plate with a frown.

"This isn't what I ordered. I need the dressing on the *side*, and I said no feta." She pushed the plate away from her.

Thomas gave a terse nod. "Right. Sorry about that."

"This is ridiculous. Appalling service," she said.

Thomas went to serve the rest of the food before he snapped and said something rude to this woman. One table complained that their dishes were cold. The table that hadn't given their order got up to leave.

Thomas's head pounded. This had gone from chaos to a disaster in record time. With his bartending experience, this really shouldn't have been so difficult.

But thoughts of Julia and his conversation with his dad swirled in his mind, transporting him out of the Coney Island and back to the basement couch. When the tears filled her eyes, her cheeks got all splotchy. He felt terrible about the whole thing. He should have been more considerate in choosing the film. The last thing he wanted to do was make her feel uncomfortable. He'd tried to make it easy for her, but he messed up.

Of course he had. Just like right now.

Letting down the restaurant and letting down his family. He really would never be able to live up to his dad's legacy. Maybe that's what he'd been hiding from all along. The real reason he left for New York City: to make some name for himself. To prove to someone, anyone—himself, his dad—that he could do it.

Some name alright.

He shook his head, walking back to the kitchen. A thin trickle of sweat dripped down his back. "Idiot," he muttered.

"You're making a real mess of it out there."

Thomas looked up, a grimace already on his face. Ari popped a hip leaning against a counter in the back, a plate of chicken tenders in one hand and a Coke in the other.

He grunted, not keen to verbally spar with his baby sister right now.

"I wouldn't quit your day job," she laughed, her voice far too full of mirth.

Heat lanced through him. Guess he didn't have a choice in ignoring her.

"Whatever, Ari." Thomas pushed past her to make another salad for the picky customer.

"No seriously, you're like really bad at this. I saw that table get up and leave." She bit on her straw, smiling wide around it.

"Well, I'm glad you finally showed up to get a fucking snack," he growled, his patience already thin and mood plummeting by the second. He didn't have time for sibling taunting.

"Ooh." She pouted, her brown eyes sparkling, obviously enjoying terrorizing her brother. "Someone's upset, huh?"

"He's testy." Danny leaned through the kitchen window to add to the pile on, his face still serious as ever.

"Right?" Ari tilted her head toward her middle brother as her mouth dropped open in faux shock.

"He saw Julia yesterday."

Thomas flashed his brother a deadly look, and Danny just chuckled.

"Shut up!" Ari's eyes widened and eyebrows lifted nearly off her face. "*The* Julia. How is she?"

"That's *not* what this is about." Thomas grabbed a

couple kalamata olives too tightly between his tongs and the extra pressure sent them flying from his grasp, rolling across the counter and onto the floor.

"Fuck," he hissed.

"Like I said, big bro, don't quit your day job." Ari aimed finger-guns at Thomas and winked.

The energy built inside him, like a rubber band pulling taut and about to snap. Being home flooded his nervous system with memories and worries, stuff he hadn't thought about in years and stuff he wasn't ready to think about yet. It all dammed inside his chest, the conversation he had with his dad this afternoon really the cherry on top of all of it. He wasn't ready to think about what it would mean when his dad dies, what moving back to Starling Hills would look like, and he sure as hell didn't need this shit from Ari.

Especially not in the middle of dinner rush.

He put a palm flat on the counter and leaned toward her. "You know what? Why don't you put on a damn apron and take some orders? Maybe roll up your sleeves and wash some dishes? If you didn't notice, we're all busting our ass around here to stay afloat, and you're not carrying your weight."

Thomas ground his teeth, his heart rate pounding, as he glared at his sister.

"Phew," Danny whistled like a cartoon bomb dropping off a cliff.

Maybe Thomas had said too much.

"Whatever, Thomas. You think you can just waltz back into town and suddenly you're the first-born golden child again?" She stepped toward him, her chest puffed out. "You may have convinced Mom and Dad into thinking you're all that, but you can't fool me. Who do you think has been around since Dad first got his diagnosis? Who drove him to appointments while Mom managed Callaghan's? Who cooked and cleaned and kept up on their housework, because Dad was weak and Mom was depressed?"

"Come on, Ari, give him a break," Danny said.

"A break? That's all he's had for the last ten years, Danny. He's been off living his fancy New York life or whatever." She fluttered her hands at him. "Ran away, hardly came home. Nuh-uh, let him flounder. It's good for his constitution."

She patted Thomas on the chest and turned away without another word.

Thomas opened and closed his mouth, at a momentary loss for words. "So you're not gonna help?" he yelled after her, a pathetic comeback to the vitriol she flung at him.

Ari just kept walking toward the back door, her middle finger waving high in the air.

Danny wrinkled his nose. "She's got a point, man, but I know you're trying."

The rest of his shift continued to be a clusterfuck, but it was nothing compared to the mental tracks his brain spun over and over. Ari's words grinding deeper into his bones and settling in.

For so long he'd been running. Away from Starling Hills to New York City, chasing down his dreams. With each success, nothing changed inside. The pride, the sense of having "made it," would sear bright in his chest and then fizzle out. The illusive happiness—whatever that meant—still evaded him.

Maybe it was time he started chasing something new.

TEN

JULIA

"I'M STARVING," Julia moaned, leaning her elbow onto the bar. "These olives aren't cutting it."

She stabbed a rogue bleu cheese stuffed olive from her dirty martini with a red plastic toothpick. The Gratzi! happy hour rush fluttered around Julia and Susan as they sat smack in the middle of the bar, reveling in the drone of people happily sipping their discounted drinks. They preferred the middle. The perfect position to be visible to their favorite bartenders who never forgot them anyway. It put them in an optimum place to order more drinks. And free bread.

Susan took a piece of soft, warm sourdough bread, dipped it in herbed oil, and then handed it to Julia.

"Eat some bread."

"I'm saving myself," Julia paused and cut her eyes to Susan, "for pasta."

"You shouldn't be saving yourself. You should be enjoying yourself at the only happy hour I can make this week. And, if I do say so myself, you should be enjoying yourself with whoever sent that text last week."

Susan sipped her dirty martini and Julia coughed, sputtering over her vodka.

"I know it got your panties in a...well, I don't know what it did exactly, but it did something to your panties. You've been off at work all week. Haven't even obsessed about your interview once. All this to say: I'm worried," Susan said.

Julia felt warmth trail across her collarbone and not up into her face from embarrassment, but further south, settling low in her gut. She adjusted her hips in her seat and bit her lip, her palms suddenly slick.

Susan was right: she hadn't thought about the promotion much since Thomas first texted her. A jump in pay and work hours was the next logical step in her career. It required travel time and more dedication to the job. Not obsessing about the interview could be considered a good thing though?

Because yeah, this whole thing definitely left her distracted. Instead, her free hours had been consumed with writing. Despite the epic failure of their first movie study, their burrito bet lingered in the back of her mind. Except that she didn't know *how* to write anymore, the old muscle memory forgotten. Instead she googled things like "how to get started writing fan fiction" and trawled fic sites for inspiration. The promotion faded into the background as she launched herself into her old hobby again.

Should she tell Susan all that? Even considering it made her insides flutter. She'd never been able to successfully talk about her writing in real life, especially at sixteen. Well, except to Thomas, who understood completely. Non-writers didn't get it the same way. But maybe Susan would. The woman who supported her and cheered her on through everything.

"Wow." Susan nodded, watching her friend. "Wow, Juju. You're guilty," she said before huffing with laughter.

"I—there's nothing to be guilty about. I didn't *do* anything." Julia slid an olive off the toothpick with her teeth, swallowing thoughts of writing with it. Susan's mind lived eternally in the gutter—Julia knew what her friend implied. The same electric nerves that Heather had triggered fizzed to life in Julia's stomach.

Sex with Thomas.

She swallowed. Thinking about it made her feel giddy and nauseous at the same time.

"No? Sure looks like it. And, hey, I don't begrudge you, girl. Sometimes you gotta bang it out of your system. I would have banged my way through my post-divorce blues if it wasn't for my girls. So let's just say there was a lot of self-love done on my part." Susan gave Julia a deadpan look, and they burst into laughter as Chad served them their plates of fettuccine Alfredo and cracked a mini mountain of fresh pepper on both.

Julia shoved her dinner fork into the noodles and twirled it against her over-large spoon, her stomach growling. She hoped that Susan forgot about their conversation now that the food arrived. Julia enjoyed marinating in her little Thomas secret, which, she noted, was no longer much of a secret at all.

"Okay, but seriously, you need something fun," Susan said. Her hair swung, free of its usual tortoise shell barrette, dangerously close to alfredo. She pleaded with her eyes, pushing her bottom lip forward. "Come on, do it for old Suse."

Julia shook her head, mouth full of pasta. "It's complicated."

"That's not an excuse. Everything is complicated."

"What about the best things in life being free?"

"Money free, sure. Drama free, growing pains free, heartbreak free? Not so much."

Julia frowned. Not what she wanted to hear. Sure, she'd already learned her fair share of that lesson but weren't things like this—whatever this was—supposed to be easy? Wasn't the right love supposed to be uncomplicated? A simple answer to a mammoth question?

She couldn't see around this hazy, amorphous, Josh-shaped blob blocking her way forward. His betrayal shattered her intuition. She didn't trust herself anymore. Those little gut feelings? They could point her in the entirely wrong direction, and she wouldn't know again before it was too late.

"I can see those stars in your eyes fading as we speak." Susan leaned toward her and squeezed her hand. "Don't let them go."

"Easier said than done." Julia couldn't help but pout. She washed her petulance down with the rest of her martini.

Even if Josh hadn't ruined her ability to trust herself, her heart now deadweight instead of soaring to new heights, Thomas would soon be back living his *fabulous* NYC author life. She couldn't let herself forget that very inconvenient fact. He was home for some reason but still hadn't said why. The longer they avoided that conversation, the more nervous Julia became about it. He sashayed back into her life with a simple text, only a guest star making a cameo reappearance.

And then he would be gone again.

Her stomach fluttering inconveniently with butterflies whenever she was around him wasn't helping. But soon he'd be back to New York City and have his cocktail dates and important meetings, rubbing elbows with other publishing professionals and chasing his dreams.

And Julia would still be in Starling Hills, having cocktails at the local Italian joint, potentially with a promotion and less time to date than ever.

It was easier when her life was all laid out before her, clear and simple. The suburban dream. Be Josh's wife—or wifey as he used to call her, even though they weren't married yet. Buy the house with the proverbial, and perhaps actual, picket fence. Keep working, make the money, get a dog, buy a second house, a boat, have kids.

But that was all a lie. Easy and false. She lived in a fantasy world and hadn't even realized. The memory made her throw up in her mouth a little, bile souring the back of her throat.

The vodka and the bitter memories of Josh sparked through her veins, tipping toward the edge of euphoria. Just buzzed enough that good and bad ideas looked the same. But...she just had a brilliant idea.

"Maybe you're right." She took a huge bite of pasta. God, she loved pasta.

"I know I am." Susan gave a self-satisfied smile and took a drink of her martini. "What exactly are you referencing though?"

"That I need something...fun. Something exciting." Julia leaned toward the bar, limp as a noodle.

"Yes!" Susan laughed. "Yes, exactly. I'm always right. Mostly always anyway."

"And you know what! I think I'm ready for casual! Yeah, this is a great idea." Julia nodded, her head bouncing steadily, tapping out a manic rhythm. "Speed dating!"

Susan whipped her head up from her pasta dish, eyebrows furrowed. "What is this, the 90s?"

But Julia didn't hear her. She scrolled her phone, looking for the Instagram post she saw the other day from Salt Cellar Distillery. They recently started twice monthly speed dating events, the perfect place to meet someone *casual*. Easy. Simple. Speedy.

"Bang it out of my system, right?"

Susan narrowed her eyes, obviously weighing the idea. "That wasn't exactly what I meant…"

"No. It's perfect." Even as images of Thomas rubbing his hand through his beard swam to the surface, Julia submerged them back to her unconscious. "You and Heather are coming with me. This was your idea. And it'll be fun! Maybe you'll meet someone, too!"

"Fun. Right." Susan twisted her fork into her pasta and pat Julia's leg under the bar. "Because I love you, I'll do this with you, my sweet, sweet Juju. Heather better come too."

"Don't worry, already texting her." A crazed grin spread across Julia's face. "This might be the best idea I've had in years!"

"Mmm," Susan murmured a partial endorsement and continued to pat Julia's leg.

Just as Julia sent off a text to her sister, another one from Thomas flashed across her phone screen. Three simple words that sent a thrill straight to her core. A thrill that she promptly forced herself to ignore.

I miss you.

* * *

STANDING in front of the Salt Cellar entrance, Julia stared at the event flyer on the door. She jangled her car keys in one hand, camel leather bag dangling in the crook of her opposite elbow.

Speed Dating! For Professionals! it read. A $15 entry fee included one cocktail ticket and two hours of forced small talk. A small note at the bottom highlighted queer friendly and no age restrictions.

Casual small talk. No strings, no drama, all fun. Exposure therapy to recalibrate her instincts. Exactly what she needed to bleach Josh from her mind and erase the temptation of Thomas.

Specifically, erase the image of Thomas's shirt riding up as he leaned forward on the couch the other night.

That perfect mole she wanted to run her fingers over.

And the cinnamon candy scent on his breath.

No. Don't think about that. Off limits, remember? She set her shoulders at the door.

For some unholy reason, this event was on a Thursday. As if love-starved, "professional" singles needed to be more humiliated and reminded of the dateless weekend that loomed just out of sight. Julia had rallied the troops, donned a sexy but simple long, grey body con dress that left none of her ample curves to the imagination, threw a grey cashmere sweater jacket over it to keep out the growing October chill, and left her hair loose over her shoulders. She and her sensible but stylish three-inch mules came prepared.

But still, she froze mere feet from the door, literally questioning every single moment in her life that had led her to this Thursday evening of *Speed Dating! For Professionals!*

"Do you think she's okay?" Heather whispered.

"She may have short circuited," Susan said.

The two snorted and giggled behind her.

"I can *hear* you," Julia moaned. "And you're not helping."

"It's fine, sis, take all the time you need," Heather said. "I'm getting pretty thirsty though."

Julia had roped Heather and Susan into attending this event by promising to pay for their happy hour tab, knowing that one "complimentary" drink ticket wouldn't get the trio very far at all.

Susan took a step forward, looping her arm through Julia's.

"You're ready for casual, remember?" Susan said, her voice soft and encouraging like speaking to a newly hatched, perfectly precious, fluffy yellow chick.

"It's gonna be great." Heather nodded, now on Julia's right side. "Butterfly moment, remember?"

God, she loved these two. Neither of them was the least bit interested in this thing, but here they were, right by her side buoying her with friendly jabs and words of encouragement through whatever happened tonight.

"You're right." Julia smiled, her lips pulling wide and crinkling the corners of her eyes. "It is gonna be great."

Julia broke away from them and stepped toward the door, arm outstretched. She could do it. She opened the door and crossed into the vestibule, a mix of the October evening air and her vanilla perfume swirling around her. She nearly bowled right into the folding card table that doubled as a name tag station.

"Hiya!" A very chipper person with long brown hair, arms covered in tattoos, and a clipboard waved Julia down. Her name tag read "Kit, she/her."

"Here for the *Speed Dating! For Professionals!*?" Kit put a little too much upward emphasis on the "professionals" part.

Julia shrank back, folding just slightly into herself.

"Uh yes! Of course!" Heather chirped, corralling her sister around the waist and pushing her toward the table.

"We've been looking forward to it all week!" Susan leaned toward the clipboard gal in a show of effusive camaraderie. She even winked.

"Excellent! We just ask that everyone put their preferred name on their tag and their pronouns for ease of introduction. Once you have your name tag good to go, I'll take your payment!"

Kit's enthusiasm did not wane.

Susan and Heather leaned obediently over the table, getting right to work. The two whispered back and forth, their bodies shaking with laughter as they both wrote down fake names.

Julia squared her shoulders. Even if Susan and

Heather only pretended to enjoy this whole thing, they did so convincingly. Julia begged them to come, dragging them downtown. But now as she disassociated standing before the name badges with a thick black Sharpie in her hand, they plastered their stickers dutifully to their chests.

"Come on, it's gonna be fun, okay?" Heather, pseudonym Cosette, pinched Julia's elbow through her sweater.

Right. Fun. Julia exhaled, scribbling her real name and pronouns on the tag. "Okay! I'm ready for a drink!"

A round of drink-ticket dirty martinis got Julia buzzed just enough that she glistened with a sheen of confidence. She would face this *Speed Dating!* with at least the amount of enjoyment she got from going on the occasional run. Getting out there always proved to be the hardest part.

Not the most experienced in the dating department, this kind of event, in truth, terrified her. After all, she'd been with Josh since senior year of high school. High school sweethearts.

The thought turned sour in her stomach. But she could pretend. This couldn't be much more complicated than forced mingling at holiday work parties and chatting up a client at dinner, right?

Julia took a look around the space. Thankfully, there was no one she recognized. Starling Hills was a small town, but not the smallest, and its cute and quirky downtown drew in folks from around the area. Maybe some of these folks were from out of town.

"We're just about to begin!" Kit-with-the-clipboard called. "This is a queer friendly event, with color coded stickers indicating orientation. So if you sit down with someone of a gender you don't date, just chat! We're here to make friends too! As a guideline, we'll have all of our she/hers and nonbinary folk take a seat and stay seated. Any order, totally random. Then the he/hims—and anyone specifically looking to speak with any she/hers—will rotate around the chairs in a clockwise fashion. If you'd rather stay seated or circulate, please do! We just need two groups of ten or so. We've had a great turnout for tonight!"

She paused to look around the room of about twenty *professionals*.

"We'll do the speed dating portion for one hour. Every five minutes you'll get a new chatting partner. While we can't guarantee you'll speed-date everyone, there will be a one-hour mingle sesh to continue any chats or tie up any loose ends!" Kit winked and gave a little shimmy.

"Alright!" Julia took a steadying breath and forced it out, widening her eyes at Susan who leaned against the bar in her *professional* pantsuit, decidedly less enthusiastic about participation.

"Go get 'em tiger," Susan, code name Marsha, said, raising her glass to Julia with one forceful nod of encouragement.

"This sounds kind of fun, actually. Right?" Heather said, a fresh martini in hand, as she looked around the room. She smoothed down her own mahogany brown hair over her shoulders.

Of course it did: Her sister shined in these kinds of settings, maintaining the *je ne sais quoi* from her youth that helped earn her the leads in all of the high school plays and musicals. She loved the spotlight, the attention. Julia had always preferred the unseen work of backstage magic.

But Susan shot daggers at her supportive partner-in-crime. Heather just shrugged.

"I'm all about supporting our JuJu, but this is a one-time affair for old Suse," Susan said. "These folks really aren't my, uh, speed." She cracked a wry grin at her own joke.

"Okay, how many times do we have to cover that thirty-eight is not old? It'll be *fun*," Julia said, reapplying her shimmering rose nude lip gloss.

But she wondered how many times she needed to keep reinforcing *that* statement until the truth seeped through.

"Yup. That's the goal." Susan threw back the rest of her martini.

Julia made her way to the most prime open chair in the two rows of empty seats that stretched across the bar. Luckily, there were empty chairs on either side of her, too. She wasn't here to chat with Cosette and Marsha, but she wanted them at her side for this. This...whatever this was. This casual speed dating thing. She tried to play cool and casual—with varying degrees of success—but her insides wiggled like her mom's Thanksgiving Jell-O salad.

It's gonna be fine. None of this means anything. You're ready for this.

She repeated the words over and over like a mantra, plastering a hopefully convincing smile on her face. This being the first, and legitimately only, forced dating experience she ever participated in, she wasn't sure how to act. Would she be good at this or terribly awkward?

It dawned on Julia that she only wanted to talk to Thomas. She internally groaned. No, that wasn't a convenient or helpful thought at all.

The clean cut, floppy-haired blonde "Peter, he/him" who just sat down across from her, on the other hand, could definitely be casual, fun, and convenient.

"Hi." He flashed an extremely white and toothy smile. "I'm Peter." He settled into a very man-spreading position and leaned forward on one knee. She couldn't hold his spread against him, he had over six feet of body to wrangle. But still.

Julia swallowed, tamping down thoughts about his *body*. She fixed her gaze on him, but in her periphery, Susan whipped her head around so fast, Julia thought she'd get a crick. Heather mirrored her craned neck and wide-eyed expression on Julia's other side.

She could basically hear their internal screams. *He's perfect.* She knew them well enough that she didn't need verbal confirmation.

"Julia," she nodded, her cheeks only slightly warm.

"What do you do, Julia?" Peter asked, flashing that saccharine smile once more. He flipped his hair out of his eyes, repositioning his boat-shoed feet. With such long legs and a tight space, his feet settled on either side of hers. She tucked her feet further under the chair.

Small talk. Right. How many times would she need to explain her boring work life to these random folks?

"I work at Contrakale Logistics as a buyer," she said. Boring. But she flashed the flirtiest smile as she could muster over her fresh drink. "You?"

"I'm an entrepreneur." Another flip of the hair. Another flash of the smile.

An entrepreneur, oh god. Julia concealed the eye roll just begging to come out. "Oh yeah, what's your line of work?"

"Health and fitness mostly." Peter set back, his arms seemingly involuntarily flexing. He didn't provide any more info.

"Oh?" Did Julia really have to beg? She sipped her drink, eyes wide over the rim.

"Yeah." He exhaled through his teeth. "I'm really trying to get my fitness training business off the ground, but until then I work at the gym a town over. As a shift manager. And I sell protein shakes. I mean, not your average protein shakes, like, actually nutritious stuff. Shakeology, have you heard of it? Changed my life, I swear to god."

Inside, Julia screamed, her chest burning with the strain of keeping it in. She shifted in her seat. Cosette and Marsha chatted with their partners, completely unaware of the multi-level marketing pitch Julia was about to receive. Sirens blared in her mind, *change the topic*!

"Haha, that's wild," Julia said, hoping that her feigned interest wasn't too obvious. "Um, what do you like to do in your free time?"

Peter ran his fingers through his hair, raking it back off his forehead. "Work out, mostly."

Julia grimaced, hopefully in a moderately friendly way. She walked right into that one.

This guy was not the perfect fun and casual option; he was annoying as hell.

Thankfully, at just that moment, Kit blew her whistle. "Alright! Switch!"

"Nice to meet you, Julia. Maybe we can catch up again later?" Peter winked, his glowing grin feeling more and more affected by the minute.

Julia barely nodded, suppressing a groan.

Susan leaned over. "MLM? Seriously?"

Julia gritted her teeth, a perma-grin plastered on as the next person sat across from her. "I know. He was like a walking Facebook message."

Susan suppressed a guffaw, covering her mouth to keep the martini inside.

"Hi, I'm Julia," Julia said, taking in her new chatting partner.

"Louis, he/him" read his name tag and he wore a simple dark navy sweater, perfectly tailored jeans, and buttery soft leather loafers. By all definitions, this man was sexy as hell and he knew it.

"Hello," he said, his French accent immediately apparent. "I am Louis."

That explained the unaffected sex appeal. Despite the fact that he absolutely was not Julia's type, she couldn't suppress the thrill of attraction that fluttered through her.

Except that he barely looked at her, seemingly more bored than interested in conversation with her.

"Louis," she liked the way his name felt, though, that was for sure, "what's your life all about?"

He sighed, crossing one leg tightly over the other. "Well, film mostly. I have a blog, you know? About *film noir*, specifically. There is a sad number of *cinémas* in Michigan, but there is one I like. The Maple Theater? Have you ever been?"

"No! But what about the theater at the outlet mall? It's huge! Tons of IMAX screens," Julia said, knowing this would likely vex the man, but she was two martinis in and he was pretentious.

Heather, eavesdropping at her side, stifled a laugh.

Louis actually rolled his eyes, then focused his gaze on Julia. "They don't show the kind of films I enjoy."

Their conversation ended there, neither caring to get to know the other one. Julia slid the olives off her toothpick with her teeth, one at a time, taking her time chewing, in order to pass the rest of the five minutes.

The rest of the hour slipped by in a blur. Julia met a zookeeper, sous-chef, professional gamer, car salesperson, nurse practitioner, high school teacher, veterinarian, security consultant, mechanical engineer, and hair stylist, all of varying genders. And none particularly fitting for Julia's quest of *casual* and *fun*.

Julia leaned both elbows onto the bar, her forehead cradled in both hands.

"This has been a disaster," she groaned.

"Nooo," Heather said, wrapping her arms around her sister's shoulders. "It definitely has not. You put yourself out there and that's the main part, okay?"

"I'm proud of you, Juju. You put up with some real pieces of work out there." Susan sipped on the last of her drink, the button of her pantsuit jacket finally undone.

"I don't need a pep talk, okay?" Julia bristled, shaking her sister off. "I just...I think I want to go home."

She found herself comparing each person she talked to not to Josh—the logical choice for her to weigh future partners against—but to Thomas. Thomas and his beard, and his earnest, guileless eyes. The way his curls fell over to the side and how he swept them back and damnit, she wanted to run her hands through them, too.

"Maybe I'm not so ready for casual." Her shoulders slumped.

"And that's okay. You don't have to make any decisions

tonight. Let's just get you home." Susan held Julia's sweater jacket as she shrugged into it, and Heather grabbed Julia's purse.

"We got you." Heather bumped her sister's hip.

Julia knew they did, and for that, she was very, very thankful.

ELEVEN
THOMAS

"I'M NEVER GOING to get this shit off me," Ari complained, holding up a nest of wispy faux spider web. "It's just like the real thing except worse. There's more of it."

Thomas's baby sister held up a wad of the white cottony stuff and frowned, her brown hair piled in a massive, wobbling top knot outlined against the sun.

He'd taken their last conversation to heart—he wanted to step up for his family. He wanted to support them through this…this. So Thomas rallied his siblings to help put up the Halloween decorations in their parents' yard.

Ari had been working on some pole routines when Thomas called. In a gesture of good faith, he offered to buy her a fifth of Grey Goose to help get the decorations up while the weather was inexplicably warm for October.

Danny, on the other hand, ditched his bowling practice and turned down the bribe of free alcohol, ever eager to please his parents as the middle child peacekeeper.

Fall was flying by. Already October, his parents, who traditionally decorated for Halloween after Labor Day, had missed out on a whole month of enjoying their set-up on the lawn. A few people on their street would decorate for the holiday, but his parents' had always been the most intricate. Not this year. Dad didn't have the endurance to do such a chore anymore, and Mom was so busy managing the restaurant, it had fully slipped her mind. But late was better than never.

Thomas sighed as he wrestled with a string of purple and orange lights. "I miss Halloween."

"It didn't go anywhere, man," Danny said, grabbing one of the ends to help untangle the knotted cluster.

"There were never any kids in my apartment building to trick-or-treat. And no one decorates. It's sad." Thomas frowned at the memory of Halloween in New York, and at the ball of lights which seemed to only get more knotted. "It's like the holiday barely existed. At least not in the way I'm used to."

"But the parties? There have to be some amazing parties? In warehouses? Secret raves?" Ari turned misty-eyed and looked skyward, sending up a faux prayer.

It was a look he recognized. He'd had the same pie-in-the-sky feelings toward New York City in his early twenties too. Though he definitely found worthy pizza pies, his dreams were more about the hustle than illegal parties and dropping ecstasy.

To be honest, his position on the publishing mid-list barely garnered him a blip on anyone's radar. Dad's question of coming home for good was beginning to feel less absurd. He'd always been a master at inception.

"Nothing on par with Theatre Bizarre," Thomas said.

New York had costume parties alright, not that Thomas ever had the energy, money, or time to go, but Theatre Bizarre was something else entirely. An epic twenty-one and over live-action maze masquerade mash-up that weaved through the tower of Detroit's Masonic Temple theater, it brought guests to themed rooms of performers, with costumes and masks required for all attendees. Thomas had never actually been, but his brother and sister worked it. His beefy brother as a bouncer for the last couple years and his sister performed her burlesque routines.

"That reminds me. I got you some tickets," Danny said.

"Don't come to my room, okay? My performance isn't sibling appropriate," Ari said as she skipped around the lawn like a little Halloween fairy, blessing each shrub with a generous handful of gauzy spider web.

Thomas wrinkled his nose. "Thanks for the warning. Proud of you, though."

Where writing was Thomas's passion, dancing—pole

and burlesque—was Ari's in between her business school classes.

"Thanks." Ari flashed a wide smile. "Are you gonna bring Julia?"

"Oh yeah, bring Julia." Danny lifted his eyebrows at his brother.

Prickling heat flashed through his body at the mention of her name. The memory of his last unanswered text, *"I miss you,"* sent another pulse of warmth. He knew the risk in sending it, because they weren't anything to each other, but being home and flooded with so many memories left him adrift. That same aching, gaping hole he had at sixteen when he thought about his future and what shape he wanted it to have. He just didn't know anymore.

But Julia...well, Julia was the person who'd sent him on this trajectory in the first place and could maybe help him crystalize what he wanted going forward. Maybe she could help him shape it. He knew he couldn't push her though, after how she'd reacted at their first movie night. The memory of her eyes welling with tears made his ribs constrict tight around his lungs.

"What's up with all of you—is my entire family conspiring on my love life or what?" Thomas threw the string lights on the ground and pointed. "Fuck these things, by the way."

"No, not conspiring on your love life so much as just wanting you to be happy, you know?" Ari intentionally adjusted a particular glob of web. They hadn't talked about their fight at the restaurant the other day, but in typical Ari fashion, she said her piece and was over it.

Danny walked a skeleton across the yard and artfully rested it on the garden bench. "Mom wanted us to ask you about Julia," he said, his tone bored.

Ari slapped her brother on the arm. "You're not supposed to tell him that part."

Danny shrugged, unconcerned.

"Is that all you all have to think about right now?" Thomas kicked at the bundle of lights, which was a far less satisfying move than he intended. His toe sunk into the strings and got tangled there.

"No, Thomas, but it's better than the alternative of constantly thinking about Dad, and Mom needs something good to focus on. Something to hope for. So, naturally, she's projecting onto you." Ari crossed her arms. "But honestly, I don't blame her. I want my brother home, too."

"Just so I'll buy you vodka to get you to do things with me?" Thomas smiled ruefully.

"Don't be an ass." She popped her hip to the side, shaking her head. "But yeah, I'll always take a fifth when you need a favor."

"What I think Ari's trying to say," Danny said, "is that she misses you. And I miss you too, man."

"Well you all have certainly cornered the market on guilt trips, that's for sure." Thomas towered over the ball of lights, staring at them, not wanting to look at his siblings and also contemplating how the hell to unravel the knotted mess.

"That's not what this is." Ari pouted, clutching the gossamer spider webbing close to her chest.

"It feels like it."

"Just think about it," Danny said, bending over to start battling the lights again.

"That's what Dad said."

"And he's usually right." The mass of lights seemed to unravel nearly on their own as Danny tugged on one end. "Hey, I think you kicking it was the magic move."

Ignoring his brother's snarky comment, Thomas stayed on topic. "I'm thinking about it, okay? But that doesn't mean anything. Just *thinking*."

"Keep thinking. It might be good for you." Danny's brown eyes were warm and sincere, and Thomas gave him a thin-lipped nod.

Ari smirked. "Yeah, like think about Julia in a hot costume, masked up, and you two spending the evening getting lost at Theatre Bizarre."

"Shut up." Warmth climbed up Thomas's neck and he threw a handful of spider webbing at his sister, which fell short in a sad attempt at a curveball. Danny laughed at his brother's pathetic effort.

But the more he thought about it, the more tempting the thought became. Could they go just as friends? There was no harm in inviting her, at least, and he would do just that.

* * *

THOMAS STARED at the computer screen, his cursor blinking. He had an idea and an outline and a deadline to meet, but the words weren't flowing. The creative block he kept ramming into still solidly in place.

The burrito bet swam up to the surface of his mind. The first to get to 50,000 words would win a burrito. A harmless bet, a fun bet. Low stakes, he'd said. So far, he had a couple thousand words. He wondered how Julia was doing on her end. They hadn't talked about it. In truth, they hadn't talked at all in the last couple days. Had he scared her off with his "*I miss you*" text? He hoped that their attempted viewing of *When Harry Met Sally* hadn't been too much for her. He probably should've picked something a little more…lighthearted…for their first go. But that movie would always be his favorite, which is why he picked it first. A timeless classic of long-time friends realizing how much they love each other.

Thomas's stomach twisted, and he forced his attention back to the computer screen.

Usually 50k wouldn't take him long to bang out. First drafts were his favorite. Usually. The initial creative spark carrying him through to the end. But this time was different.

Between the very loud quiet of Thomas's parents secluded street, Dad's cancer, and disruptive thoughts about Julia, the words were logjammed somewhere inaccessible.

His days had become this: work at the restaurant for eight hours a day, blessedly only bussing tables after his serving debacle, spend time with family either before or after work depending on his shift, and then retreat to his room to glare at his computer screen until some ungodly hour when his eyeballs rubbed like sandpaper with each blink.

He sat in the middle of a novel, his sixth, but fourth that was primed for publication. It was a romance, as they all were. Happy endings for everyone! Yet his own plot was anything but *happy*. Even writing a happy ending felt impossible right now. It all felt like twisted fiction.

But still, he hoped that this next novel would be it. Maybe it would be his big break off the mid-list. His agent, Sandy Thorne, remained unerringly positive that it would be, talking about marketing tactics and his backlist and ways that he could increase his social media engagement, as if that could actually move the needle on his sales. Sandy Thorne, cheerleader as ever, only meant to help encourage Thomas, but it certainly didn't help with the mounting pressure. The expectation.

Tonight he was extra distracted by thoughts of Julia after his conversation earlier with his siblings. The way her brown hair flowed around her shoulders. Her peachy-cream skin that looked so soft he could barely contain himself from touching her. How she still wore the warm vanilla body spray that had driven him wild at sixteen. The hurt layered in the storm of her cloudy-day eyes.

He wanted to pulverize Josh for being the cause of that hurt. Why the hell that guy had done what he did, Thomas would never know. Not unfamiliar with polyamory, Thomas knew that intimate relationships came in all different shapes and sizes. But they had agreed upon monogamy, and Josh had broken that trust. Douchebag Josh. The popular boy from high school who continually ignored Thomas, Julia's best friend, until slowly he was expunged from her life completely.

Thomas cracked his knuckles over the keyboard. The flickering cursor still taunted him.

The image Ari had planted burned in his brain, too. Of Julia in a costume and mask, in the dark maze of Theatre Bizarre. In his imagination, she was holy in her hotness. His mind ran with it, lost in veneration to her. Desire prickled over his skin until he had to adjust himself in his jeans.

Shit. *Stop.*

It was late, and his mind became lazy. The safeguards he had during the day could keep thoughts of Julia firmly on the friend side of things, but at night, all bets were off.

He clicked over into his email inbox for a different distraction and scrunched his eyebrows. There were two unread messages there. One from Micha and one from his agent. His stomach plunged. Micha. He still felt like a bit of a douche because of the way he ran from the city. But when his mom called him sobbing, there really wasn't anything else to do.

He clicked on Micha's email.

Subject: Hey

Thomas,

Thought this article might interest you. Haven't seen you around the bar. When I asked about you, they said you went home. Would've been nice to know, but I suppose we don't really owe each other anything. Hope the writing's going well. Send me anything you want read.

Cheers,
Micha

Thomas's chest tightened. He had run out of town quick, that was true. Which meant that beyond his roommates, the brewery, and the unpaid publishing internship he ditched, Thomas left his social circle largely in the dark about him going home.

And since he had been home, he hadn't thought much about the people he left there.

Maybe that meant something.

But Micha's email shuffled the feelings from that chaotic week of getting out of New York to the forefront. Was it guilt? He *had* been sleeping with Micha for a couple months, and while the sex was great, they had never talked about a relationship. Seeing Julia again confirmed that, despite the years, *those* feelings had never really gone away.

What was left in New York for him again? It was becoming more difficult to remember.

He clicked to the next email. Sandy had always been the perfect champion for his work, but he began to doubt how much longer his repeated assurances of "you'll have pages soon" would tide her over.

Subject: Deadline time

Thomas,

Take your time, but not too much time. Think of your deadline as a soft deadline, but a target nonetheless, yeah? We need to build some momentum with your books, so the sooner we can get your brand built, the better. Send me anything you have, when you have it!

Best,
Sandy Thorne

Thomas rubbed at the back of his neck, absently

trying to work out some of the knots there. Brands, momentum, deadlines. He didn't want to think about that stuff. There was a time in his life when he was naive enough to believe that being an author was just about *the writing*. But being in the publishing world was a different beast entirely. It was a strange conundrum that his dream, his passion, had to directly translate into dollar bills in order for his career to get off the ground. Each day brought a new fresh rejection in the publishing world.

Thomas scrubbed his hand over his face and beard, pulling at the skin around his eyes. It was probably time to cut his losses and try again tomorrow. As he yawned wide, mouth uncovered, his phone flickered on the bedside table. Julia had finally responded. Thomas bit his lip, fiery energy coursing through his body. He clicked on the new message.

Today 1:30 AM

I miss you too

I didn't expect to see you like ever again

What I'm trying to say is, I'm glad you texted

:-) it was a bit of a gamble but I'm glad too

> Oh, you're awake, too. You owe me a romcom. I'm dying to know what you'll pick next.
>
> Unless we're going to finish When Harry Met Sally?

> Still working, actually.

> No, I think we got enough out of that one. Though we could do an entire masterclass on Meg Ryan films alone

> The romcom queen of our hearts

> Truly

> Sometime this weekend, then? If you're free?
>
> My parents are going up north so you could come over here?

Sweat prickled Thomas's brow like he was a teen sneaking around. At thirty, after years living on his own, it's not like he needed permission to do anything. But the thought of being all alone with Julia in her house made his mouth dry with possibility and rattled his nerves.

Except that, try though his fantasies might to convince him otherwise, there was nothing between them.

The sordid expectations his mind had built up would need to be sledgehammered if he was going to survive being just friends with Julia Ward. And he wanted to be her friend. Above all else, he missed their friendship.

Today 1:45 AM

> I'm in

Saturday, 6 pm. I'll get pizza. See you then :-)

TWELVE
JULIA

JULIA PACED AROUND HER PARENTS' kitchen waiting for Thomas to arrive. She had the pizza and the beer ready to go, and if she could just control her jittering nerves, everything would be fine. Great, even.

But Thomas would be in this house for the first time since her high school graduation party.

It was the last time they saw each other.

She had worn a white eyelet dress and espadrilles as she sweated in the backyard under the huge tent her parents had rented, greeting all of her guests: family, friends, some of her parents' coworkers. The setup was complete with folding tables and chairs, en masse mostaccioli catering, a huge cake, and a keg from which Josh and all his buddies kept sneaking red solo cups of beer.

Already then, she and Thomas had drifted apart, no longer the inseparable duo from the past two summers.

Because by mid-senior year, she was fully entrenched in Josh's world.

And by the time of her party, Julia and Thomas had had their big blow-out, where she revealed the big secret that she'd kept from Thomas for months. The one that changed their future.

Through the party, Josh had stayed glued to her side as she greeted her guests and took their gifts, smiling in the dress that her mom insisted complemented her peach cheeks and long, mahogany hair.

Thomas hadn't stayed long that day. She didn't blame him. She virtually ignored him, but she told herself then that it was because she was so busy hosting.

Now, she wasn't so sure that was true.

Now, she could admit that she didn't want to talk to Thomas then.

Now, she could see how foolish she was.

That day, she saw him, standing to the side, eating a piece of cake in his jeans and black t-shirt even in the ninety-degree sticky Michigan heat. Afterward she had found his gift tucked among all the others. An autographed copy of her favorite book—their favorite book—*The Perks of Being a Wallflower* by Stephen Chbosky, which Thomas, too, had inscribed.

Her thank you card apologized for not being able to talk with him that day. A couple lines that felt pathetic in the light of their once close relationship.

And that was it. She never saw him again. Until a couple weeks ago.

The doorbell rang, shocking Julia from her memories. She wrung her fingers, nervous because after the *Speed Dating! For Professionals!* event, she only had one person in mind for her fun and casual exploits.

She and Thomas could be casual, right? If that's what he wanted too? And she could have sworn there was tension between them. Now the fact that he would one day leave for New York City again seemed like the perfect opportunity to flex her casual muscles. No obligation. Perfect.

Julia padded to the door in her rubber ducky patterned socks, worn to complement her cozy buttercup yellow cardigan that she wore over a creamy, faux silk camisole.

She opened the door, and there he was, standing on her doorstep. He pulled his lips between his teeth as his shoulders hiked high under his black zip up hoodie. His hair was perfect, his beard neat and trim. A small parcel peeked out from under one arm.

Julia smiled, her glossy lips parting and her stomach flipping. God, he was gorgeous. In a casual, grungy kind of way that really hadn't changed since high school. She definitely appreciated that.

"Hey," she said. "Come in."

She waved him through the door, and Thomas bent

down to give her a hug. Her nose rubbed against his hoodie, which smelled like clean laundry. She stopped herself from sighing into him. That smell did something strange to her body as nostalgia coursed through her veins. When they pulled apart, his nose twitched like a bunny.

"Mmm pizza," Thomas said as he looked around. "Well, this looks nothing like I remember."

"My mom gets bored easily," Julia said, her eyes tracking the changes from all those years ago as well. The walls now updated to a dark greige with fake hardwood floor replacing all of the old carpet. Though the lonely upright piano still graced the family room, and Julia and Heather's now-dated senior photos still plastered the walls.

More than ten years later as different people all alone in her parents' house, it felt all *Twilight Zone*-esque to stand here in the foyer. Eerily the same, and yet completely different. A twisted kind of déjà vu.

Thomas cleared his throat and held out the small wrapped package. He immediately shoved his fists back into his pockets when Julia took it.

"What's this?" Julia asked.

"A gift. Sort of."

"You didn't have to."

"I know. But I wanted to."

Julia smiled as she remembered his graduation gift again.

"Come on." She nodded deeper into the house. "Let's get a beer and some pizza, then I'll open it."

She lifted the lids of the Jet's pizza box on the kitchen table as she flitted by. Though a chain, Julia firmly believed it was the best pizza in Starling Hills. This one was one half pineapple and jalapeño, the other half pepperoni and onion.

"Help yourself. I assumed pepperoni and onion is still your favorite? Mine's changed, so it was a bit of a stab in the dark."

"I see that, jalapeño and pineapple—quite the combo." Thomas smiled, his shoulders finally relaxing down his back. "Everyone says pizza in New York is the best, but I'll be forever partial to Jet's. There are Jet's in New York, but people die every time I want to get it. As long as the pizza's got eight corners and there's Jet's ranch, I'm good to go."

"Remember who you're talking to, buddy. I always get a whole bottle of ranch from them, okay? We're set." Julia grabbed the ranch and two Coors Light from the fridge.

Julia set the ranch on the table and twisted off the beer caps. She took a deep drink from hers as she reached the other to Thomas. The lingering awkwardness and the years-dormant magnetism now buzzing under her skin left her antsy.

Thomas took his beer, the ghost of a smile on his lips. "Open your gift."

Julia ripped open the plain brown paper wrapping.

She turned the gift over in her hands: a pack of brown Moleskine cahier journals.

"I always loved these. Thanks, Thomas." A smile crept over her face, crinkling her eyes. She put her hand on his forearm, energy fizzing between them. Did he feel it too?

"They're for notes while we're watching the movies. Or for your writing. Both. Whatever." After a lingering moment, Thomas moved from under her touch. He grabbed a piece of pizza straight from the box, took a huge bite and grinned around it.

They filled their plates and moved to the living room. Julia let him pick where he wanted to sit first and she'd follow his lead.

Except that he settled right into her dad's recliner chair, immediately isolating himself from her, crushing her opportunity to make any kind of *casual* moves.

She cleared her throat, barely concealing her frown. *It's fine.* "So what movie are we watching?"

"Another Meg Ryan classic, as discussed. *You've Got Mail.* It's on Netflix."

"Ah, and another Nora Ephron," Julia said, dropping into the spot on the couch closest to the recliner—the next best option. She tucked one leg under her bottom, the other one bobbing free in midair. "Perhaps the most Nora Ephroniest offering we have?"

"Very good." He nodded and tilted his beer bottle toward her. "Who says you need a romcom education?"

"Only my bleak and depressing outlook on love and enduring happiness."

"Right, that." Thomas huffed a light laugh through his nose. "Not sure we've done much to help on that front."

"Not yet." Julia's lips crooked mischievously.

The barest flush crept over Thomas's beard and into the visible portion of his cheeks. It sent a flutter through her insides.

Good.

Still rusty with flirting, the *Speed Dating! For Professionals!* unhelpful on that front, Julia lifted her chin, pleased to know she could still make a man blush.

She toggled through screens until she found the film. "Ready?"

Thomas nodded, mouth full of pizza.

Julia finished her two slices of pizza in record time, before the credits were even over. She walked back into the kitchen with her plate, facing the TV, her eyes never leaving the screen. She'd seen *You've Got Mail* before, but this time it was somehow even more charming. Late 90's Tom Hanks and Meg Ryan? Downright dreamy.

She moved back to the couch with two fresh Coors Light, one Moleskine journal, and a pen rummaged from her mom's junk drawer.

"Thanks," Thomas said, taking a beer from her.

A little zing travelled straight to her core as his thumb brushed hers in the handoff.

As she pulled the pen cap off with her teeth, he

watched her. She felt his attention tickling over her body. Out of her periphery, she watched him too. Thomas stared, pushing his sweatshirt sleeves up his forearms, but she couldn't tell what his face said. His forearms drew her eyes to where they rested on his lap, and she wanted to run a hand over his soft, hairy arms. Her heart skipped over itself, and she drew a sudden breath, the wave of her desire overwhelming her.

She'd worn her skimpiest camisole underneath her sweater and her most flattering jeans on purpose. Her outfit didn't leave much to the imagination, outlining every curve of breasts, stomach, and hips. But Thomas physically avoided her, seating himself in the single chair, even if his attention lingered on her.

Her change in tactic was giving her whiplash, but maybe he wouldn't suffer from the abrupt change. Before, she couldn't even sit down and watch a whole movie with him and now she was ready to go.

Just a couple casual moves, and we'll be on our way to pound town.

Julia cringed. Pound town? Who was she anymore? Even her inner monologue sounded utterly embarrassing and incapable of seduction.

She cleared her throat, readjusting in her seat. Putting pen to paper, she wrote the date on the inside cover and the movie title on the first page, feeling like she was in school again taking notes.

"*We're seeing the end of Western civilization as we know it.*"

"Wow, Greg Kinnear, you soothsayer, you don't have to be so right about it." Julia scribbled her first comments. "This movie's like a frigging time capsule."

"Yep, 1998. It's certainly pre-9/11, pre-Obama, pre-2008-recession, pre-Trump, pre-pandemic. It's a 90s relic that's for sure." Thomas crossed his arms, beer crooked into his elbow. He was tall enough that his large, black stockinged feet sat flat on the floor with no effort.

Julia wet her lips. Why did the sight of his black socks under dark blue jeans feel so intimate? How was *that*, of all things, turning her on?

She snorted, focusing again on the film. "Right. It's like a goddamned fairytale where big box stores are the big bad guys. Too bad Amazon was a bigger baddie."

"A very distinct snapshot of a moment in time. Amazon had just started selling CDs in 1998." Thomas nodded along to Tom Hanks's on-screen voiceover. "But also fuck Amazon."

"I would live in Meg Ryan's shop if I could." It had the perfect independent bookstore motif, something well-suited for Ann Arbor. Something right out of Julia's daydreams.

"The Shop Around the Corner." Thomas nodded. "Me too."

"Okay, so wait. I have a feeling this movie might be...

problematic?" Julia chewed on the end of her pen. "I mean, this whole email setup is an emotional affair."

"Problematic? Probably. Nora Ephron classic? Yes, still true." Thomas frowned. "I didn't think about the email thing though. Is that going to be triggering for you?"

Julia's stomach clenched. She was getting better about not thinking about Josh every damn day. Or at least, not constantly daydreaming about painful ways for him to suffer. She'd basically fabricated an entire ring in hell solely for her ex-fiancé. Josh couldn't ruin everything for her. And she especially didn't want him to ruin their movie night. Again.

"No," she said. "Thanks, but I think it'll be fine. They don't really go into the whole *cheating* stuff anyway. That's what's interesting about Nora Ephron: there's these big breakups mid-movie and not even a tear shed. It's virtually conscious uncoupling."

Julia wrote some more notes, and Thomas straightened, leaning toward her notebook. "Whatcha writing?"

"No cheating." She shielded the page with her hand. "If watching this film is necessary for my education to win this bet, you better not be peeking at my notes."

Thomas laughed. "Fine, fine."

And they didn't compare notes again for the rest of the film.

* * *

"SO, WHAT DID YOU THINK?" Thomas asked as the credits rolled, not moving from his chair.

"Hmm?" Julia said. "Oh, hold on. I'm having thoughts."

Her pen flew over the paper. A frenzy of ideas poured from her brain. That was unexpected. But she supposed that was the point of all this. Teach her something about love and happy endings, get her interested in writing again. Was it working? Against all odds it seemed to be.

"Okay, tell me more about New York City. How'd the movie do?" Julia looked up from her journal to find Thomas waiting patiently for her attention.

"It's a version of the city, that's for sure, but it's not the version I know. I don't know if anyone ever knew it, but set in 1998 with 30-somethings living like that? I don't buy it. And I live in Brooklyn, so the idea that young people wouldn't want to move to Brooklyn is ridiculous. That's where all the cool shit is now. Another thing is that the film portrays a completely sanitized version of New York. No poor people, no struggle. And all that Starbucks placement? Fuck Starbucks. Their coffee is trash."

Julia lifted her eyebrows at him. "Though, in fairness, Starbucks was at their peak in 1998?"

"In fairness. The film is nostalgic, soothing. I just don't know if it was ever really like that." He took a drink of beer. "Rose colored glasses and all that."

Rose colored glasses. The kind she'd kept on for most of her life. It kept her blind to what a shithead Josh was. Or was it willful ignorance? At one time, Julia really did want that Le Creuset butter dish and everything it represented.

Didn't she?

She swallowed. "I thought you said you love this movie?"

"Oh, I do. Nora Ephron is a master class of dialogue, wit, and character-based comedy. But it's weird as hell. Almost a fantasy. Though that's of course viewing it through today's lens and not 1998. Different times. And I fell in love with this movie in a different time." Thomas shrugged. "What about you?"

"If something like this was made today, it'd probably be considered propaganda for capitalism." Julia snorted a laugh at her little joke. "Economics aside, this movie isn't about that at all. It's about the internal journey of Kathleen, and Joe to some extent, but I only really care about Meg Ryan right now. The complacency versus vulnerability themes stick out most. That line: 'You are daring to imagine that you could have a different life.' Chills." Julia looked down at her notes, flipping pages back and forth.

Thomas stood, taking their empty beer bottles and moving to the kitchen. "Exactly. I think that's why I love this movie so much. Or any romcom worth its salt. It's not about the *love* of the love story but the arc of the characters themselves. That's why I love writing them, too. When Kathleen wonders if she hasn't been brave? I love it."

Thomas came back with two more beers. This time he

sat on the couch next to Julia. Her lips pulled into a true smile, so wide that her cheeks ached from it.

"I think about that a lot." Julia played with the corner of the page.

"What?"

"If I've been brave. Daring."

"And what do you come up with?"

Julia shrugged. One of her cardigan sleeves fell down, exposing her shoulder. For a moment, Thomas's gaze burned into her expanse of bare skin there, but he blinked and met her eyes once more.

"Nothing. I don't think I've done a single brave thing in my life. At least, not for the last ten years. Maybe I was brave once. I used to post spicy fics anonymously on the internet for fun! But I folded and molded myself into a certain shape to be with Josh, and then that all blew up. I can't trust myself anymore. My instincts, or lack thereof, are what got me into this whole mess..."

She trailed off, too close to saying something she wasn't ready to admit yet, especially to Thomas. Too close to talking about the secret that she kept from him all those years ago and the blow-up fight that it led to.

"I think you're brave." Thomas's voice was hoarse, but he held her gaze.

She wrapped a finger in her sweater and looked away, feeling too seen. "You don't know me, Thomas. Not anymore. I'm a different person than I was when you knew me. We haven't even talked in years. You're viewing me through those rose-colored glasses."

A white-hot anger built in her chest, and like a lightning rod, Thomas focused it and gave her something to channel it into.

"We're talking now."

"We are." Julia rolled her eyes and rearranged herself on the couch. There was so much that she wanted to say. She wasn't mad at him specifically. She was mad at everything. Mad at Josh. At being thirty-one and feeling completely rudderless. The words bottlenecked on the way from her brain to her tongue.

She took a drink of beer to lubricate her thoughts. "I just have this opportunity to be someone different, become something different, and I already feel like I'm wasting it. Like maybe I'm doing something wrong. Heather keeps calling this my butterfly moment. I hate that, but it's kind of true. Except that I have a knack for making the wrong choices."

"So, what are you doing about it?"

Julia cocked her head, appreciating the way Thomas subtly challenged her. "I've got that interview this week. The promotion is the next logical step in my career. But is that just the complacent move? Nothing else has presented itself, but it doesn't feel very brave."

Julia pulled the cardigan back up on her shoulder and wrapped it tighter around her middle, crossing her arms. This conversation was certainly vulnerable. More so than she'd ever been with Josh. Did it always feel so icky?

"I don't want this to end in crying again, but it easily could." She sniffed.

"Don't worry about it."

Her downcast eyes found his hands on the beer bottle in his lap. His fingers worked the label, peeling it back off the glass.

She pointed. "In college we used to say that means you're sexually frustrated."

Oh god why did I say that? Julia bit her lip and her cheeks heated all the way up to her hairline. The words just flew out. She couldn't stop them.

"Yeah, well." Thomas fumbled and placed the bottle on the couch-side table and crossed his arms, hiding his hands. "Listen, I should probably go."

With that, he stood, swinging his arms in the air, hands swiping on his jeans as they went by.

"Oh. Okay. Umm, I got dessert, but..." Julia pointed a thumb over her shoulder toward the kitchen, but her words were already trailing off.

She didn't want their night to end. She wanted the mint chocolate chip ice cream and Saunders hot fudge topping. And then she wanted him as second dessert.

Thomas ran his hand over his beard and grimaced. Literally grimaced. "I have some writing to do. Ya know, deadline and all that."

Julia widened her eyes and nodded. "Mmm, yep, deadline. Sounds important."

It didn't sound important. It sounded stupid. Julia felt like shit. That anger clawed from the inside again, the evening spiraling out of her control. She had a plan and she was prepared. She'd even shaved for Pete's sake. Julia was ready to have the fun that Susan and Heather wouldn't shut up about, and Thomas was ready to run.

"I'm sorry I can't stay. Right now. I need to get this work done and…let's hang out again?" He shoved his hands into his pockets. "I know this has all been rocky with this stuff going on with my family and this deadline breathing down my neck."

He paused, looking beyond her for a moment.

"I have tickets to Theatre Bizarre in like two weeks and want to take you. Would you want to go with me?"

"The Halloween masquerade at that theater in Detroit? Costume required?" Julia scrunched her mouth to one side.

"Yeah, costume and mask required. Do you have one?"

"I have something that I can pull together, I think, yeah. But I don't know." Julia suddenly felt so unsure about everything. Maybe she was reading this totally wrong.

"I just feel like things didn't get off on the right foot, and I want things to be good between us."

What does that even mean?

She stood and stepped toward Thomas; the energy between them made her heart soar like a kite floating on the breeze. This feeling was impossible to make up. He had to feel it too, surely? The way his breath caught in his chest convinced her that he did.

But it wouldn't be the first time she felt one-sided attraction between them. She squashed that thought.

Thomas licked his lips as his eyes lasered in on her mouth. "I think it's better if I go, Julia, but come to the masquerade with me."

The masquerade would mean getting to spend a lot of time with Thomas in the dark, meandering through the theater, masked, and in—she fantasized—extremely sexy costumes. "Alright."

Thomas smiled down at her and he let out a breath, as if he wasn't sure she would agree. "You're not going to regret it, promise. Thanks for the pizza."

Julia padded back to the living room after she saw him out, sighing as she braided her hair over her shoulder. Tonight hadn't gone the way she wanted at all. Her expectations had wildly outpaced the reality. Her mind played back the separate reels like in *500 Days of Summer* and she groaned, afraid that she had miscalculated after all. But he invited her to the Theatre Bizarre, meaning he did actually want to spend more time with her, so maybe all wasn't completely lost. Maybe he really did just need to get some work done.

She unlocked her phone as she plopped onto the couch, and there was already a text from him.

Good luck with the interview. Rooting for you.

THIRTEEN
JULIA

JULIA SAT AT HER DESK, head hanging as she stared at her phone inhaling, holding, and exhaling breath with a meditation app. This little powerhouse guided her through today, the only thing keeping her sane.

That and a grande oat milk pumpkin spice latte.

Under her curtain of hair, she sipped autumn's sweet nectar, willing it to fuel her through the next three hours of interviews.

Yeah. The virtual calendar invitation had really blocked off three freaking hours for this interview.

One would think that interviewing internally would bring somewhat of an advantage, but it didn't feel that way. They were putting her through the damn ringer. They said *jump* and Julia said *how high*? She'd been going through this process for months now—how could it have been months already?—and this interview was the final one.

Until three weeks ago, the upward mobility of her career was the bright spot of her post-Josh life.

Now, she craved the evenings and late nights she put in with her laptop, tapping out scenes and outlining story ideas. She'd even picked up some craft books and dedicated time to learning how to write again. She loved it. Something she'd completely forgotten.

Still, she was only 5k into the 50,000-word total. She'd texted Thomas little crying emojis, and he'd likened writing to working out. The more she practiced, the easier it would be. The muscles just needed some toning.

It made sense, but part of her was jealous of his career and mad at herself for letting her writing get rusty. He was a published author living out the dream they'd planned together, and she was still in their small hometown, back at her parents' house, and slogging it out in the corporate world. Wow, stellar.

Breathe, just like the little app coached her. It was almost time for her interview.

At five minutes to eleven, she stood, pulled her hair back into a neat, low pony, and gave Susan a thumbs up across the aisle. Susan gave her two enthusiastic thumbs up in response and growled like a tiger. Julia laughed, her shoulders relaxing a little.

She walked to the boardroom, her pulse pounding just under her jaw. She'd interview in a long room with one massive table and a wall of windows. The inner walls were glass too so that everyone could see everything that went on in that room. Julia would be on full display for her entire interview, where anyone on her floor could peer in at any moment. She just hoped Michelle didn't waltz by. The last thing she needed was her office nemesis as a distraction.

Her palms started to sweat. Through the glass window, three executives and one executive assistant, present to take notes, huddled around the end of the table, waiting to conduct the interview. She pulled the door open and four heads swiveled around to her with wide smiles.

"Thank you for meeting with us today, Julia. Have a seat," Christopher said, a Korean-American man who was all pinstripe suit and wavy curtain bangs. He stood to shake her hand across the table. Julia would directly report to him if she got the position. He also had the final say in who they awarded the role.

The other three also stood and shook her hand, white teeth flashing and eyes sparkling.

"Hello. Of course, happy to be here." Julia smiled, her teeth clenched and aching, as she sat in an extremely ergonomic rolling chair. She whitened her teeth on Sunday and wore a cool-toned pink lipstick to make her teeth look even whiter. The women professionals at Contrakale Logistics always looked so put together, and she wanted to be one of them too. Or convincingly look the part at least, immaculate white teeth and all.

"Of course, we're so happy to have you, too," Denise said, a Black woman with long braids and a bronze pantsuit. She would be a peer on Julia's new team. "So, we're going to start the interview with some more zoomed-in personal questions, and then we'll zoom-out and talk about the job and cover some technical questions. And at the end there will be an opportunity for you to ask questions. Does that sound alright?"

The four professionals bobbled their heads, all smiles and positive reinforcement. Did their cheeks hurt as much as hers?

Julia chose to be here, but suddenly she felt trapped. Sweat prickled her elbow creases under her navy blazer. She forced a smile back on her face. "Yep, great!"

It didn't feel great. This was miserable.

"So, we all know you, Julia, but tell us, who *is* Julia Ward?" asked Tamora, a white woman with a blonde bob and gold hoop earrings, who functioned as Christopher's counterpart on Julia's would-be partner team. Tamora narrowed her eyes and leaned in toward the table as she finished her question.

These "zoomed-in" questions proved tricky. Especially now. Julia had the technical stuff locked down. Memorize a couple of buzz phrases, use power verbs, tack all that together with some metrics about her performance and boom, done. But questions like *who is Julia Ward* were basically a panic attack on a platter.

Julia took a deep breath before answering. "First of all, thank you for the opportunity to interview today."

She made eye contact with each person around the table, their smiles plastered on and eyes blinking widely back at her, observing her like a zoo animal.

"Well, I'm from Starling Hills, born and raised. I still live here, in fact." Her throat ached. She couldn't swallow, so she kept speaking. "I graduated from the University of Michigan. I love to travel when I can. And— "

And what? She had barely said anything and she'd already run out of things to say about herself.

Before she would have filled in the blanks with stuff she picked up from Josh. Lies like 'I'm a huge football fan' or 'I love boating.' Now, she was slowly figuring out who she was without him, and she still had no idea. *I did theater in high school? I used to write fan fiction and it's a hobby I just picked up again?*

Yeah no, none of those answers would work here.

"And yeah," she continued, suppressing the rising panic, the executives still politely smiling with ogling eyes, "fall is my favorite time of year, because I love pumpkin spice lattes."

Which was true but, fuck, that was a stupid thing to say.

"Great, thanks." They all bent their heads toward their notepads, scribbling quick notes. Beth, a white assistant with straight brown hair and a very large, very sparkly solitaire diamond on her ring finger, never stopped writing, transcribing every single ridiculous word that came out of Julia's mouth.

Julia rubbed her hands on her navy trousers, willing her palms to dry up, and braced herself for the next question.

"Tell us about some of your goals. Where do you see yourself in five years? Ten?" Denise asked, raising her eyebrows.

Julia's stomach curdled. She'd prepared for this question but hated it nonetheless.

Five-year and ten-year goals? What did that even mean? As if ten years ago her goal was to be in this chair having this conversation.

No. It wasn't so long ago that she dreamt about a life in New York City with her best friend. When she still hadn't made that final decision that would change everything.

Five years ago, she wanted the Le Creuset butter dish, the quartz countertops, the suburban dream. She wanted to be Josh's wife.

And now, she had none of that. Goals meant nothing.

"With this job as a stepping stone, I hope to expand my knowledge of Contrakale Logistics operations so that within five years, I'll have moved comfortably up the corporate ladder. While my focus is sales now, I would love to get into marketing so that in ten years, I will have built a meaningful and lasting career here. Personally speaking..." Julia swallowed, words turning to dust on her tongue.

Sour bile crept up her throat, making her chest burn.

She didn't know what she wanted *personally speaking* anymore. Even the answer she'd just given was a relic of her life with Josh. 'Buy a house and start a family' was the cookie cutter future she'd dreamt of and clung to for years. But now that felt hollow and wrong. And in this economy? Downright unattainable.

It was just a stupid answer to a stupid interview question, but it sent her into a spiral. The smoldering ashes of her life didn't care about five or ten-year plans.

The three executives blinked at her, waiting patiently. Christopher even gave an encouraging nod. Good Lord, she was making a fool out of herself.

Julia took a breath and started the sentence over. "Personally speaking, I just want to be happy, whatever I'm doing."

"Great! What more can we ask for?" Christopher beamed, opening his hands and twirling side to side in his chair.

Denise, Tamora, and Beth murmured in agreement.

Julia wanted to sublimate and float out of this room in a gaseous cloud.

The rest of the interview passed in a dissociative haze. Julia shined with metrics and numbers, Excel sheets and bottom-lines, lead times and cost reduction. She wasn't worried about that part. As she sprouted it all off without breaking a sweat, she turned over her answer to the goals question.

I just want to be happy.

She didn't even know what that meant anymore.

But after work, Julia knew what would make her happy.

She sat down with her laptop and started writing. The words came easier that night, flying from her fingers. She didn't doubt or self-censor. She didn't think about rules or how she was supposed to write, but she went back to her roots, lassoing the joy of the frenzied fan-fiction smut she wrote back in the day.

Julia took her OT3—her One True Throuple, a Rey/Finn/Poe pairing inspired by *The Force Awakens*—and gave them the steamy scene of her dreams.

Bottom lip skewered between her teeth, she copied and pasted it into an email and sent it on to Thomas before she could second-guess it. Sending him a sex scene set her insides vibrating, full of kinetic energy, but his response five minutes later made it all okay.

This is hot. I love it. Keep going (and send me more).

Julia smiled, her bottom lip slipping free. She picked up her phone, inspired.

She still needed a costume for Theatre Bizarre, and there was only one person who could help her now. Heather, whose bedroom still fit the definition of a dress-up box.

ALAINA ROSE

Today 7:02 PM

Help! I need a costume. Like a good one

> What does that mean? And why?

Thomas invited me to Theatre Bizarre

> Imagine the eyes emoji, and then imagine me as that emoji and now you know my reaction to that statement

> That's hot

Shut up it's not hot it's just…fun

> Mmhm

> Anyway then what do you need?

Something…hot?

> HA! See I told you. Hot.

> I got you

I'll bring some stuff over to mom and dads

You're a lifesaver

> I know. See you soon <3

"SOME? STUFF?" Julia picked up a leather corset and held it up to her body. "I can't believe that you just own all of this?"

Piles of colorful fabrics and varied textiles covered Julia's bed, which Heather lovingly organized *by* color and textile.

"Impressive right? You can take the girl out of the theater, but you can't take the theater out of the girl. It's all about the aesthetics." Heather tossed a silk scarf in the air. "Now what are you going for?"

Julia made a non-committal squeaking sound and waved her hand. All of the options overwhelmed her.

"You were so obviously part of the stage crew."

"You can take the girl out of the backstage, but you can't take the backstage out of the girl?" Julia repeated Heather's phrase with the necessary modifications and far less enthusiasm. "That's why I need your help. And your treasure chest of costumes."

"Okay, I can see you're desperate here, and calling me was one hundred percent the right move." Heather cleared a space for herself on the bed and sat, crossing one leg over the other, her pointer finger tapping her chin. "First, we need a vision. And with these curves, you'd look banging in a corset."

Julia raised a corner of her lip. "A corset?"

"Don't be like that, corsets are great. And actually, they're comfortable, or rather shouldn't be uncomfortable." Heather rubbed her hands together. "Do you know how long I've wanted to dress you?"

"That sounds weird." Julia dug her hands into the piles of fabric on her bed. "How do you afford all this? Doesn't it seem a little...superfluous?"

"Don't yuck my yum and I won't yuck yours. I didn't make fun of you when you were all decked out in Lions football gear." Heather twirled a finger up, down, and around her sister.

Julia frowned, remembering the Honolulu blue leggings she used to wear to all of the football tailgates. She made a mental note to gather all that memorabilia and burn it. "That wasn't my yum."

"Even worse." Heather rolled her eyes and picked a stray hot pink feather off her arm. "Anyway, do you want my help or what?"

"Yes. I'm sorry. *Yes*," Julia groaned, a little humiliated by this whole thing.

Her sister visibly perked up. "Okay, goals. What are your goals for this outfit?"

"Goals? Well, I need to be comfortable but," she hesitated as heat climbed up her neck, "hot."

"I knew it." Heather began re-organizing clothes in fresh piles, but what the theme of each group was, Julia couldn't tell. "How are things going with Thomas anyway?"

"There is no 'thing' to 'go.' We're just friends." Julia crossed her arms and popped a hip to the side. A defensive front eased the simmering burn under her skin. Thomas's vanishing act from their last hang out made her dizzy as her instincts swiveled around in search of her true north. Until things settled, maybe she just shouldn't make any moves. So far, all of their hang outs ended in cringe mode.

"Sure, sure." Heather widened her eyes as if she didn't believe her sister. "Okay, I'm thinking steampunk sharpshooter. Showcase your body type, flattering, hot, and pretty easy in the grand scheme of costumes. And no skirt, you can wear leggings, so it's comfortable too."

"Oh! Leggings?" Julia perked up. "Yeah, that sounds perfect."

"And— " Heather squealed and jumped from the bed. "I have the perfect mask!"

She brandished a plastic mask, painted in burnished silver to give it an aged look. The details curled over the surface like curving wrought iron, with metal-like dragonfly wings sprouting from the bridge of her nose.

"It'll go perfectly with this tunic." She pulled a gunmetal gray top with puff sleeves from the pile. "And this corset."

"You have more than one corset?"

Heather fixed her sister with a deadpan look. "Yes, I do. They're necessary."

The one she handed over to Julia wasn't the traditional kind of corset of Julia's nightmares, but more like what she would consider a bodice. A curve-hugging, dark brown leather vest and a grommet belt that cinched around her waist. Julia held it up to her body, still suspicious of the thing.

"Oh my god, yes! You're going to be a vision in steampunk." Heather clapped and danced around the bedroom. "Julia Gulia goes to the haunted ball! It's like all of the rom-coms and fairytales are combining. I am one hundred percent living vicariously through you. Come on, let's test run it."

"It's not like that, I'm telling you." But even as she said it, something tickled deep in her gut. Julia slid off her jeans and pulled her sweater over her head.

"Please tell me you're at least going to have some hot sex. You deserve hot sex."

"You sound like Susan." Julia wiggled into some black pleather leggings that had plenty of give.

"Susan is very wise."

Julia sighed, dropping the tunic over her head. "Well, I'm working on it, okay? Not like it's any of your business."

"As your younger sister, my business is very much you being happy, and I think a couple great orgasms would make you *very* happy."

"I got the orgasms covered." Julia waved her fingers in the air.

Heather whipped a hot pink feather boa at her sister. "It's not the same, and you know it."

Julia shrugged and put her arms through the corset, bringing it around her and doing up the latches.

"How'd that interview go by the way?" Heather asked as she fluffed and arranged the tunic top to artfully showcase Julia's ample cleavage.

"Great, I nailed it," she sighed. "I just don't know if it's what I want anymore. Thomas got me thinking about writing again and I do miss it. I don't know if it could be like a career thing but this promotion would be a huge change in my work-life balance, and that's not as appealing when I don't know what I'm working toward anymore."

"A conundrum as old as time. Work sucks— "

"I know!" they said together, quoting the iconic Blink-182 line, and laughed as Heather spun Julia around to the full-length mirror. She lifted the mask over Julia's eyes from behind and tied it.

Julia gasped. "Wow."

Her pulse quickened as she looked at her reflection. Heather was right about all of her editorial fashion choices and what they did to her curves. She looked *hot*.

"Yeah dude, you look hot, okay? And I'm not just saying that because you're my sister and I'd really like for you to get some. I'm saying that because it's true. The corset was an excellent idea." Heather fussed with the outfit, adding a holster slung low on Julia's hips. "Here, put these on too."

Julia inched fingerless, above-the-elbow leather gloves up her arms. "You're good at this whole costume thing."

"I know." Heather smiled and shrugged in a self-satisfied way. "You just need a hairdo. I'm thinking pigtail buns on the top of your head."

"Right. I think I can manage that." Julia nodded, an exhilarated feeling racing through her veins. She was truly excited now and deeply curious about Thomas's costume.

"Thomas won't know what hit him." Heather winked at her sister in the mirror.

Julia thought her sister might be right.

Later that night, she texted him while brushing her teeth.

> Alright. Got my costume all set.

> Oh? Pics?

> Spoilers! You're just going to have to wait and see ;-)

FOURTEEN
THOMAS

THOMAS STEPPED into the kitchen freezer carrying a crate of tomato slices that slammed against his quads with each step. After an entire mid-afternoon spent slicing all the vegetables they needed for the week, he didn't have the will, or upper body strength, left to lift the plastic tub higher than his waist.

The cool freezer air whipped around him, snaking under his apron and t-shirt. A blessed change from the heat of his slicing station tucked in the back, right in the sweltering triangulation created by his spot, the dishwasher, and the industrial gas griddle. Plunged into the chill, he swore the beads of sweat on his neck instantly froze as he slid the container of tomatoes in its place.

He trudged to the drink machine, the musty-soapy dish room smell and the scent of roasting hot dogs clinging to him. He desperately needed a shower. Thomas slammed the button for Coke, his mouth watering. He desperately needed pop.

"Uh, hey, T," Danny called for his brother's attention, the affected casual tone immediately putting Thomas on guard.

Thomas, suspicious, sipped his drink as he regarded Danny who leaned through the kitchen window. But being that they were between the lunch and dinner rush, there weren't any Coney dogs or chili fries or Greek salads to bring out. "What's up?"

"Is that your girl?" He pointed with his chin, a goofy grin popping up on his face.

"My girl?" Thomas wrinkled his brow. Then thought, *Julia?*

Sure enough, Julia sat at a booth, hair clipped back from her face wearing a fuzzy grey sweater with her laptop open in front of her. Ari stood next to the table chatting with her.

Thomas's eyes widened. *Ari stood next to the table chatting with her.* He nearly choked on his pop. What could they possibly have to talk about...other than him? He put the drink down and tried to untie his apron, which got promptly knotted as Danny watched and laughed.

"Oh, you're in trouble, man. Ari can be *brutal*." Danny tapped his metal spatula on the edge of the griddle, emphasizing his enjoyment. This, of course, caught Ari and Julia's attention. Thomas heard their giggles from across the dining room.

Thomas finally got the knot undone and threw the apron on the counter. He walked toward Julia's table, smoothing back his curls and catching the awful, unique back-of-the-house smell.

He cleared his throat. "Hey, Julia."

Did he sound casual? He hoped he sounded casual. Like that seeing Julia unexpectedly in his dad's Coney Island wasn't whipping up all sorts of strange and confusing emotions in him. He hadn't seen her in here since...well, since just before their fight. He leaned against the tall coat hanger that rose up out of the bench opposite her and crossed his arms and ankles. *Casual.*

She smiled. Radiant, transcendent. It hit him square in the chest. He literally felt it colliding with his heart.

"Hey, Thomas. Ari was just telling me all about her routine for Theatre Bizarre! I didn't know she performed. It sounds fantastic." She picked up a fry, making sure it had sufficient chili and cheese on it, and folded it into her mouth, somehow still smiling while chewing.

Ari stuck her pen in her massive nest of hair. "You can come check it out, Julia, but Thomas can't. Might give the old man a heart attack."

The two of them laughed, but Thomas just scowled. Nodded. Tight lipped and afraid of what else these two talked about before he had intervened.

But Ari saw right through him. "Oh my god Thomas, don't look so uptight. I didn't show her, like, embarrassing baby photos of you. Though I have plenty on my phone.

Mom was just going through all these old boxes and, honestly, he was a cute baby."

She snatched her phone from her back pocket, swiping through a couple screens at true millennial speed before Thomas could realize what she was doing. Ari shoved the phone under Julia's nose.

Ari looked her brother up and down. "I don't know what happened to him."

Julia broke out into peals of laughter, slapping her hand on the table, tears prickling the corner of her eyes. "Aww, you weren't joking!"

"Gimme that," Thomas mumbled, more insatiably curious which baby photo his sister had revealed than angry that she had.

About one year old in the photo and round as a bowling ball, he stood in front of a massive aquarium. His small, pudgy hands pressed flush to the glass, he faced the camera over his shoulder. He didn't smile, but the wide-eyed look on his chunky face was distinct awe.

That day, his parents had brought him, still a single child, to the Detroit Zoo and let him stand in the penguin house for hours. He remembered it. Vaguely. Or maybe thought he did just because of the photos and because his dad never tired of telling the story. How Thomas cried as they left after spending nearly half a day watching the penguins diving and porpoising. Maybe it wasn't Thomas's unique memory at all. Just something cobbled together from other people's lenses.

"You really were sweet, Thomas," Julia said.

Thomas handed the phone back to his sister. "As much as I love you helping out around the diner, *Ari*, I don't appreciate you showing off my baby photos without my consent. Now run along."

He pushed her away, both hands on her shoulder blades, despite her protests.

"But I was just starting to have fun!" she whined, stomping away to the back.

Thomas rolled his eyes. "Sorry about that."

Julia still dabbed the tears from her eyes. "No, it's fine. Ari's cool. She was like twelve years old when I saw her last..." She trailed off, adjusting herself in her seat. "Anyway, it was a while ago."

Thomas paused for a beat, unsure if Julia would say anything else. When she didn't, he shoved his fists in his pockets. "What're you doing here? It's a Monday? Midday?"

"Ah, Indigenous Peoples' Day. Contra gives it to us off every year, and for the correct holiday too."

"Rightly so." Thomas eyed the laptop. "So...you're off work, but working?"

"Writing." Her cheeks flushed peach. "But I think I'm ready for a break."

The color of her skin had a direct reaction on his pulse. It bounded wildly through his body. "Want to go outside? I'm up for a little break, too."

"Actually yeah, that sounds perfect."

"Milkshakes?"

Julia nodded vigorously, eyes wide.

"Give me two minutes."

Thomas rushed to the back, washed his hands, and put on an extra layer of deodorant to combat the back-of-the-house smell. Then, he made two chocolate milkshakes, complete with mini mountains of whipped cream and Maraschino cherries.

Back out front, Julia opened the door for him, and he led them to the far edge of the parking lot. They settled on the curb, her legs stretched out in front of her and his bent up so that he could rest his elbows on them. The October sun shone down in the bright, golden, slanting way of autumn. A couple trees stood around the parking lot, their leaves winking a riot of fall oranges, purples, and reds.

"So, writing," Thomas said, after a few minutes of contented milkshake sipping.

"Yep. Trying out a couple different pairings and one shots, just creative brainfood to get me thinking. Inching my way to the burrito bet finish line. Oh, and," Julia pulled her bottom lip between her teeth and squinted one eye closed, "I'm thinking maybe I might start posting some stuff online?"

"Seriously? That's amazing. A huge step for any artist. Tell me more."

"Just a blog. Tumblr probably? Nothing exciting or fancy. I don't know if I'm ready for like *real* fan fiction sites or anything, but I just want to keep a record of it all. Maybe start up an Instagram account too?"

Thomas nodded along, processing. "Okay, the real question is: what's your pen name? Unless you want to post smut online under Julia Ward, which, no shame."

"Oh no, I need a pen name." Julia ducked toward her milkshake, avoiding his gaze. "I've thought about this one, and I think I've got it. Don't laugh—"

"Never."

"But Jewel, from 'Jules,' your nickname for me, and last name Parrish from—"

"Adam Parrish."

"Raven Boys. Exactly. My favorite character. He reminded me of you when I read it. Minus all the trauma." Julia's cheeks flushed, and Thomas smiled in response.

"Jewel Parrish." He tried out the whole name.

"How does it compare to T. Callaghan?"

Thomas pressed a hand to his chest, feigning offense. "It doesn't, of course. But I love it. Just flirty enough with a niche reference. That works for fan fiction."

He knocked his shoulder into hers, surprised at the sudden ease they'd settled into. Their last hangouts were stilted, awkward. Despite being as casual as they tried to be, it wasn't the same as it was when they were kids. How could it have been? It had been twelve years since they'd seen each other the last time, a long time since they were normal with each other. Whatever normal even meant.

But now, sitting at the edge of the parking lot drinking

milkshakes, Thomas relaxed, stretching like a cat in a puddle of sunshine, kicking his legs long and leaning back on his elbows. The heat from the sun curled inside him, energizing him. Sitting here with Julia, he felt more like himself—the self he imagined—than he had in years.

"That baby picture was seriously cute though," Julia said around her straw. "I'm going to have to sweet talk Ari into showing me more."

Thomas groaned. "She'd show you anything, bathtub pictures and all, with glee."

"Precious." Julia pouted, just a little. "She told me your dad hasn't been around the restaurant much lately."

So, Ari had said something. He knew he'd eventually have to tell Julia what was going on; he was just procrastinating. As if because there was someone who didn't know about Dad, maybe it wasn't really happening.

But it seemed that eventually was now. To not say something would be too much like lying. Thomas didn't want to skirt the truth with her anymore.

He took a deep breath and sighed it out. With it came the words. "He has cancer. He's dying, Jules."

Their eyes met. Julia's wide and stormy blue, glassing over with a sheen of tears. Her eyes that had meant so much to Thomas over the years, the excitement they held, the fire and joy. And now the sympathy.

"Are you serious?" she asked, her voice thick.

Thomas frowned, running a hand over his beard. "Unfortunately so."

"Thomas, I'm so, so sorry. Are you okay?"

His chest shuddered, tight and hot. "Not really."

The corners of his lips involuntarily pulled down. His eyes burned, about to cry, too. Fuck. He sniffed, trying to keep it in.

But why? He hadn't cried about it yet. He didn't know how. Part of it was denial. The other part: fear.

"I'm not ready."

Thomas curled his legs back up and leaned over them, forming a protective ball. Julia's arm wrapped around his shoulders and the other around his own arms stacked on his knees. She didn't say anything, waiting, as his tears fell silently into his lap. After seeing that photo that Ari had on her phone, it's like all of his emotions were brought to the surface, raw and boiling over. One day, too soon, he would lose his dad, and then what?

He finally sniffed and sat up, dragging a hand across his eyes to wipe the tears away.

"He's just so strong, so proud. Always has been. Seeing him like this, so sick and weak, it's been a lot. So much that I'm afraid to really put it into words."

Thomas balled his hands into fists. "And then...it's me. I'm the oldest and the one who should be here to help out my mom and Danny and Ari. And Dad's Coney Island. Callaghan's Coney Island. But my life's in New York."

Thomas paused as a dark cloud of emotion flickered across Julia's face. There one fraction of a second and then gone just as fast.

He swallowed, brushing the thought away. "Dad's so many things that I'm not. When I began to sense who I was supposed to grow up to be, what was expected of me, it only pushed me further to the city. To create my own independent life."

"But you're strong, too, Thomas," Julia said.

Thomas scoffed, thinking about how easy it had been for him to go away—run away?—to New York and make any excuse to stay there. "Hardly."

They sat in silence again, drinking their milkshakes. Thomas's tears dried up, but he still felt flayed open, exposed and tender.

"He used to watch all those romcoms with me, you know? No one else in the family cared about that shit. But we'd browse the Blockbuster aisles for forever, him patiently trailing behind until I picked out a movie. *10 Things I Hate About You* was my favorite. I rented it a million times; we should have just bought the damn thing. But browsing was part of the ritual. He enjoyed it as much as I did, which is what's so great about Dad. He doesn't have to fake it. He just kind of loves everything. Especially anything that his kids love."

Julia smiled, staring off into the distance, letting Thomas talk.

"That movie was my bisexual awakening. When I saw it at eleven years old, I knew that I liked guys and girls all thanks to Patrick Verona and Kat Stratford. I didn't tell anyone until I was sixteen. But Dad was the first person I told, and it didn't change a thing between us."

"I love that." Julia crossed her legs and slurped the last bit of her milkshake.

They'd been out here longer than he expected, and Thomas felt drained. But when they looked at each other, Julia's eyes searching over his face with a soft smile, Thomas felt truly seen.

Not T. Callaghan published author. Not the shy sixteen-year-old with a buzz cut. But the Thomas of this very moment in time. Her gaze held him. Thomas's stomach swooped, and he wanted only one thing.

"Can I kiss you?" he whispered, voice hoarse.

Julia's lips wrapped over her teeth. Her eyebrows lifted up in the middle, and with wide, pleading eyes, she bobbed her head yes, giving him permission.

Still side by side, they curled toward each other, Thomas hunching down to meet her height. His hand ran along her jaw, his fingers curling around the shell of her ear. Before their lips even met, she leaned into his palm, which cradled her entire cheek. She closed her eyes and audibly sighed, sending a spark of electric heat down Thomas's spine. They stayed like that for a moment as Thomas memorized her face, the Julia of now. He rubbed his thumb across her cheekbone, and she smiled, eyes still closed.

Thomas inched his way toward her, savoring this

moment that he had dreamt of. Fantasized about. Written different imagined versions of into his novels.

When their lips met, soft as butterfly wings, she tasted like chocolate milkshake. He pushed his tongue tentatively between her lips, and they both laughed into each other's mouths, sheer bliss pumping through Thomas's veins. Then their teeth knocked together, and they laughed some more.

The spell broken, he kissed her again, a quick peck, then dropped his hand and leaned back on the curb.

"That was nice," she said.

"It was, wasn't it?"

His hand found hers, resting on the pavement, and he laced their fingers together as they sat in silence for a couple more minutes.

It happened. It had finally happened. It was real.

And it was better than he had ever dared to imagine.

FIFTEEN
THOMAS

THOMAS PULLED INTO JULIA'S PARENTS' driveway and turned the car off. The windows glowed warmly from the inside out in the October evening chill, as the purple-pink colors of sunset melted in the western sky, framing the night in watercolors.

Sitting in the Corolla for a minute, he collected himself. He'd been stuck in a loop since Monday remembering the unbelievable feeling of his lips on Julia's. All of his senses vibrated in awareness. He still felt the cool fall breeze of that day tickle his cheeks, carrying a faint smell of frying oil, as the sunlight dappled on his skin under the trees. The crumbling concrete warming the back of his thighs. His fingers tangled in Jules's hair. Their soft tongues making contact.

He pushed it all aside. Or tried to. It didn't really work. Every nerve ending reverberated the reality of it.

Thomas really had kissed Julia. But now what? He was still going back to New York City, and she was *not* ready for anything after her ex. He ran his hand through his beard, squeezing at his chin. This was fine. Everything was fine. They were going to have a great night.

Thomas felt silly kicking open the driver's side door and walking to Julia's door dressed in costume for Theatre Bizarre. At least he left his mask and black feather shoulder cape in the car.

To his complete horror, Julia's mom opened the door.

"Thomas! You've grown." She looked Thomas up and down, lingering an extra fraction of a second on his black eyeliner.

"Hello, Mrs. Ward." Thomas inclined his head toward her, feeling every inch the awkward teenager that he was the last time he spoke with Julia's mom on their doorstep.

"Oh please," she brushed a hand at him and laughed, "it's Anne. We're all adults here. Come in, come in."

He accepted the invitation and resisted the urge to fiddle with the faux gold pocket watch dangling on his front.

"Julia told me you're a published author now. I had no idea! That must be so exciting," Anne said, not quite asking a question.

Thomas cleared his throat and plastered a smile on his face. "Yeah, it's great. I get to daydream for a living, what's bad about that?"

It was the rote answer that he typically gave folks.

What does Julia's mom actually care about his career? She won't know that he doesn't make anything close to a livable wage writing books, and people only want to hear about how amazing it is.

"Do I know any of your books?" She clasped her hands in front of her.

He was saved from answering Anne's question by the appearance of Julia's father. As a single bead of sweat rolled down the back of his leg and met with his dress sock, Thomas admitted to himself that he was still very frightened of the man in front of him. Though Thomas had several inches on him, he didn't have Julia's father's stoic, formidable presence fueled by minimal words and a Roman nose.

"Sir." Thomas nodded to him and extended his hand.

Anne looked adoringly at her husband, as her husband looked unblinkingly at Thomas, who clamped down on the impulse to flee the premises immediately.

"It's been a while. How are you, son?" He took Thomas's hand and gave it one firm shake, staring him straight in the eyes. Though he didn't seem like the kind of man who would be impressed by Thomas's eyeliner application skills.

"Yes, it has. I'm very well, Mr. Ward, thanks. And yourself?"

"Well." Mr. Ward gave a single nod and didn't give Thomas permission to use his first name.

Pleasantries taken care of, the three of them stood in

awkward silence as Anne smiled, expectantly looking between them all.

"Okay! I'm all set!" Julia cried as she waltzed down the stairs.

Thomas's heart stopped, forgetting to breathe.

Julia was a vision in steampunk and downright sinful. The perfect combination of playful, nerdy, and sexy as hell. All of her glorious curves were on display, including her cleavage. A black lacy bra peeked out of her top and left little to the imagination under her corset. Her hair sat in buns on the top of her head, and though she otherwise looked nothing like Princess Leia, Thomas's mind ran away with inappropriate thoughts muddling his two biggest teenage crushes. One fictional and one very, very real and standing in front of him. He swallowed and felt every movement of his neck muscles.

"You look fantastic."

She beamed under her mask that was a mix of whimsy and machinery as she smoothed down the front of her corset, betraying some of her discomfort. "You too. A little like Thomas Shelby?"

"Just don't call me Tommy. I hate that." He shifted his weight into his heels. "Wait until you see the rest of the costume, then you can guess the reference."

The two giggled until Mr. Ward cleared his throat, interrupting them. Anne's eyes bounced between Thomas and Julia.

"No drinking and driving," Mr. Ward said, bringing his

hands to his waist, upping his intimidation points by at least ten.

"No, sir, of course not." Thomas crossed and uncrossed his arms, eager to get out of there.

Julia slipped her feet into knee high leather boots, bending to zip them up. "We got it, Dad."

"Well, just have fun. And you do look great, honey. I just wish you'd cover up a little more," Anne said, the image of suburban handwringing.

Mr. Ward grunted in agreement.

Julia groaned loudly. "We're leaving now."

She yanked the door open and stomped out before Thomas knew what was happening.

"I'll be safe." He looked around. "Uh, bye."

Speaking of no chill, he definitely had less than zero. As he stepped out the door, he went to run his hand through his hair but at the last second remembered all the pomade he'd used to tame his curls, and instead rubbed his beard. That didn't go terribly with her parents, but as far as second first impressions go, it definitely could have been better.

Julia waited by the passenger door with her arms crossed, and she huffed as they both got in the car. Now that they were alone, he wasn't sure if he should kiss her, or give her a peck on the cheek, or just hold her hand. The one-time kiss between them didn't necessarily mean anything. It's not like they debriefed afterward. In fact, they'd hardly spoken all week except to set the time for the pickup. It wasn't awkward though.

Thomas's old fear of Julia's rejection had crept right back into his mind, keeping him company all week. If they didn't talk about the kiss, maybe nothing had to change. Not that anything could. Thomas didn't want to be the one to bring it up, and he hated himself a little bit for it.

"Sorry about that." Julia grimaced. "They treat me like a teenager now that I'm back home. It's like they forgot about my years of living in sin with Josh."

Thomas pulled out of the driveway, and at the mention of Josh, he wondered if Julia's ex would be caught dead in an outfit like the one he wore now. The thought elicited a rise in his body temperature.

"Sorry, I didn't mean to bring up Josh." She folded her hands in her lap.

"Don't apologize. He's a big part of your life."

"Not a part I want to think of."

In the growing darkness, speeding down the highway, Thomas couldn't discern her facial expression, but he could hear the disappointment in her voice.

"Don't worry, you won't be thinking about him tonight. I've heard so much amazing stuff about this event from my siblings. Danny's been involved for years, but it's only for folks over twenty-one so I've never actually been."

"Ah, so we're both Theatre Bizarre virgins, eh?"

"Ha, I suppose so." The neck of his dress shirt suddenly felt tight, and he changed the subject. "Oh—I forgot to ask the other day," another flush of warmth pulsed through him at the mention of *the other day*, "how did the interview go?"

"Mmm." She shrugged. "Fine."

So, Julia wasn't in a talkative mood. Was it her parents or thinking of Josh that made her quiet? Maybe the interview? Hopefully not Thomas.

It didn't matter. They didn't need to talk. They didn't need to talk all night if they didn't want to. It wouldn't be long before they were so distracted by the performers and the wonder of Theatre Bizarre that talking wouldn't matter.

After a couple minutes of silence, Thomas turned up the Lord Huron album he had on Spotify. The sun had set totally, and the dark grew inkier as they flew from Starling Hills to Detroit. On the opposite side of the highway, the oncoming headlights looked like fallen meteors speeding toward them.

Julia sang along with the music so softly that Thomas wasn't sure if she was singing at first. She rolled her window down and breathed in. Thomas put down the rest of the windows, and the autumn air swirled around them, crisp and cool. He kept his hand on the shifter, gripping it with white knuckles, as Julia's perfume circulated around the car too. Julia looped her arm around behind his, where his elbow rested on the console, and latched on to his bicep. So touching was okay. *Good to know*.

The drive downtown was smooth. Thomas's heart rate

ratcheted up a few notches as they parked and he hopped out of the driver's seat. From the back, he grabbed his black feather shoulder cape, mask, and leather gloves. Securing the cape over his shoulders and the plain black matte mask over his eyes, he felt extra extra, as planned.

"Wow, I love it!" Julia's eyes widened as she got the first full look at this costume.

"I know you said Tommy Shelby, but this is my take on Kaz Brekker."

"Six of Crows!"

"You've read it?"

"All of them! And watched the show. I love it!"

"Don't worry," Thomas extended an arm to Julia, "I don't have skin-on-skin phobia like Kaz." His stomach flipped at the implication of skin contact with Julia.

"You look great, too, by the way. I didn't know what to expect from your costume, but it's fantastic," he said.

She smiled demurely, her grey-blue eyes behind the mask utterly hypnotizing, and took his arm. He led them through the parking lot to where the queue snaked around the corner of the building. Thankfully, the line moved fast, and it wasn't long before they were standing in another line, this time for cocktails. He handed Julia a gin and tonic as he sipped his own.

The Theatre maze had a twisted funhouse feel, everything washed in a muted red-gold light. Under masks, their identities slowly slipped away. The space was so packed with people that it became a writhing sense of bodies all moving along the same general trajectory. Thomas had the familiar feeling of anonymity that he had whenever he had to go to Times Square. He blended in, part of the milieu, no one special.

But the person beside him was someone. For the first time in a very long while, he didn't feel alone or isolated. So often in New York, his connections were fleeting and relationships temporary. This woman on his arm, though not a constant through it all, was a connection to parts of him he'd long forgotten. The parts that knew how to be happy.

Disorienting as it was to admit: with Julia, Thomas was happy.

A man dressed as a circus monkey with a tiny red fez crouched and clanged two symbols together as they passed, calling Thomas back to the present moment. He placed a guiding hand on Julia's lower back so they wouldn't get separated. Even through her corset—*corset*—and his gloves, he could feel her shiver from his touch.

Like when they sat in the restaurant parking lot earlier in the week, a spark kindled between them, fueled by their hidden identities and oxidized by surreal displays all around them. Their bodies magnetized toward one another.

He felt the shift as they watched a person covered in tattoos undergo body suspension. The hooks that dug into their skin were attached to linked chains and slowly lifted the person off the ground, where they remained motionless.

Julia stepped toward Thomas, her feet interlocking with his, and she buried her face into his chest. "Ooh, I can't watch this."

Automatically, his arm encircled her, drawing her warmth closer, until her hips bumped his thigh. Her nearness flooded his senses.

She looked up into his eyes, hooded under her mask. For a moment they pleaded to be closer. His heartbeat pulsed through his entire body as she pulled a corner of her lip between her teeth. He wished he was that lip.

But she blinked and the moment passed, hazarding a glance back to the performance.

Thomas watched the person suspended by their skin, with Julia still tucked against his side, and he thought that maybe he knew what that person felt. Thomas, too, knew deep and pleasurable pain. Except that his had spanned over a decade. Maybe it would be easier to be rigged up by hooks buried deep in his skin.

They continued on through the rooms.

There was a pair of male presenting fire breathers in fishnets and red, lacy corsets who shot jets of flame toward the audience. Thomas's external warmth reflected his growing internal desire for Julia, still molded to his side.

Fire spinners dressed like porcelain dolls in black and white dresses juggled burning sticks, balancing two opposite ends, like how Thomas balanced two opposing realities. One in Starling Hills, and one in New York City.

Sword swallowers dressed as demented clowns in black and white performed feats seemingly against all laws of biology. Thomas swallowed involuntarily, remembering all the time he'd swallowed words he wanted to say, confessions he wanted to make to Julia. Especially during that junior year Homecoming dance. Unlike these sword swallowers, his body acted as a cage and wouldn't let the words out.

A band of topless undead musicians wearing nipple pasties performed on a stage. Nearly nude folks of all sexes and genders lounged on all performing surfaces, occasionally miming suggestive gestures to passersby.

Thomas's world spun with the heady blend of juniper from their drinks, Julia's vanilla, and the cinnamon, sage, and lavender that permeated the autumnal ambience of the space. His senses heightened to take in all of the sights and sounds. With Julia's body so close to his, in these costumes, he almost believed that they could be anything.

She tugged on his arm, her fingers pulling the tiny hairs there. When he looked down at her, her eyes were wide, all white and all pupil, the remaining blue-grey sliver of her iris sparkled in the red light. Julia smiled and pushed up onto her tiptoes to reach his ear. Her breath tickled the short hairs at the base of his skull, sending goosebumps scattering over his body. He shivered, and her grip tightened on his forearm.

"This is amazing," she yelled into his ear, but over the music and the din from thousands of folks surrounding them, he barely caught the words.

He met her eyes and nodded, enjoying the hell out of the whole thing, too. They were pressed together—so close that he could feel her breasts pushing against his stomach—when her hand snaked around his waist and found his dress shirt between his vest and trousers and slid one finger under the edge of his waistband.

Thomas crooked his head in question, one brow quirked high. Julia stared up at him, her eyes shining like glittering beetles in this odd masquerade world, and nodded, mouthing—or maybe yelling, he couldn't hear either way—the word *yes*. She was giving him permission. He nodded in return, a spray of electric tingles racing over his skin, suddenly rudderless.

There was no road map for what would happen next.

But he knew he wanted her closer.

He made a show of pulling off his gloves and shoving them deep into his vest pocket with the fake pocket watch. Her eyes sizzled watching his every move.

Then, Thomas slid his palm up along her back, across the soft leather bodice, crossing onto the linen of her tunic. He finally came to rest, grasping at the base of her neck. He squeezed, gently applying pressure. Julia's breath hitched in response, a move made even more impressive by her breasts spilling over her corset.

He leaned down to her ear and dropped his hand, once again cradling her against his large palm.

"Come on, Jules, let's go in deeper."

And he clasped her hand, leading them further into the labyrinth.

SIXTEEN
JULIA

JULIA'S EYES WIDENED, large as saucers, trying to take in everything that she could. She hadn't known what to expect from tonight, but the displays and the effect of everyone in costumes and masks, completely enchanted her. Her own mask allowed her to blend in with the rest of the crowd, becoming just *someone* to everyone else. No one knew her here. Except for Thomas.

Her hand fit in his and he held fast, guiding them through the twists and turns of the different rooms. She surrendered herself to it all. When he ran his hand up her back and held on at the base of her neck, she knew that something had shifted between them.

Tonight, they weren't Thomas and Julia, the sort of adults who used to be best friends trying to figure things out between them. The pair who shared an achingly sweet, vulnerably perfect, chocolate milkshake flavored first kiss—*first kiss!*—just days ago. Though she had played the memory over and over in her mind all week, a sweet burn blooming in her chest, tonight was different. That kiss, though seismic in its own way, didn't have the charged energy of tonight.

Tonight, they were dapper, demented Kaz Brekker and his sexy, steampunk sharpshooter.

Under her mask, Julia grew bold. Under her mask, Julia knew how to ask for what she wanted. Though she had no idea what Thomas thought about their kiss, masked-Julia was willing to risk the rejection of *something casual* between the two. Casual, because even that day of their kiss, Thomas verbalized returning to New York. And she'd risk it tonight, because, by some twisted masquerade-fueled logic, it wouldn't be *her* that he turned down, if he did.

So, as they held hands watching a new stage of musicians, all dressed up like different versions of Pennywise, Julia ran her fingertips up Thomas's forearm. A thrill shot through her body as his skin pebbled with goosebumps from her touch. It had been a long time since just holding hands with someone made her mouth go dry.

Thomas looked down to her, meeting her gaze, his brown eyes wild and sparking with desire.

She lifted her hands like a cup to her lips, miming that she wanted another drink. They'd long given up trying to speak to each other; it was so loud and overwhelming that it was hard to hear anything other than the performers. He nodded and pulled her along until they found another bar.

Julia sucked down the gin and tonic, twirling as they passed under a neon rainbow tunnel and came out onto a dance floor. A DJ in a skeleton onesie and a half-face skeleton mask spun from a platform above the crowd. The fluorescent violet of black light made the whites of everyone's costumes and the drink in her hand glow. When she looked at Thomas, his lips parted into a wide grin, making his teeth the only thing that lit up on him.

Julia drained the rest of her drink, and now it was her turn to lead. She threw her plastic cup on the ground and stomped on it, where it now lived with the rest of the cups that crunched underfoot. Julia grabbed Thomas's hand and plunged them into the dancing crowd. It was sweatier here than the rest of the rooms as each body bounced and gyrated to the thumping electronic beat. The music vibrated up through her legs.

Once they reached some ambiguous point in the crowd that was so dense she could move no further, she stopped and smirked up at Thomas.

"Let's dance," she yelled, but she was certain that he could only read her lips.

She spun in a circle with her hands in the air. She wooed into the sound, her voice eaten up by the musical abyss. A firm grip on her biceps stopped her rotation, and Thomas slid in behind her. He was so close that she could feel his entire body up against her back.

"Is this okay?"

Julia jumped at the nearness of his voice in her ear, his beard soft against her neck. She turned into his body and cupped a hand over his ear to be sure that he heard her answer. "Yes. *Please*."

His hand splayed on her abdomen and held her close to his body as they bobbed to the beat. It was less dancing so much as Julia melting into him and Thomas holding her up.

But his hands—oh his hands—they ran all over her body, touching every inch that he could manage from this angle. Up and down her arms, over her shoulders, and down her front, just skimming the crests of her breasts that peeked out over the corset. Her hands rested on his thighs, moving up and down as they bounced with the music. Through his trousers, his quads contracted and released with each dip to the beat. A fever pitch built between them, their nerve endings flooded and tingling from their over-the-clothes caressing.

At first, she thought she imagined his lips on her neck, a gentle fluttering against her skin. But then he persisted, and it was sweeter than her fantasies.

Moving up and down and along her shoulder, he nipped at every bit of exposed skin that he could. His opposite hand moved to hold her chest against him, his fingers wrapped lightly around the base of her throat. She reached up to snake a hand around his neck. With an exhale he moaned gently into her skin, and she could feel his hardness growing at her back.

More.

She wanted more, and, suddenly ravenous, she turned to face him, both arms reaching up to cradle his neck. Her brain, for a second, expected to see Josh behind her, but when her perception caught up to her, she bit her lip.

This was Thomas. This was a years-old crush blooming between them in this black-lit, costumed, electronic dance floor in the middle of a masquerade funhouse, and she laughed. It was the most delightfully absurd scenario and, in this moment, she couldn't be happier.

They danced facing each other, Thomas resting his forehead against hers. This close, Julia couldn't figure out where to focus, her eyes bouncing over his mask. She settled for his lips.

Swallowing a giggle, she moved her hips closer, like a puzzle piece settling into his body. One hand traveled down the front of his vest, over the pocket watch chain, and found that same place as before. She snuck her fingers between his vest and trousers, and, finding skin, she hooked under his waistband and pulled him closer, if that was even possible.

She wanted to tip her lips up. Julia wanted them to connect. But this tension, this *almost* moment right before, sizzled lava through her veins that pooled between her legs. Pure masturbation fodder that would last her for months.

Sweat dripped down her face, the salt clinging to her lips. Darting her tongue out to lick the sweat was just the opening that Thomas needed. He ducked down, and she pulled him in at the same time, their lips smashing together.

Thomas infiltrated her senses, the spicy cardamom of his cologne enveloping her. He sucked her lower lip between his teeth and bit down, causing her to shiver. His touch pulsed all over her body. Julia's hands travelled up his back in direct response to Thomas's lips tracing along her jaw. He breathed heavy in her ear, nibbling the soft skin down her neck. Julia palmed the back of his head and swung her hips closer to his, causing their center of gravity to tip backward, and they stumbled apart.

Quickly righting themselves, they laughed. Another sound lost to the booming bass. Separated, Thomas's eyes roved her body. She never felt so sexy as right then, seeing desire open and clear on his face.

Julia grabbed his hand, leading him off the dance floor. The crowd faded away as her blood burned, sweat dripping down between her breasts and collecting at the small of her back.

This was the fun that Susan and Heather kept talking about. Behind the mask, her exhilaration mounted. All of her urges and impulses inside screamed to do it. All she needed was a dark corner or an empty stairwell. An abandoned closet. Anywhere semi-private would do.

They passed a bearded lady in a gilded corset. A woman dancing with a yellow and white boa constrictor. A person with tattoos covering their entire body. Around each corner was another mystery. They didn't stop for any of it. Julia had a singular mission in mind.

Thomas and Julia's fingers tangled. He rubbed his thumb across her palm, sending shivers up her arm. Thomas tugged her toward him. He caught her with a hand at the base of her back, and together they fell through a stairwell door.

The scent of wet cement tickled her nose. Julia shivered in the cooler air, looking up at Thomas in the fluorescent glow of a faraway light, his olive toned skin turned a garish yellow. Her chest heaved, breathless. Thomas openly stared at her breasts. His eyes filled with reverence more than anything else, the downturned corners of his eyes pulled tight.

"Hi," Julia said. She didn't know what else to say. Sweat plastered her forehead underneath her mask.

"Hi." Thomas smirked, roguish and playful at the same time.

Her stomach twisted into knots.

"You want to do this?" He was nearly as breathless as

she was.

"Yes, I do." She mirrored his wicked grin, shoring up her confidence. Julia's skin buzzed. Hot, casual fun.

In the next moment, Thomas pressed her up against the wall. His damned knee worked her legs open and pressed up, creating delicious friction in just the right spot. Thomas braced his hands on the concrete, over each of her shoulders, pinning her there. Julia took two breaths to savor this feeling of Thomas physically holding her in place. Then her hips arched over his knee, her body involuntarily begging for more.

When their mouths met, they couldn't do anything fast enough. Julia wanted to taste all of Thomas, and she opened her mouth against his, her hands on his hips as leverage.

Thomas pulled back slightly and bit his lip, bringing a flush of blood to the surface. "What is going on with this outfit? It's so hot. How do I get it off?"

Julia laughed. *This is fun.* "Umm, it's a lot of layers. The leggings don't make this easy."

"Never mind. I don't need to take them off." Thomas dove for her neck again, causing Julia to gasp and clutch on to him. He growled against her skin, "I'll get you off with them still on."

Heat pooled in her pelvis. That was the hottest thing anyone had ever said to her.

Thomas ran a hand up and down her inner thighs.

"Please," Julia whimpered, the teasing exquisite. She wanted this to happen so badly.

He laughed, the sound rumbling in his chest.

"Usually, I'd draw this teasing out a bit more," he flattened his palm against her body, "but since anyone could walk in on us at any time, I'm going to cut this part a little short."

Julia's heart rate ratcheted up at the thought of being caught.

When Thomas ran his hand up over her corset, she clenched, anticipating his bare touch. His fingertips worked between her layers, hunting. When his rough fingers found her hidden skin, lightning crackled over her body.

"*Oh*," she whispered, hoarse and feverish.

Julia melted, giving into Thomas entirely as his touch moved south, under her leggings and lace panties, brushing through her downy hair.

"God, Jules, you're so fucking wet," Thomas groaned, his words dripping like honey down her spine.

And she was. Warm and melting, barely able to stay upright and aching for more of his caress.

Thomas's middle finger found her most sensitive spot and applied firm pressure as he rubbed back and forth, eliciting the softest pleas from Julia, already seeing stars. When he rocked his hips against her, she palmed his hardness through his trousers.

"Christ," he ground out the word, and as he did, he

entered Julia with two fingers well lubricated by her own wetness.

"Fuck," she cried, drawing out the vowel until the word ended in a low mewl. The sensation pulsed through her entire body.

With his thumb, Thomas circled her clit as he pumped two fingers in and out, bringing Julia to the edge with just his hand. She teetered there, not quite wanting the release yet. She wanted this pleasure to last forever. Closing her eyes, she leaned her head back against the cool concrete, and Thomas traced his lips up her neck, alternating kissing and licking.

When he pulled her earlobe into his mouth and started sucking, she knew she was close. So close.

"Don't stop, please, oh god." Her chest grew heavy as her pelvis tightened, and Thomas, sensing her closeness, thrust deeper with a third finger.

"Oh god, I'm coming," she hissed the words, pulling Thomas closer, her insides exploding and melting like butter.

Thomas rested his forehead against hers, keeping his fingers inside her until the aftershocks ceased and she came back down to earth.

"Thank you," Julia sighed, leaning her head against his shoulder. And she meant it.

"The pleasure was all mine." Thomas pulled back and gave her a heavy-lidded look, sweat glistening on his upper lip. "You're so beautiful, Julia, do you know that?"

The emotion behind his words made her eyes burn.

This is just hot, casual, fun. He's going back to New York.

She'd convinced herself that she could do this. Some harmless fun. But Thomas's smoldering brown eyes, and how they directly affected her heart rate, suggested that maybe she was in over her head.

SEVENTEEN
JULIA
FOURTEEN YEARS AGO

THE CLOSEST JULIA ever got to believing something might happen between her and Thomas was Starling Hills High School's homecoming dance their junior year. It was certainly the closest she ever came to saying the words that would change their relationship forever.

I love you.

Not that seventeen-year-old Julia really had a solid grasp on "love," but she believed that she was in it.

Homecoming was never what they made it out to be in the movies. No coordinated dances, no impassioned Homecoming Queen speeches, hardly any fun if she was being honest. Even being in their darkened high school on a Saturday evening felt a little odd. Like trespassing almost. Most of the gymnasium's bleachers were accordioned up to the walls, with one section open, dotted with some who refused, or just didn't care, to dance.

A shocking number of metallic silver balloons studded the space in arches and bunches of all different shapes, with orange streamers, ribbons, and tinsel weaving through it all. Besides the fact that Student Council ignored that the school's colors were in fact *grey* and orange, Julia wondered if decorations in the name of school spirit actually conveyed a good time anyway.

She stood awkwardly, pondering the conundrum and surrounded by her peers in the middle of their high school's gymnasium. She danced as well as any fresh seventeen-year-old could. Which is to say, not very well. It was more of a bopping back and forth to the beat than anything else. She added in a shoulder wiggle every now and then when she felt particularly bold.

Unlike her sister, Julia blended in with the rest of the inelegantly limbed high schoolers. Heather dominated the dance floor with her date; naturally, the boy who played opposite her lead in the fall play, *A Midsummer Night's Dream*.

Of course, Julia didn't have a date. No one had asked her, as much as she'd hoped that someone would. *Someone.* Not just any someone. The only other dateless person in their little group of theater friends that did the whole homecoming thing together, limo and all.

Thomas. That someone. Since they met at the *Les Misérables* wrap party, the two had been basically inseparable. They spent most of their time getting Slurpees and swinging at Starling Hills's Municipal Park, with not much else to do in their town. Or by maintaining a never-ending stream of consciousness text message conversation.

Thomas was her best friend, yeah, but she couldn't shake the thought: *maybe I'm in love with him?*

Despite all of the hints—some of them not-so-subtle in her opinion—he didn't ask her to be his date, so, like all of her other crushes, Julia knew this one was also unrequited.

But she would make the best of tonight. As much as feeling like a princess felt like an archly unfeminist goal, Julia did tonight. She loved her dress, and she wasn't going to waste it by pouting, terrible dance moves and all. A floor-length, satin gown, the fabric shimmered between purple and blue depending on how the light hit it. It had a halter neckline but cut down low in the back, exposing a wide expanse of her skin.

Thomas shuffled across the group toward her. Despite the general awkwardness of a bunch of high schoolers dancing around, Thomas looked cool in his dark navy suit and his hair buzzed short. His jacket long discarded, he still wore a vest with his tie loosened and top button undone. It honest-to-god made her stomach flip at how handsome he looked. He smiled, his eyes soft and open, almost always pleading in some way, and leaned close to Julia's ear.

"This isn't anything like the movies," he yelled over

the music. His breath tickled the baby hairs that hadn't been shellacked or corralled with bobby pins into her updo. "All this school color decor is really sending some odd messaging."

Julia pulled back and met his gaze, laughing. "I was just thinking the same thing! I'm trying to have fun, not think about the Comets' losing football record."

She rolled her eyes; not like she ever cared about their record.

Just then, the song changed. From the first chords, Julia recognized *I'll Be* by Edwin McCain. Her skin flushed hot. A slow song. There'd been a couple already tonight, and, being dateless, the whole thing was just a cringeworthy situation to navigate. Usually, she took the opportunity to use the bathroom, but there were only so many times she could sneak away without that itself becoming concerning.

But now Thomas tilted his head toward her, eyebrows raised and eyes latching onto hers from the top of his gaze. And then he offered his hand, an open and waiting palm, with a little shrug.

Might as well, he seemed to say, though he didn't need to use any words at all for Julia to drop her hand right into his.

With a shocking amount of force and grace, Thomas pulled her toward him and rested his hands on either side of her waist. Thomas was tall, but Julia could still loop her arms around his shoulders. She laced her fingers behind his neck, careful not to touch any more skin than was strictly necessary.

One slow dance didn't mean anything anyway. Julia didn't want her fantasies getting away from her. Yet, in this sweaty gym with low lighting, Thomas fixed his intense gaze on her, and she couldn't help it.

Naturally, all she could think about was her breath. She ducked her head. "I maybe shouldn't have gotten that garlicky pasta at dinner."

Thomas shrugged his shoulders, lifting her arms, and with it she raised her head. "What are you talking about? You love garlic."

"I didn't think I'd be slow dancing with anyone tonight."

"I don't think that would have changed your decision." Thomas smirked.

"You're right. What my stomach wants, my stomach gets."

They wobbled around in a circle, not too fast and not too slow, the scenery revolving around them. Julia reminded herself to breathe.

"What do you think 'love's suicide' means?" Thomas asked, thick eyebrows lifting, referencing the song lyrics.

Julia threw her head back with a deep belly laugh at the earnestness of his question. Her inertia pulled her away from Thomas just slightly, and in response his hands moved from their stabilizing position on her waist to encircle her more securely. She righted herself and her heart seized at the closer contact, even as she tried to play it cool. If the change in touch meant anything to Thomas, he didn't show it on his face. Cool as a cucumber.

"I have no clue, and I have a feeling it will be a mystery that will plague me for the rest of my life."

Now Thomas ducked his head, snorting a little laugh between them. When he raised his head again, his soulful brown eyes met hers, shadows cast across them in the gymnasium's attempt at mood lighting.

"Me too, I think," he said. His breath hit hot in the hollow of her neck.

But was he talking about the song lyrics anymore?

The next chorus built up, the song's emotion mounting, and despite Julia having no real clue what was going on between her and Thomas, she felt like maybe this was the beginning of something. This moment representing a branching trajectory into her future. She felt silly, goofy, utterly elated.

"And I'll be your cryin' shoulder. I'll be love's suicide," Julia sang, laughing between the lines, swirling her head back and grinning at the ceiling as Thomas clung to her. "And I'll be better when I'm older. I'll be the greatest fan of your life."

When she finished her solo, Thomas pulled her close. Closer than they were dancing before. Julia instinctively moved her hands from his shoulders to around Thomas's middle, making it easier to close the gap between their bodies. Julia rested her cheek against his chest.

He whispered the lyrics between them, so low he almost hummed along. Her breath hitched as she felt Thomas's fingers inch along the skin of her back, where her dress cut low.

Julia stayed silent, still, frozen in fear like a wild animal.

Is this happening? Is this happening? The words repeated on a loop in her mind.

Thomas, growing more bold, splayed both hands completely flat on her back, taking up as much of her skin as possible. Goosebumps raised over her body. So close to him, she felt his breath catch too.

This was it. This was the moment. The words teetered on the edge of her tongue.

Julia's heart swelled, bordering on painful. She thought the damned butterflies in her stomach might make her throw up. The song ended, and Thomas dropped his arms, stepping ever so slightly back from her. He pulled a lip between his teeth, his eyes fluttering to her lips.

Was he going to kiss her?

It was exactly like the movies, the world around her evaporating. The moment stretched on, just them in their magical little bubble.

She wanted to say the words but couldn't force them out.

And then Thomas blinked. He actually shook his head, running a hand over his cropped hair.

The gravity in Julia's center pulled her chest concave. And she smiled, shakily, before she could let herself feel foolish, so naive. Her instincts always failed her.

Because why would Thomas Callaghan want her? What a ridiculous thought.

EIGHTEEN
THOMAS

BEYOND BUSSING tables and helping out in the back of the house, Thomas had taken to finding odd jobs around the Coney Island and getting them done. Nasty jobs, like the one he did right now: scrubbing the unisex bathroom's grout with a toothbrush, crawling around on his hands and knees, his nose burning from the bleach smell.

This, and a bunch of other jobs that got repeatedly pushed off. After spending most of his time at the diner, it had become clear just how far behind things had fallen with the decline of his dad's health. He used to be the one that kept up on the little things—the caulk that needed to be redone, the windows that needed washing—and Mom couldn't do it all on her own. All these tiny projects were a perfect outlet for Thomas's anxiety which pressed in on him from all angles.

Anxiety about writing, anxiety about Julia, anxiety

about Dad. The only way to escape it was to make himself more and more useful, whipping himself into a Tasmanian devil tornado of chores. To be fair, most of his thoughts about Julia were decidedly not anxiety laden, filled with the soft mewls she made as she came on his fingers in the stairwell at Theatre Bizarre. But then his thoughts inevitably turned to New York and his eventual return to the city...after Dad died.

Because that was still the plan. That had always been his plan. He didn't abandon the plan twelve years ago. Now, the more his stubbornness latched on tighter to his imminent return, the less appealing it seemed, making him his own worst enemy.

So when Mom burst into the bathroom, Thomas startled, lost in thoughts on his hands and knees with a toothbrush in hand.

"Thomas, you don't have to do that," Mom fussed.

"Of course I do. Dad's not going to do it." He didn't look up from his progress.

Mom tutted. "I'm sure there's someone else who can do it."

"One of the waitresses between orders? Or maybe a kid from the back? Or Danny? Ari? Yeah right," he scoffed.

And anyway, these chores felt more productive than staring at his keyboard, forcing out a couple hundred sad words every evening just to have something to send to Sandy Thorne. At least while doing work like this, visions of Julia coming undone underneath his fingers weren't much of a distraction. The highlight reel from their night at the Theatre Bizarre could play on a pleasurable loop without completely derailing his progress.

Until he remembered New York. And that returning to his place and his roommates in Brooklyn meant leaving Julia behind in Michigan.

Just like he did all those years ago.

They hadn't spoken since Sunday morning when he drove her home from Detroit after four AM. The eastern horizon lightened to the faintest shade of pale blue as their hands laced on Thomas's thigh.

Thomas waited to text her, because he didn't want to pressure her. And because his own stubborn streak made his future as clear as mud.

When Mom didn't go away, Thomas leaned back on his heels, coming out of his spiraling thoughts.

"What's up?" He smiled, more thin-lipped and impatient than a true smile.

"Your father and I want to speak with you. In the office. When you're free." She nodded at her son and disappeared without another word.

That wasn't a good sign. Usually a talkative person, Mom clammed up when something was bothering her.

Great. Thomas looked around him. He'd made good progress that afternoon and only had the small square left under the wall-mounted sink. Standing up, he raised his arms overhead and pushed up on his tiptoes, stretching after being hunched on the ground for so long. He washed his hands and ignored the darkening circles under his eyes. More diner coffee would fix that.

He pushed through the swinging "Employees Only" door, behind which there was a small line of lockers, a tiny room that doubled as a break room and changing room, and, at the end of the hall, Dad's office. It was a cramped thing, with a tiny chrome and faux wood desk, an ancient computer, and a fabric rolling chair covered in pills from years of use. At least there was a window that faced the parking lot beside the restaurant.

Dad sat behind the desk, nasal cannula coiled down under it and attached to the faintly whistling oxygen tank. Mom perched in a folding chair, silent and her fingers clenched. An empty one sat beside her, and Thomas plopped into it, attempting to quell the uneasiness that surged in his gut.

Thomas slouched a bit in his chair, manifestly casual. "Bathroom floor's looking good."

No one said anything. Through the walls, the dishes clanged and the commercial dishwasher whooshed as the kitchen called orders. Dad didn't look up from his lap. Mom fidgeted in her seat. Thomas's chest prickled.

This couldn't be good. Thomas blew out a breath, eager to break the tension. "Okay, what's going on?"

Dad inhaled deeply, his shoulders rising up toward his ears. He met Thomas's eyes and held them.

"I know we talked about you moving home before, but

I want to officially start the conversation about you taking over the restaurant," he swallowed, "after I die."

Thomas blinked, his throat immediately tight. Beside him, Mom sniffed and pulled a tissue from her pocket. She always had tissues on her these days. Without looking away from Dad, Thomas put a stabilizing hand on Mom's knee and squeezed. It only made her shoulders shake more.

"Just blindsiding me with this at four PM on a Tuesday?" Thomas clenched his jaw.

Sure, he expected it, but he didn't know, well…he didn't know when to expect it. Somewhere in the corner of his mind, he clung to the childlike belief that if they never had the conversation, they'd never *need* to have it. Dad would never die.

"I'd hardly call this *blindsiding*, Thomas. Your father is dying, and we need to figure this out before then." Mom dabbed at her eyes again, shattering any barriers of disbelief that Thomas still had erected.

He bristled, sitting upright in the chair and crossing his arms protectively over his chest.

"What I mean is, it's not in my plans to move back to Starling Hills. This was never supposed to be permanent." Though he tried, Thomas couldn't keep the steely edge out of his voice. He sounded like a dick, and he knew it.

"You got a subletter. What's left there for you?" Mom asked, her eyes pleading in the same guileless way that his own did.

Thomas seethed but kept his words strained. "It's not as simple as that. I have a whole life in the city. In Brooklyn."

It was the line he kept saying to himself, using it to remind himself that he was going back. He wasn't staying in Michigan. His future was in New York. The life of a novelist, glittery and gritty at the same time.

But it felt less true each day. There was good in Starling Hills. There was family and Julia. Sure, he could write anywhere, but leaving New York felt like failure. Like if he came home, he was giving up this New York City dream that he had since his teen years. And he wasn't ready to admit defeat.

Yet, he still hadn't emailed Micha back. And his agent must surely be convinced by now that Thomas was virtually avoiding her. (He was.) Even scrolling his friends' feeds at night didn't elicit the same FOMO as when he'd first come home. Dinners with his family and time spent with Julia was quickly usurping the pseudo-homesick for New York feeling that had hung like a cloud over him the first couple weeks he was home.

But it was *his* plan to go back. And he didn't want to be forcefully stripped of it.

"I know this is a hard conversation to have, but I ask you to be open-minded. The fact is, your mother can't run this place on her own." Dad laid his palms flat on the desk. "We have to at least have the conversation."

Heat prickled over Thomas's scalp, and he furrowed his brows.

"Have the conversation? Changing my life like that right now…it's…" He didn't know what it was. Didn't know what he could say right now with Dad's death looming over the room, the Grim Reaper lurking just offstage to take his dad into the wings. "Why can't one of my siblings do it?"

"Ari's getting her MBA, and Danny's got his own career and side gigs and hobbies," Mom said.

"But they already live here." Thomas squeezed his eyes shut, pressing his thumb and forefinger in the corners, hoping to relieve some tension. He didn't like the whining tone building behind his words, but it all felt so unfair. Daydreaming about a life in Starling Hills was a different story than actually living out a future here.

"You're our oldest," Dad said, as if that made it all clear. "Surely you can write here? You don't need to be in New York City?"

The oldest. This was the real reason neither Danny nor Ari could take over. Thomas was expected to fill the shoes of the man across the table. Not that he ever could.

Thomas drew a deep breath through his nose to keep his emotions measured. His whole life he'd been reminded of that mantle. It was part of the reason why he left for college. Going to New York was the dream, but it also meant that he didn't need to worry about what his parents thought about his life. He didn't have to be "the oldest" out there. He didn't have to try and live up to the precedent that his dad set. In New York, he could pretend that his family didn't exist, for better or for worse.

He would always be the first born, try though he might to forget it. And moving to New York and pursuing a writing career wasn't their idea of what the oldest did. At least not in the long term.

Thomas sighed, his mouth twisted as if of its own will. He hated the hot anger that settled in his chest. In some ways, he always knew that this day would come, when his parents would sit him down and ask him to take over the family business, to come home. To give up any dream he had.

Sixteen-year-old Thomas thought that thirty-year-old Thomas would have figured out how to deal with it all by now.

Yet here he was, every inch the petulant teenager.

He scooted his hips back in the chair and leaned forward, his elbows on his knees as he ran a hand over his beard.

"It's a big change. Huge change. I know it looks like I left it all behind, but getting a subletter for while I'm home just made financial sense. My plan has always been to go back." He paused. "What happens if I don't take over?"

"Then we sell." Dad didn't blink. Didn't even move a muscle.

"And I find another job. There's always work for a

dental hygienist." Mom frowned as she said it. She had quit her career after Dad's cancer diagnosis, helping out at the restaurant full time.

Thomas couldn't meet Dad's eyes as he asked the next question, his voice low.

"Would selling be so bad?"

Mom clicked her tongue and sniffed again.

"You know about dreams, Thomas? That's what you're going after in New York City, right? This restaurant was my dream." Dad's jaw quivered as he spoke, the effort apparent in each word. "After years of pulling this family up to where we are, working double shifts at the General Motors plant while your mother took care of you all? Then putting her through dental hygiene school? Working to put you kids through college? All those years I dreamed of this place." He stamped a finger into the desk.

"Does that mean it has to be my dream too?" The words came out more sour than Thomas intended.

Dad held his gaze, his mouth popping open into a soft O.

Thomas wanted to take the words back the second he said them. He meant them, but they sounded so harsh, so terrible, spit at the man who raised him and provided for him. His mouth sweat, nauseated that he could be so selfish, so uncaring.

And yet.

All of his muscles tightened, primed to launch. He

pushed his chair back and stood too fast, his head spinning.

"I'm sorry, I don't know if I'll ever be able to give you the answer that you want."

Thomas shoved through the door, whipping off his apron, and banged open the heavy door that spit him out in the back parking lot next to the dumpster.

This question, this life-altering decision to make, served on top of his deadline with thoughts of Julia cycling endlessly on the treadmill of his brain? Great. Love it. No sweat.

And underneath it all, guilt mounted that while they were all losing Dad too soon, Thomas had the audacity to worry about his own silly little problems.

He got in his Corolla and slammed the door.

In the sun-warmed car, sweat prickled his forehead. The very un-October-like heat gave him an outward sensation to focus on. He sat there, absolutely still, breathing in and breathing out, before sliding his phone out of his pocket. When his email loaded, he saw one from his agent marked urgent.

"For fuck's sake," he said under his breath, his stomach plummeting like a rock. His agent used "urgent" very judiciously, and this letter could bring no good news.

Thomas,

I know you have a lot going on at home, but we need to

chat, and soon. I don't mean for this to sound so ominous, so I guess I'll just let you know now that I have bad news to share.

Let me know when you're available to hop on a call.

Best,
Sandy Thorne

"Fuck fuck fuck fuck *FUCK*." Thomas slammed his hands on the steering wheel, shaking the entire car with his force. "Goddamnit."

He threw the phone in the seat beside him and started the car, angling the vents for the air conditioner to blow directly on him.

Everything all at the same time.

When it rains it pours.

What other stupid conciliatory phrases could he come up with?

It didn't matter, because they were all bullshit.

Grabbing his phone again, he responded to Sandy with the best times for them to chat this week. If he was in New York, they would have met for a drink instead of having a video meeting. Boozy meetings in swanky New York bars, another perk to living in the city, always made bad news land a little more softly.

Either way, there'd be booze during this meeting. If he couldn't down a fancy martini while getting shitty news, he'd at least have a Coors Light clenched in his fist at his desk.

He leaned his head back against the headrest. The faint scent of bleach and frying oil clung to him.

There was another social email in his inbox. One from Micha telling Thomas all about a northeastern tour with his punk band that would bring him to Toledo, Ohio. Which wasn't far from Starling Hills, Michigan, where Micha heard at XYZ Brewing that he'd jetted off to. And maybe they could meet up?

I know we don't owe each other anything, but I hope you're doing alright.

Thomas ignored the email. Micha, being non-monogamous, always went the extra step for his friends. But Thomas wasn't interested. He didn't want a part of his New York life showing up here in Starling Hills. He needed the stark delineation. This life and that life. He'd message him back later.

Waiting be damned, there was only one person he really wanted to talk to right now. Only one person who maybe would identify with this rudderless feeling.

> I've had a terrible day, but I can't stop thinking about you. Which is not related to the terrible-ness of this day.
>
> When can we hang out again?

I'm sorry you've had a bad day, Thomas. Honestly mine's not great either. My brain is still at Theatre Bizarre

Are you free Friday night? I've got a secret plan

NINETEEN
JULIA

JULIA LET out a breath as she picked up her phone from beside her cubicle keyboard. Her lungs ached with release.

Finally, Thomas had texted.

She didn't want to be the first to reach out, seeing as she didn't trust her dating impulses anymore. Not that this was really dating. Inside, she had no chill, and she didn't want Thomas to know that. Her fingers itched to text him minutes after he'd dropped her off Sunday morning. But she didn't. Instead, she fell into a hazy sleep, hair still in two high buns.

Admittedly, Saturday night had gone off without a hitch. They'd had fun alright. Hot, casual fun. The memory of Thomas bringing her to orgasm in that stairwell was unbelievably hot. Blood rushed to her pelvis at the thought even now. *The pleasure was all mine,* he said.

Those earnest words paired with the blatant desire scrawled across his face made her melt all over again.

The problem here wasn't that her libido had revved up, but that her heart thudded in her chest at the thought of him. A sure sign that Julia's feelings were getting involved. A fatal sign.

Don't think about it.

Don't think about how he's going back to New York City. Don't think about how he makes her feel more seen and validated than Josh ever had. Don't think about how teen Julia would scream that something had finally happened between the two of them...and then pen a fic about Rose Tyler and the Tenth Doctor based on the experience.

Which is exactly what thirty-one-year-old Julia did. She didn't send Thomas that fic though. That one was just for herself. And her growing Tumblr following. Subtitled "based on a true story." It was her most shared post thus far.

Pair all this Thomas anxiety with her mounting nerves about the promotion that should be announced any day now, and Julia wasn't getting much work done at her cubicle. She pulled her cardigan closer around her shoulders and settled deeper into her comfortably ergonomic chair.

"Jeeeesus." Susan leaned into Julia's cubicle, abruptly ending her daydreaming. Her eyes rolled up so far into her head that Julia could see only whites. "You'd think getting married is end game for some people."

"God, what now?" Julia craned her neck to see around Susan.

Susan crossed her arms over her chest, as she indicated what she was talking about with a flick of her head. Behind her, Michelle squealed with some other coworkers clustered around her left hand.

"He did such a good job." Michelle fluffed her precision highlighted white-blonde hair over her shoulder.

"Well, uhh, it appears that Michelle got engaged over her long weekend." Susan frowned. "Does it make me an old crotchety divorcee that her happiness makes me salty as hell?"

"Then I, too, am crotchety." Julia crossed her arms over her stomach, turning in her chair. "Ugh."

It wasn't so long ago that Julia's coworkers fawned over *her* around the proverbial office water cooler, everyone desperate for wedding planning details as her princess cut diamond sat pretty on her left ring finger. But when she'd stormed out of her and Josh's apartment, she'd thrown that ring with all her might, aiming to hit him square in the forehead. Instead, it went far left, pinged off the wall, rolled under the couch, and hopefully tumbled down a vent.

A five-foot-eight blonde and lithe creature, Michelle was, in many ways, Julia's polar opposite. But they were both good at their jobs and together had completed many successful deals, despite Julia's judgey thoughts about her coworker.

"Just think, I'm supposed to work with her on the next launch. If I don't get the promotion, that is." Julia crossed her arms. "She's insufferable."

Susan leaned closer. "Do you need me to put in a bad word for you? Get her fired or something?"

"No." Julia snorted. "I mean, like, *yes*, but that would probably just get us both fired, so please don't."

"I'm joking. Don't worry, I'm far too lazy for such office espionage." Susan brushed a hand at the air. "Not like they'd listen to Grouchy Office Mom's opinion anyway."

"Shut up. You're not grouchy." Julia smirked. "Most of the time at least."

"Okay, grouchy maybe not. But I'm honest, Juju. And let me tell you, I've seen a lot of you entry level kids come through here, and you're nothing like Michelle. Nothing like the rest of them." Susan rested her elbow on her arm crossed over her stomach, picking at the cuticle of her right pointer finger. She eyed Michelle from across the floor. "And that's a *good* thing. This corporate thing is a scam."

Julia pushed her rolling chair back from her desk to better face Susan. "As much as I appreciate ranting against capitalism, I'm not up for it right now. This job, this promotion, it's all I've been working toward these last couple years. Without my career, I have nothing."

"Well, that's not fucking true. For one, you have me. And we'll always have our sacred dirty martinis and fettuccine Alfredo. And for two, Thomas? Your writing? There's more to life than just work, you know."

Julia pinched her lips together. "What do you have then?"

Susan had her answer primed. "My girls. I love those little shitheads. And my Dungeons and Dragons group. If my divorce taught me anything, it's that nothing is certain and to chase joy when I can. And I chase my joy while roleplaying a barbarian on the weekends. Well, one weekend per month." Susan lifted her eyebrows at Julia as if to say, *so there.*

Chase joy. Wasn't that exactly what she was doing with Thomas? Following what her body wanted. Remembering forgotten passion and sharing her writing again. Allowing her heart to feel something.

But her body was finicky. Her heart, timid. She had Josh to thank for all that.

Julia sighed. This promotion was a chance to wade out of the kiddie pool and into the deep end—for better or for worse. "The promotion's a means to an end, Susan. That's all."

"Mmhm. And hell is just a sauna, my friend." Susan patted Julia on the head, a move which made Julia furrow her brow.

"You're ridiculous."

"I know, but I'm also, usually, very right."

Julia rolled her eyes as she picked up her rainbow unicorn mug to take a drink, only to find it empty.

"Okay. Well then, thanks for the encouraging chat. I hardly feel better." Julia stood and smoothed her cardigan. "I'm going to make more tea for this last hour of work. Need anything?"

"All set, thanks. Just need to finish up these last emails and I'm out of here."

"Jealous."

Julia made a beeline for the kitchenette on their floor, giving Michelle and her admirers a wide berth. She wasn't in the mood for any water-cooler chats, and definitely not in the mood to hear anything about Michelle's engagement.

She stared out the window, waiting for her water to boil for her green tea, when the kitchenette door opened and closed.

"Julia!" Michelle squealed.

Julia closed her eyes and took a deep breath before turning and aiming her toothiest smile right at Michelle. "Michelle! Oh my god, congratulations! I heard you all talking about your weekend."

"Oh, you're so sweet." Michelle pouted and put her left hand on Julia's forearm, the massive diamond sparkling right in Julia's face.

"Wow that's—" But Julia stopped mid-sentence as she actually, begrudgingly, looked at the ring.

She knew that ring. Julia found that ring by spending a not-negligible amount of time scouring obscure shops on the internet. She'd stared at it on their

Instagram page for months. Left Josh extremely unsubtle hints about that ring. She swallowed. "That's a beautiful ring."

"Isn't it? He did good." Michelle eyed her ring fondly, and Julia tried not to roll her eyes at the oft-repeated sentiments of the freshly engaged.

Michelle produced her phone. "Want to see some pics?"

She didn't wait for Julia's response before she shoved her Instagram under Julia's nose. "At sunset! Up north! He hired a photographer and everything." The pitch of her voice reached supersonic.

The first photo in Julia's face was mostly Michelle, her arms wrapped around the shoulders of her nondescript fiancé who faced away from the camera. With, of course, her left hand on top to showcase the new jewels. But Julia's Spidey sense began to tingle, her stomach suddenly roiling.

Snatching the phone from Michelle's hands, Julia scrolled to see more photos. The pair of them in the sand, outlined against the orange and purple sunset, him on his knees and Michelle's hand pressed to her chest in surprise. Her fiancé's profile was eerily familiar.

Julia's throat tightened.

"What did you say your fiancé's name is?" she asked mid-scroll to the last photo in the series, and then Julia didn't need the answer.

There, the two of them on the beach, holding hands

and looking every bit the perfect photo-ready couple, was Michelle and Josh.

Julia's Josh. Her dishonest, conniving, scum of the earth ex-fiancé.

"Josh Kempton." Michelle beamed.

Julia thought she was going to be ill. She swallowed the impulse.

"How long have you two been together?" Julia's words were thin and shaky, but Michelle didn't seem to notice or care, sucked back into her world of *congratulations!* notifications on Instagram.

"He proposed on our one-year anniversary! Isn't that romantic?"

Julia grabbed the edge of the counter, now certain that she would be sick as her mouth sweat.

Michelle looked up and reached toward her half-heartedly. "Whoa, Julia, are you okay? You look pale as a ghost."

"I'm fine." But she launched toward the counter, putting a hand over her mouth, as her stomach heaved.

"You don't look fine." Michelle backed toward the door.

Josh. Fucking Josh.

Barely four months after their engagement imploded and he's engaged again. To a woman he'd apparently been cheating on her with for eight months prior to that.

Her stomach convulsed, and this time she couldn't hold it back. Her burrito bowl came up right into the sink.

* * *

WHEN JULIA RANG Thomas's doorbell on Friday, his dad answered. Julia wasn't prepared for the sight of Mr. Callaghan; he was much smaller than she remembered him, with a nasal cannula trailing to a rolling oxygen tank. All thoughts of Michelle and fucking Josh shattered, scattering like the dry October leaves on the wind as she saw Mr. Callaghan standing in the doorway. Dying, Thomas said. She opened her mouth, but nothing came out, momentarily speechless.

"Julia." His face broke into a warm, wide smile.

"Mr. Callaghan, it's so good to see you." She returned his smile in kind, but her stomach swooped. Should she say something about the cancer? His diagnosis? "Thomas told me—" she started, but Mr. Callaghan cut her off with a wave of the hand.

"Ah, it's nothing."

It obviously wasn't nothing.

"But it's Sean to you now. No more Mr. Callaghan. Come in." He stepped back, his foot nearly catching on the entryway rug. "T's just outside finishing up a job for me. Would you like some coffee? Just made some."

He shuffled through the living room to the kitchen.

"Sure, that'd be great, thanks."

She took a steaming mug from his hands.

"I sweetened it for you." Without pretense, he walked back to the living room, and Julia followed him.

If the basement hadn't changed at all, the upstairs sure hadn't either. Mr. Callaghan—Sean's—Lay-Z-Boy recliner still sat in the corner, the table next to it piled high with books, crossword puzzles, and old coffee mugs. A pair of readers perched on top of it all. The floral-patterned couches, looking a little aged, still corralled all the furniture around the TV, next to which sat a basket of Mrs. Callaghan's knitting projects. The coffee table in the middle of the room held a backgammon set, more books, and empty mugs. It had a sense of homeyness that Julia had deeply missed. A feeling that she didn't even get in her own parents' home.

"Please, sit, sit." Sean dropped into his chair that rocked back and bumped the wall with his inertia. Julia sat in the opposite recliner that flanked the crowded side table.

They sipped their coffee in silence, Julia unsure of what, if anything, to say. The grandfather clock ticked by the seconds, and Sean's chair clicked as he rocked gently back and forth. Julia hoped that Thomas wouldn't be long. Not that they were late, just that, nice though Sean certainly was, she didn't want to sit awkwardly with his dad for much longer. Which of course made her feel guilty. The man was dying, after all. Shouldn't she try and make conversation with him? She floundered around for a safe topic, but Sean broke the silence.

"Thomas has enjoyed having you around. I can tell."

"Oh?" She wasn't sure how to respond to that.

"Being home's been hard for him, I think. Misses New York. The stress from all this has been a lot." He picked up the tube of his nasal cannula and dropped it again to indicate the *all this* that he meant.

Julia nodded along, ignoring the *all this* and focusing on Thomas. "It's been great to see him."

"Sometimes it feels like he's still my little boy." Sean lifted his chin toward a decade-old family photo that hung on the wall.

Julia studied the picture. All five of them were there, years younger, and a lot less worries ago. Sean held his head high, strong and proud, with a warm smile on his face. The photographer caught Thomas's mother mid-laugh that came out as a flattering expression. Thomas looked about the age when she first met him, with his buzzcut and pleading eyes and soft smile. Danny with a very serious, near scowl. And Ari who nearly vibrated right out of the frame.

"A lot has changed since then."

"It has and it hasn't." Sean fixed her with a knowing look. "Some things never change."

Julia fidgeted in her seat. She knew she'd changed over the years. But writing again and seeing Thomas again got her thinking that maybe Sean was right. At least a little bit. A kernel nestled deep inside her that was still that teenager with stars in her eyes. The one that came alive in the blue glow of her laptop as she typed words away until too late at night. Sure, getting less than eight hours of sleep per night was definitely more rough now than as a teen, but it was the same feverish passion that made her fingers tingle to keep going.

Not to mention, her undeniable crush on Thomas. That hadn't changed. Her cheeks blazed with warmth as the memories from Theatre Bizarre flooded her while sitting with his dad.

She cleared her throat. "Some things do."

Sean nodded. "Considering the circumstances, I haven't seen Thomas this happy in a long time."

The base of Julia's neck tingled. She was more intrigued than she wanted to admit.

"That's good." She kept her answer as neutral as possible, but she felt silly as she danced around the conversation.

"Will you take care of him?" Sean's words were brittle, so tissue-paper thin that Julia turned to him with her head cocked to the side.

Sean's eyes shone bright and wide, clasping his coffee mug in his hands.

Take care of him? How could she take care of him in New York, when he was hundreds of miles away?

For the first time in years, something unfurled inside her. New York City. The dream she'd tucked away, as she did so many other parts of herself when she was with Josh. She always wanted to live there, to try it. Maybe not forever, but for a little while. Maybe she could take a sabbatical from work, an extended vacation. She could take care of Thomas in New York...

In the span of a few seconds, so many possibilities blossomed into Julia's future. She opened her mouth to respond, but the moment shattered when Thomas came in through the sliding door. Her stomach swooped at the sight of him, a sheen of sweat on his forehead.

"Oh! You're here," he said. "Let me just wash up real quick and I'll be ready."

He walked away before she said anything, her heart thudding and everything suddenly looking a little differently than it had a few minutes ago.

Julia turned back to Sean. In the span of a few seconds, he'd dropped his head back against the chair and fallen asleep, mug still clutched in his hand. She stood to untangle the handle from his fingers, more gnarled and spotted than they should be for someone of his age, and put both mugs on the coffee table.

Thomas's palm on her lower back made her jump, but he was looking at his father.

"He's always so tired now." His voice was soft, barely a whisper.

Julia wanted to say something, anything, desperate to comfort him, but the icy flash in Thomas's eyes put her off it. Instead, she turned over her shoulder and pecked his cheek, lingering for an extra moment against his sun-warmed skin. He smiled, his cheek muscles tightening under her lips, before stepping away from her, his hand leaving behind a ghostly warmth on her back.

Julia's stomach twisted. It was clear that Sean wouldn't be with the Callaghan family much longer. And she knew, in answer to Sean's question, that yes, come hell or high water, she would take care of Thomas.

TWENTY
THOMAS

THOMAS SAT in the passenger seat, his hands pulled inside his dark denim jean jacket.

Thankfully, the brief October heat had broken and it was back to seasonally appropriate crisp fall temps. He frowned out the window, visions of Dad cluttering his mind.

The emotions from conversation at the Coney had mellowed out a bit in the couple days since, but Thomas still clenched his jaw at the memory. Turning over different scenarios in his mind. Trying to figure out how everyone could get what they wanted.

If only he could turn down his stubbornness a couple of notches.

"So, this surprise isn't all that much of a surprise. It'll be kinda obvious when we get there," Julia said, turning up the last word like a question. She narrowed her eyes, focusing on the oncoming traffic as she waited to turn left.

"That's fine. I'm excited. I like surprises. And sorta surprises." It had been a while since someone had planned a surprise date for him, and he liked it.

Was this a date?

He and Micha had never dated in the standard definition of the word. Micha dated a lot of people, so it was hard to tell if Thomas was one of his many paramours or fell more on the friends with benefits side of things. It didn't matter—they both got what they needed out of it. But together they only ever wrote in trendy coffee shops or stylized dive bars and otherwise worked off their excess energy in Thomas's too small twin bed. Being taken somewhere felt good.

Thomas settled back. The vents blew warm air on his feet, tickling his ankles. Things were comfortable between him and Julia, just two adults hanging out, a week after one brought the other to a stunningly successful climax.

"How are you?" Julia flicked her eyes to him, smiling quickly before looking back at the road.

Shitty? Stressed? Anxious? Depressed? All of the above?

He ran a hand over his beard, unsure of how much to tell her. One orgasm didn't mean anything in the grand scheme of things, but the flame he carried for Julia Ward burned like a wildfire in his lungs. Opening up to her would open him up to rejection. More rejection than he could handle right now.

"Peachy," he said with a slight frown.

"That good, eh?" Julia side-eyed him, but he kept his mouth shut. "I didn't have the best week myself."

She frowned, and all of his worries about rejection faded away. Instead, a fierce animal rumbled in his chest. Flexing his fists in his lap, Thomas would fight tooth and nail whoever, whatever, had wronged her if he could.

"Well, we're here anyway." She shut down that line of conversation and pointed with her chin over the steering wheel.

Here being an empty parking lot in downtown Starling Hills. People milled about, a field of blankets and camping chairs covered the asphalt and the grass around the lot. Julia bounced in her seat at the sight.

"Movies in the Moonlight. Fall edition." A wide grin spread over her face, and her stormy eyes sparkled.

"This is cool. What movie?" Thomas looked around for any hints.

"Nope! That's the true surprise." She quirked an eyebrow at him and hopped out of the car, grabbing a tiny cooler and two overlarge blankets.

Thomas laughed and swung out of the car. His breath caught at the two rosy spots that had spread over Julia's cheeks. Visions of them cuddled under a fuzzy blanket on the grass, their hands clasped and sweating, danced in his head.

Damn, he had it bad. Real bad. Worse than teen Thomas ever had.

Because now the stakes were real. Before it had always been some fantasy. Some far-off version of Julia and himself living out their half-baked plans.

But now she was the person he'd always envisioned in those dreams.

He was the person of that far-off sometime.

"Come on, slowpoke." Julia turned back toward him, her brown hair loose and flying in the autumn breeze around her, contrasting against her chunky red sweater and dark denim jeans. She looked like magic.

He shoved his fists in his jean pockets and did a little awkward jog to catch up with her. They found an empty spot on the grass toward the back, and she laid one blanket flat, tossing the other one on top. Julia sat first, cross-legged, and patted the ground beside her. When Thomas flopped next to her, she pulled the purple blanket over their laps. She slid what could only be described as wine juice boxes out of her cooler, one for each of them.

"Shh, don't tell." She twisted off the cap and took a deep drink, leaving behind the faintest trace of red wine on her cupid's bow. Julia leaned closer to him, and he could smell the wine on her breath. "Are you okay?"

Thomas grimaced. "Define okay."

"In a place, mentally, where you can enjoy a good movie."

"Sort of." He considered how much he should tell her. In truth, he wanted to share it all, everything about Dad and Callaghan's Coney Island, and the bad news Sandy had given him this week over Skype. But how much could his heart handle?

Opening up to Julia would be an exercise in vulnerability, something New York and his career in publishing had trained out of him. He could play calculated games with his career, something Sandy Thorne helped him figure out, but with his heart? There was no playbook for that. He considered not saying anything. Because if he didn't wager it all, there was nothing to lose.

But even as he thought it, he knew that was wrong.

He already had so much to lose. Now he could lose her for good. This was going to hurt.

"There's just a lot going on right now," he said, running a hand back through his curls.

Julia pulled her knees up to her chest and leaned into them. "Do you want to talk about it?"

"Yeah." He took a deep breath.

If he couldn't tell her, who could he tell? The publishing news was humiliating, and he definitely didn't want to tell Micha or anyone else in his New York circle.

"My publisher pushed back the date of my next novel. I guess my first two books aren't selling well. And so that means my advance is getting pushed back too. I haven't told my parents. They'll just use it as ammunition to get me to move home."

Beside him, Julia noticeably stiffened. He glanced at her sideways, but didn't say anything.

"Oh. Well, there's a lot to unpack there," she said. "First of all, I'm sorry. That fucking sucks. Secondly, is moving home something you're considering?" Her voice fluttered just slightly on the end of the question.

He deflated under the stress of the week.

"I don't know." He huffed out the answer. He truly didn't anymore.

"Starling Hills isn't so bad." Julia took another drink of wine and didn't meet his eyes, instead surveying the crowd.

What wasn't so bad was sitting here with her.

What was bad was feeling trapped. He could never live up to his dad. A failure before he even tried. He dropped his chin to his chest, already feeling like he'd disappointed his family.

"It's not as easy as that." Thomas swallowed, his Adam's apple bobbing.

"Tell me about it," Julia sighed. "My engagement exploding and moving back in with my parents hasn't been easy. It's fucking miserable. And guess what? It gets worse."

She took a steadying breath. "I just found out that Josh is engaged, again, already, to my *coworker* who he's been *dating* for a *year*."

His own troubles forgotten, white hot rage scorched through Thomas's veins, incensed that anyone would treat

Julia like this. His nostrils flared and his voice pitched dangerously low. "What the everliving fuck, Julia?"

She shrugged, her voice toneless. "Yeah, I know. I don't know. Just thinking about it makes me queasy again."

Blood pounded in Thomas's ears. "Josh is a fucking moron."

"Josh is...well, he's something. I'm not quite to the point of casually disregarding that the whole thing happened—is still happening, apparently—but, good fucking riddance." Julia pulled her legs up and wrapped her arms around her knees, wine juice box still clutched in one hand.

Thomas wanted to shatter something. Not the least of which was Josh's nose with his fist. He smiled tightly, his eyes flat and empty. Between his pain and Julia's heartbreak, he saw red, but in the next second he was so exhausted by the heaviness that just didn't seem to let up. By the sheer gravity of adulthood and responsibility. He was desperate for something to be easy for once. All he wanted to do was have his arms around Julia.

So that's what he did. Thomas closed the space between them and wrapped her in his arms, like when she held him in the diner parking lot and he cried about his dad. It took a second for her to melt, but then she did, her shoulders releasing and arms winding around his middle.

"I'm sorry," he mumbled into her hair.

"Me too," she said, her words moist against his neck.

They inched closer and stayed there, tight in each other's arms. It had been a while since anyone outside his family had truly held Thomas like this. So tight and true.

In this moment, everything changed for him. He felt a seismic shift, his deformed pieces slipping back into their original form. One word repeated on a loop in his mind: *hope*.

Julia was his hope. The vanilla scent of her. Her red sweater against his cheek. Her chest moving up and down as she breathed. It all anchored him to this spot.

Julia released him, sitting back. "Now are you okay?"

"I will be." He meant it. He believed it.

They sat in silence after that, as the dusk grew more purple-grey and the parking lot more crowded, waiting for the movie to start. Vendors fired up their machines, popping kettle corn and spinning cotton candy, their roasted-sweet scents carrying on the wind. Underneath the blanket, their pinkies touched, side by side. The gentlest friction sent electric shocks up Thomas's arm.

When the screen flickered to life, Julia tilted her head sideways, smirking. "I love this movie."

She slid her hand into his, and he laced his fingers with hers.

The first thirty seconds were credits, and he already recognized it. "*Amélie*."

* * *

"OKAY, so not an American romcom, but we didn't define the rules of what we were studying." Julia leaned back on her elbows as the end credits ran and people packed up their blankets and chairs around them.

"It was an excellent choice." Thomas leaned back, too, his shoulders less tense than they had been in weeks.

"It's funny how it makes me nostalgic for a time and place I never knew." Julia smiled softly. "I've always wanted to go to Paris."

"You've never been?"

She shook her head. "I wanted to go for our honeymoon, but…"

Thomas pulled his eyebrows low. "You should go. At the risk of sounding cliche, it truly is magical."

"The film certainly makes me believe that." Julia sat up and ran her hands over the plush blanket. "When she breaks the crème brûlée, the montage of all of her little pleasures, I wonder how someone so lonely can still find the good stuff. Find the joy. I feel like that's all totally inaccessible for me now."

"Is there nothing that makes you happy now?" The question coming from him was rich. He didn't even know how he'd answer it.

Julia half-shrugged, non-committal. "Writing's been fun. Seeing you…" She trailed off, a blush creeping from underneath her sweater.

He wanted to know how she would finish that

sentence. He wanted to know what exactly made that pleasant color wash over her skin. But he didn't ask.

"The film does give me hope though," she said.

"So maybe our experiment is working?" Thomas smirked, a similar sense of calm radiating through his limbs.

"Maybe." Julia pulled her hair over her shoulder and played with it around her fingers.

"It's packed full of yearning for me." Thomas's cheeks warmed. He knew what it meant to yearn. To wait and wish for something good to happen. And maybe—his eyes flicked to Julia's—maybe something good finally was happening.

His gaze burned into her, channeling the power of his unasked questions. She smiled, soft and sweet, and he wanted to kiss those lips. He remembered how those same lips brushed his ear as her breathy whimpers sent shivers down his spine in the stairwell at Theatre Bizarre. How he'd ached for days after remembering her sweetness. Her saltiness. That sexy as hell steampunk outfit she wore.

"It makes me wonder if what I ever actually yearned for was real. What I had with Josh wasn't real. He was never really mine. Was I just deluding myself?" Julia snaked her arms under the blanket. "Like, I fixated on this beautiful Le Creuset butter dish, of all freaking things, in this gorgeous ivory color. Meringue, it's called. It was a symbol of everything I thought I wanted with him and look at me now."

"No. Fuck Josh," Thomas growled. "You weren't the wrong one there, Julia."

"But how was I to know? If I never got that email, I never would have known. And now he's with one of those other women." She shivered beneath her layers.

"You left though. And that took courage. That's not nothing." Under the blanket, his fingers found hers, lacing together and pulling their palms flush. His whole body tingled, electrified by her skin on his.

"Maybe I am a little like Amélie."

"I think you are. More than you know." Thomas swallowed. "Being around you reminds me what happiness feels like. I have something good to hope for every day. A text from you, your smile. Your dirty stories in my inbox—not just bad news from my agent."

Julia laughed and squeezed his hand. "You weren't happy in New York?"

Thomas squeezed back and didn't let up the pressure. It grounded him to this spot. "I thought I was. Published author, with cool friends, in the coolest borough. But I could barely even afford my rent. It was all very devil-may-care. No substance. Don't get me wrong, I loved it. For a time. And for some people it works forever. But I started to feel hollow. Here."

He knocked his free hand, balled in a fist, to his chest and held it there. The hollow feeling lingered. It would be a long time before he forgot that empty ache.

"I didn't even realize it until I got some distance from it. Some perspective."

At the time, he didn't know what that hollow feeling was. He didn't know what it meant.

Now he knew: New York City wasn't what he wanted anymore.

"In my social circle, it was all about who was going to be the next meal ticket. The big breakout star. It was a whole rat race. Those people didn't see me. I felt so alone."

"You're not alone now." Julia's eyes blazed hot with their own sincerity. "We're not alone."

"No, we're not," Thomas said, a comfortable weight settling into his chest.

They sat for a little while longer as the crowd and traffic cleared. The damp-leaf autumn wind blew away the popcorn and spun sugar scents that lingered from the vendors. Thomas felt that same nostalgia swimming in his veins that he'd had during *Amélie*. A cotton candy sweet, bone deep ache.

They walked back to the car, holding hands, until Thomas pulled Julia under his shoulder. Her warm curves fit perfectly against his body. Somewhere, sixteen-year-old Thomas rejoiced.

"Will you drive me?" Julia asked, looking up at him.

He ran his hand over his beard. "Of course."

When they got in her Jeep, the fresh cool air blew in as

they closed their doors. He sniffed and turned to her. "Where do you want to go?"

"Anywhere." Her pink cheeks rose with her wild smile. The mane of her hair was windswept.

He thought he might follow this woman anywhere.

He drove without a destination, like when they first got their driver's licenses, reckless and free. He drove, passing under the fluorescent lights lining downtown Starling Hills, with Julia in the passenger seat, and the growing dark and the music to keep them company. He drove until the paved roads turned to dirt. Roads that had tall tree canopies. And even though it was getting cold, they opened the windows.

Julia grabbed his phone and put Death Cab for Cutie's *Transatlanticism* album on Spotify. She turned it loud, the music breathing the night air with them. It was just like when they were kids.

They drove until they were two towns over. Ahead, Thomas saw a school, glowing otherworldly almost-purple at way-too-late on a Saturday night.

"Should we check it out?" He pointed with his finger from the top of the wheel, tilting his head. His right hand clutched Julia's on the center console as he adjusted his hips in his seat, his motives for wanting to pull into the parking lot entirely sinful.

"Let's go," she laughed, flashing him a wicked grin.

He pulled into the lot and parked the car, letting it run so their music would keep going. His pulse pounded as they sat there and just listened. When Thomas shifted to look at Julia, she turned to him too. Her lower lip pulled into her mouth, just a sliver of her teeth visible. Her eyes flashed mischief, and it sent a thrill right through him.

He brought his hand up and ran it through the tangled ends of her hair, pulling just slightly until her lips popped open, letting out a tiny gasp. The sound sent blood rushing between his legs, his jeans instantly tight over his hips.

Thomas moved his hand to her jaw, rubbing his knuckle along it until he reached her ear. She leaned into his touch until he opened his palm and cradled her chin. Licking her lips, she turned to his palm and kissed it. Her touch rippled through his body.

They leaned toward each other and kissed over the center console, awkwardly straining against their seatbelts. Julia laughed, snorting air through her nose, and broke off, undoing her seatbelt.

"Should we get into the back seat?"

Thomas eyed it. It looked big enough for him to sit comfortably. In response, he turned off the engine and jumped out of the little SUV. When he opened the back door, Julia was climbing over the seat.

"Oh my god, I'm gonna get stuck. I'm too fat for this." But she twisted and landed in the back, pulling her legs over.

Thomas laughed as he slid onto the bench beside her and pulled the door shut. Julia immediately scooted closer. He snaked his arm behind her back, and she swung her legs over one of his, tucked as close to his side as she could get without being on top of him. With both of them back there, there wasn't much space, but it worked.

"Hi," he whispered, his voice breaking in the middle of the word, and he let out a little cough.

"Hey," she murmured.

Thomas put his hand on her knee. "Is this okay?"

She nodded.

He moved his hand further up, stopping mid-thigh. "Is this okay?"

"Yes." It was a gentle whisper.

His hand travelled across higher, coming to rest under her sweater at her hip. Her soft stomach brushed the back of his hand. "And this?"

"It's all okay," she said, her voice like velvet.

Thomas dipped, their noses coming close until they breathed the same air, their lips just barely touching. The heat built between them until Thomas was sure that he would combust and it would be all Julia's fault. Just when he couldn't stand another second of the blistering torture, she turned her chin up, and their lips came together.

His hand moved over her curving stomach and reached her soft bra. Desperate to cup her breast, he plunged his hand into her bra. His pointer finger found the hard pebble of her nipple and pinched. She froze, moaning into his mouth. When he applied pressure, the sound became a high whine. The sound made him groan, his cock aching blissfully.

Julia moved, flipping impressively onto all fours. Unbuttoning her jeans, she kicked off her shoes and shimmied her jeans around her ankles. In a flash of white socks and pink cotton panties, she swung a leg clumsily around again to straddle Thomas's lap.

"You're going to kill me," he groaned, his hands braced on her bare thighs.

"That's not the intention." Julia smirked, a waterfall of hair cascading around her shoulders.

He breathed in. Warm vanilla and the night air tickling his lungs. Inching his hands up her legs, he teased her through her underwear with both thumbs. Julia tilted her hips back and forth against him. Pushing aside the thin strip of her cotton underwear, his fingers worked her into a frenzy.

Her fingers tugged to undo his belt. "Is this okay?"

"Yes. And yes, you are definitely going to kill me, Jules."

"Then it will be a good death." Julia's voice was low and coarse, the button of Thomas's pants releasing and zipper purring as she released his hardness. She grabbed him through his briefs and he tipped his head back, moaning.

"Condom?" she asked.

Curling an arm around her waist for stability, Thomas reached for his wallet before he lifted his hips and Julia helped push down his jeans. He hooked the waistband of his briefs, shimmying them down, too. From his wallet he produced the condom he kept there for exactly these kinds of emergencies.

He held the foil wrapper between them. "Are you sure?"

"Yes." It was dark, but there was lightning in her eyes.

Thomas rolled on the condom, and Julia lifted herself up, pushing aside her panties. She bent toward him, using his shoulders for balance, and began to lower herself onto him.

When he first entered her, they both gasped. As she inched down, slowly pulling him all the way inside her, Thomas held her waist, not daring to move himself. Finally, their hips were flush.

They froze. He savored the feeling of being inside her. His thumb worked her sweet spot, as she settled into a steady rhythm.

"Oh fuck, you feel so good." Her hot breath sent goosebumps scattering over his body. She made little excruciating noises in his ear.

A strangled, guttural sound escaped the back of his throat, and Julia laughed, picking up speed with her hips. Thomas increased the pressure of his thumb, eager for her to orgasm before he did.

This was Julia. His *Jules*. The girl he'd loved back in high school, now a full-fledged woman. Real and melting under his touch, controlling her pleasure on him.

"I love the way you're riding me, Jules. So good."

She hummed in response.

Thomas reached around to pull her closer, moving his hips to match her pace. He dug his fingers into her soft, rounded back as their gaze locked, and he knew he was a goner.

She was everything about Starling Hills that he had loved and grew to hate in the end. In some ways, he'd stubbornly clung to their New York City dream, because he knew that she'd given it up. She chose Josh over him, over their dream. Maybe it had just been two naïve kids with silly ideas, but from the moment they hatched the plan, he wanted it. So badly. He wanted it with her, but he couldn't have her, so he went alone.

What would it mean now to give it all up?

What would he gain if he did?

Her eyes flashed, thunder rumbling right down to his core, and he shuddered.

"Don't stop," she demanded. "I'm so close."

"Me too," he whispered the words, and she changed her angle just enough that it pushed him over the brink. "Fuck, I'm coming."

"Oh god, me too." She moaned through it, each wave of pleasure drawing out a new, delicious sound.

When they were both spent, they stopped moving, still joined together. Their heart rates eventually returned to normal.

Julia laced her fingers into his hair, humming along to

the music that still played. Thomas's mind was quiet, empty, as he ran his fingertips up and down her back underneath her sweater.

"This isn't so bad," he whispered against her skin. "This, right here."

This happiness. This bliss.

And he was so, so happy.

TWENTY-ONE
JULIA

JULIA SPENT most of Sunday holed up in her bedroom, daydreaming to music and scribbling notes in her Moleskine journals. She moved back and forth between her laptop and the journal, adding over three thousand words to her 50,000-word total in one day.

By the end of the day, she'd have another story to send to Thomas. She hadn't heard from him today, but she wasn't worried.

The feedback he gave her was great, invaluable. Notes and questions and little word changes. He understood what she was trying to do completely, and she loved that.

She loved smashing together characters from her favorite fandom's head canons and giving them the steamy scenes they never got. The romances and redemptions that didn't always fit the actual canon but were fun and spicy to write.

Oddly enough, as she posted more and more to her Tumblr and Instagram with aesthetically curated snippets, she was slowly creating a little following online. Each like, comment, and reblog from her readers gave her a little shot of dopamine.

Burrowing into her comforter, she smiled to herself, wide and toothy, her heart fluttering. Her daydreaming often led her back to Thomas. There was something so wild and unbelievable about having sex with him. In the back of her Jeep. In a random school parking lot like a couple of teens with nowhere else to go. Something that would have been so awkward between them as teens was now instead so freaking *hot*. Tingles raced over her body and settled low in her pelvis. Her pussy throbbed from being so well-fucked.

But it wasn't just the sex.

Thomas respected her and listened to her. He inspired and encouraged her. And—her stomach flipped—he mentioned moving back to Michigan. Maybe there could be a future between them after all.

Her heart banged inside her chest, still tender, and yet everything looked a little brighter today. Like some kind of magic weaved through the autumn air. She stayed in her cozy pajamas all day, cocooned in her bed, only throwing on a cardigan when she slunk downstairs for dinner.

Sunday dinner. In the past, Julia had been busy on Sundays with Josh's football fanaticism—going to home games and tailgates or hosting parties for away games—so

Sunday family dinner hadn't become a thing until recently.

"Mom's not happy you've been hiding out all day," Heather whispered out of the corner of her mouth as she walked around the table, setting places.

"Whatever." Julia rolled her eyes and grabbed the open bottle of red wine that stood on the table, overfilling one of her mom's crystal glasses.

"Smell's good, Mom," she called into the kitchen with a criminal wink to her sister. Julia nabbed a piece of bread from the basket and ripped it apart, suddenly ravenous.

Heather snorted a laugh out her nose.

"You couldn't have gotten dressed?" Her mom's lips pulled down with the ghost of a frown. "You're a mess."

Julia plopped into a chair and shrugged as her mom flitted around the table with dishes.

"I've just been working upstairs."

"What kind of work are you bringing home now, Julia?" Her dad came into the dining room, a mug of some dark beer clutched in his fist.

"Oh, it's not like work-work, just some writing stuff I'm doing." Julia took a deep drink of her wine.

"Writing? Why are you wasting your day doing that? Maybe there's something more *productive* you can do?" Her mom placed the roast chicken on the table, and her eyelashes fluttered with a delicate roll of her eyes.

Julia didn't respond. Heat chased itself around her

chest. It was just like every other conversation she'd ever had with her parents about writing.

Heather caught her eye across the table, her expression tight and pained. *Sorry*, she mouthed.

The irony was that they'd never shamed Heather for her enduring love of theater or her penchant for costumes. Julia always had to be the responsible one, with a real job right out of college, paying off her loans. Her writing dreams shriveled up and rotted long ago. To them, Heather's hobby was cute and if she spent her time and money on that, it was her choice. Yet, when Julia absorbed Josh's love of sports, to them, it was fine to spend all day Sunday tailgating and at the football games.

Heaven forbid Julia wanted to spend her time writing.

They passed dishes around the table in silence. Julia wondered why they even bothered with family dinners when none of them seemed to truly enjoy the forced bonding time. Not to mention the resentment her mom would hold onto for the rest of the day about cooking all morning, as she would passive-aggressively leave the dishes mounted up for someone else to do after dinner.

The quicker this was over, the better. And if she could get drunk during it, well, then that would be a bonus. Julia drained her glass and grabbed the neck of the wine bottle to refill it, her mom eyeing her under heavy brows.

Julia cleared her throat. "They should announce who gets the promotion this week."

Her dad grunted an endorsement as he fisted a drumstick and ripped the dark meat off with his teeth.

"That's great." Her mom stabbed a forkful of Caesar salad.

"How are you feeling about it?" Heather asked, looking up from her food to make eye contact with Julia.

Julia shrugged, her wine glass clutched in her hand. "I used to want it really badly."

"And now?"

"And now I don't know."

She shrugged. Heather shrugged. Their parents kept eating.

Now working more of her day job didn't seem so desirable. Julia made pretty good money as it was; she didn't need the raise that came with the new title. Her online writing was doing well. Well enough that people asked for more chapters before she had them done or gave her ideas for new pairings she hadn't considered. She valued the engagement from her readers, getting more fulfillment from folks online than her job at Contrakale had given her in years.

"That just seems silly, Julia," her mom said.

Her dad continued attacking his drumsticks, not saying a word.

Julia rolled her eyes and scoffed. "It's not like it's your decision."

Her mom didn't look at Julia as they carried on this

pseudo-conversation, but Heather watched them volley back and forth.

In Julia's sweatpants pockets, her phone vibrated in a ringing pattern. No one called her except for the people around this table. Who was calling her? Probably a spam call. She let it go to voicemail; she wasn't about to back down from this conversation.

"It just doesn't seem worth it to me, losing the work-life balance that I have now to *probably* be more miserable and hate my life more anyway." Julia took a drink from her wine. "It's dumb."

"Well, you're rather flippant all of a sudden about this promotion you've been going after for months." Her mom sniffed.

"I'm actually considering taking some time off work. Taking a leave for a couple weeks or something? Maybe go on a vacation. Get my head back on straight after all this Josh stuff," Julia said.

"Oh, that sounds fun!" Heather said, jumping back into the conversation. "Where to?"

"New York City." As Julia said it, her heart stuttered in her chest. Maybe that meant this was actually a good idea.

"Oh, don't be ridiculous, Julia. A leave? That hardly seems like a good idea," her mom sneered. "I hope this doesn't have anything to do with that Thomas Callaghan being back around again."

The familiar cloud of her mother's disdain settled over Julia, and she concealed the wince she felt in her soul.

Instead, she narrowed her eyes, her hackles immediately raised and readied to fight.

"What are you talking about?" She spit the question.

"Just that you've been very distracted lately and I know you're staying up until God knows what time doing... whatever you're doing." Her mom's fork pinged as she dropped it onto her plate, and she paused before picking it back up again to continue eating.

"I'm not a fucking teenager." Julia dropped her free fist to the table, waving around the wine glass with the other for emphasis. "There's hardly such a thing as being *distracted* from my miserable job. I basically spend my entire work day *trying* to be distracted from it."

"Welcome to being an adult, dear. Did I ever say that it was going to be fun?"

Her mother's simpering tone made Julia want to bare her teeth in rage. She was just about fucking done with this family dinner.

"You certainly seemed to think that it was *fun* with Josh."

"Marrying him would have been fun." Her mom gave her head a little shake.

Julia slammed her glass of wine on the table, two drops splashing over the side. She breathed slow and steady through her nose. "What are you implying?"

Her phone buzzed against her leg. This time, just once. A text.

"Nothing, honey, just the facts." Her mom's head tilted

at a quizzical angle, finally making eye contact with her daughter, as if Julia was the outlandish one here.

"It seems like you're implying that I should have stayed with my dishonest, disgusting ex?"

Heather stared at her plate, not eating, her eyes wide. Julia's dad reached for the other drumstick.

Her mom laughed—a polite little thing that curdled Julia's stomach—but her eyes flashed venom. "Don't twist my words, Julia."

A second vibration from Julia's pocket reminded her of the message waiting for her.

"Gah!" Julia pushed back from the table. "You know what? I'm not hungry."

"You're not excused." Her mom sat up ramrod straight, her eyes wide.

"As we've already covered, I'm not a child. I don't need to be fucking *excused* from the table." Julia downed the rest of her wine and stormed out of the dining room up the stairs.

Slamming her bedroom door, she cringed, realizing the irony of acting exactly like a teenager in this moment. Wasn't she thirty-one? Wasn't she learning to trust herself to make the right choices?

Except for the fact that life fucked with her and now she was stuck here in her parents' house because she literally had nowhere else to go. There was the offer of Heather's couch, but she hardly wanted to crash in a house with four other former thespians who played way too many musical soundtracks. And sang along.

She was just getting back up on her feet. This wasn't forever. She'd be out of here soon.

Right?

She paced around her bedroom and then suddenly remembered her phone buzzing in her pocket.

Missed call from Thomas. *That's weird.* They never called each other. The text was from him too. Her stomach flip-flopped with anticipation as she opened the message.

There, at the bottom of the screen, sat two words that meant Thomas's life would never be the same.

Dad died

TWENTY-TWO
THOMAS

THOMAS STOOD in front of the mirror that hung behind his bedroom door. Tousled curls gelled somewhat into place. Beard that he didn't quite have the energy to tidy up that spread into a pretty impressive neck beard. Bags under his eyes that pulled down toward his cheeks more than usual, betraying the depths of his sorrow. Black suit, white shirt, and a thin black tie.

On a normal day, ties didn't pose an issue. But today, his fingers fumbled, numb from grief just like the rest of him.

His body lamented his loss. From the scratching pain behind his ribs when he breathed to his shoulders that insisted on curling inwards. The blood that circulated through his body came from the hollow space of his chest where his heart once lived. His eyes burned. Mouth twisted.

Dad was dead.

And it hurt so fucking much.

He thought since he knew it was going to happen, had anticipated his death for months, years, that this wouldn't be so bad. Boy, was he wrong.

The man Thomas had idolized his entire life, the strongest man he ever knew, just...gone. Who after squarely beating Thomas in a late-night game of backgammon, just went to sleep and didn't wake up the next morning.

And now—what?—Thomas was still here. The oldest, suddenly the patriarch, who was supposed to take over the restaurant? As if Thomas could ever fill Dad's shoes. Thomas would never be enough compared to his dad. The man he ran away from for years. He built a life without his dad, away from his family.

Now, Thomas realized what a mistake that had been. He knew he could never measure up to his dad.

Thomas slammed one of his useless, blundering hands flat onto the wall. He hung his head, the muscles on the back of his neck tingling from the stretch.

There was a soft knock on his door, and it opened slowly.

"You okay?" Ari whispered, sticking her head around. A rhetorical question at this point, really.

But Thomas nodded. Once, tight.

"I can help you with that." She pointed at his tie with her eyes.

"Thanks," Thomas mumbled. "My fingers just—"

He didn't finish the sentence and instead just flexed his fingers in the air.

"It's fine." She squeezed around the door since Thomas still stood frozen like a six-foot-four statue behind it.

She picked up the ends of the tie, and he dutifully turned toward her as she got to work.

"Are you doing alright?" he asked, in a feeble attempt to be the supportive big brother despite the fact that he was obviously falling apart himself.

"I don't know." She shrugged, her lips wringing into a painful half-frown, half-smile. "Feels weird that Dad's actually gone now. Like an extinguished candle, ya know? Just poof."

Thomas's throat closed up, puffy and painful. He nodded. "Yep."

"I'm not sure it's hit me yet," she whispered, keeping the conversation close, between them. "I'm not really sad. I haven't cried. But just thinking, like, for the rest of my life he won't be here? All those milestones he'll never get to see? That really hurts."

The rest of their lives without Dad. The thought made Thomas dizzy, like he had felt when he and Dad stood on the edge of the Grand Canyon. A never-ending expanse of grief.

Ari tightened his tie and patted his chest. "All done."

In response, Thomas wrapped his little sister in a hug.

"Thanks," he said, resting his chin for a moment on top of her head. Then he released her.

They both turned and looked in the mirror.

"We don't look too bad for a wake, eh?" Ari said with a smile that didn't quite reach her eyes. She wore a long sleeve turtleneck dress, her hair pulled back into a low ponytail.

Thomas gave a noncommittal huff.

"Love you, T," Ari said, giving his hand a little squeeze.

He squeezed back. "Love you too."

And Ari slipped out the door.

Thomas prowled his room in an attempt to work off his agitated energy without much success. On his bookcase, he spied the flask his dad had given him for his twenty-first birthday. Something fancy and expensive that he never really had a use for. Until today. He grabbed the thing and shuffled all the way down into the basement where his family stashed the extra liquor. Thomas didn't want his mom to see him filling up the flask.

His dad had always been a Scotch man, before the cancer and he lost his taste for alcohol. Seemed like the perfect booze to drink today. Thomas browsed through the labels, looking for his dad's favorite.

The last basement stair creaked, and he looked to see Danny creeping around the corner.

"Ah, great minds," Danny said, shaking his matching flask.

Danny looked far more put together than Thomas,

with his face shaved smooth and his white shirt clearly ironed. Damn, why hadn't Thomas thought to iron his shirt?

"Showing me up," Thomas said, waving a hand up and down. Danny even had on cuff links.

His brother snorted. "Not like it's hard, man."

"Alright, that's fair." Thomas smirked. Danny always dressed more stylishly than Thomas when he finally changed out of his gym shorts.

"So, it's a Lagavulin kind of day, I guess," Danny said, frowning at the bottles. It only took him a couple seconds to search out Dad's favorite and grab the unopened fifth.

They carefully filled their flasks and then held them out to each other.

"To Dad," Thomas said, and Danny echoed him.

The whiskey burned like a bonfire all the way down, leaving Thomas with a mossy taste on the nose. He imagined if Scotland had a taste, this must be it.

"Dad never did get to Ireland, did he?" Danny asked, pursing his lips.

Though he preferred Scotch, Dad had always dreamed of seeing where his great-grandparents came from before they immigrated to Detroit in the 1930s.

"No, he didn't." The thought shattered Thomas's heart.

"Hey, maybe we could go? All of us kids and Mom?" Danny took another sip from his flask.

"That's a great idea. I'm sure she'd love it," Thomas

said, though his words were devoid of any enthusiasm. Plans for the future seemed so unattainable right now.

Danny eyed his older brother then clapped him on the arm. "We're gonna be okay, you know?"

Thomas nodded, the corners of his lips pulling into an involuntary frown.

"Yeah," he sighed the word out, deflating like a two-day-old balloon, once again feeling like a pathetic caricature of the oldest sibling.

Upstairs the doorbell rang and their mom's modest heels clapped across the hardwood as she went to answer it.

"I guess we shouldn't leave Mom to handle everyone on her own," Thomas said, lifting his eyes to the ceiling.

"Nope. Can't hide out in the liquor cave forever, as fun as that sounds," Danny said, elbowing his brother.

They tucked their flasks in the same pocket in the inside of their respective suit coats and trudged upstairs to greet the guests.

* * *

IT DIDN'T TAKE LONG for the house to fill up. Thomas's mom wanted to host the wake at the house before the official funeral in a couple of days. Tons of family, friends, people from Callaghan's Coney Island and his first career at the General Motors plant were there to celebrate Dad. Dramatic flower arrangements, casserole dishes of all shapes and sizes, and at least one Honey Baked Ham came through the door. They wouldn't need to cook for at least a week.

His aunt immediately sucked him into conversation, and Thomas didn't even get a chance to take a breath. He had dull mask shuttered in place as everyone chatted with him. They all shared their favorite memory of his dad, all taking turns pouring Scotch and other assorted drinks at their bar cart in his honor.

But there was only one person he wanted to see and he hadn't spotted her yet. Maybe Julia wasn't there? They hadn't texted much since Dad died, since he was so busy with the arrangements that he didn't want Mom to face alone. But he made sure to text Julia the details of today, eager to see her, to touch her, to have her by his side for this. There was no one else he could imagine supporting him through it all.

So where was she?

But then someone brought dishes into the kitchen, and the swinging door that separated the kitchen from the living room opened and closed. Opened and closed. A twisted kind of stop-start animation.

And there she was. At the sink, in her sleeveless black velvet dress and black tights without shoes, up to her elbows in sudsy water. His lips parted, caught off guard seeing Julia doing the dishes in his family's kitchen and surprised that she was in the house and he didn't even know. His knees went weak, and he leaned back against the couch to steady himself.

Thomas's mom came up next to him and folded her soft arms over her stomach.

"She showed up early and shooed me right out of the kitchen, insisting on doing all the work."

He didn't say anything, just watched Julia, hyper-aware of every single tingling atom in his body, as the swinging door slowed and then stayed closed.

"She's a keeper, that one." His mom nodded to the door.

Thomas turned to Mom and opened his mouth, but she cut him off.

"I know, I know. I shouldn't say things like that, but I'm sentimental today. So sue me." She grinned coyly at her oldest son.

Though Thomas's insides gnawed him hollow, his mom appeared surprisingly chipper. He furrowed his brows. "How are you doing, Mom?"

"You know? I'm okay." She huffed, heavy and loud. "Ask me again in a week. But today I'm okay."

Mom smiled at him, the kind of comforting Mom-smile that said so much without any words at all. And Thomas knew what Danny had said was true: they were going to be okay. Maybe not today. Maybe not next week. But eventually, they'd be okay.

Then he and Mom both got sucked into conversations in opposite directions.

Thomas heard a lot of good stories about his dad, mostly ones he heard many times before but loved to hear again. Memories from his cousins about growing up as poor, second generation Irish immigrants in Detroit. How moving out of Detroit as a kid meant their family moved to a trailer park. Stories of his time working on the assembly line. How he helped out with the union there, too.

"He made the best coffee of anyone I know."

"Always had the perfect piece of dating advice for the kids."

"I never did beat him in backgammon."

"His pancakes? Chef's kiss."

Once Thomas knew Julia was there, he felt where she was at all times. Like a compass, his awareness pulled toward her, searching for his true north. She flitted around as part of the background, going in and out of the kitchen as the visitors filtered around. She cleared dishes and filled drinks. Set out more food and kept the little kids from knocking over the flowers. When he caught a glimpse of her in the kitchen, she was portioning and freezing leftovers. Emptying and refilling the dishwasher. She took care of everything with impressive ease and grace.

His conversations kept him busy enough that he didn't have a chance to say a word to her. But whenever she looked at him, their eyes met. Held across the room between the guests and over the flowers, casseroles, and the bottles of liquor. He didn't smile, didn't wave, just rested his eyes on her, drinking her in. She held him with her gaze, conveying so much without saying a word. The gravity of her magnetized him.

He couldn't imagine losing Julia again.

Watching her now, it seemed impossible that anything had ever come between them. Impossible that anything would ever again.

It wasn't until hours later, when Julia stood at the kitchen sink all alone, that Thomas pressed a heavy hand to her lower back. Her heat radiated through her dress, and she melted right into his touch.

"Thank you." Thomas curled around her, his mouth nearly flush with her cheek as his voice rumbled low.

He slid his hand along her back, grasping onto her waist, as all of his nerve endings crackled. When she turned, her back flush with the counter, her mouth popped open soundlessly.

His hands grasped the counter on either side of her body. Though ample space yawned between them, he pushed her back toward the counter, not so much with his weight but with his presence. She hooked her thumbs through his belt loops, her hands still wet from the dishes and upper lip sprinkled with sweat.

"Thank you," he repeated, "for being here for my family. You know Dad loved you." His voice nearly cracked at the end.

Thomas's heart clenched as they stared into each

other's eyes. She swallowed, throat jumping, but otherwise didn't move. Suddenly, he couldn't hold himself up anymore, and he collapsed into her, nuzzling his head under her chin. Her arms wrapped around him, and he fell even more into her, his ribs expanding and contracting with each breath.

"You're welcome. Of course. There's nowhere else I'd be," she whispered into his hair.

They stood there clasped, frozen in space, somersaulting deeper into intimacy.

He pulled back, rubbing a hand over his beard, his eyes burning into her. "Let's get out of here."

"And go where?" She crossed her arms, as he stepped back, leaving space between them, but his hand was still on her waist. "There are still people here and cleaning up to do."

"Everyone's leaving. My aunts can finish." He looked over his shoulder. "Let me just go talk to Mom."

He slipped his hand from her body and instantly missed her warmth under his touch.

His mom sat with the aunts in the living room. They sipped Bailey's and coffee.

"Yes, get out of here, go go," she shooed him. "Julia's done enough today already, that girl! Bless her."

He ran to his room, hanging up his suit coat and grabbing a plaid blazer for Julia to wear over her dress, preferring to see her in his clothes than whatever jacket she brought. At the front door, he picked up her flats and her purse from the coat closet.

"We're good to go," he said, waltzing back into the kitchen.

"You want me to just stop what I'm doing?" She held up her hands, pruny from the washing.

He didn't answer. Instead, he held open the blazer to her, and a blush creeped over her cheeks.

She stepped into her shoes, and turned, slipping into the jacket. As he slid the sleeves up her arms, time slowed. His fingers dragged along her bare arms, his warm breath on her neck. Goosebumps appeared on her skin.

The last time he breathed her in this close, they were in the back of her Jeep, just last week, as they came one right after another. He swallowed and lightning flashed over his skin, causing his desire to spike. Neither of them spoke until the jacket was all the way on, and then Julia turned to him. Thomas cleared his throat.

"Yeah, it's fine." His eyes darted left and right, and he jangled car keys in his hands. "They've got it covered."

"Hey, are you okay?" Julia stepped toward him and reached for his hand. He gripped her fingers tight like iron. "We've barely talked at all today. You don't...look good."

Thomas snorted through his nose and shrugged. Yet his eyes darted around the room, wild, not meeting hers. "I don't know what I'm feeling, Julia. Dad's gone, and today's been a lot. I don't really want to talk about it right now. I just want to take you away from here and keep drinking. Maybe get some nachos?"

"You're hungry? Haven't you been eating all day?"

"Not a damn thing." His eyes landed on their hands, and he rubbed his thumb along the inside of Julia's wrist, the friction sending fire down his spine. "Too much talking."

"Alright, well I'm driving." She tapped the outline of the flask now in his pants pocket. "I know you've been drinking. You reek of whiskey."

He pulled it out and took a swig. "You caught me." With the flask back in his pocket, he turned her around, grabbing her shoulders. "Come on, let's go before Ari catches on and begs to come along. I know you don't want to bring her too."

"Yeah, she is not coming to any bars with us. I will not be the one to corrupt that little angel."

Thomas snorted. "She's hardly an angel."

Julia's mouth dropped open in faux offense, the tension breaking just slightly between them. "Don't you dare speak ill of your sister! I say she's an angel, so she's an angel."

"Whatever you say, kid." He pushed past her, heading out the back door. "Let's go, I'm thirsty."

TWENTY-THREE
JULIA

IT HAPPENED to be Friday so Betty's Billiards Bar in downtown Starling Hills was crowded. They managed to get a table at the edge of the room, tucked into just a sliver of shadow—the corner with the worst lighting in the whole place. A beer sign glowed green, casting rippling neon ghosts over Thomas's white shirt and suspender get-up, highlighting the deep furrow of his impressive brows and imploring eyes. Everything about him just looked so heavy.

But Thomas wanted to play pool. So they would.

"You know I'm shit at pool, right?" Julia grabbed the cue stick and rubbed blue chalk on the end.

"Excellent, because I'm a shark." Thomas drank his Scotch on the rocks and narrowed his eyes at Julia. "Should we make it interesting?"

"Interesting?"

"A bet."

"Another bet? Isn't one enough?"

"Oh, that 50,000-word bet? Yeah, I passed that like last week, Jules, just didn't want to tell you. Thought it might make you bitter and not want to hang out with me." Thomas looked serious under heavily lidded eyes as he chalked his cue.

Julia's jaw dropped open. "You're joking."

"No way. I'm a *professional*, remember? Writer's block can't hold me back." He leaned back against the pool table with a playful grin.

"Granted, all 50,000 of those words were extremely painful to write, and my relationship with writing at the moment isn't what I'd call healthy, but I did it."

"Oh my god!" Julia laughed. "Okay, first of all, you sound like an asshole."

"But you like it," Thomas growled.

Julia's mouth dropped open at his blatant flirting, ignoring how her stomach absolutely flipped at his words.

"And second of all, here I've been busting my ass, and you've completely lapped me." She stuck her tongue out at him, and Thomas laughed wryly, his mouth quirking in a delicious way. "Well, congratulations. You're a seriously impressive and very professional writer."

She stepped toward Thomas, and he palmed her lower back, pulling her between his legs where they spread out from his perch against the table. Julia stumbled into him, but she braced herself on his thighs, fingers splayed for more purchase.

His muscles jumped under her touch. Thomas wasn't laughing anymore. He studied her.

"Thank you, seriously, for everything today." His words melted into one another. "You owe me a burrito, though."

Julia flicked her eyes up to meet his, the laughter dying on her tongue at the seriousness of his gaze. This close, she memorized the different shades of brown in his eyes, from umber to russet. Julia never wanted to forget the way that they glittered when Thomas looked at her.

During the wake, one of his great aunts had grabbed Julia's wrist, the elder woman's skin cool and soft against hers.

"You're Thomas's girlfriend?" she said, her eyes crinkling as she smiled.

She caught Julia completely off guard. "Oh no, we're just friends."

Which is exactly what they were. Not even a sort of *thing*. They couldn't be.

"My late husband and I were just friends once, too. Celebrated our sixtieth wedding anniversary just before he passed," the great aunt crowed. "I've seen the way Thomas looks at you, honey. I wouldn't be so sure on the just friends part."

Julia's cheeks flushed now at the memory, heat settling low in her pelvis.

Maybe this was what that woman meant.

This look that burned into her. *This* was how he looked at her. A way that held her. Accepting every odd little thing about her. Who was she before Thomas came back into her life? He stripped her bare under this gaze. She shivered, a pleasant prickle coursing through her veins. Every fiber in her body screamed to trust *this* look.

"You're welcome," Julia said, and then dipped closer to his ear. "I'm so going to kick your ass in pool."

She twirled away from him, wanting to keep him distracted tonight. Not thinking about his dad or his publishing contract. She didn't want to think about him leaving. Now that his dad was dead, he would leave Starling Hills just like he planned, destined to return to his regular life in New York City.

"Okay, I can't decide if you're hustling me or not." Thomas rearranged the balls in the rack.

"There's only one way to find out." Julia beamed from across the table.

She, in her black velvet dress, and he in his white shirt and tie, both overdressed for Betty's Billiards Bar. She imagined they'd just come from a black-tie affair instead of a wake. He'd left his coat at home, his glorious suspenders on full display. He was unbearably sexy, even though his eyes held more sadness than usual.

"Wanna break then?" Thomas twirled the cue ball in one hand and sipped Scotch with the other.

"You bet."

He rolled the ball across the table. Julia lined up the shot with extra showmanship. She pulled her cue back and let it fly, the cue ball spinning erratically until it connected with the rack, sending the balls zigzagging across the table. None of them seemed to be moving purposefully toward any pocket. But just as she was about to give up hope, one striped ball tipped lazily over the edge into a pocket.

"Would you look at that." Julia bent to line up her next shot.

Thomas tracked her, his eyes leaving a trail of fire behind.

Julia hit the cue ball a little too hard, and it jumped off the table.

"Oops," she giggled.

"Okay, so not a shark? Lucky first shot?" Thomas picked up the ball from the ground.

Julia shrugged. "What can I say? I like playing pool. I'm just terrible at it."

She took a sip of her neat Scotch as she watched Thomas setting up his turn. With his shirt sleeves rolled over his elbows, his forearms flexed under the table lights. His eyebrows pulled seriously low as he considered the angle. Julia's heart rate ratcheted up a couple of notches.

But then someone laughed, loud and pompous across the bar. Heat raced up her back and over her scalp.

She knew that laugh.

Don't look. If you don't look, you won't know for sure.

She had to look. Julia needed the confirmation that he was there, that she wasn't making him up. Turning, her eyes scanned across the bar, landing on Josh, surrounded by a handful of his dudebro friends.

Thomas cracked the balls on the table. She wasn't paying attention to him anymore, but distantly heard him call her name. Gripping her rocks glass, she stared at Josh across the room. Her ribs squeezed her lungs. Julia could barely breathe.

Then Thomas was beside her. "Jules? Are you okay?"

"Uhm." She wet her lips. The booze in her stomach roiled. "It's Josh."

She just stared, and Thomas followed her gaze.

"That fucker." Thomas cracked his knuckles and stormed away.

"Thomas! Wait, what are you doing?" Julia ran after him, but Thomas got there before her.

Josh looked up in surprise, eyebrows high, as Thomas caused a commotion, plowing his way through their group. He barely got out any words as he made his way to Josh, just incoherent grunts.

Josh's eyes held no recognition. There wouldn't be. He didn't know Thomas in high school and wouldn't deign to remember him now. Everything happened so fast that Josh's friends didn't have time to mobilize. Thomas pulled back a fist as Julia shouted.

"Thomas!"

His concentration unbroken, her voice instead caught

Josh's attention, and his eyes flitted off Thomas, landing on Julia. They went wide, comically all white.

It was just the opening that Thomas needed. His punch landed squarely on Josh's chin, and his friends all *oohed*, taking a step back from the action.

"That's for Julia, you son of a bitch," Thomas growled, gearing up for another punch. But he stumbled, losing his balance, giving Josh the extra time he needed to recover.

A menacing glint flashed in Josh's eyes as he wound up. Julia screamed as Josh's fist hit perfectly, using Thomas's inertia to send him to the ground. Josh lifted his foot, ready to kick him in the ribs.

Before she could think twice, Julia launched herself over Thomas and grabbed onto Josh's shoulders, yanking away his attention. For a second that passed in slow motion, their eyes locked and Julia's pent-up rage and hatred exploded from her. She channeled that energy into her leg. Which she brought directly up into his groin.

The crowd collectively hissed and winced, as Josh doubled over.

"Don't touch him again!" Julia yelled and dropped to her knees. "Are you hurt, Thomas? Can you walk?"

Thomas half moaned, half whined, but started to move to his feet.

"Come on, let's get out of here."

Josh's friends circled around him, and the rest of the crowd didn't pay Julia and Thomas any attention as they slipped out the back door.

* * *

THOMAS FUMBLED with the keys to the back door in the darkness. The back porch light hadn't been left on. Julia fished her phone from her purse, fingers brushing her lipstick and a foil condom wrapper she'd slipped in there after Theatre Bizarre, and turned on the phone's flashlight. She aimed it at the lock, though Thomas still struggled, his fingers shaking.

"Let me." Julia grabbed his hand and steadied it. Despite her heart pounding against her sternum, the key slid into place.

They stumbled through the door and into the kitchen in the dark, the only light coming from a fluorescent under-microwave lamp. Thomas laughed, an uncontrollable giggle building in his chest, and he pulled Julia along behind him.

"Shh! You're going to wake up your mom," she chided him.

He spun around the kitchen, teetering on his feet. Julia clenched her jaw. The alcohol combined with the adrenaline of his fight with Josh sent Thomas careening toward mania.

She crossed the room to the freezer for some frozen vegetables for his eye. Peas.

"You need to calm down." She handed him the frozen veggies.

"I don't." But he leaned against the counter and put

the bag against his eye, grinning at Julia like a demented pirate.

In the half dark, he was still the shy new kid Julia met at the *Les Mis* wrap-party when they were both sixteen. Except that there were fourteen years in between and the shadows cut his face in sharp relief, reminding Julia of each second of those years gone by.

She narrowed her eyes and shook her head, trying to clear the memories before she fell in too deep.

"Your lip is split too." There was a trail of dried blood down his chin.

"I think that's from when I fell on the floor," he laughed, touching his lip gingerly.

"How rude of the floor," Julia snorted. "Hold on, I'm going to find some rubbing alcohol."

The floor print of the Callaghan house was burned into her brain, and she made it to their linen closet in the pitch dark. The house was silent under the hush of the moon, ghosts of shadows lurking in the corners. Julia rummaged for the first aid supplies by the dim light of her cell phone. When she padded back to the kitchen, Thomas was humming but still dutifully holding the frozen peas to his eye.

"You're a mess." Julia's voice pitched lower than intended.

The corner of Thomas's mouth pulled into a smile as his eyes burned into hers. "But I was fighting for your honor."

"Yeah, well." Julia rolled her eyes. "Exactly like the plot of a romantic comedy."

"That's me, your hero."

He was joking when he said it, but Julia's stomach actually fluttered. *Oh my god.*

She stepped toward him with a gauze soaked for cleaning.

"This is going to hurt." She pulled her lower lip between her teeth, bracing herself, as if it was going to hurt her too.

"I know," he whispered, and her stomach tensed.

Thomas dropped the peas from his face, both hands bracing on the counter, and inhaled loudly through his nose. As the gauze touched his lips, his eyes fluttered shut and he exhaled.

Time stood still. It was just them in his silent childhood home. The home haunted by their memories and the ghost of his dad and their dreams. The clock in the kitchen ticked slowly, keeping the pace, a metronome that mirrored her heartbeat thudding through her veins. For a wild moment, everything was inescapably perfect, bittersweet in its torment.

As she dabbed around his wound, she felt his eyes on her though she concentrated specifically on cleaning his lip. She tried not to think about how close they were. About the heat building between them.

And then, just as Julia thought she imagined his warmth coming closer, Thomas's hand connected with her thigh, right at the hem of her dress. His fingers splayed wide, taking up as much thigh real estate as possible through her tights. Her mouth fell open as heat spread through her body from underneath his fingertips.

"Is this okay?" he rasped, raw with feeling.

Julia thought she might break, shatter into a million pieces right on the floor. But she couldn't, because she still needed to be the strong one right now. She couldn't speak, so she nodded. Whether this was a good idea or not was a question that she couldn't answer at almost three in the morning, but it was what she wanted. And Julia needed an outlet for everything that she kept locked up tightly, too.

She swallowed hard. "Are you okay?"

Thomas rested his forehead against hers, his whiskey-tinged breath filling the space between them.

"Yes," he ground out, rough as stone.

With the blood cleaned off his chin, Julia's fingertips grazed his lips. She took another step closer as his hand traveled under her dress, over her tights and the curves of her thigh, hips, until he found the bare skin above her waistband. His fingers tucked over the band, searching for more purchase.

She gasped at his touch, her dress bunched over his arm. He laughed, a devilish thing, before his other arm shot around her back and pulled her even closer. His eyes scorched into her depths, dark pools of longing.

Julia dropped everything from her hands onto the counter, her palms coming to rest on his strong forearms.

She ran her fingertips over his bare arms, through the hair, then grabbed a small handful in each fist and gave a tug.

Now he gasped. "That was unexpected."

She quirked an eyebrow. "I'm full of surprises."

His laugh rumbled in his chest more than out loud as he laced a hand into Julia's hair, cradling her skull before running his hand down around the curve of her jaw and under her chin, lifting her lips toward him. Thomas's tongue snaked along his lips, and desire flickered through her body. Julia bit her lip, knowing what inevitably came next.

This quiet moment, standing in the kitchen with only silence between them, crackled like a live wire. She took a breath, and her chest shuddered. The need for release built between them.

They inched toward each other, and she closed her eyes. His lips brushed gently against hers, warm and rough. After first contact, a hunger took over both of them, and they kissed messily, sloppily. Julia's fingers entwined with his beard, and his hands pulled her hips flush to his. Thomas's tongue pushed in her mouth, and she sighed against it.

They stopped kissing for a moment, just to breathe, and Thomas picked her up. She giggled as her legs wrapped instinctually around his waist. Thomas's hands supported her on her bare back under her dress, and she trusted him to hold her weight. Her warmth pressed up against his stomach. His belt rubbed sensuously through her tights.

"Can I take you to my bedroom?" Thomas breathed.

Her arms encircled his neck. "Yes."

It was clumsy, him walking down the hall and carrying her. His thighs hit the bottom of her ass, bouncing her along. Julia's fingers laced into his hair at the nape of his neck.

At first Thomas still laughed, smiled. The adrenaline and the joy of this moment a powerful tonic for his grief. But as they got closer to his room, he grew quiet.

His eyes tracked to his dad's chair, his brow darkening, and Julia knew Thomas was thinking about him.

Now in his room, he set Julia down. She stood and watched him pace a small circle around his childhood bedroom. Still the same wallpaper, the same massive bookcase stuffed with books, old journals, and DVDs. Vintage movie posters plastered on the walls. It was the same as it had always been, but now they were different. Lifetimes away from their younger selves who still had big dreams.

And then life got in the way. Those years between pulled them apart and flung them back together at high velocity.

The fire of the moment before was all but extinguished, and Thomas sat on the edge of his bed.

When he put his head into his hands, his shoulders heavy, she sat down on the bed next to him. There were no words to say. The fire from moments before doused under the shroud of grief.

Instead, Julia pulled his shoulders under her arm in a side hug, the only thing she could do. He crumpled into her chest, and she cradled him there.

He pulled back, his face glistening with tracks of tears. "It hurts so much, Julia."

"I know it does." She rubbed a thumb across his cheek. "I know."

Thomas's eyes were still the same, wide and pining, as when they were younger. As if the years hadn't passed and they were still the same best friends that they were in high school. Julia bloomed fresh and innocent here with him. She was who she wanted to be when she was with Thomas. He didn't laugh at her or belittle her. She was free to be herself.

He nuzzled his cheek into her hand, kissing her palm. "Thank you for being here."

She locked onto his gaze. "I wouldn't be anywhere else right now."

When their lips met again, his wet cheeks brushed hers. Their kiss roared with hunger and pure need. Full of sadness and loneliness. All of their hurts laid bare between them.

Thomas pushed her shoulders back onto the bed, and Julia scooted up toward the pillows. She pulled his suspenders so that he followed, chasing her up to the head of the bed.

Everything was hard, vibrating. The tension between them, the years, the memories, all iced with sorrow and loss.

She pushed her hand under a suspender. "Is this okay?" asking him for permission like he did for her.

"Please," he whispered, a confirmation and a prayer.

Once they were off his shoulders, Julia slowly undid the buttons on his shirt one by one. Then reversed the button and the zipper of his trousers and pushed his pants below his ass. He shimmied the rest of the way out of them, his boxer briefs bulging and tight against his erection. Thomas's hands found the waistband of her tights once more, but this time he pulled them down, helping them off. They popped off her feet at the end. They peeled off the rest of each remaining piece of clothing, an intense amount of skin-on-skin contact building friction between them.

Propped up against the headboard, Julia spread her legs, and Thomas's fingers entered her without much preamble. He groaned as he slid two fingers in up to his hand with ease.

"Julia," he whimpered, inching closer to her. His erection brushed her thigh.

She sighed and opened wider as his thumb caressed her most sensitive spots. He bit her lip as she reached down and grabbed his hardness.

"I've wanted you for so long," he confessed as he nibbled Julia's ear lobe.

The memory of what happened last time he tongued her ear lobe sent sparks of heat cascading down her spine.

"Me too," she said, the truth tumbling out. She arched her hips up and Thomas swelled in her fist. She bit her lower lip, wanting to be closer to him. She wanted all of him. Her voice came out as a whimper. "Thomas, fuck me."

He didn't need to be asked twice. His weight shifted above her as he rolled on a condom, his forehead resting against hers. Despite it all, he hadn't stopped crying, but she didn't say anything. Julia cupped his neck, as sweat and tears all became the same on her chest.

When he entered her, they both shuddered. Julia moaned and cried as each stroke lodged deeper into her. Closer and closer to the truth of her.

She took his tears with the pleasure, both of them building until his hot breath tickled her neck right below her ear. It was this sensation that put her over the edge. With her ankles locked around him, she came quietly and spectacularly, melting into the bed underneath him.

Thomas's orgasm followed closely after, his moans of pleasure almost breaking under the strain of grief. When he collapsed next to her, his arm draped over her chest, keeping her close.

They didn't talk. They just stayed like that with Thomas's tears drying on her skin, until Julia finally fell asleep.

TWENTY-FOUR
THOMAS

THOMAS LAY IN HIS BED, breathing slowly in and out in tandem with Julia's soft snores. He started out on his side, one arm over her chest, cupping her left breast as she lay on her back. Eventually, their heat dissipated into the room and he pulled the duvet over them both. He thought maybe he could fall asleep like this.

But his brain never quieted. Though he'd acclimated to the silence of his parents' house, his mind still had a hard time slowing down.

And how was he supposed to calm down after this? This love making? There was nothing else to call it. The sensual rhythm that built between them and knocked down the final wall Thomas had built between himself and Starling Hills—and all the familial strings that came attached with it.

Between himself and Julia.

Himself and his happiness.

Eventually he rolled onto his back, his mind running...running. He stared at the ceiling with one major thought looping through his mind...

With Julia curled up naked against his side, sleep never came, and eventually the morning light turned blue. Slowly it became a reasonable hour to make breakfast.

Thomas pulled on navy gym shorts and a black t-shirt, picking his way through their funeral blacks scattered around his room. Julia nuzzled into his pillows, deeper under the covers, her hair strewn everywhere. Hopefully her vanilla scent would stay behind on his sheets. He couldn't believe the sight of her naked in his bed. If he thought about it too long, he'd get hard again, so he slipped from his bedroom and padded down the hall to the bathroom.

Overnight, his eye had turned a stunning shade of purple. His split lip dried and cracked. But punching Josh out had been worth it. Something he dreamed of doing since his first drink with Julia a couple weeks ago.

Though Julia got her retribution, too. From his spot curled on the ground, Thomas had an upside-down view of Julia nailing the asshole in the crotch. That made the whole situation downright pleasant.

Of course, the sex afterward was even better.

Thomas couldn't believe what had blossomed between the two of them. It made him so undeniably happy; he could actually see a future for himself that wasn't just a miserable, lonely slog.

He knew what he needed to do.

First, he would make breakfast. Then, talk to Mom. And finally talk to Julia. Tell them both about the decision that he made. And maybe, just maybe, talk about the future he hoped for between him and Julia.

Thomas got to work on Dad's secret pancake recipe, one of the first recipes his dad had taught him all those years ago. Callaghan's used the same pancake recipe, consistently the most popular breakfast item on their menu. People raved about them, coming from neighboring towns just to have them on the weekend. Cooking was one of the first things he and Dad loved to do together. This was before Thomas could really understand the rules of backgammon. But he could definitely understand licking the batter off of the hand mixer's beaters.

So as a little five-year-old, Thomas stood on a chair, the too-long white cook's apron wrapped three times around his waist, as his dad measured out the ingredients and Thomas dutifully stirred it all together with a wooden spoon. The memories burned in his chest, searing him right through like the morning sunrise cutting through the curtains.

Thomas spooned a dollop of ricotta cheese into the mixing bowl: the secret ingredient to make the pancakes just right. From the cupboard, he pulled the cinnamon, shaking a healthy amount into the bowl, as well. They didn't use the cinnamon at the diner. But at home, Thomas loved to make this snickerdoodle version of Dad's pancakes.

Bacon sizzled in the oven. Coffee dripped through the Chemex. The sun shined, and the leaves rustled, and Thomas more than half expected his dad to shuffle into the kitchen in hunt of a steaming cup of coffee.

Thomas exhaled the gnawing pain through his nose, clenching his fist around the spatula as the griddle pan sizzled with butter.

He sipped his black coffee. The whole house still slept. The quiet was—oddly enough—extremely satisfying. It gave him some time to digest the house as it would be now, without Dad.

Thomas's chest took on the familiar hollow, heavy feeling. The same one he'd begun to associate with going back to New York. The feeling that had always haunted him, but he couldn't name it until he was far enough away to truly examine it. To turn it over in his hand like a stone he found on the shores of Lake Michigan as a kid.

Was it a symptom of his anxiety? Or depression maybe?

Whatever it was, it wasn't good. And in Starling Hills, that feeling ebbed.

He plated up some golden pancakes, placing a little pat of butter between each, and doused the stack with maple syrup. On the breakfast tray, he also put a mug of sweetened coffee and two rashers of bacon. Perfect.

After putting everything else in the oven to keep warm, he picked up the tray and walked down the hall, knocking lightly on the bedroom door before entering.

"Oh," he said, surprised to see Mom awake, sitting upright and reading on her Kindle. Fresh, cool November air blew through the open window, stretching the gauzy curtains into the room.

"You didn't think I'd be able to sleep through the smell of bacon, did you?" She smiled, her eyes crinkling. "This is so sweet, Thomas, you didn't have to—"

She paused, getting a closer look at him as he situated the tray over his mom's lap.

"—and what is going on with your eye?" she asked, abruptly switching topics. "Is that a black eye? Have you been fighting, Thomas? You're thirty years old and the head of this house now. I can't have you—" She would have continued as she grabbed a piece of bacon and took a huge bite, but this time Thomas cut her off.

"Mom, it's alright. Relax." He ran a hand through his hair, pushing it back off his forehead as he sat down on the bed. "Yes, I got in a fight. It was…important. I don't plan on making a habit out of it."

He swallowed, pulling one leg half up on the bed in front of him.

Mom clicked her tongue. But then she took a sip of

coffee, and her demeanor changed instantly, humming her approval.

"And anyway, I couldn't sleep so I made breakfast." He jazz-handed to the tray over his mom's lap.

He cleared his throat, remembering what had kept him up so late. Or rather, who.

"Julia's here. She spent the night," he said.

Mom choked on her coffee, her eyes widening. "She did? I know Dad and I pushed that a little bit but...you're happy about this?"

Thomas nodded, his throat suddenly dry. "Happier than I've been in a long time."

"Dad always liked her." Mom's eyes turned starry. "We just want you to be happy."

"I am. Honestly. For the first time in a long time, I truly am." He looked toward the ceiling, stretching out his neck. It felt good to say out loud. "And there's something else I wanted to talk to you about."

"Oh? Breakfast wasn't just a nice favor you did for your mom? There are strings attached to this stack of perfect pancakes?" She smiled crookedly and put down her utensils, giving him her full attention. "Let's hear it."

Thomas's pulse bounded through his veins. Blood rushed in his ears.

"I'm going to move back to Starling Hills."

Saying the words, admitting it to himself and his mom for the first time out loud, transmuted the last of the stagnant energy tucked into the darkest corner of his ribs. He found he could truly breathe now. Tears leaked from Mom's wide eyes as Thomas exhaled.

"But I want to talk about some conditions," he said. "Dad and I were figuring it out, but we didn't get it settled."

Thomas started the conversation during their last backgammon game. Before Dad went to sleep and didn't wake up. The memory of relief plain on his dad's face crowded Thomas's mind like fog.

Mom nodded, encouraging him to continue.

Thomas's hands shook in his lap. "My writing career comes first. It needs to. That's still my dream. If I'm not going to be killing myself to make New York's godforsaken rent, then I want to have more time to write than I did there."

"Okay," Mom said, letting him continue.

"I'll help out with the restaurant, and I want to. But I don't want to do it full time." He laced his fingers together. "Would you continue as you have through Dad's illness as owner and acting manager? We can work out a schedule for me. And a wage. I can do all the odd jobs, fill in on the schedule, help out with the bookkeeping behind the scenes. But I need my focus to be writing right now."

Mom sniffed, pulling a tissue from the sleeve of her fuzzy robe. "You talked to Dad about this?"

"Started to. We never got to finalize it. We ran out of time."

Mom blew her nose loudly into the tissue. "We never wanted you to give up your dream."

Thomas smiled, his hand ruffling his beard.

"Okay." He nodded, his head bobbing seemingly of its own accord.

Mom reached out and grabbed his hand, giving it a squeeze. "I'm so happy."

"Me too." He squeezed back. "There're some things I need to wrap up in the city, but I think I can be back here full time after the New Year. Do you think you can make it work until then?"

"It's November already. As long as Danny and Ari are able to keep helping out, I think we'll be totally fine until after the New Year."

Thomas looked down at his hands. "I'll talk to them. Make sure everyone's on the same page."

The Dad-shaped hole in their lives would never be truly filled, but maybe it would get smaller over time. Stepping into his shoes, committing to the family in this way, felt right. Kismet.

"And what about Julia?" his mom asked. "Does she know yet?"

Thomas's pulse jumped, ticking time next to his jaw. "No, I haven't told her yet. I wanted to tell you first, make sure you and I agreed before...before I say anything to her."

"And?" Mom raised her eyebrows.

"And I'm going to tell her now." Thomas's lungs

pumped like when it took him a minute to catch his breath after climbing up his seven-floor walk-up.

Mom leaned over and squeezed Thomas's knee. "I'm proud of you, you know that?"

"Thanks," he said.

On an actual fucking cloud of bliss, powered by purpose and fate and destiny all coming together in some kind of otherworldly way he'd always written for his characters but never believed he'd actually achieve for himself, Thomas breezed from his mom's room.

Thomas whirled around the kitchen table, setting it for four, because maybe by the time he got Julia back down here, his siblings would be awake and ready for breakfast. They stayed over last night, too, after the wake. Maybe they'd beat Thomas and Julia down, depending on how long the conversation would take with her, and the table would be ready for them. Either way, he wanted to tell Julia his news in private, like he had his mom.

So, he poured a cup of coffee and grabbed a perfect piece of bacon and damn near floated down the hall. He reached for the doorknob as his stomach fluttered and his limbs tingled.

It felt good. It felt like hope.

TWENTY-FIVE
JULIA

JULIA'S LIDS FLUTTERED OPEN. For a moment, she forgot where she was, but then she immediately remembered exactly where she was.

Thomas's bedroom. His cedar-cardamom cologne wrapped around her, closer than the sheet tangled around her naked body, and her nipples hardened.

Oh, she had it bad if just the scent of his cologne on her bare skin could turn her on. Grinning like a maniac, she rolled over and stretched long in Thomas's bed. Sliding along the cream and black windowpane sateen sheets, she pulled the duvet with her. They'd fallen asleep, limbs entwined, in his childhood full-sized bed. Otherwise they wouldn't have fit. But she didn't mind one bit.

She'd fallen into an easy sleep, melting into the sheets, earnestly held by Thomas. Whatever happened between them, whatever was happening or would happen between them—she trusted him. Over the last week she gave free rein to her impulses. She leaned into the hot, casual sex that had, somewhere along the way, turned out to be not-so-casual feelings. But this was Thomas, and she felt safe in his arms.

As momentarily disorienting as waking up alone had been, she enjoyed having his blankets all to herself.

The faint scent of bacon wafted into the room, and her stomach growled. But she stayed in bed, more than a little afraid about who she might run into padding alone through the house.

No, she'd wait for Thomas to come back to get her. Hopefully with coffee in hand.

Sliding from bed, her bare feet landed in the carpet, and she wiggled her toes. She plucked her dress from the floor and slipped it over her head, falling into place down her hips. Where were her tights? The morning-after outfit was a teensy bit humiliating, but maybe she could borrow something from Thomas when he returned.

Their clothes littered the floor, and as she picked her way through them, her eyes landed on Thomas's bookshelf. It was packed tight with cracked-spine novels, not in any discernible order, all bookended by an old shoebox with its own mini pile of books atop it.

A couple shelves of decidedly more organized journals stood below the mismatched books. The thick, black Moleskine ones that he always scribbled in, not the thin cahiers that Julia preferred. Each one had a thick piece of tape along the spine with dates. She bit a thumbnail, her curiosity blooming as a tingle at the base of her neck.

Without much thought, Julia reached for one, sliding the one dated from the summer they met off the shelf.

Her gut tightened, immediately second guessing what she was doing. Tiny little alarm bells clanged loudly, but she shut them down. The book was already in her hands, anyway. Would it be diary-like thoughts in the pages? Fictional story ideas? Or something more mundane like lists and dates and homework assignments?

Julia wasn't snooping. No, no, of course not. She was just eager to know Thomas better.

For some reason, in that moment, she believed the blatant lie.

Her interest caught like wildfire, and before she could turn back, the pages flipped open, nearly of their own accord. She held the covers with her thumbs, the pages fanning out before her. Thomas's tidy scrawl filled the pages, keeping near perfect lines on the blank paper.

She picked a random page in early autumn of their junior year.

> *I don't know if I'll ever get the courage to tell her. The risk of losing her is too great. What if she doesn't feel the same way at all? And she thinks I'm disgusting and then never wants to see me again?*
> *I can't risk that. She's my best friend. The best friend I've ever had.*

Does that make me a coward? Or does it make me smart? Smart to keep things as they are, knowing I can have her as a friend? I don't know.
I can do friends. I can be friends with Julia Ward but if I tell her that I love her and lost our friendship... No, I can't take that risk.

Julia swayed slightly on the spot, blood rushing from her head. Her mouth dropped open as her eyes lifted from the page. Did she read that correctly? She blinked and looked back down at the page.

I love her.

Yep, right there. Words Thomas had never said to her.

She flipped forward a chunk of pages to mid-October, in flagrant violation of whatever semblance of trust she and Thomas had two minutes ago. Her stomach flipped, knowing she was wrong. Yet she couldn't stop.

We went to the Homecoming dance with a bunch of other theater kids. Julia didn't have a date and neither did I, so we hung out with each other all night. In pictures, in the limo, at dinner. On the dance floor, her naked shoulder rubbed my arm.
I'll Be came on (what's with the saxophones in that song?), and we looked at each other, just kinda shrugged, and then put our arms on each other to slow dance. We talked about dinner and laughed at every-thing. I couldn't bring myself to compliment her dress, a

shiny purple thing that had straps around the neck, but I wanted to. She looked really pretty, as always.
I wanted to tell her right then and there that I love her. But the words wouldn't come. I can't tell her. It used to be easy enough to ignore but now sometimes it hurts.

Julia sat down on the edge of her bed, too dizzy now to stand. Her grip went slack, and the journal fell to the floor. In that moment, her worldview shifted entirely. Did the earth still turn? Did the sun still rise in the sky? Maybe—but her memories transformed, shifting into some kind of funhouse alternate universe.

She remembered the Homecoming dance junior year. The way everyone else in their group was coupled off except for them, and they laughed watching the couples take awkward photos together. The memory of them dancing to *I'll Be*, a song she still quite liked, shuffled to the surface. They'd laughed through the dance, feeling silly and singing to each other. Though many of the sensory details were lost to time, she still remembered the swoop she'd had in her gut as Thomas ran his hand along her bare back. Her stomach still flipped now.

For weeks after that she had thought maybe something would happen between them. She wished and hoped it would. Maybe, she had thought, she could find the courage to confess her crush.

But it never happened. He never said anything, and she couldn't handle the assumed rejection. Much like

Thomas, she settled for *just friends* when she'd really wanted so much more.

Not long after that, Josh came into her life.

Josh. That bastard who was never honest, never faithful. Who had ruined her life, leaving her a shell of a person stuffed full of someone else's hobbies and personality. Someone who couldn't trust herself, because she always made the wrong decisions.

What if Thomas had confessed his love when they were in high school? What would have happened if Julia had never met Josh? Never dated him? Never got destroyed by him?

What if Julia had gone to New York City?

The heavy, numb feeling ebbed away, and her limbs began to shake. She tried to swallow, but she couldn't.

The bedroom door creaked, and Julia didn't even move. She stared straight ahead, anger vibrating through every inch of her body. Anger at Thomas, yes, but at herself most of all.

If Thomas lied back then, so did she. She always made the wrong decisions. And she'd been doing so for a long time. What little trust in herself that she'd started to cobble together, crumbled right before her eyes. She didn't trust what she felt about Thomas then—when maybe it would have actually made a difference—and now? What now?

Julia was once again the bad guy. Apparently she never learned. Her stomach hardened with resentment.

Thomas carried a mug of steaming coffee and a piece of bacon, but his eyes immediately fell to the open journal on the floor, with the spine up and the date obvious. His gaze stayed glued there as he stood in the doorway.

"What the hell is that?" she whispered, pointing at the journal. A frown pulled at her lips. Pure disgust. She wanted to scream. Not denying that she read his private journal with the evidence right there, she knew she should feel guilty, but she didn't.

Instead, she wanted to fight.

"My journal." Thomas froze to the spot but swallowed audibly.

Julia laughed through a clenched teeth smile, still pointing. "What the fuck?"

"I can explain." He put the coffee down on his desk and bent to pick up the book.

I can explain, the same words that Josh had said to her when she got the encrypted email. She jumped to her feet, raw energy coursing through her veins.

"There's nothing for you to explain, Thomas." Her voice rose to an impressive pitch. "It's clear. It's all right there. Everything has been a lie."

"A lie? Hardly." Two deep lines cut between Thomas's eyebrows, the corner of his lip drawing up in a small sneer.

"Hardly? Very much so, extremely yes, Thomas. Do you know how fucked up it is that I just read that you *loved* me when we were kids, and you never said anything!" She gestured around her. "Look what happened!"

"Okay, so I didn't confess my love when I was a stupid fucking sixteen-year-old, but don't blame your shitty life on me. You picked Josh all on your own. Remember? Your own little secret, your own choice that you made. You made that choice to follow him, Julia. I had no part in what Josh did to you." He sliced a firm hand through the air.

Julia sucked a breath through her teeth. It was almost like they were graduating seniors again and having their huge blow-out fight in front of the school. The fight when Julia revealed her secret back then.

"How dare you," she whispered.

"What about you reading my fucking journal? How's that for fucked up?" He pushed the book into her chest. "Take it. You can have it. Read it again for fun if you want."

"That's disgusting," Julia spit. She didn't touch the book again as it clattered to the floor.

"No, actually I'd give you the ribbon for 'Most Disgusting' in this situation." He shrugged, watching Julia gather up her things, as if he didn't have a care in the world.

Julia stomped around the room, grabbing her tights and phone and shoving them all into her bag.

"You know what, screw you, Thomas. Go on back to New York City. Have fun." She flitted a hand in his face, her heart shattering as she said the cold words.

Thomas opened and closed his mouth. Once. Twice. And then left it shut for good.

"That's what I thought," Julia huffed, and she stormed down the hall to the front door. She just slipped on her flats when the doorbell rang.

Thomas rushed in front of her and opened the door. There was a beat of silence, and then the person on the other side cleared their throat and spoke as plastic rustled.

"These are for you. For your loss." A pause. "And because I miss you. I was worried about you."

Miss you? Julia yanked the door open. "Who are you?"

A tall Black man with long braids stood on the threshold, and Thomas now held a massive bouquet of roses. Motherfucking *roses*.

"I'm Micha. Thomas's...writing partner?" Micha tilted his head to the side before looking Julia up and down.

"Oh, I thought you were Ari for a second. You're not Ari." Micha extended a hand, a pleasant smile on his face.

Julia took in the scene. Thomas holding flowers from a man. Because that man *missed* him. Thomas not saying a word. Just standing there. His skin wasn't even a shade of olive anymore, just deeply red, as he stared at the ground. Offering zero explanation. None.

Heat surged through Julia's body, still ready to fight.

"Oh. Well. I'm Julia. Thomas's...nobody? I'm nobody to Thomas?" She stared at the top of Thomas's hung head, waiting for someone, anyone, to say something.

Thomas didn't raise his eyes.

"What are you doing here, Micha?" The words rumbled in his chest.

Micha's smile faltered as he looked between Thomas and Julia. "I saw a post on some social media that you were tagged in. Said your dad died and, ya know, the band's in Toledo for the tour, so I just wanted to be here for you."

Julia couldn't believe it. Thomas had someone in New York who was worried about him, and here he was fucking her in Michigan? Making her fall for him without giving her the whole truth? He was just as evil as Josh.

Julia had gotten right into bed with another dishonest man. She gave an exasperated laugh, and Thomas met her eyes. His eyes were drooped and expectant and, above all, sad.

When he didn't say anything, she shook her head. "Whatever."

She pushed past them off the porch, not willing to wait for an explanation. She didn't need one.

Micha. *The writing partner.* What a joke. Had this been a game to Thomas the entire time? After knowing what Josh had done to her?

Add this to the list of lies between them. They were good at lying to each other by now.

She didn't look back as she got in her car and left. She didn't need to.

This time, Thomas Callaghan was the liar.

TWENTY-SIX

THOMAS

TWELVE YEARS AGO

THE DAY THINGS all fell apart between Thomas and Julia, Thomas was, humiliatingly, wearing an ugly New York University hoodie. Even at baseline, Thomas wasn't much for school spirit, if he was being honest. Considering that the sports gene had essentially missed him—that was more Danny's thing—it made sense.

But Senior Spirit Week was kind of fun. Even though scheduling "fun" "senior things" for the senior's last week of school that May was a thinly veiled charade to get the seniors to actually attend their last week of school, Thomas was surprised to find that he actually felt a little rah-rah about the whole thing after all.

Maybe it was because it was a sign of the end. So close. They were so freaking close to being done with high school forever, and his adventure with Julia in New York City could finally begin.

It was the Wednesday of Senior Spirit Week: "College Spirit Day," another kind of spirit that Thomas would inevitably fail to curate when he finally landed on New York University's doorstep. But on this day, he would play along. It was meant to be a reveal of sorts, a chance for everyone to show off their chosen college. So, since NYU purple really wasn't his color, he went online and found a heather-grey-purple-lettered NYU zip-up that he liked alright enough.

And, as usual, he waited out front of school for Julia to show up in her likely more purple than his NYU apparel, since she seemed partial to the color. He pulled his hands into his sweatshirt, oddly nervous about the whole reveal aspect. But Julia would be by his side and with him in New York for the next four years and presumably beyond. Best of all, Josh wouldn't be by *her* side next year in New York. Win-win-win.

This morning, she was late though. Usually quite a punctual person, this, too, was another of today's oddities. He wouldn't let it get him down though. It was almost the end.

Squinting toward the sky, he did a little mildly embarrassing twirl.

And there she was.

Head bent against the breeze and over-large bag tucked under her shoulder, she walked briskly across the parking lot toward him in her New York—

Wait. Her sweatshirt wasn't any shade of purple. It also

didn't say New York University anywhere on it. Instead, it was a gaudy maize and blue, emblazoned with The University of Michigan.

Thomas's stomach dropped into his toes. Just as she met his gaze, she bit one corner of her lip which would have been cute in another circumstance, but in this one screamed *guilty.* All of the pieces clicked together with an ominous clang.

Is this why she'd been so cagey the last couple of weeks? The last couple months, if he was being honest. He stared as she walked up the sidewalk, tucking her hair behind her ear, and finally looking up at Thomas as she reached him.

Immediately on the defensive, he didn't tiptoe into the conversation at all.

"What the fuck is this, Jules?" He gestured up and down to her sweatshirt.

Julia looked down at her sweatshirt, as if checking it out herself. Her hair fell around her shoulders. "It's my school, where I'm going next year. I didn't know how to tell you."

"Are you serious?" Thomas pulled a hand down his face, stretching his skin. "With Josh then, right? You know that guy's a piece of shit, right?"

"You don't even know him, Thomas. If you just gave him a shot..." she nearly begged, but the sentence died on her tongue. She often asked this of him, and he outright refused to entertain the thought. He didn't want to get to know that guy. No way.

Thomas scoffed. "Nah. I know who you are with him."

"What's that supposed to mean?" Julia narrowed her eyes, her cheeks flushing peachy-pink.

"It means—" He paused, a lightning bolt of sense causing him to censor himself.

Her eyes thundered in response. "No, no. Finish that sentence. Tell me. Tell me what you really think. Might as well let it all out, Thomas."

She knew exactly how to taunt him, tease him, rile him up. And as they stared right into each other's eyes, something inside Thomas begged him to wave the white flag and surrender. To shut the hell up and instead tell her what he really had wanted to say all this time: *I love you, Julia Ward.*

But she pushed her chin up, and he knew that her decision had already been made. He had already lost her, so there was nothing else to lose.

"It means I don't like who you are with him, Julia." The words were ash in his mouth, a bitter, burnt marshmallow degrading into nothing. His last hope—poof—gone.

"Wow." She drew the vowel out and spun in a half circle away from him, hiding her face.

The first school bell rang in the distance, and they both ignored it.

"Yeah, wow." Thomas ran a hand over his buzzed

head, awareness settling into his bones of what this decision really meant, and he decided to go for broke. "I mean, really, you're not the same person I knew two years ago. Wow, like. I can't believe you're changing your whole life for him. I bet you mom's real fucking pleased."

"Alright, that's enough. I'm the ass, but leave Anne out of this."

"No," Thomas steamrolled on, "she never wanted you to go to New York. But we were gonna go anyway, because it was our dream. The dream. Your dream. You and me, Jules. That was always the plan."

"Dreams change." Julia crossed her arms over her chest and avoided his gaze now.

He weaved around her, trying to get back into her line of sight.

"No they don't, Julia," he said. "Mine didn't."

"Sometimes they have to."

The second bell rang across the parking lot as another realization dropped into Thomas's humiliating bucket: Julia had kept this from him. Intentionally. A secret. The whole time letting him believe a lie. Colleges required notification months ago for incoming freshmen in the fall. And she'd just let him believe everything was status quo.

Thomas fought his growing nausea. "So, this whole time you've just been lying to me?"

"Not exactly."

"Not exactly?" His eyes nearly bugged out of his head.

"I didn't think it would be a big deal." A blush flushed Julia's cheeks and down her neck.

"Awesome." He laughed bitterly. "You know what? Screw this."

Thomas stormed away from her, leaving her rooted to the spot where they'd met outside school for the last two years. The third bell rang. The late bell. Great.

Her graduation party was a month later. Thomas bitterly regretted every single stupid word he spit at her on College Spirit Day, but she wouldn't respond to any of his texts or phone calls. He knew he deserved it, but they needed to talk it out, and her graduation party was the perfect time to apologize. He had it all planned out, even reinforcing his rehearsed speech with a written card.

Thomas barely noticed any theater people at the party. It was mostly Josh's social circle, and there were a lot of them, and tons of parents and family. People he'd never see again after that day.

Julia wore a short white dress and these strappy wedge sandals, her hair cascading over her shoulders in perfect contrast. She looked beautiful even as she was plastered against Josh's side as he led her around her own party. Thomas wondered what she saw in him, how he had lost his partner in crime to *that guy*.

Julia waved to Thomas across the party with a thin-lipped smile but seemed to pointedly avoid him after that. Every time Thomas thought there might be opening for them to have a private chat, he tried to catch her eye, but her gaze ping-ponged in the space around him, refusing to acknowledge him further. Eventually, someone absorbed her into another conversation. He couldn't blame her, really, considering the last time they talked had quickly devolved into a yelling match. Mrs. Ward definitely wouldn't be pleased if Thomas caused a scene at her daughter's grad party.

A huge piece of buttercream frosted cake was a weak consolation prize to the humiliation of sitting alone on a plastic folding chair and sweating under the circus-sized rented tent. This party was torture.

He left his gift, a signed copy of *The Perks of Being a Wallflower*, which he personalized "to Julia" along with the date of her grad party.

But he didn't leave the card. That went into a shoebox. A tattered and battered shoebox of gilded memories that Thomas brought to every place he lived in New York City and eventually tucked safely back on his bookshelf in Starling Hills.

After her party, they didn't see each other for over twelve years.

TWENTY-SEVEN
JULIA

JULIA MOVED through the next couple of days in a haze. Work, home, eat, sleep, repeat. She was on autopilot. It was a testament to how well she did her job that she met all her deadlines that week with time to spare, responded to emails with utter professionalism, and no one at work was the wiser to her turmoil.

She hated that she was so good at her job.

At her cubicle, she input data in a fugue state. Her fingers here, doing the work, but her mind fixated, fuming and decidedly elsewhere.

Josh's betrayal had been one thing. She had been naive, tricked.

But regarding Thomas: she knew better. She knew better than to trust her instincts about him.

Her instincts lied. That's what Josh taught her. Yet still she listened to them. Believing that Thomas was safe, that her heart was true this time. Even still, as she sat here miserable and unbelievably pissed off, she had that same heart-clenching, stomach-swooping, tingles-all-over feeling that Thomas elicited from her.

His calloused fingertips over her curves. His gentle tugs on her hair. Two of his fingers curling inside her.

Nope. She had to put a stop to it.

And Thomas knew her story. He knew their story. Their history. He knew the exact trap that he set for her, and he let her walk right into it like a helpless, cuddly bunny.

She was so mad that she could scream. Her skin felt like a husk. She shivered, pulling her cardigan tighter. Why did their damn floor still have the air conditioning on? It was November, for Pete's sake. Julia sipped her now-cold pumpkin spice latte and frowned.

The shrill ring of her desk phone nearly shocked her out of her seat.

"Julia Ward," she answered, the corded receiver clutched in her hands.

"Christopher Wu would like to see you at your earliest convenience," the pleasant voice chirped on the other end.

Shit. Christopher Wu was the big boss, the one she would report to in her new role. If she got it. If she even accepted it.

What started as a vague possibility—withdrawing from

consideration for the promotion—had become an itch she couldn't quite scratch. Since she couldn't put a stop to her brooding about Thomas, she thought, maybe turning down the role and taking time off would satisfy her.

"Right now?" She looked at the clock, mind buzzing. Nearly three PM on a Friday. Did that mean good news or bad news? She didn't know what she wanted to hear anymore.

"If that works for you!" This person on the other end was way too happy.

"I'll be right over." Julia hung up the phone and stood, smoothing her pants and adjusting her hair over her shoulders.

How do I look? she mouthed to Susan who watched her from her cubicle across the aisle.

Susan grinned broadly and gave her two enthusiastic thumbs up. *Amazing*, she mouthed.

Deep breaths. The walk across their floor took ages. She stared straight ahead, avoiding eye contact with anyone else. Was she going slow or just imagining it? Her brain whirred, calculating, rehearsing the words she wanted to say. They wouldn't be easy to get out, but it was really the only actionable option left to her. Finally, she made it to the secretary's desk.

"Julia Ward for Christopher Wu." Did she sound as miserable as she felt?

"Oh, I know who you are, sweetie. Hold on just one

second." The secretary actually giggled as she picked up the phone to call inside.

She said only mmhmms into the receiver, pushing her horn-rimmed glasses up her nose as she did so.

"Go on in," she said, hanging up the phone.

Julia's palm slipped on the door handle, and she gripped it more tightly to turn it.

Christopher Wu sat behind a large desk and a very large computer screen. Laughably large, it seemed, to Julia. His face broke into a congenial grin as Julia crossed the threshold.

"Ah, Julia." He stood, flipping his black hair out of his eyes, and extended a hand as Julia crossed the room feeling absurdly on display. "I have to start by saying, everyone was deeply impressed with your interview."

She wiped her sweaty palm on her pants as incognito as she could before she brought her hand up to his for a handshake. His grip cinched like a vice.

"Please sit." He indicated with his hand at one of the chairs in front of his desk.

They spoke at the same time.

"Well— "

"I— "

Julia snapped her mouth shut, cold sweat trickling down her back.

"Please, you first," Christopher Wu said, amiable as ever.

"Right." Julia rubbed her palms on her thighs, swallowing thickly. *Please don't let my words shake.*

"I wanted to officially withdraw my application for consideration. I'm sorry, I know this is last minute and may upset some decisions and conversations you've had. But after careful consideration, this role is not something that I'd like for my life right at this time." She swallowed. "So I must rescind my application."

Christopher Wu raised his eyebrows. "You're sure?"

Her chest tightened. Julia forced herself to nod, suddenly feeling too hot, but the words kept coming.

"I know it seems rash and rushed and probably a little silly to have gone through this entire process to then just all of a sudden withdraw, but it's not. I've actually been thinking about it for a while, and this seems like the best move, you know?" She cleared her throat.

Christopher Wu flashed that charming smile again, taking her decision entirely in stride. "Your needs come first, Julia. You know what's best for you."

Julia nodded, picking up steam. "I do, yeah. I just don't think *more* work right now is what's best. I've lost my center. Or maybe re-gained it? But either way, it's all off balance, and I need to reassess...my life. My entire life. Starting with withdrawing my application. And you know? I'm going to take some time off too, a little three-week vacation to recalibrate. Focus on me for a little bit."

He rubbed his chin, actually considering her words, as if Julia didn't just word vomit on his desk.

"This is great. I respect it. We'll always support you, because you're still one of our employees, Julia," Christopher Wu said. "I think this is why you're so good at your job. You listen to your gut. Your instincts are good."

Julia quirked an eyebrow, tilting her head. "Sorry?"

"You don't believe me?" Christopher leaned back in his chair. "It's all anyone could say about you when we asked. And your performance evaluations consistently reflect it."

He opened both palms toward her as if to say *that's that*.

"I just never heard that before is all. It's unexpected, I guess you could say."

Christopher nodded. "Understood. Well, I thank you for your honesty."

She stood, offering her hand to Christopher, and he took it for another firm shake.

"Thank you," she said.

The walk back to her desk felt lighter, easier. That promotion was the final relic from the old Julia that she needed to scrub from her life. She didn't want it anymore. She didn't want career prestige that glimmered like a facsimile of happiness. Julia wouldn't settle for something fake anymore.

Blonde hair flicked out of the corner of her eye, and she turned to see Michelle in the kitchenette. The damned kitchenette. Still humiliated and eager to avoid a run-in with Michelle or any of her friends, Julia had avoided the common space since she threw up in the sink in front of Michelle.

But here she was walking into the kitchenette, following those damned instincts of hers. And her instincts said she should talk to Michelle.

"Hey, Michelle, do you have a second?" Julia swung her arms in an attempt to work off nervous energy.

"Julia, hi!" Michelle flipped her hair over her shoulder dramatically.

Did she need to do that so much?

Julia's stomach tightened as she considered the words she was about to say. There wasn't really any other way to say it, except to be uncomfortably blunt.

"Josh is a cheater."

Michelle blinked, her absurdly long lashes fluttering. "Sorry?"

"I used to be engaged to Josh." Julia gestured to Michelle's left hand. "Umm, not too long ago actually, and I got an encrypted email that said he cheated on me, and," she shrugged, "well, I broke it off."

"Oh." Michelle pouted, her eyebrows turning up in concern. "You're so sweet. Yes, of course I know. Who do you think sent that email?"

Julia's head spun. "Excuse me?"

"I sent it, because I want to be Josh's wife. Not his mistress. Not his sidepiece. His legally wedded wife. And I knew he'd never break it off with you, so I sent the note to get you to break it off with him." She eyed her ring. "I knew you'd recognize the setting when you saw it. I guess showing you the pictures was probably a little over the top, even for me, but your face—oh, it was priceless. But, don't worry, before I dared put the ring on my finger, I made sure Josh upgraded the stones."

"That's fucked up, Michelle." Julia shook her head. "You two really fucking deserve each other."

Julia backed out of the kitchenette, clutching her stomach and desperate for a bathroom. Weaving through the maze of cubicles, Julia made a beeline for the most private one.

She'd been right about Michelle. That lurking suspicion that something was *off* about her that wasn't just thinly veiled occupational rivalry.

No, Michelle was a bottom dweller just like Josh.

Julia pushed into a bathroom stall just in time to aim her projectile vomit into the toilet.

* * *

"IT'S gonna be a four martini kinda night." Julia sloshed some of her drink on the bar.

"You know what that means? Lotsa pasta." Susan nodded and pinched Julia's arm lightly. "I'm proud of you."

Julia sighed deeply. "I don't know what I'm doing, Suse."

"Here's the irony: no one really knows. We make it up as we go along."

Julia frowned. Between Thomas, the job, and Michelle, this week was a serious buzzkill.

Susan knocked her shoulder into Julia's. "I know. It's not what you want to hear. But nothing is certain in life, Juju. Just gotta find our people and hang on for dear fucking life. Like I'm hanging on to you. You'll never get rid of me."

"Well, thanks." Julia ate an olive from her drink.

"You trusted yourself, okay? You did it. You turned down the promotion, you put in for your leave, and you're taking your trip. That all takes a lot of bravery, too."

"I don't feel very brave." She ripped apart a piece of bread on her plate.

"Have you talked to Thomas?" Susan asked.

"No." Just like all those years ago, when they were both young and immature, he'd texted her plenty.

Were they any more mature now? She wasn't ready to read the texts yet, wasn't ready to figure out what it all meant. If she even wanted to talk to him again. He'd go back to New York City soon, and she didn't need to reconcile with him for it to just break again when he left. "He'll be gone soon, and it won't matter anymore. I can go back to how I was before."

"Mmhmm." Susan nodded, her head bouncing like a bobble head, eyes wide.

"What." Julia side-eyed her. "Ugh, what?"

"So, you're not going to see him when you're in New York?" Susan tore at a piece of bread.

"No. I mean, I don't know. Probably not." Julia frowned, her insides all jumbled up. "I don't even know if he'll be there. And I don't care if he is."

"Granted, I'm not in that beautiful head of yours, but that just doesn't seem right."

"What do you mean?"

"It doesn't seem truthful. I don't think you're being honest with yourself."

Julia pursed her lips. "It's complicated."

"It always is," Susan sighed. "Tell me about it."

Julia unloaded on her. Complete word vomit. She told Susan everything: how they met in high school, about their plans to move to New York City together, how meeting Josh sent Julia's life tailspinning in another direction. Julia recounted their fight back then and how they just stopped talking afterward. How he left for New York and she didn't. The middle bits she knew: the whole Josh thing and everything that had happened with Thomas this fall, the Theater Bizarre, their movies, the hot Jeep sex, the wake...

She recounted the way it all ended. How Julia had really fucked up by reading his journal. Guilt churned in her stomach, but she didn't want to listen. Julia wanted to cling to her naïve belief that she wasn't wrong here, Thomas was.

"If he'd just fucking said something at the time, when

we were kids, then maybe things would have been different. I would have gone to New York with him. Never would've hitched my wagon to Josh's." Julia slammed back the rest of her martini, willing what she said to be true.

"You don't *know* that," Susan said gently. "Hindsight is 20/20, but this isn't hindsight; this is fantasy."

When Julia scowled into her empty drink, Susan kept going.

"Thomas is just a person, too, doing the best he can. Josh fucked you up, yeah, but healthy relationships take at least two people working together to keep it that way. What you did, reading his journal, that wasn't right either. You're talking about him being dishonest? That's a huge violation of trust, Juju. And I say that, because I *love* you and I don't want you to delude yourself. You have to be honest with yourself, too. Then you'll really be able to learn to truly trust yourself again."

Susan's words buzzed with truth.

Julia sighed, her lips still puffed out in a pout. "How did you get so wise?"

"I paid a professional therapist a lot of money so that I didn't lose my goddamned mind while going through a divorce and learning how to single parent two little girls." Susan sipped her drink noisily. "And now you get to benefit from it, little grasshopper."

Julia leaned into the bar, resting her chin in her hands, and groaned loudly. "I don't like it."

Susan patted her back. "I'm sorry. If it makes you feel

better, no one likes this part. That's why so many people are bad at it."

"What do I do now?" Julia moaned.

"I can't help you there, but I have a feeling you'll think of something." Susan continued to rub small circles on Julia's back.

That night, Julia tucked into bed with her laptop, phone, and notebook. She nestled her AirPods in her ears and blasted *Transatlanticism*. Her heart fluttered as she clicked "book" on a three-week solo vacation to New York City. With or without Thomas, she was going to have her adventure, her New York moment. And that felt like the beginning of something.

Then she opened her notebook, grabbed her pen, and began to write.

TWENTY-EIGHT
THOMAS

IN THE IMMEDIATE aftermath of Julia storming out of his parents' house, Thomas booked a plane ticket back to New York for a week from then. His gut coiled into knots as he clicked the "purchase" button.

He then sat his siblings down, plying them with stacks of snickerdoodle pancakes, bacon, and fresh coffee. Thomas detailed the plan, outlining how the family needed their help around Callaghan's Coney Island until the end of the year and then he'd be home to do the lion's share of the work, stepping fully up to help Mom run the place. His siblings agreed, and the first weight lifted off Thomas's shoulders.

Seven days. In that week, his pathetic attempts to write anything productive just ended in a hamster wheel of shame, playing back the events of his last hours with Julia and wondering how it got so royally fucked up.

So, instead, he preemptively threw himself into the role Dad left behind.

In the couple days that Thomas had left in Starling Hills, he worked at the Coney Island from before open until after close, distracting himself with manual work. Standing in the deep freezer he took food temps, and he shivered. Not from the cold.

Micha sneaking away from his band's tour and showing up on his parents' doorstep was a surprise. Micha had always been considerate and sentimental, and he routinely went out of his way for his friends as much as his dedicated partners. But still, the shock of seeing him on his front porch, the epically terrible timing of it all? Thomas still wasn't over it.

If Julia thought that Thomas was a liar before, well, coming face-to-face with Micha in that scenario certainly solidified it. To someone who didn't know Micha, it would definitely look like he and Thomas were committed partners.

Of course, all of Thomas's text messages trying to explain went unanswered.

Not that his explanation would really solve everything.

Julia still read his journal—an epic violation of *his* trust. Since then, he'd burned them all in their backyard fire pit in a fit of desperation. Something he should have done years ago. He wasn't willing to risk someone unintentionally reading them again.

Still, he kept his shoebox of mementos stuffed with

old photos and ticket stubs, collected stickers and patches, pretty rocks and trinket souvenirs. And, of course, the apology letter that he never gave to Julia at her graduation party.

Thomas sighed, re-focusing on the trays of sliced veggies and cold cuts that he temped and logged. Honestly, there had to be a better way to do this. But it kept his hands busy and his mind mildly occupied. Just a part of the routine. Along with cleaning the bathrooms, refilling all the condiment bottles and shakers, wiping down the menus, and a hodgepodge of other jobs that often fell to the wayside.

He pushed out of the freezer and nearly ran into Ari holding a basket of freshly fried french fries. At twenty-five, she ate like a dump truck but still managed to keep her dancer physique.

"Oh, hey," Thomas said. "I'm surprised to see you here today."

"Just came for food before class." Ari smiled brightly, her dark brown hair piled on top of her head in her trademark top knot.

"And french fries at nine in the morning is a good idea?"

"The heart wants what it wants, Thomas. Who am I to judge?" She booped him on the nose with a fry before stuffing it in her mouth.

"You're gross," he said, but his own heart skipped in his chest, not thinking about morning fries or how nasty it was that his sister just booped him with a one and then ate it, but because his heart remembered exactly what it wanted. The memory of Julia at the outdoor movie, looking over her shoulder at him with her red sweater and her hair flying all around her, flashed hot and fierce through his bones.

Ari leaned back against the counter. "So, you and Julia had a fight, huh? Decided to leave those dirty details out of the family meeting?"

Thomas shoved his fists into his pockets. "Where'd you hear that?"

"We all *heard* it, T. Mom just had a front row seat to it all and thankfully has no filter and gives her favorite daughter all the good dirt. You know she can't keep anything to herself."

He groaned. "Unfortunately true."

"Also unfortunately, she heard literally every single word between you two." Ari's lips turned into a smug grin as she continued to dip her fries in mayo. "Then, she said some guy showed up at the house? Micha?"

"Jesus, she really never does shut up, does she?" Thomas grimaced.

"So Julia read your journal, eh?" Her eyes widened, entirely too excited as she recounted the whole thing like watching a horror movie over a bucket of popcorn.

The whole thing was admittedly pretty horrific if he was being honest. "Yep."

"Brutal. That's one of many reasons why I don't keep

one. No evidence." Ari tapped her temple with her pointer finger. "Plus like, sixteen-year-old Thomas? Blech," she stuck out her tongue. "I bet he was boring."

"He was in love with Julia." His ears burned impossibly hot.

"Some things never change." She fluttered her eyelashes at the sentiment. "It's kinda romantic actually."

Ari gasped and stood bolt upright, putting her hand on Thomas's forearm as she stared into the distance, her eyes wide and starry.

"Oh my god Thomas, this is your chance." She turned to her brother slowly, her eyes still wide.

"My chance?" He wasn't exactly following her logic.

"Your chance to make a fool out of yourself like in those romantic comedies you love. Like in your books!" She smacked her hand playfully a couple times on his arm, the excitement building in her. "Yes yes yes! You have to do it!"

"Do what?"

"Do something big and ridiculous to win Julia back." She flailed her hand around, drawing erratic air circles with a french fry.

"Back? I never *had* her." Thomas ran a hand over his beard, half-convinced that Ari had lost the plot.

She lowered her chin and fixed Thomas with a glare from under her eyebrows. "You are literally ridiculous."

He opened his mouth. And then closed it.

"Did you even tell her that you're moving back home?

That she's like the only thing in years that has made you even sorta happy? That publishing romance novels pales in comparison to getting your dick wet?"

Thomas made a face. "Ew, you're my sister; please don't speak like that about," he half coughed, half gagged, "me."

Ari continued to glare at him.

"Mom's been talking a whole lot, hasn't she?" Thomas frowned. He frowned so much in the last couple days that he suspected it might become permanent.

Ari shoved her weight against his but he didn't move very much. "Come on, I'm being serious. We all just want you to be happy. And Dad most of all would have wanted this. You're being intentionally difficult."

Thomas turned away. "It's not that easy."

"I'm not saying it is, but I'm saying y'all need to talk. You're just gonna let it all end like this? Not even try to figure it out?"

"What if it's not enough?" His voice was small. "What if I'm not enough?"

Ari frowned for a moment but didn't take the bait, choosing zillennial pragmatism instead.

"You won't ever know until you try." She leaned back against the counter to finish her fries, as if this was all very casual for her.

"How are you so good at this stuff? Shouldn't this be, like, reversed?" He drew a circle in the air between them with his pointer finger.

"Thomas, I'm the last of the millennials and the first of gen Z, okay? I know nothing matters, because we're all just going to end in the flames of a major climate disaster and capitalist collapse anyway, so you might as well swing for the fences until then."

She gave him a little pout that suggested she pitied him, but really said that he was just being silly. Ari reached up to pat his head.

"Grand gesture. Think about it."

* * *

A COUPLE WEEKS later and hundreds of miles away, Thomas still hadn't heard from Julia. The chance of a *grand gesture* for Julia seemed more bleak with each day that passed. If she wasn't responding to his messages, it all felt impossible. Would she even want to see him when he moved back to Starling Hills? She still didn't even know he planned to move back. That wasn't news that he wanted to send in a text message.

Thomas slipped easily back into his city life, which somehow felt both brand new and soothingly familiar at the same time. Except that he wasn't there to slot back into his old life; he was there to tie up the loose ends—figure out what to do with his furniture, ship home boxes, go over career logistics with Sandy Thorne, say goodbye to the city and his flatmates. Settling back into a rhythm wasn't exactly the goal, but it happened.

Thomas's flatmates surprised him one Wednesday in late November with a flurry of activity in their kitchen. Janet, a white woman with bottle-red curls, tapped a massive box of red wine, filling what could only be described as a goblet up to the brim.

"We're making homemade Thanksgiving lasagna!" she yelled as Thomas peeked into the kitchen. "And on the night before as a form of protest!"

Thomas raised his eyebrows. They typically ignored Thanksgiving, considering it celebrated genocide and forced family bonding.

But Thomas wouldn't look a gift horse in the mouth, especially if it took the form of homemade lasagna. "Thanksgiving lasagna, eh?"

He stuck his nose into the kitchen, the comforting smell of oregano beamed him directly to his dad's kitchen. Automatically, a frown pulled at the corners of his mouth at the thought of Dad. Thomas hadn't talked to his flatmates about him, about Michigan, about anything that happened when he was home. They knew he'd be gone after the New Year, so why bother? Would they even care? The thought settled heavily in his chest.

"And garlic bread!" Rick said, beaming. Short, Black, bald and clutching a box of frozen Texas toast garlic bread, he twirled in the middle of the kitchen. "But not homemade, because Texas toast is already perfect."

"Why mess with perfection?" Trixie asked, boiling water for the layers of lasagna noodles. "We're using my mom's recipe, Thomas." A Korean-Chinese-American genderqueer person with a buzzcut, their mom had a homemade recipe for everything, it seemed.

"But with Beyond Meat instead of veal and pork." They shuddered. "We're gonna have so much food. I would have invited Micha and the band over, too, but they're still on the road. Somewhere in Nebraska or something. Can you imagine?"

"Woof." Rick snorted. A born and bred New Yorker, he could barely imagine Michigan.

"Wanna help cook?" Janet, who wasn't actually helping herself, just drinking, wiggled her eyebrows to entice Thomas further into the kitchen. She held out a second equally full goblet of wine for him.

All three of his flatmates stared at him, varying levels of expectation written on their faces.

"Uh." He pulled his bottom lip between his teeth and ruffled his beard with his hand. "I'm good, thanks. Looks like you all got it covered, really."

He took the wine, though, and stole into the living room, leaving his flatmates abuzz in his wake. The ancient couch that got passed down with the apartment sagged under his weight as he lay down and placed the wine on the table next to the couch.

He'd timed his edible perfectly, and his body and mind dropped into a fuzzy wormhole. Thomas floated between the waking world and sleep, his consciousness bringing forth a patchwork of images.

Julia in a corset, writhing under his fingers in the stairwell. Julia at the diner, laughing with Ari at his baby photo. Julia coming undone in the back of her Jeep. Julia begging, pleading, for him to *come home, come home*—not a memory but a hazy, fabricated dream.

Home.

Something he ran from for so long. Confused and scared and never ready to live up to Dad's reputation. A place filled with backgammon boards and pancakes and Chemex coffee. A pair of readers on a stack of mail. A wad of faux spider web and chocolate milkshakes. His siblings and his mom, still in Starling Hills. Waiting for him to return. This time for good.

The couch sucked him in like a vortex, pulling him deeper into this ethereal realm, unraveling him at the seams. He was going home. He would be there soon. Going back to his family—and Julia, if she'd have him—to face up to the person he'd become while he was away for so long.

Thomas woke with a start, Rick's hand grasping his bicep. "Dinner's ready," he said with a kind smile.

Trixie insisted that they all sit at the dinner table for once. "It's Thanksgiving, after all," they said, as if that meant something to any of them.

They stuffed themselves with the home-cooked meal, finishing one box of wine and transitioning right on to the next. For a while they didn't talk, just ate the food to the soundtrack of a random jazz playlist that Janet was obsessed with.

Thomas ate the delicious food in contended silence, but he couldn't deny that it seemed like his flatmates were waiting for something, springs primed and loaded. Each one stole sideways glances at him every couple minutes. The tension wafted between the flickering LED tealights on the table. His mild paranoia could have been from his edible, but he didn't think so.

"So, your dad died," Rick said eventually. He never could stand the silence for long.

Trixie groaned, rolling their eyes.

Janet slammed her silverware down and picked up her wine instead. "Nice one, Rick. Smooth."

"What?" Rick looked around the table, playing innocent as he shrugged. "I mean, that's what this is all about, right?"

Thomas looked around the table. His flatmates watched him back. "I—I mean, yeah he did."

Trixie delivered another piece of garlic bread to Thomas's plate. "Do you want to talk about it?"

He opened his mouth, but no words came out. Did he want to talk about it? What was there to say? Thanks to stumbling upon this flatshare through Janet at XYZ Brewing, these were the closest friends he made in the last couple of years. But it just…didn't seem like it mattered. He ran a hand through his hair.

"I don't think so, but thanks." He ate the fresh piece of garlic bread to do something with his hands.

Janet shrugged, raising her goblet in the air, and sighed.

"Well," Trixie leaned toward Thomas and patted his hand, "we're here for you if you want to chat or whatever."

"I think we should have a party," Rick said.

Again, his words were met with a groan, and this time Thomas joined in. Rick always wanted to have a party. And always disappeared for the 12-24 hours after them to avoid cleanup.

"Oh, you all suck, but I'm serious. Hear me out." He took a drink before continuing, "Thomas is leaving our blessed city, and we need to remind him of everything he's going to miss. New. Year's. Eve."

Rick bounced in his chair, just about ready to go blast off.

Eventually his pure excitement won them all over, and they agreed to host a New Year's Eve party at the flat.

"But you have to help clean up this time," Trixie said, their one stipulation.

Rick winked at them. "Sure."

After dinner, they all ended up in the living room, lounging on the couch, or sitting cross-legged on a pouf, or laying on the floor. They took turns playing DJ, queuing up their favorite ballads and singing along. "American Pie," "Piano Man," "Tiny Dancer," "Don't Stop

Believin'." Each rendition more dramatic as they continued to drink.

Thomas drank too much that night, not because he was sad, but because he had a great time. Through his gauzy, maudlin thoughts, he wondered if New York had always been this fun and he'd just been missing out on it this whole time.

*** * ***

"THOMAS," Sandy Thorne said, leaning across the table. "I've missed your face. Truly."

He smirked in response. Sandy Thorne had so many clients that he found it difficult to believe that she missed his one face specifically, but he'd take the compliment. Because today they met in midtown Manhattan at some swanky steakhouse right around the corner from the Empire State Building and Bryant Park. Because Sandy Thorne had *news*.

News that, since Thomas was back in New York City, she refused to deliver over some digital form of communication and insisted on sharing it in person with two Scotch on the rocks and two medium-rare ribeyes.

How could he refuse?

"It's good to see you too, Sandy."

She pouted in response before taking a sip of her drink. Her outrageous flirtation skills that she passed off as doting concern made her particularly good at her job.

"Now, listen, you know publishing is a very meticulous and finicky blend of art and math, right?" Sandy Thorne dropped her drink and began cutting her steak, attention somehow laser-focused on both her meal and their conversation at the same time.

"I do," Thomas said, unsure of the direction of this chat, as his brain fiendishly cataloged their recent emails for clues. The emails definitely implied some kind of *good news*, but her ominous beginning didn't inspire confidence.

"Sometimes," she waved a fork in the air, "things fall more on the side of art. Passion projects, writing for the love of it, you know what I mean."

Thomas swallowed. He did. Oh, did he ever.

"But sometimes," Sandy Thorne slammed two fists onto the table, flashing a borderline maniacal grin, "things fall more on the side of *math*, and, baby, this one is definitely on the side of math."

Thomas thought he followed her metaphor but... math? It was never his strong suit. He nodded along, knowing that the chips would fall eventually. When he clearly wasn't giving the desired reaction, she steamrolled on.

"Your proposal, Thomas! It sold!"

Thomas's stomach dropped as if cresting the big hill of a rollercoaster. "What? I thought you said my other books weren't doing well and this one was going to be a long shot—"

Sandy Thorne brushed his words away. "Forget all that. Ancient history. Your proposal just happened to land in the lap of an editor who *loves* the forced proximity trope *and* all of your backlist and just went to frigging bat for you. She and I make a good team, it seems."

"Okay..." Thomas let the news sink in. "Okay, my book sold. That's great."

But Sandy Thorne still grinned wildly, waiting for Thomas to catch up.

"It sold for six figures, Thomas."

His stomach buoyed back up too high into his chest so fast that his vision prickled at the edges. "Six figures?"

"SIX FIGURES!" Sandy Thorne stage-whispered before going back to her steak, leaving Thomas still dazzled in the wake of the news.

His proposal for his latest romcom, a madcap combination of unexpected roommates turned rivals who ultimately learn they are, of course, better as a team than by themselves, had been his fun distraction project. Definitely more on the *art* side of things. He sank all of those 50,000 words from the burrito bet with Julia into that book. The book had changed so much over the last couple of months, but so had he. Thomas dumped all of his anxiety and tension into the novel, and the words buzzed off the page in the best way—if he did say so himself.

"I'm...shocked," Thomas said, which was a ridiculous understatement. None of his other novels had sold for nearly as much.

"Don't be shocked, you deserve this. Revel in it. You worked for this. We worked for this!" Sandy Thorne raised her glass toward him. "Onward and upward, Thomas."

He lifted his glass to cheers her.

"Onward and upward," he echoed. And as the Scotch blazed a trail of warmth down his throat, igniting a fire in his stomach, promise and possibility vibrated out from Thomas's center. Something good finally happened. More good would come. He knew it.

Onward and upward, indeed.

* * *

THOMAS SHARED most of his shifts at XYZ Brewing with Janet, and tonight they closed down the bar together after another Friday in December. Not that pulling pints had ever been a passion of his, but Thomas's tips had suffered lately, and he could only blame his own distractedness. Not working fast enough, not chatting enough, not up-selling the limited edition taps.

His mind ran on a loop: Starling Hills, a dream of his future, a memory of grief, a vanilla-scented ghost that chased him all over the city. Repeat into infinity.

Or whenever he got back to Starling Hills. Whichever came first.

"Earth to Thomas…" Janet tossed a towel in his direction and grinned when he looked up. "Come on, let's get this shit shut down. I need to drink copious amounts of red wine, and I need to have started ten minutes ago."

"Sorry. Just totally out of it," Thomas said, shaking his head.

"Yeah, we've all noticed," she said as she heaved a crate of clean glasses out of the dishwasher.

"What?"

Her statement caught him off guard. Who was noticing what?

"I mean, dude, your *dad* died, and you don't even want to talk about it? Even when plied with grief-lasagna and sadness-garlic-bread for Thanksgiving?" She didn't look at him, just kept going about her job. "Like, I have dad issues and mostly try to ignore the man, but his death is not something I'd want to keep close to the chest, ya know? Sometimes you gotta let that shit out."

Is that what their untraditional Thanksgiving meal was all about? Rick had brought his dad up, but the whole thing was about him?

Of course, Thomas had been too obtuse to see the gesture for what it was. Instead, he had completely turned in on himself, full of carbs and power ballads.

"What I'm saying is: we care about you, okay? This town is fucking rough, but we got your back, okay? Me, and Rick, and Trixie. We're not just your flatmates. We're your friends, and just...I know you're leaving soon, but we're here for you if you need it. No pressure though." Janet popped her hip, one hand on her waist.

In that moment she so reminded him of Ari that his stomach swooped with an awful, unending sense of homesickness.

"I appreciate that." He swallowed. "I really do."

"Are you ready to leave New York?" Janet whispered the question.

Thomas ducked his chin, ignoring the tension in his muscles.

"I think so. I," Thomas sucked in a breath, "I haven't felt like myself here in a while. I don't even really know who I am or what that means anymore. But I'm not sure I'll find it here."

"Too noisy?" Janet smirked.

"Something like that."

But there would never be a whole truth. Since coming back from Michigan, New York felt more like a home than it ever had. The irony that Thomas finally felt a part of something in this massive, writhing city now that he had plans to leave was not lost on him.

"You'll find yourself again, I know it. It's not out here," she gestured around herself, "but it's in here." She pointed to her chest.

Janet finished her jobs and ducked out, blowing a kiss behind her as she went. Thomas slowly completed his own tasks and locked up. He had nowhere to go but back to his apartment with the tiny bed and the tiny desk and the sagging common room couch. So he took his time. Why not?

With his fists shoved in his pockets and his peacoat collar pulled up high around his neck, he finally trudged back to his apartment around four AM. Snowflakes fell thick and perfect as a snow globe. His breath frosted around him. He passed the shuttered cafes and bars where he'd written and drank himself into a stupor—sometimes at the same time. Places where he schmoozed and hooked up and got lost in the noise of the millions of folks living, breathing, and dying all around him.

This was the glittering, nighttime New York City that he always imagined sharing with Julia, somehow before he even knew that such a space-time actually existed. This quiet in-between time when he could peek into the softly glowing apartments and wonder about who lived there. When his imagination ran away from the facts laid plain before him and he could muse about the endless possibilities in this world.

His heart thudded in his chest, and he thought maybe this is what Janet meant. Little bits of himself knitted back together with each beat in his chest.

He would miss this expansive wonder back in Starling Hills. The magical thinking that only seemed to happen after four AM in the middle of a sleepless city.

But in return, he gained a foundation. Solid ground in which to root. And he couldn't wait to see what kind of flower he would blossom into.

TWENTY-NINE
JULIA

ON THE 26TH OF DECEMBER, Julia sat in the passenger seat, seatbelt firmly in place, as Heather sped to the airport, displaying impressive driving skills and a healthy respect for the wintery roads.

"I'm so proud of you." Heather grinned, peeling her eyes from the highway and lingering her gaze a little too long on Julia for her liking.

Julia flicked her finger toward the windshield.

"Eyes on the road." She smiled, albeit a little strained. "Thanks though."

The whole withdrawing from her promotion and three-weeks-leave from work thing didn't go over so well with her parents. Her mother launched into a tirade, the thesis of which built on their argument at the dinner table a couple months ago. Julia was wasting her time and being *imprudent*—her mother's exact word. And, anyway,

Julia was an adult now, what did she expect? Adults can't just run away from their responsibilities. None of this would have happened if it weren't for Thomas Callaghan. And did her mother not teach her anything about time and money management and being the least bit reliable?

Her dad, for his part, grunted his agreement on key points.

In the end, Julia only doubled down on her decision to go to New York City. She'd already booked her plane ticket and a dope Airbnb in Brooklyn by then anyway. She was following her instincts. Something she was trying to get better at.

Julia sighed, long and loud, in an attempt to undo the lingering knot of tension in her shoulders from the whole thing.

"Don't worry about Mom and Dad," Heather said, zeroing in on the source of Julia's exasperation. "They don't get it. They don't see the world the way us millennials do. They're unhappy people, afraid of change. Forget them. This is a good thing. Have your *Eat, Pray, Love, big butterfly* moment in New York. Maybe get some writing done? Find yourself, ya know?"

Heather flashed a smile at her older sister. Her pep talk was remarkably similar to Susan's when Julia had told her the whole plan. Maybe that meant she was on the right path.

Three weeks and a full itinerary to experience the city she'd always dreamed of. Armed with the best outfits

Heather pulled together and a list of restaurants, museums, and points of interest, Julia was prepared. She prepped more for this trip in the last couple weeks than she had actually done work for her job.

Of course, Julia's to-do list spanned Manhattan and parts of Brooklyn, so she ended up booking an Airbnb in Bedford-Stuyvesant that met the parameters of cost, triangulation of activities, and ease of public transport. The place, a to-die-for artist's loft, had a living room painted navy blue, almost black, a loft with walk-out roof-deck access, and a neat little room for Airbnb guests, decorated in an artful blend of vintage minimalism and cheap Ikea furniture flair.

On the flight, Julia tucked her AirPods in and put on *Transatlanticism*. She listened to this album more in the last couple months than she had in the last twenty years. Goosebumps prickled up her arms as she remembered Thomas's hands holding firmly onto her hips in the back of her Jeep.

"This isn't so bad," he'd said, his breath ghosting across her skin.

She remember how he looked at her, seeing every part of her. Accepting her despite all of her flaws.

Her breath caught as if Thomas was right there with her now. God, how she missed him. She couldn't even fully admit how much.

More than anything, Julia wanted to apologize for violating his trust. But she'd been awful and didn't deserve his forgiveness. She wanted to finally say out loud how she felt about him. Because if Thomas was a liar, then she was, too.

But would he have her? She wasn't ready to know his response, so she left his texts unanswered.

The plane landed at JFK at almost ten PM on a Friday. From the backseat of her Lyft, she watched the neighborhood speed by, the streets still of people. Groups of Hasidic Jewish folk. Julia squinted out the window.

Where are they going? she wondered with each person or little group she passed. All Julia could think of was going to sleep.

Julia diligently set an alarm each morning, so she could spend the day exploring New York City. Though she slept in later than she planned each day, she still managed to check things off her list. She combined each day with a classic tourist activity, like moseying around the Met or walking the Highline, with visiting some restaurant or bar she read about on a food blog. Like drinking espresso at Abraço and sampling the tasting menu at Atoboy.

It didn't take long for her annoyance of needing public transportation or a rideshare app to get anywhere set in. She missed hopping in her car and arriving somewhere easily. And though she knew that the city could smell, she never imagined so many unique trash and, horrifyingly, urine stenches existed.

By her fifth day, Julia woke still exhausted and a little grumpy. Last night, as she tossed and turned, she realized with startling clarity: she could never live in New York City and maybe three weeks here was too long. The city was too much, too loud, too everything.

But since it was New Year's Eve and she had a cake class booked at Milk Bar, she refused to let this realization ruin the last day of the year. The class granted her unlimited access to frosting—best eaten by spoon—as she worked, so it was easy to ignore her grumpiness.

Later that evening, Julia unlocked the apartment door, finally getting the hang of her host's sticky lock, and pushed it open with her shoulder, balancing her cake box against her chest in the process.

"Oy! Julia!" her host, Saige, called, popping her head over the loft's metal banister.

"Yeah?" Julia called back, looking up with furrowed brows.

"Ah, thought that might be you." Saige said, bubbling with warmth. Her skin glowed white-gold in the strategic mood lighting in the apartment.

"Come on up here if you want to chill some," Saige said, waving a bottle of wine and pulling her pastel pink hair over her shoulder. "My friend Yasmin is up here, too."

"Okay! One sec."

Julia hadn't crossed paths all that much with her host, but the listing said she was friendly and always willing to hang out. Julia dropped her bag off in her room, looking in the mirror to quickly refresh after a day spent around the city. She grabbed the cake and, since Saige insisted that everything in the kitchen was fair game, rummaged around the kitchen for a couple forks and paper plates before teetering her way up the tight spiral staircase to the loft.

Julia hadn't been up in the loft yet, but she saw pictures of it on Airbnb. In real life, it was even cooler. Built-in bookcases lined the space, with a couple scattered mid-century modern accent chairs and small tables. Large pillows and poufs lined the perimeter. Yasmin lounged on one of them. A sliding glass door made up one wall that opened onto the little roof-deck. Snow dusted the outside space as the last orange fingers of the sun burst across the sky.

Saige busied herself pouring a fresh glass of wine for Julia. Yasmin, with brown skin and thick, dark brown hair, reached a delicate, perfectly manicured hand out to Julia before realizing that Julia's hands were full. She hopped up from the floor.

"Oh my gosh, let me help you with that." Yasmin gathered the box into her hands as Julia clutched the forks.

"What is it?" Saige whirled around, her colorful silk robe flaring out over her black tank and wide leg pants. Her eyes widened, zeroing in immediately on the cake box.

"I took a cake decorating class today," Julia said, taking a glass of wine from Saige and pulling her knit cardigan close around her shoulders.

"It's Milk Bar!" Yasmin cried. "I love you already."

"You made this?" Saige pointed at the wonky frosted cake coated in sprinkles.

"'Made' is a bit of a stretch. 'Assembled' is more like." Julia passed around the forks and plates before settling down into a worn leather chair. "Help yourselves, honestly. As much as I'd love to eat this whole thing, I think I'd get sick of it before I could finish."

"It looks amazing!" Yasmin said, forking out a massive slice. "I've always wanted to do one of their classes but never had the time."

"Well, I definitely have the time. Three weeks flying solo in New York will do that to you." Julia sipped her wine before taking the slice of cake Saige passed to her.

"That's really cool though," Saige said. "Any special occasion?"

These people didn't know her. How much did they really care about the mortifying details of her life? Probably not much.

But Julia leaned into it, sighing morosely. "Oh, I don't know, just running from my life."

As much as she hated to admit it, her mother had at least a partially accurate read on her eldest daughter.

"Well," Yasmin nodded enthusiastically, "spill! It's five PM on New Year's Eve, and we have wine and cake and nowhere else to be for at least five more hours."

"And we love harrowing details," Saige added, raising her glass.

"Hear, hear," Yasmin said.

Julia groaned but smiled, entertained by these two and feeling just loose enough at the end of this hellish year to recount the whole damn saga. Saige cursed at the appropriate spots, and Yasmin gasped as if on cue, the whole situation mirroring her therapeutic happy hours with Susan.

Yasmin scooped a forkful of frosting into her mouth. "I don't know, Julia. It doesn't seem finished."

"What doesn't?"

"This story." She shrugged, eyebrows jumping up her forehead. "Your story."

"I agree." Saige sipped her wine, her spine curled slightly, with a far-off look in her eyes. "New York's a magical place. Who knows what could happen here in the next couple weeks."

Julia ate cake, pondering Amélie's bravery and Kathleen Kelly's vulnerability from the movies she studied with Thomas. If they could get their happy endings, maybe Julia could too.

A sour taste raced up her throat, and she swallowed it back down. It was impossible though. Sure, she was in the same city as Thomas, but what was she supposed to do? Hunt Thomas down and confess everything? Stalk him and make him hear her apology? She didn't even know where he lived. For all she knew, he wasn't even here.

Susan said relationships take two. Healthy relationships do. Julia had acted like an asshole, and she knew it. Not only would Julia have to apologize for reading his journal and violating *his* trust, but she had her own secret left to confess: the crush she harbored back then, too.

"I don't know." Julia pursed her lips.

"That's what I'm saying," Saige said. "Don't think about it. *Magic*. What's meant to be will be. The city always has a way of working things out in the end, I swear to god."

Julia laughed. "That easy, huh?"

"Oh no, never easy. Just...serendipitous."

"Oh my god!" Yasmin sat upright like a prairie dog. "You have to come to the party tonight. Some friend-of-a-friend artist is having this huge good riddance party to send off this dumpster fire of a year."

"Aren't they all dumpster fires?" Julia asked, and Saige pointed at her in agreement.

"That's beside the point. It's gonna be a good party. You have to come!" Yasmin crawled over to Julia and rested her chin on Julia's knees. "I know we just met you and all that, but you have to."

Yasmin pleaded with a megawatt smile, and Saige nodded vigorously in the background.

Julia's gut said, *Go*.

"Alright." Julia giggled, and heat prickled in her cheeks. She was pleased to have made fast friends in these two. She thanked the cake for being a good common bonding denominator.

"So, what do you do?" Yasmin asked, sing-songing the question as she sat back on her pouf.

A current of electricity licked through Julia's stomach. To these people, she was no one. She could tell them anything, any story she wanted to. So she did.

"I'm a writer." It was the first time she said it like that, like that's just what she was. The first time she ever claimed the title out loud.

"Ooh fun! Have I read any of your stuff?" Yasmin tucked her feet underneath her as she continued working on her cake.

"How much fan fiction do you read?" Julia's heart raced. Confessing her side hobby made her sweat.

"TONS." Saige leaned forward as Yasmin pointed her fork across the loft at her pink-haired friend. "A surprising amount if I'm being honest."

"She is being honest." Yasmin laughed.

Julia plunged right into it. "I write as Jewel Parrish."

"No shit!" Saige nearly launched out of her seat.

"You know my stuff?" The heat from Julia's cheeks now tingled over her entire body. Was she really meeting a fan for the first time IRL?

"Know it? I love it! That stairwell piece about the Tenth Doctor and Rose Tyler—hot. Fuck! This is wild." Saige bounced in her seat.

"Yes!" Yasmin snapped her fingers. "Magic! I'm feeling it."

"Wait! That fic was based on a true story, right? Don't tell me it's based on this Thomas guy you were just talking about." Saige narrowed her eyes, fitting all of the pieces of the puzzle together.

"The very same."

"Holy shit! Goddamnit, I love this city." Saige drained the last of her wine.

Julia had a couple more glasses of wine and another piece of cake before heading back down the spiral staircase to get ready for the party, still laughing about the coincidence of her Airbnb host being a fan of her fan fiction. What were the odds?

She opened her suitcase and realized she hadn't exactly packed anything suitable for a New Year's Eve party. Julia had completely anticipated falling asleep with her laptop open, curled up in bed at eleven-thirty PM… but apparently the city had other plans. Pushing aside a few sweaters, a flash of black sparkles caught her eye. She pulled out a strappy, slinky shift dress covered in black sequins. Of course Heather would have tucked some stunning number into her suitcase when she wasn't looking. Julia made a note to text her sister tomorrow to thank her for the forethought.

Julia straightened her hair and opted for a jewelry-less look, instead playing up the dramatics with cat-eye eyeliner and a matte brown lip. She laced up her Doc Martens, which Josh didn't like but she did, and pulled on her pleather jacket. Damn, she looked good.

Yasmin and Saige waited at the front door, ready to walk across Bed-Stuy. Saige didn't change—staying in her all-black outfit and silk robe—and just pulled a teddy coat over the whole thing to stay warm. Whereas Yasmin changed into a wildly patterned, vintage get-up that made her look like she walked off of a seventies mood board.

They clamored down the three flights of stairs and out onto the street. The two women looped arms on either side of Julia, making her feel a part of something.

Something. A nebulous, changeable *something*. The kind of sparkling magical *something* that only happens in a foreign city on New Year's Eve with new friends.

Saige kept up a stream of consciousness conversation as Yasmin navigated them on foot. When they arrived, Yasmin challenged them to a race up the seven floors to the apartment. Even though she was the only one in heels, she beat Julia and Saige, who gave up around the third floor, panting and laughing the rest of the way together.

Standing in front of the apartment door, some kind of deep house beats radiated from the speakers. Julia's heart fluttered. Somehow it felt like a threshold, begging her to cross.

She shook her head, diffusing her thoughts, ready to enjoy this last party of the year. Julia took a breath and followed Saige and Yasmin through the door.

Compared to her tight, though gorgeous, Airbnb apartment, this place sprawled. From the entry way, a hallway turned off to the right that led to at least three other doors, the left opened into a large living room, with the kitchen right in front of her. People mingled everywhere. On and in-between the mismatched furniture, perched on the radiator and kitchen counters, and dancing in the living room that had a wonky Christmas tree and some festive lights up. The music vibrated through her legs, reminding her of the last time she danced—with Thomas at Theatre Bizarre. Her stomach flipped at the thought.

Julia considered taking off her boots, scanning the sprawling mound near the front door. A pair of beat-up checkered Vans stuck out of the coat closet, and she thought of Thomas again and his signature shoes. *Damnit.*

But she decided to keep her boots on. The floor looked stickier than it was worth.

Saige tugged her arm, pulling her into the party. "Come on, Jewel, I need a drink."

They weaved into the kitchen, one counter stacked with an assortment of hard liquor and boxes and bottles of wine of all shades. Bags of potato chips, a huge bowl of guacamole and tortilla chips, and a plate of chocolate chip cookies lined the smaller counter next to the fridge.

"Oh, I recognize this one. It's expensive." Yasmin pulled the cork out of an orange-tinged bottle of wine and filled solo cups for the three of them. She leaned close to Julia. "These parties are great, because even though we're all broke, most of us work some gig in the service industry and can get this great booze for cheap when they get rid of it."

Yasmin winked and passed around the cups. They

toasted their drinks in a silent cheer, and as Julia sipped the funky wine, she spied a magnet on the fridge. A Michigan-shaped magnet. Stepping closer, it read, "Someone in Michigan loves you."

She furrowed her brows and then blinked, trying to control the fluttery sensation in her stomach. She leaned toward Saige. "Who did you say lives here again?"

"I don't think I did, but this artist we know, Trixie, and some of their friends that we've only met a couple times," Saige said.

Julia nodded, biting the lip of her plastic cup. A couple random coincidences didn't mean anything. To be fair, she thought about Thomas a lot on this trip, so this was basically just confirmation bias at work. Thomas couldn't possibly live here. In this apartment. And yet...

"Jewel's got a look in her eye, Saige!" Yasmin gestured to Julia with her drink.

"I don't have a look."

"You totally have a look," Saige agreed.

"I—" What? *Think the man from Michigan that I'm in love with might live in this apartment?* No, that sounded ridiculous. "This is just good wine."

"Mmhmm." Yasmin looked her up and down, still skeptical.

"Come on!" Saige shouted over her shoulder, diving into the mass of folks sort of dancing, sort of mingling, in the living room.

Still, a bubble of possibility grew in her chest, and,

spellbound, Julia followed Saige out of the kitchen, as she looked around the apartment. Random art and posters lined the walls. Most of the furniture—a mix of clearly well-loved pieces—lined the perimeter of the room, as if someone rearranged it to accommodate the party. In the corner stood a towering bookcase. Even from across the room, Julia spied the colorful spines of T. Callaghan's romances. And not just one of each copy. Each of his previous releases had an entire shelf to itself.

She wedged through the crowd, her heart pounding as she gaped at the collection. Julia ran her fingers along the edges of the pristine copies.

It couldn't be.

It had to be.

Magic.

THIRTY
THOMAS

THOMAS WALKED around the apartment with a stack of red solo cups in one hand and a pitcher of some noxious punch he and Trixie had mixed together in the other. Combining his bartending skills and their nose for flavor after years working in fine dining, the duo always made some deliciously lethal punch for their apartment parties.

"Who needs a drink!" he called, weaving around the already-packed party, trying not to spill anything on his black plaid button down. Which was mostly an exercise in futility since no one else paid attention to where they spilled their own drinks.

Thomas's question was met with a call of responses: seemingly everyone could use another drink. It was New Year's Eve after all. Thomas and his flatmates always threw the wildest parties. And since this would be Thomas's last party as an official resident of New York

City, his flatmates had really pulled out all the stops. Nearly everyone from their social circle was here. And their social circle had all told their social circles, so the party was packed. In a marked display of irony, Rick turned the TV on to see the Times Square Ball Drop, a place none of them would dare venture at this time. Everyone writhed to the beat of Janet's house playlist that she favored for parties.

Thomas turned on the spot, scanning the living room. Someone stood in front of the bookcase stuffed with the remaining author copies of his two novels. Someone with long, straight brown hair wearing a sparkling black dress and Docs—a stunning combination.

A tingle spiked through his body, recognizing this person's curves before his mind caught up. When she turned, he nearly lost his grip on the punch-pitcher in shock.

All cognitive and motor functions failed. Thomas's still stone-cold sober mind somehow wildly supplied the word *angel*. Julia's vampy brown lips parted, and she looked around the room with wide eyes.

She must have put it together—that Thomas lived in this apartment.

By all rights, she shouldn't even be here.

Not in New York. Not in his apartment. And certainly not in his living room. Especially not in that dress. She must be some kind of blessed mirage.

But then, Julia caught Thomas's eyes across the party

as he juggled the pitcher of punch and tower of solo cups, and lightning struck him to the spot. Her mouth fell open, disbelief laid plain on her face.

Thomas pushed through the sea of partygoers, desperate to make his way to her, as if she might evaporate into a puff of smoke at any second.

"Jules?" Her name felt hurried and rushed on his tongue, almost panicked. Did she notice?

"My Airbnb host brought me," Julia blurted and stuck her thumb over her shoulder.

Thomas followed where she pointed. Two people he recognized from Trixie's shows laughed over their solo cups as they watched their exchange.

"Oh," Thomas said, hands still full. "How random."

"Magical, one might say." Julia's eyes, tonight almost as grey as wet concrete, flashed.

"One might." Goosebumps raced down his neck and arms. "Uh—" Thomas tried to free a hand from the punch and cups, tangling Julia up in the whole mess as she tried to help. "Sorry. Um, do you want some punch?"

He set the pitcher and cups on the bookshelf, but she ignored the question. "Do you live here?"

"I do." Thomas swallowed instead of offering more information than she strictly asked for. Like the crucial bit about him moving home in two weeks.

"Cool." Julia looked around, shaking out her hands as she did.

Somewhere in the back of Thomas's mind, Ari whispered *grand gesture, think about it,* and he felt her phantom pat on his head. In the movies, and even in his own novels, he favored the understated kind of grand gesture. His brain whirred into overdrive. Stuck in his apartment, in the middle of a blowout party, there wasn't much he could pull off in the way of gestures—if Julia was even interested in that.

She was the one that stormed off, he reminded himself.

Then he remembered the old shoebox tucked under his bedside table. The letter addressed to Julia tucked in there so long ago was his best chance to apologize. It was his best chance to show her that he tried to make things right all those years ago. He just never got the chance.

Thomas leaned in toward Julia, bending so that his mouth was mere centimeters from the shell of her ear. Like mini antennae, his beard hair caught her skin. The same shiver careened through both of them, which intensified when Julia grasped onto his forearm as she gasped in surprise.

"Do you think we could go somewhere to talk?" His words came out thick, his mouth as dry as the dying Christmas tree that stood in the corner of the living room.

She nodded, offering no words. But they stood so close that he felt her nod through his entire body.

Taking one of her hands in his, Thomas led the way through the party to his bedroom, hoping to find some quiet.

When they were both in the room, he shut the door

and faced it for a moment, his hand gripping the doorknob. He had no idea what he actually wanted to say. No idea if this would work. He just knew he needed to apologize, tell Julia the *whole story*, so that she'd understand everything that went down between them. He couldn't control what happened after that.

When Thomas faced her, Julia worried her hands. His question just came out.

"What are you doing here, Julia?" he asked, running a hand through his beard. It surprised him how tired he sounded.

She pointed her thumb over her shoulder like she had before. This time just his twin bed and a row of windows were behind her. "My Airbnb host…" but she trailed off.

Thomas stepped closer to Julia, his head bent, focused on the thrifted Urban Outfitters rug that had been passed down to each resident. He took a breath. His shoulders rose and fell with it.

"I mean, why are you in New York?"

She ran her hand up and down the sequins of her dress. The movement hypnotized Thomas.

"Well," Julia started. "I decided I didn't want that promotion at work and thought maybe I'd take some time off and do a little something for myself. Spend some time in New York City like I always dreamed of."

Thomas nodded then opened his mouth—even though he still wasn't sure what to say—but Julia powered on instead.

"I'm sorry I read your journal. It was a dick move, and I know I violated your trust. It upset me, because I was mad at myself, too. I could have written those journal entries, Thomas. That could have been me saying those same words. I loved you back then, too. It's just, nothing ever happened between us, and then Josh came along, and everything changed so quickly. I thought maybe I'd made up that there was anything between us. If you want nothing to do with me, I get it, because I've been terrible. Back then and now. But I just really needed you know how sorry I am and will be for the rest of my life."

Julia stopped and took a breath.

Thomas's mouth fell open, shocked. Her confession burned in his chest. His body heated slowly, rolling through him like hot caramel.

"Say something," she pleaded, back to wringing her hands.

He cleared his throat. "There's a lot that I want to say. So much. But before I do, you deserve an explanation too, okay?" Thomas rubbed the back of his neck. "It's all I've been thinking about for weeks. I need to tell you. I need you to see."

He left Julia standing in the middle of his room and knelt to rummage in the shoebox under his bedside table. Buried underneath his treasured relics sat the card Thomas wrote to Julia as part of her high school graduation gift.

Thomas wet his lips as he stood, holding the envelope

in both hands. "There's this letter. I wanted to give it to you at your high school grad party, apologizing for all the shitty things I said to you on that college spirit day. It says a lot of things I never got to say to you."

He couldn't meet her eyes, carefully keeping a couple feet between them, still unsure how this would go. "I was supposed to apologize to you first, to your face, and the card was a reinforcement. We never got a chance to talk that day, so I never gave you the card. We never talked again."

Julia stared at the envelope, her brows furrowed, not saying a word.

Thomas took her silence and the fact that she hadn't stormed out on him again as a good sign. He kept going.

"And—just so you know—Micha's my writing partner. We *were* sleeping together, strictly as friends though. It was never anything more than that. When he stopped by, his band was in Toledo playing a show, and he came to check on me, because he's a good guy. But we're platonic. No strings. I wouldn't lie to you about that. Not ever.

"And you know, you were right. Maybe things could have been different between us back then. But maybe not. It's impossible to know. We were young and dumb. We didn't know any better." The words tumbled out, his stomach fluttering.

"What I'm saying is: it's you. I love you, Julia Ward, and I'm not sure that I ever stopped loving you. I'm so deeply sorry for any sorrow I ever caused you, and I'll do everything I can to make it up to you, today and every day. If you'll let me."

Thomas pushed his chin up to stare at the ceiling and pulled his lower lip between his teeth. When Julia opened her mouth to speak, he let out a small gasping cry, his eyes flicking to hers and shining with tears.

Time stopped. Thomas's chest ached as he literally held his breath.

And then the moment snapped.

They both moved and wrapped each other up in a bear hug. He pulled Julia close, covering her shoulders with his arms. She held him around the middle, her cheek flush to his chest. For the first time in weeks, Thomas felt like he could breathe easy.

"I'm moving home, you know? Back to Starling Hills," he said, his voice wet and heavy.

"Oh, thank god." Julia laughed into his chest. "I don't think I could ever live here."

"You get used to it. But fair." Thomas laughed, too, then pushed back from her. "Do you want to read the card?"

"No. Thank you, but no." Julia narrowed her eyes at the envelope. "Burn it or save it or do whatever you want with it, but I don't need to read it. You're right—we'll never know what could have been. We're here together now."

She grabbed two fistfuls of Thomas's button down, pulling him down so his lips met hers. She ran her fingertips up into his hair, eliciting a growl from deep in his chest, as she opened her mouth and let his tongue in. Thomas nibbled lightly on her bottom lip, and she pulled on his hair in response. Thomas walked backward two steps onto his bed, and Julia landed in his lap, without once losing lip contact.

As his hands roved her bare thighs, her dress riding up, Julia broke away.

"I love you too, by the way." She smiled. "And I still owe you a burrito, you know."

He laughed, palming the back of Julia's head to bring her lips back to his. After fourteen years, Thomas finally said the words that he swallowed down and held back too many times to count. So many times that it was physically painful.

And now he ran his hand up under Julia's dress, over her little red panties. The softness of her belly never ceased to amaze him. His hand inched higher. The curve of her breasts made his cock stiffen. She wiggled her hips on top of him, and he knew that she felt it too.

"You like that?" He laughed into her mouth.

She took his bottom lip between her teeth and applied pressure. "I love it."

Thomas groaned. "Such a tease."

Julia smirked, her eyes stormy and smoldering. He flipped her onto the bed in one deft move. She turned onto her side, ass to his erection bulging in his jeans. Julia looked over her shoulder at him, eyes wide and innocent.

"Definitely a tease."

He dove for her neck, his hand caressing up and down her stomach. Julia worked her hips back into him. Even through layers of clothes, the grinding drove him wild.

He breathed warmly into her ear, letting her know exactly how turned on he was with his uncontrollable guttural moans. With his palm flat on her stomach, he pulled her backside into him, enjoying the extra pressure on him from her ass.

Julia snaked her arm behind her and cupped his neck, urging him closer. As if they could get any closer with clothes on.

Thomas slid his hand between her legs, up and down her thighs and over the warmth between her legs.

"Now who's teasing?" she choked out.

Thomas chuckled into her ear, pleased to have her right where he wanted her. Taking a torturous amount of control, Thomas slowly worked his way down her stomach and under her panties. She opened her legs wider, trying to give him more space as he made circles around her most sensitive spot with his middle finger.

Julia rolled onto her back then, keeping steady eye contact. Thomas leaned on his forearm, balancing on his side, as he looked down at her. He pulled a lip between his teeth. His pulse thundered through his body.

All the moments before had brought him to this one.
Right here.
With her.

"We'll never know what could have happened

between us, Jules. But, fuck, I'm so happy that I'm here with you now." Thomas dropped his face and nuzzled her neck, into her hair.

Her warm vanilla scent was like a time portal, beaming him directly back to all of the best, most nostalgic parts of his adolescence. The Slurpees and the stargazing. The night drives and the mixed CDs. Texting and writing all night. All of it with Julia.

"Me too," Julia whispered. "I'm happy too."

Thomas moved south and lifted her dress above her waist, kissing her stomach. It was warm, and with each touch of his lips, she jumped, giggling.

Repositioning, he grinned crookedly up at her from where his chin rested on her stomach. As he held eye contact with her, he pulled down her panties and entered her with a single finger. She gasped, holding his gaze. Keeping one hand on her lower abdomen to measure her reaction, he moved in and out. Julia's wetness coated his fingers. His thumb pulsed on her clitoris, alternating pressure, encouraged by Julia's breathy whimpers.

Thomas shifted, moving further down her body until he settled between her thighs. He kissed a trail up her inner thigh, teasing the entire way.

Another finger slipped easily inside her, stretching gently. With the way she responded, he knew she was close, and he wanted to send her over the edge this way. Thomas wanted to taste her as she came.

Thomas's mouth found the right spot, and Julia

gasped. He timed his tongue in tandem with his fingers and thumb, loving working her into an absolute frenzy. Her hips bucked into the air until she froze, her abdomen tightening under his palm.

"I'm coming," Julia whispered, grating herself against him softly until she palmed the back of his head.

When he popped back up, fire burned in her eyes. Thomas reached his two fingers up to her mouth, and she wrapped her tongue around them, closing her eyes.

"You taste so good," he whispered as she nodded, agreeing. Almost instinctively, she reached down, rubbing her hand over his jeans.

"You're so hard." She laughed huskily and flicked an eyebrow. "I want to taste *you* now."

She pushed him onto his back, slowly undoing every button on his shirt, exposing his white undershirt, before undoing his pants and taking them off. Thomas laced his fingers into her hair, pulling as she took him into her mouth. He watched her progress as she took his entire length, causing him to grunt with pleasure.

"Oh god, Julia," Thomas moaned as she moved up and down. "You're so good."

Julia's hand worked together with her mouth, her own pleasure obvious in her tiny mewls that vibrated over his cock.

It wasn't long before he wanted more. "Please let me have you, Jules."

And she paused, a wicked grin spreading over her face. "I love you."

He groaned and pushed her hair back from her forehead. "I fucking love you."

Julia flipped onto her back as Thomas slipped a condom from his bedside table drawer and rolled it on.

Thomas situated his forearms over Julia's shoulders and braced his knees inside Julia's splayed legs. He looked down at her, her eyes shimmering. She gripped his biceps, her fingertips sinking into their softness. They held each other's gaze as he entered her, moving in and out slowly and shallowly at first, enjoying the buildup. Using his upper arms to push herself, Julia moved with Thomas, increasing the friction between them. His breath came faster as he picked up speed, going deeper with each thrust, until Julia raised her eyebrows and gave a tiny gasp with each movement.

"I'm gonna come." She bit down on her lip but still held his gaze.

Her words sent Thomas cascading into oblivion, and he shuddered as he came too.

They stayed connected as their breathing returned to normal. And only then did Thomas roll off Julia to lay by her side. He picked up her hand and kissed the back of it. They danced their fingers, tangling and untangling in the air.

As the clock got closer to midnight, the guests out in the living room shout-counted down from ten. When the clock struck midnight, Julia sat up and turned to the window.

"Do you hear that?" Her eyes sparkled from the glow of the streetlights outside his window. Leaning over, she wrenched open the pane.

The guests from the party cheered and whooped, but from outside, so did millions of other people all at the same time. A fuzzy haze of celebrations cocooned around them. Two people wrapped up together in a city of millions.

Julia smiled.

Thomas touched the corner of her lips. "The first smile of the new year."

And it spread wider. She rested her chin in her hand and half covered her lips as she giggled. "The first of many." Julia shifted to stare out the window again, awe written on her face. "Think of how many stories we'll write this year."

There were a lot of stories that he wanted to write, and there never would be enough time to write them all. Just like there could never be enough time with this woman, one of his oldest friends. His best friend.

"Nah, I'm not thinking about that." Thomas sat up and kissed her forehead. "I'm thinking about you. And all the stories we already have."

SIX MONTHS LATER
JULIA

JULIA SIPPED the hot diner coffee, her thighs sticking to the booth's bench where her soft shorts ended. She and Thomas had created a tradition of late Saturday brunch at Callaghan's Coney Island each week, and they always kept the date. Since he usually worked in the diner all day Saturday, and she spent most of Saturday doing writing work, their standing date made it so they could see each other a little more on the weekend.

Sometimes Julia even wrote at the restaurant—like on this day. She spotted Thomas coming with her food, so she saved her work and shut her laptop, running a hand over the stickered top.

"One stack of pancakes for the lady." Thomas winked, placing the plate down in front of her.

"And, I don't know, whatever this thing is for me." Thomas plunked into the bench opposite her.

"A skillet?"

"Yeah, I guess it's a skillet, but it's like all this random shit from the fridge. No guarantees what I'll find." He twiddled his fingers in the air before side-eying his dish.

"You're very brave, love." Julia reached across the table and patted his hand. "Anyway, my pancakes look good. Thanks."

The diner quieted down between the lunch and dinner rush. That golden hour lull that the restaurant staff craved. When the sun dappled across the dining room pleasantly and they got to eat their meals in peace for once.

"What are you working on today?" Thomas shoved a forkful of eggs dowsed in hot sauce into his mouth.

"A one-shot. I'm back on my golden throuple shit. It's like catnip to me. I'm sorry. I can't say no to the power of Rey and Finn and Poe. *Together*." She took a bite of pancake and continued talking with her mouthful. "I like what I like, and goddamnit, my readers like it too."

Which was true. She had *readers* now. And that's what she always wanted for her writing: an audience, excited for her work, where she couldn't produce fast enough for the most voracious of them.

This feeling, this buzzing kind of coming alive that she had for the last eight months? Thomas had reminded her of it. Within a couple rounds of drinks, Thomas had seen what she needed so much more clearly than Josh ever had. Thomas saw something that she forgot about herself.

With their simple burrito bet, she rekindled the parts of her she had forgotten over the years.

Since then, she managed to build up a decent chunk of engagement with her writing between her Instagram and her TikTok. With luck, most of the readers then got funneled either to her Tumblr full of cleaner fics of her favorite pairings, AO3 for most of her smut, or her Wattpad for her original short stories. Eventually she hoped to put up a novella that had spitballed from one of the more well-received short stories.

And she enjoyed the hell out of it.

"It's a shame Disney never went there." Thomas shook his head, referencing the throuple.

"I mean, you're right. But it was so obvious it almost would have been annoying if they *did* do it." Julia waved her fork and knife in the air as she spoke. "Ya know?"

Thomas sipped his black coffee noisily instead of responding, and Julia rolled her eyes at him.

"Yep, I know." He reached across the table to pat her hand this time.

"Whatever." She wrinkled her nose, fully aware that he was pushing her buttons in the playful way that she adored.

She wiggled her hand from under his. This girl had to eat. "Anyway, it's gonna be fun."

"I know it is, dear." He nodded, hiding his giggle behind his coffee mug.

"What about you? How's the novel?"

"Well, the deadline for my edits is next week, so still banging those out." He cleared his throat and readjusted himself in his seat.

She liked asking him about his writing in public, because it made him so antsy. It kept him modest, reminding him that a world existed outside of his social-media-based writing community. The deal for his proposal was, in fact, huge. It gave him wind in his sails, and it meant that the publisher breathed life into his backlist.

Everything felt good.

"Do you ever miss New York?" Julia asked for the millionth time. The question that gnawed at her constantly.

She traced the "I <3 NY" sticker plastered on her laptop. An inside joke because she didn't end up loving New York City. But she saw how much Thomas loved it in his own way.

After the New Year, Thomas showed her around his New York for their next two weeks in the city. They explored the bars and shops of the Brooklyn neighborhoods of Bushwick and Bedford-Stuyvesant. He brought her to Greenwich Village, and they checked out all his old university haunts.

And while she knew that Thomas didn't leave the city for her, she just had to check every couple weeks to make sure that he had no regrets.

"No. I don't." Thomas met her eyes. "We've been over

this. *I* made the decision to come home, and I'm not disappointed. Far from it."

"I know, I know. Sorry," Julia said, ducking her chin. She knew she needed to stop, needed to trust Thomas's words and his actions. At least, that's what Susan said her therapist said.

Susan, for her part, was trying to get Julia to start therapy herself, but she wasn't quite there yet.

"I'm right where I want to be." Thomas lifted his head, his eyes soft and round and pulling down at the corners. His forehead wrinkled as he raised his eyebrows. The look, molten and sincere, sent goosebumps skittering down her arms.

Julia widened her own eyes, expectant, wanting to take it all in.

This was the way that he looked at her, and she would never get enough of it.

But Julia laughed and broke the tension, stabbing at her pancakes, as Thomas ducked his head to his phone in his lap.

"Oh yeah? Right where you want to be? Living in that house with Danny? I know he's your brother, love, but he and Camden do have some questionable cleaning techniques," she said.

Her phone buzzed on the table next to her pancakes.

With you, eating pancakes

Julia smiled and sat back in the bench, sliding slightly along the slick plastic cover. She crossed her arms over her stomach and watched Thomas eat. She thought she could still see the sliver of that sixteen-year-old in there and that this man in front of her was in there all along, waiting all that time to unfurl his wings.

If she allowed herself that same kind of grace, she'd probably think the same about herself.

They continued their meal in companionable silence.

This wouldn't be so bad for the rest of my life, she thought.

Pancakes, too many story ideas, and her best friend.

THE END

MORE FROM STARLING HILLS

Danny & Ari will return with their stories

Sign up for my newsletter for the latest updates, to get exclusive content, ARCs, & more

ACKNOWLEDGMENTS

Writing and self-publishing a novel has been an absolutely delightful fever dream. I won't bore you with my whole writing history, but just know that holding a physical book chockfull of my own lovesick brain-children is something I've dreamt of for a long time. To say I finally did the damn thing is kind of wild!

First and foremost, I have to thank my partner, Andrew, who only laughed one time when I told him "I'm a writer" all those years ago. Little does he know that chuckle fueled years of spite-writing to prove him wrong. All jokes aside, he never doubted me, constantly supported me, and played hours of video games while I furiously typed away on my laptop. Thank you for being my first pre-order. I love you boo!

Thank you to Ash, the first person I really shared my writing with. I think you were only mildly shocked when you learned I was writing a romance novel. This adventure would be way boring without you and our little discord chat where I can scream/spiral with you 24/7. Thank you for putting up with my endless stream of consciousness messages.

Thank you to Sammy, my first "online" friend, who I can talk story with for literally hours. Our chats have inspired me in so many ways! Thank you for proofreading for me.

Thank you to Livy who saw something in that first version of Relative Fiction. Thank you for loving *them.* Thank you for always responding when I have something to scream about via text.

Thank you to Rach who reads all my early drafts and still manages to find something to love.

Thank you to MG Buehrlen for all of the writing dates, sprints, and Negroni spagliato with Prosecco and Pedro Pascal TikToks.

Thank you to Jessica Costello for beta reading Relative Fiction and always being excited for me!

Thank you to Sarah T. Dubb for reading and encouraging me.

Thank you to Miranda Valentine and Hailey Harlow for helping with my blurb.

Thank you to the WTS Squad for being such a supportive bunch and giving me a space to explore *me*.

Thank you to Amy M for asking repeatedly to read this book. And thank you for reading!

Thank you to the rest of our girl gang, Emi and Hil, for being two of the best friends a gal could ask for.

Thank you to Kara A who laughed when she read the first chapter in front of me.

Thank you to my sister Kassy and brother-in-law

Collin for asking questions about my book and being curious about the process.

Thank you to my beta reader, Gen. And my cover illustrator, Ashley, and designer, Murphy, for honestly creating the cover of my dreams!

And, of course, thank you to Mom and Dad for fostering my love of words from a young age. Love you both oodles and boodles!

Thank you to all of my family, friends, and followers for every like, comment, and share on social media over the last couple of months. Online interaction and excitement really does buoy my spirit!

Finally: thank you to the readers of this book. Especially the early ones and the champions! Please share about this book if you loved it (and tag me)! Or even if you didn't (please don't tag me)!

Thomas & Julia are yours now.

ABOUT THE AUTHOR

Alaina lives in Michigan with her spouse and grumpy cat, Gary. She's proudly self-published. Relative Fiction is her debut novel.

Find me, memes, links, & more on my Instagram.

instagram.com/alainarosebooks

Made in the USA
Monee, IL
01 April 2023